Praise for
Bad Boy Boogie

"Thomas Pluck is a crime writer to watch. Steeped in the genre's grand tradition but with heart and bravado all his own, his writing is lean, smart and irresistibly compelling."
—Megan Abbott, author of *You Will Know Me*

"Thomas Pluck has launched himself into the rare category of... must read novels...must re-read...Just tremendous."
—Ken Bruen, Shamus and
Macavity Award-winning author

"A vivid dose of New Jersey noir with heart, soul and muscle."
—Wallace Stroby, author of the Crissa Stone series

"...a superb, taut, little thriller that hits all the right notes and sustains its central conceits to the very last page."
—Adrian McKinty, author of the Sean Duffy trilogies

"Tough, tight, and taut, *Bad Boy Boogie* is a standout. A damn fine read from start to finish."
—Hilary Davidson, bestselling
Author of *Blood Always Tells*

"Beautiful bad-assery. Thomas Pluck may well be the bastard love child of James Lee Burke and Richard Stark."
—Josh Stallings, author of Anthony and
Lefty Award-nominated *Young Americans*

"*Bad Boy Boogie* is the kind of explosive book that makes life-long fans."
—Bracken MacLeod, author
of *Stranded* and *Mountain Home*

BAD BOY
BOOGIE

ALSO BY THOMAS PLUCK

Blade of Dishonor

As Editor
Protectors
Protectors 2

THOMAS PLUCK

BAD BOY BOOGIE

DOWN&OUT
BOOKS

Down & Out Books
3959 Van Dyke Rd, Ste. 265
Lutz, FL 33558
www.DownAndOutBooks.com

The characters and events in this book are fictitious. Any similarity to real persons, living or dead, is coincidental and not intended by the author.

Cover design by James Tuck

ISBN: 1-943402-59-0
ISBN-13: 978-1-943402-59-5

*This is not a true story. The names have been
changed to protect the guilty.*

*Dedicated to my sister Danielle, who saved little J,
and to my wife Sarah, who helped me write again.*

PART ONE

BACK IN BLACK

CHAPTER 1

When Jay Desmarteaux walked out the gates of Rahway Prison, the sun hit his face like air on a fresh wound. The breeze smelled different, felt charged, electric. A rawboned middle-weight, he was broad at the shoulders and hips, as if God had attempted to halt his growth and he'd thickened out of spite.

"Go on," the guard said. Jay couldn't remember his name, but he was all right, as far as COs went. "Ride's waiting for you at the curb."

Jay squinted at the road. The only vehicle waiting in the early summer heat was a black Suburban parked at the yellow curb. The wind played with his shock of black hair. He had spent twenty-five years as a monk locked inside a dank Shaolin temple dedicated to violence and human predation while the men who put him there lived free from fear.

Men who needed killing.

Mama Angeline raised him to understand that some folks just *needed* killing. There was nothing you could do for them.

And she'd been right.

He'd met many such people, both in prison and the real world. He didn't make a habit of giving them what they needed. There were too many of them.

He hadn't been all that surprised when he'd been unable to convince either the police or the jury to agree. The friends he'd saved from the rotten son of a bitch's rape and torment had either been too afraid to speak the truth, threatened out of doing so, or in one case, had twisted things around to ensure Jay's imprisonment.

But that didn't change the fact that Joey Bello had needed killing.

1

Jay had been vocal about it, before he had expectations of ever walking free. The sentence, delivered a month past his six-teenth birthday, had been life without parole. Then after twenty years behind bars, thinking it was his forever-home, the Supreme Court ruled that sentencing a juvenile to LWOP was cruel and unusual punishment.

He wasted no time finding a jailhouse lawyer, and after years of appeals, they got the attention of a bleeding heart named Martins, who did pro bono work for lost causes such as Jay's. There'd been pushback, from law enforcement and the Bello family; Jay's case got bounced from court to court as defense and prosecution appealed, until a circuit judge ruled that despite the infamy of his crime, Jay had served more time than any other juvenile in the state, and sentenced him to time served.

After that it was all paperwork, according to Martins. They put him in reentry classes, but Jay had been one step ahead: after he'd beaten the rage out of his young hands in the yard or in the boxing ring, he'd gotten his GED and taken every me-chanic and repair course the prison offered. Five years back, the governor had even given him a special award for having more certifications than anyone in the country, free or imprisoned. The man's rubbery smile had been fake as plastic fishing worms, but he'd used Jay's example to get the prison a new auto shop, built by one of his cronies. The old shitbird warden, unfazed by Jay's newfound penitence, made life hell for him until the day he retired, but the inmates and even some of the guards gave him respect.

He'd get none of that outside. The best he could hope to be was to be anonymous, which would be difficult given the infamy of his crime.

All he could do was live well. Okie, his old con mentor, always said that was the best revenge.

Jay felt otherwise.

The air electrified his lungs. He left the guard without a word and pointed his brogans toward the pickup area, following a chain fence topped with a Slinky of razor wire toward the row of waiting cars. Okie had told him it was bad luck to look back on freedom day, so Jay didn't even peek over his shoulder once at the dirty brick castle he had called home since his eighteenth year.

He flipped it the finger.

Two men got out of the black Suburban wearing jeans and black T-shirts. They had the scoured faces of men who'd endured the desert sun. Black fanny packs at their belts. They smelled like cop.

"Martins sent us," the driver said, and held out an envelope.

Jay opened it. Greyhound ticket, Newark to New Orleans.

The passenger, a big man with a brush cut, opened the rear door for him.

Jay obeyed out of habit, then cursed himself, holding his duffel bag possessively in his lap. He'd have to get used to doing things his own way. No one out here could put black marks in his jacket, or take away his privileges. Get him thrown in Ad Seg, alone with four green walls until he punched the bricks to feel anything other than bugshit crazy.

Brush Cut got in beside him. The truck smelled of mint chewing gum and new leather. The air conditioning felt like heaven.

"First class chauffeur service," the driver said. "Only the best."

The truck rumbled toward the highway.

That morning two guards had taken Jay to administrative segregation with the punks, psychos, and informers, where the reentry counselor told him his release date had been moved up, citing good behavior. Jay found that hard to believe, but hadn't argued. The little man rushed through his spiel and gave him a duffel containing safe sex pamphlets, a pack of condoms, a cheap fleece hoodie, and a spare pair of socks and underwear. Then the bursar gave him a sizable roll of twenties. His gate money, minus fees.

"We took the liberty of purchasing you a bus ticket to New Orleans," the social worker said. "Martins said that's where your family's from."

Jay hadn't spoken to Mama Angeline or Papa Andre for twenty years. Their silence had burrowed inside him, a cold creature with sharp claws that squirmed its way behind his belly. Late at night, ravaged by hope, he would dream they were all back at the fishing camp tipping beers and swatting mosquitos, and the thing inside would twitch and gnaw.

Jay asked for a phone call, and the social worker said there'd be payphones at the bus station. Jay told him to give his radio and paperbacks to his celly, a Dominican who was in for installing secret compartments in dealers' rides, but the man didn't even look up from his papers while the guard escorted Jay out, straight to the gates.

The truck's door locks snapped shut.

A familiar paranoia cinched a ring around Jay's abdomen. He had been under the complete control of others for most of his life. He'd walked a tightrope between an alpha dog's bravado and a coyote's fine-tuned sense of danger, and his hackles rose as they trucked toward Newark Penn Station.

An unbroken stretch of strip malls, diners, and motels scrolled by. Working-class beaters jockeyed with sleek black sedans. Grimy white trucks and semi-trailers towing corrugated shipping containers herded toward the port. The sheer constant activity set him on edge. Prison was boring. The routine kept things sane, but also drove you mad. At least one riot during Jay's tenure, started because one wild young con had been bored out of his skull and wanted to see what would happen if he stirred things up.

Jay held loose but dead still. Staying wound up like a spring would kill you; Okie had taught him to float, like when he was in the ring. No need for footwork until the opponent made their move.

The two men didn't make a move, and they weren't much for talk, either. The truck got caught in the molasses of Jersey traffic once they reached Newark.

"I want to talk to Martins," Jay said. "He said he'd be here."

"He's in court," the driver said. "Saving some other psycho killer from doing his time."

Jay had worked on modern vehicles; he knew with the child-safe lock, the rear handles wouldn't work. He'd have to elbow Brush Cut in his cinder block of a face and then heave himself up front, claw the driver's eyes and go for the door handle. He played it over in his mind.

"Don't you worry," Driver said. "You're going home. Real home. Louisiana. An old friend's making sure of it."

Jay couldn't think of many friends. There was Tony, who owned an auto shop near their hometown. He'd suggested Jay take the mechanic certifications, and offered him a job if he ever got out. They hadn't spoken since the last court case. Once Jay's release became a possibility, Tony never seemed to answer the phone.

Cheetah, his celly from juvenile, was supposed to be running a club for the Italians in Newark somewhere according to the grapevine. He sent a package once a year around Christmas and a check to keep Jay's commissary account flush. He wasn't much for letters, and Jay didn't have his number.

And his family, they'd been gone since his conviction. Mama had written a few times. Sent pralines, Jay's favorite. When her letters dried up, Jay had been high on the former warden's enemies list, so he assumed they'd been confiscated. But when the new warden came in, no letters appeared, old or new, and the letters Jay sent continued to be returned. His folks had always been on the move, so that didn't mean anything. He hoped.

Inside, hope killed. Outside, it was all he had.

The truck bullied its way through a yellow arrow and double parked near the drop-off lane of the bus station. Cars honked in vain. The driver shifted into park.

"Thanks for the ride, fellas." Jay tugged the door handle. As he expected, the lock didn't disengage.

"Out the other side," Driver said. "You been inside since what, high school?" He jacked a thumb toward Brush Cut. "Lucky here, he gets to escort you all the way to the Big Sleazy."

Brush Cut grinned and popped the door on his side. Stuck one leg out. Made a little waving motion with his hand.

Later, Jay thought that was what set him off. The condescension of it. The same smug dismissal he'd seen in Joey Bello's eyes as he'd tortured Jay's friends. The look that said, *you deserve this. You know it, too. You're the shit beneath my shoe, and you know it.*

Ice cold indignation flared in his chest and misted his eyes red at the corners. The unquenchable rage that brought the axe down on Joey Bello now fired his fists without thought of consequence or damnation.

Jay mule kicked Brush Cut with his prison brogans, one lugged sole hitting his chest and the other cracking his face. His head bounced off the door and his broad chest thumped on the pavement.

Driver tore open his fanny pack to reveal a black pistol. Jay right hooked him three times in the nose. The seat rest blocked him from using his iron left cross, but he felt the man's neck weaken on the third blow, and his head lolled onto the steering wheel.

Jay grabbed his duffel and jumped out the back door, one foot landing on Brush Cut's solar plexus. The big man was fast. He'd already recovered and drawn his pistol. Jay heel stomped him in the liver until the pistol fell, then kicked it across the pavement. Other commuters squinted and stared, unsure of what they were seeing.

Jay opened the driver's door and unbuckled the dazed man's safety belt. Underhooked his right arm and heaved him on top of his vomiting partner. Dropped an elbow or three into his kidney to keep him down.

"If y'all mean the old 'friend' who left me flat," Jay said, "You tell him it's a little late in the game to start giving favors." He half-stepped into the truck and levered the column shifter into reverse. He hopped out with the vehicle in motion, then jogged between parked cars toward the taxi lane.

Car horns blared as the big truck rolled. Pedestrians scattered as the black Chevy crunched into a utility pole.

The green cab at the front of the line was a repainted police car on saggy springs. A thin black man with gold-framed glasses and a pencil mustache sat behind the wheel. Jay slipped in the back seat.

"Whoa," the cabbie said. "Hell was that?"

"Some jagoff drove the wrong way out the parking garage," Jay said. "Nearly hit me."

The cabbie leaned out the window to stare. "Crazy."

"Let's get moving," Jay said.

"Gotta tell me where we're going first."

"Nutley," Jay said. Home. First thing that came to mind. Old cons lamented how weak the human mind became in times of stress, sending you headlong toward familiar hiding spots that were always the first place the police were sure to look. But he knew no place else. He and his folks left Louisiana when he was seven years old. New Jersey might have attempted to imprison him for life, but it was home, at least for now.

The cabbie eased away from the taxi line and paused at the exit ramp.

Jay took a twenty from his bankroll and held it over the seat rest. "This thing burn rubber?"

The cabbie snorted. "Maybe if I set it on fire."

Jay wagged the banknote. "Give it a shot."

The driver snatched the bill. When he saw an opening he revved in neutral, then dropped the shifter into drive. The tires chirped as the cab lurched into traffic. Behind them, a small crowd gathered around the two downed men, one unconscious, the other dry heaving in the street.

CHAPTER 2

Jay stuck his face out the window and breathed in the perfume of diesel soot, car exhaust, and fryer grease. Prison smelled of unwashed bodies and stuffed toilets. Disinfectant over mildewed walls.

No one else would think New Jersey smelled like heaven.

"Get your head in here," the cabbie said. "What you doing?"

Jay slumped into the worn seat and rubbed his knuckles, listened to the sweet V8 rumble of the Crown Vic's Ford 302. He hadn't thrown a punch in anger in years. It had come back all too easy. They disappeared into the crush of traffic. Jay looked back. No sirens, no police. He breathed his four fours, like the guy who ran the Zen class taught him to.

Four seconds in, four count hold, four seconds out. Four more before you breathed again. Four sets of those and the pounding of his heart settled.

"What's your name, brother?"

"Herschel," the cabbie said. "You?"

"Desmarteaux," Jay said. "I mean, Jay." Old habits die hard. At least he didn't give him his inmate number.

"Well stay inside the car, Jay. Truck mirror almost tore your head off."

Jay stretched his arms behind his head with a thin smile. "Thanks, Hersch. Needed a little thrill. Been away a quarter century."

"Where you been?"

Jay thought on it. He was a free man, at least for the moment. "Rahway."

"No shit?" Herschel tucked the twenty deep in his sock.

"What the hell you do, a white boy going to jail that long?"

"Rather keep that behind me, if it's the same to you."

"You don't wanna say, that's fine with me. Man's got a right. You done your time."

Cee-Lo Green crooned on the fuzzy stereo as they headed up Route 21. A billboard with a tricolor harem of dancers advertised *Cheetah's: A Club for Gentlemen*. Jay made a note of the phone number before looking away, watching traffic. A woman with her hair tied back passed in a Mustang convertible. The perk of her nose and gleam of her hair made Jay ache deep inside.

"Mind if we make a side trip?"

"Depends," Hersch said. "You need to score, I don't truck with that. I'll drop you off wherever you want, but you get another ride out of there."

"Nothing like that. Wasn't in for drugs."

"Lemme guess, strip club? There's one just up the road. I'll wait, but you can't bust your nut in my car."

"Nope," Jay said. "Been so long, I figure I can go a while longer."

Punks inside dolled up and offered suck jobs for barter. Jay had politely demurred. A Latin queen named Rene had grown fine little breasts on smuggled estrogen treatments, and fixed up real nice. Rene liked to say it was all the same under the sheets in the dark, but Jay never found out.

"I've done some pickups from the county jail. Most of them want to find a girl or stop for a drink right away. A drink I can handle, but you get sick in my car, I'm driving straight to the police. Tired of cleaning filth out the back. So you feel queasy, you tell me so I can pull over."

Jay's last drink had been Irish whiskey, with the girl who'd saved him from doing time a virgin. Memories of her had been enough to fend off temptation from both the punks and the throat-clenching stink of jailhouse hooch, which was usually orange juice fermented in a toilet tank.

"I'm good," Jay said. "I'm thinking Rutt's Hut. You know it?"

Herschel laughed in three short chops. "Twenty-five years in jail, man wants a hot dog. Only in Jersey."

"They better be as good as I remember," Jay said. "The food at Rahway tastes like wet toilet paper."

Herschel nosed the cab down a side street and hugged the Passaic River until he got past the traffic snarl, then popped back on the highway.

"Take the Nutley exit," Jay said.

"Next one's closer."

"I wanna see something."

"Okay."

Nutley had a new bridge and a lot more clutter, but the heart remained. Graffiti marked the overpass off the highway. Rust stains on the concrete like honey brown hair flowing down a woman's back. Houses with neat little yards huddled in a phalanx on the border.

As they cruised River Road, Jay frowned at the hole in the sky where the steel rocket of the International Avionics tower had once stood. The defense contractor's sprawling campus was gone, with townhouse condos posed in their place. Most people worked there, or across town at Roach Pharmaceuticals, makers of the tranquilizer made famous as "Mother's Little Helper" by the Stones. One side built tools for the Cold War, and the other cranked out the pills required to live in the shadow of the mushroom cloud.

They swerved past Kingsland Park's waterfall, where police had emptied their guns into a Newark carjacker when Jay was in sixth grade. The shootout stood as a warning to interlopers, an invisible moat that made the denizens feel safe in their homes. Nutley had been a good place to grow up, rich or poor. Parks to roam, ponds and streams to fish in, a pizzeria in every neighborhood. The town had been a little too proud, a little unfriendly to outsiders, but Jay felt a twinge inside at no longer being welcome there.

"Thought I recognized the name," Herschel said. "You're the guy who...you're him."

"That I am," Jay said. "You're pretty sharp, Hersch. I don't remember you from school."

"I'm from Belleville," Herschel said. "But we all heard about it."

Everybody had. Jay's rep preceded him to Annandale reformatory and followed him into Rahway.

Their eyes met in the rearview mirror.

"C'mon, Hersch. I ain't gonna kill you with a hot dog."

"Sorry, man." Herschel laughed and held up an open palm. "Looks like you'd do just fine with your bare hands."

"I only use my hands under the hood," Jay said, and slapped Herschel's palm. "You pull over, maybe I can hunt down your vacuum leak. This heap whistles like it's got a chest wound."

"You're all right, Jay," Herschel laughed again in three short chops. "You're all right."

The soot-stained brick of Rutt's Hut squatted on a ledge overlooking the highway. Construction workers rubbed elbows with suit-and-ties in its yellowed tile interior, lining up for the lunch counter. The low scent of fry oil filled the air.

Greeks in stained aprons tortured hot dogs in the deep fryer until the skins burst and split up the middle, calling out orders in clipped jargon.

Six rippers. One Frenchy, traveling. One Coke, one Marvis, cap.

Jay slathered the dogs with spicy mustard and nuclear yellow relish. They ate in the parking lot, staring out at the slick brown r̶i̶ ̶ ̶ ̶ ̶ ̶ ̶ ̶ ̶ the Passaic River painted alongside the highway. ̶ed, begging for scraps.

a bite and moaned. The snap and crunch of the

fried skin, the soft yeast roll and the sweet relish outshined his faded memories.

"Good as you remember?" Herschel said.

"Better." Jay looked over the edge at the cars and trucks roaring toward Newark.

"Lot's changed since you went in," Herschel said through a mouthful. "It's a whole different world now."

"That suits me just fine," Jay said. "I didn't like the other one all that much."

"How old were you?" Herschel asked, and picked at the paper boat of fries.

"Fifteen," Jay said.

"You even know how to drive?"

"Nope."

"They don't teach that in there, do they."

"Just how to steal." Jay watched a high school kid with spiked blond hair rumble out the lot in a red Camaro.

"I don't mean what you did was right," Herschel said, and chewed his lip a moment. "But I just wanna say, I kinda understood what you did. In middle school there was this boy named Joseph, he had it in for me. Made life hell."

"Some folks just need killing."

Herschel's eyebrows came together, then he laughed. He watched Jay like he would a strange dog.

"Well it's true."

"Yeah, but most of us just think about it. Guess twenty-five years didn't change your mind."

"Oh I learned my lesson," Jay said, around a bite of ripper. "Doesn't change the fact that the world'd be better off with some people underground. Paid my debt, but I'm glad the evil sumbitch is dead." He started on his next hot dog. The first hit his belly like a lead sinker.

Herschel cocked his head and chopped one nervous laugh. "You're something else. Making me think twice about completing this fare."

"That boy got what was coming to him for what he done," he said, and tossed a piece of hot dog roll to the gulls. One snapped it up and flew away. "You only know what you heard."

Herschel parted his lips to ask, and Jay cut off the question with a steely glare.

Joey Bello had always grinned like he'd gotten away with something, and he usually had. Flat little squirrel eyes, and fingers lumpy with burned-off warts, quick with a flick to the ear or a pinch and twist of tender belly meat. If playground torment had been the extent of Joey Bello's transgressions, Jay might have tolerated him to walk the earth. With what Joey had done, the world was considerably better off for his absence.

Jay looked out at the Passaic. The carpenter's hatchet Papa Andre had given him on his tenth birthday was somewhere in the muck. The police had never recovered it.

Herschel gave a playful smile. "So was it worth it?"

"I was a dumb kid," Jay said. "Thought I could take it. My friends' folks, one was a cop, another was rich. They said they'd grease the wheels, but they let me swing in the wind."

"You gonna do anything about it?" Herschel said.

"A good friend of mine once told me the best revenge is living well," Jay said. "Reckon I'll try to do that." He tossed the burnt dregs of the fries to the gulls and watched them squabble and fight until they tore the last one apart.

"Good luck. Ain't easy, these days."

Four rippers gone, Jay popped the hood and fumbled around until he found the loose vacuum hose. Herschel gave him a rubber band from the glove box, and Jay wrapped it around until it stayed put. The whistling stopped.

"It won't lug down so much now," Jay said. "But this thing needs more work than I can do in a parking lot."

"Ain't mine," Herschel said. "We rotate, and today I got the shitbox."

Jay brushed his hands off on his jeans. "Let's motor," he said. "If I'm gonna live well, I might as well get started. Friend's got an auto shop, somewhere in Belleville, in the valley."

CHAPTER 3

The sign for Big Tony's Auto Shop displayed a gamma-green airbrushed Hulk wearing a mechanic's cap, toting a massive wrench that read "Incredible Performance." The lot was filled with customers' vehicles, from daily beaters to hopped up Mustangs and import racers. Below the sign was parked a Hummer H2 pickup painted custom gamma green with the Hulk logo airbrushed on the doors.

"This the guy?" Hersch laughed at the sign.

"I'm pretty sure. He was the Hulk every Halloween when we were kids."

Herschel gave him his card. "You need driving lessons, you give me a call. I'll take you to the DMV and everything."

Jay palmed him another twenty and watched until he drove away.

The broken glass in the gutter resembled a trail of diamonds in the morning sun. Jay followed them to the front doors. A handful of mechanics worked the bays. The machine-gun patter and whirr of hydraulic tools echoed down the street.

A beefy gearhead with a Roman nose manned the counter, speaking to a Latin woman in pink sweats.

"You got a bad oxygen sensor. That's a buck fifty, plus labor." Tony talked with his hands, and his face ran through emotions like a hammy actor at audition. Since Jay had last seen him, Tony had molded a Big Mac and pepperoni pizza physique into muscle that hung on him like slabs of brisket, swelling his shop uniform as he nodded in sympathy with his customer.

The woman frowned at the price. Tony threw up his hands, the universal symbol for "what ya gonna do?"

"You ought to get both done," Jay said. "They usually go

16

one right after another. Save you on the labor."

"Thanks, buddy," Tony said. "Was just gonna say that. Have a seat, miss. It'll be about an hour."

Jay set his elbows on the counter and cleared his throat.

"Just a second, tough guy," Tony said, punching computer keys.

"I hope your pecker's not as short as your memory."

"The fuck you say?" Tony reared up like he was hefting two heavy suitcases. His chest nearly burst his shirt.

"Don't Hulk out on me, pallie."

Tony knitted his caterpillar eyebrows. "Jay?"

He stomped around the counter and heaved Jay up in a hug. The shelves rattled and the customer put a hand to her chest. "Holy shit!"

"Easy, hoss," Jay laughed. He slapped Tony's back until he set him down.

"How the hell are you? How'd you..."

"Long story," Jay said. "But it's legit. Free as a bird."

"Never thought..." Tony looked like a kid on Christmas opening a pair of socks.

"Look at you," Jay said. "Thought you and Matty were gonna beat Billy Gates."

"Well it turns out Gates was pretty smart," Tony said. "But this beats desk work."

"What they been feeding you?"

Tony grinned big and flexed an arm. "Like these, bro? I call 'em the Guns of Provolone."

The woman rolled her eyes and went back to playing a noisy game on her phone.

Tony walked Jay through the shop bays past a Mustang getting new rear gears. "When Matty bought me out, I went in with Uncle Sal. Then the economy went south, and I talked him into doing custom work and paint jobs, performance. If people

17

can't buy new, they fix up what they got."

Uncle Sal was a bald-headed walrus on Tony's mother's side, the closest thing Tony ever had to a father. Jay had met Tony's real father only once, at their confirmation party. He'd sneered and drank a lot, until Sal and Papa Andre escorted him out. "How's Sal doing?"

Tony kissed his first knuckle and held it to the ceiling. "Gone six years now."

"I'm sorry, Tone. He was a good man."

They walked past the paint box where a flat gray stealth coat baked on a late model Volkswagen.

"Looks like you got your hands full," Jay said. "You got a job for an old friend?"

"Uh, maybe," Tony said. He rubbed his chin between thumb and knuckle. "You'll need to get your A1 certification."

"You're looking at a Master Technician. Auto, truck, and collision."

Tony arched his eyebrows. "You kept busy in there."

"There wasn't a hell of a lot else to do."

They walked in back to the lobby. Tony told him to wait in his office while he wrote an invoice. The cramped room was lined with shelves of parts catalogs, the walls papered with old pin-up tool ads. A woman straddling a wrench, another excited beyond belief by a set of whitewalls. Above the desk, a replica of the sword from *Conan the Barbarian* was mounted on the wall, ready to fend off a Pictish invasion.

Jay sat in the office chair and winced at the stale scent that squeezed out of the cushion. The desk was a collage of pink and yellow carbon paper, a coffee-ringed desktop calendar, and a dusty computer keyboard. A yellowed photo poked out from the corner of the calendar.

Ramona.

The photo showed her with Jay and Tony, laughing in the International Avionics company pool. Mama Angeline must have taken it.

His best memories all revolved around water. Fishing in the bayous with Andre, tubing the rivers with Mama Angeline. Meeting his best childhood friends at the pool. He tucked the photo back when footsteps reached the door.

Tony carried two cups of coffee and offered one. "Maybe you can pick up a few hours here and there," he said, and stirred his coffee with a lug bolt. "I mean, I can help you out, but to hire you full time I'd have to let one of my guys go. They got families." He settled in his office chair with a creak.

"And I don't," Jay said.

Tony studied the oil slick spinning in his cup.

"Looks like you're doing pretty good here," Jay said.

"I worked real hard for this," Tony said, and set down his coffee.

"Not as hard as I did."

Tony shrank into his seat.

"I kept my mouth shut," Jay said. "And what I need now is work and a set of wheels. My folks kept in touch awhile after they got chased out of town, but it's been five years since I heard anything. Nobody came to visit. Might as well have been death row."

Tony licked his lips and looked up, slumping in his seat. A fat kid in gym class, waiting to get beaned in dodgeball.

"I got no one else, Tone." Jay bared his palm, where a white scar sliced across the meat. "No one but my brother."

Tony pinched his face as if swallowing a cockroach. He scratched at the pocket of his hand, where a matching cut shined like the nerve in a cheap cut of steak.

"I pay my guys twenty-five bucks an hour," Tony said. He rested his chin on his fists, let out a long sigh. "You're certified, but you got no experience. So let's say...twenty?"

"Thanks, brother."

They shook on it.

"As for a set of wheels, I got a shop truck we use to pick up parts," Tony said.

Jay furrowed his brow. "Don't tell me you sold the Hammerhead."

The beast hunkered in the weeds behind the shop like a reef shark cooling its fins. Four flat tires, purple metal flake webbed with cracks. The vinyl top had peeled and the chrome was speckled with rust. A dent had snapped the Challenger emblem in two and left the R/T decal a scrape of rust. The air cleaner cover was missing, and a black plastic trash bag showed through the cut in the hood where the sigils 426 Hemi were once emblazoned.

"Looks like you used up your half and mine," Jay said, shaking his head.

Tony looked away, corners of his eyes crinkling. "I blew a head gasket in a race, and had to limp back to the shop. Been meaning to restore her, but something always comes up. I only got one pair of hands."

"Mine work just fine," Jay said. He ran one along the paint, squatting to sight down the side. The door was dinged to hell but the frame was true.

"You got time to fix her up, she's yours."

"It was half mine to begin with." Jay popped the hood pins and lifted the hood. Weeds had grown up through the engine bay, and a small animal had built a nest between the alternator and the shock tower.

"Aw, Tone. It's got critters."

"I'm sorry, alright? You even got a license?"

"I will soon enough."

"See, you're getting ahead of yourself," Tony said. "I'm going back inside. I got a business to run."

"I hope you run it better than you make coffee," Jay said, and sluiced his cup's contents into the weeds. "Tastes like you made soup out of assholes."

"I wipe my ass on the filter. I should piss in it, too."

"Might taste better if you did."

Tony slapped Jay hard on the back, and pulled him along as he lumbered back inside. They worked away the afternoon. Jay helped Tony's foreman, a chunky Puerto Rican named Guillermo, work the frame straightener on a T-boned Subaru. Jay squinted at the road any time a black truck cruised by. He let the work keep his mind off the Brush Cut twins, but kept a wrench in the hammer loop of his jeans in case they showed. It wouldn't take Columbo to figure out where Jay had gone to ground.

When they broke for lunch, Jay followed the mechanics to a roach coach for a meatball sub. Tony drank a protein shake and ate from a can of tuna with fork.

Jay plucked a long strand of cheese from his mouth. "This computer you got. Think you can help find my folks?"

"I can try," Tony said, looking away from Jay's lunch.

"They're probably back in Louisiana."

"That don't really narrow it down."

Tony tapped the keys. "Google's got nothing, on either Angeline or Andre Desmarteaux. Facebook, neither."

"You might as well be speaking pig Latin," Jay said. "They didn't let me use those things. Look for woodworkers, maybe Andre's got his own shop."

"What was your mother's maiden name?"

"I don't know. Never met her side of the family. Just Andre's brothers." There was Pitou and Ti' Boy. But those weren't names, not really. "I ought to drop by my house. Maybe they left something, and the owner's got it in the basement, or the garage."

"You should stay out of Nutley." Tony belched and swatted the air. "They made Mr. Bello mayor."

"I paid my debts. More than I can say for some." He peeled a layer of melted cheese off the tinfoil and ate it like a tortilla chip. "Speaking of, what's Matty Strick up to these days?"

Tony shrugged. "He was a better programmer than I ever

was. Wrote trading software for a hedge fund startup and made big coin. Then he went into real estate like his father. You see an office park, he's probably behind it."

Matt had been the kid who killed the curve in every class. He'd lived up to expectations.

"His old man still in town?"

"Nope," Tony said. "Leo Zee's chief, though."

Leo Zelazko, the cop who'd shot the infamous carjacker, was the obvious choice for Nutley's chief of police. His twin sons Billy and Brendan had been Jay's friends since grade school. And the main target of Joey Bello's torment.

"And Ramona?"

Tony's eyes drifted over the old photo of them at the pool.

"She went back to her own. She's with a big law firm out on Route Eighty."

Ramona had wanted be an architect. Urged him to join her in drafting class, to design houses on paper. Now he was a convict and she was a lawyer who'd left him to rot. After how he'd behaved during her final visit, Jay wasn't sure he blamed her much.

"I'm sorry, pallie. Twenty-five years is a long time."

Jay stared out the dirty window at the Challenger.

"Maybe, you know, you ought to just fix her up and do like Fogerty said. *Choogle on down to New Orleans*," Tony sang.

From "Born on the Bayou." *Choogle* was a word whose meaning they'd pondered as teens while they worked on the Hemi, sneaking beers, a Creedence tape in the stereo.

"You can't fight those kind of people. It's like banging your head against the wall. Only feels good when you stop."

"I got a pretty hard head," Jay said, and rapped his knuckles on his skull.

Leo Zelazko and his partner had kept Jay up all night in the detectives' office, detailing what would happen to his folks if he didn't confess. Brought him out to see them both cuffed in the holding cell, with hangdog faces and tears in Mama's eyes.

Pleading with him not to sign. Shouting that they could take care of themselves.

Jay crumpled the foil into a tight little ball.

"You should leave it alone," Tony said. "These people were big enough shit back then and they're bigger shit now."

"Then I'll use a plunger."

"They knocked the Avionics tower down," Tony said. "You see that? Things change. And there's nothing we can do about it. Come on, let's get the Challenger on the lift. Give you something to hammer on that won't bring down a load of shit."

They roped the Hammerhead to the shop truck and pulled it out of the weeds. Jay popped the old tires off the rims and put new shoes on, performance rubber. Then he walked underneath the chassis, checking the frame for rust. He wiggled the hammer beneath the engine bay. Something gray and fuzzy tumbled onto his shoulders.

"Shit!" Tony yelped.

Jay skipped aside and stomped the lump as it hit the floor.

"The hell was that?" Tony peered at the rear axle, brushed off his hair.

"Your last passenger," Jay said, and held up the desiccated corpse of a bucktoothed squirrel. He thrust it at Tony. "Hide your nuts."

"Gimme that." Tony flipped the stiff critter into the trash bin.

They worked in silence, getting to know the car from their youth again. Wrenching seized bolts, razoring off old gaskets. The car had been Matty's father's. He'd sold it to Jay and Tony in exchange for yard work after Jay admired the wreck in his garage. It had been bent near in half from a passenger-side collision.

When Jay turned fourteen, Strick had it towed on a flatbed to his backyard. Andre chained the car's frame to the old oak next to his wood shop and spun the tires until the frame was close to true. Jay and Tony bought a Haynes manual and picked through the junkyard when they had chore money to spend, but mostly they sat in the cracked vinyl buckets and dreamed of escaping onto life's infinite highway.

CHAPTER 4

The taut clothesline ran from his swollen purple ankle to the leg of the sofa. The boy huddled under the sofa's stained yellow arm. There he didn't have to look at her. He dug at the knot with the carrot peeler. Crusted with blood.

He had to get free before the Gator man came.

Water dripped in the sink and tortured his dry throat. There was a warm glass of flat Coke on the other side of the sofa but he couldn't reach.

Not without crawling on top of the Witch.

Flies buzzed over the hum of the television's gray test pattern. The thick swamp heat had ballooned the Witch into a waxy purple slug seeping into the corduroy cushions. White holes where her eyes had been. Alive with maggots.

The stench coming off her was so thick the boy might drown in it. But it couldn't hide the factory town's rotten-egg miasma that had leached into the trailer's walls and everything inside.

The boy pried at the knot, slipped and jabbed his swollen skin with the peeler. Black blood oozed to his feet.

He reeled at the pain and passed out.

Hands on him, soft. The boy woke with a snarl and stuck the peeler into the woman's thigh.

A freckled face haloed in golden blonde. The boy bawled when he saw her face. The blood-encrusted peeler fell to the moldy carpet.

"It's okay, little Jay Jay." The woman bit her lip, wrinkled her forehead. Coughed into a bandanna. "You remember us, don't you? I'm sorry we went away. Some bad folks made us go to school." She turned to a tall man with a black beard. "Need your knife."

The boy remembered the man. They'd gone fishing. He smelled good and never raised his voice. The man knelt and squeezed the boy's hand as the woman sawed away at the rope leading from the boy's purple ankle to the leg of the sofa.

She carried the boy to the sink and held a jelly-glass of water to his cracked lips. He spat it up, then drank more.

"Sip," she cooed.

The boy cried into her tied-off shirt, enveloped by her warm breasts. She carried him outside to a purple Jeep with no roof and cradled him in the passenger seat. An ax handle stuck from between the seat and the stick shift.

The man took a gas can off the back and stalked toward the trailer. A sulfurous wind flapped his denim vest, revealing a finger-grooved knife handle at his belt. When he returned, the trailer fumed black smoke.

"Her own boy," the man said, sparkles in the corners of his eyes.

"Speak no ill of the dead," she said. "You know who put her that way."

The man nodded. He wore his hair long, tied back like an Indian brave.

The woman gently brushed the boy's swollen toes. "Feel that?"

"Hurts," the boy said, fading in her lap. The high sun gold through his closed eyes.

"No one's gonna hurt you no more," the man said.

"Baby, I'm your mama now," the woman said.

The Jeep kicked gravel, pluming dust as they topped the levee and disappeared down the swamp road.

Jay woke screaming. He sat up in bed and squinted at the dark of the no-tell motel room Tony had found. The tang of sulfur in his throat dissipated in the cool night air. His head pounded and his belly ached. He turned the lamp switch. It clicked. The bulb had died while he slept. He hadn't been in true dark for so long that it felt like a giant hand had snuffed out the world.

He stumbled to the bathroom and turned the light on.

Back in bed he stared at the bare ceiling, feeling like he'd been staked out on a desert plain with nothing for miles. Without the clang and clatter of men behind bars, the summer night-song of traffic was an abysmal silence which set him on edge.

He tore the covers off the bed and stuffed them into the tub. He closed the bathroom door and curled in the tub to sleep with the comfort of four close walls crushing in.

In the morning he sprung out of the tub with a hoot and repped out his daily workout. Topped out with single arm pull-ups on the door lintel. He took a shower, hot as it would go, for as long as he damn well pleased. Finished it ice cold and felt ready to slap the Devil and kick his ass clear across the horizon.

He was free.

Jay killed his hunger in the red vinyl booth of a sprawling chrome diner. He hunched over a Denver omelet, two fat breakfast sausages, and a mound of home fries splashed with ketchup and hot sauce until the plate resembled a murder scene.

He thought about calling Martins on a payphone but figured the last thing the lawyer would want to hear was that the killer he'd worked two years to set free had committed aggravated assault on two men who were probably off-duty police officers, even if, as Jay suspected, they'd been in the employ of Matthew Strick, the former friend who'd testified against him at his first trial.

* * *

He worked at the shop all day. Tony found him a furnished studio apartment on Craigslist. A five-floor walkup in a brick complex in North Newark, on the edge of Branch Brook Park and its towering oaks and Japanese cherry blossom trees. The room had a twin bed, a galley kitchen, a clawfoot tub converted to a shower, a five-drawer dresser, and an armchair with a lever that tilted the seat to help you get out of it.

The rent was three hundred. Jay figured the previous tenant had died and the super, a fat man with lazy eyes and a sparse mustache, was still cashing the social security checks. The room smelled clean, had a window with a fire escape that looked out to the park, and a space for the Challenger.

Now he only learned to drive the damn thing.

CHAPTER 5

Herschel drove him to an abandoned lot with weeds poking through the asphalt where they exchanged seats. The cab was another ex-cop car with the spotlight installed by the driver's side mirror. Something felt wrong about that.

Jay gripped the shifter.

"Whoa," Herschel said. "You gotta adjust your mirrors. They failed me for that. And your seat belt, put your seat belt on."

Jay cinched the belt tight. Held the wheel at nine and three, and eased into gear.

"Easy on the pedals. Smooth."

They lurched away as Jay let off the pedal, feathering it as he circled the lot and looped around the light posts.

"Slow down on the turns," Herschel said. "And don't jerk the wheel so much. Easy around that pole, don't take the mirror off."

The cab drove like a boat. The tires squeaked as Jay palmed the wheel. Nothing like driving Mama Angeline's Renegade from her lap while she worked the pedals barefoot. The Jeep had no speed but lots of torque, and it turned on a dime.

"Slower," Herschel said.

"Gonna go back and do that turn again," Jay said.

"Yeah. Try not to fling me around like Captain Kirk. Slow and smooth," Herschel said.

Jay let the wheel slide to true between his fingers. Killed an hour as he learned to feel the car around him, the way the pavement crunched beneath the tires, and how the body swayed and righted itself.

"You got the hang of it," Herschel said. "Next time maybe we'll hit the street."

"Come on, Hersch." Jay rolled toward the exit. "It's dead out there."

Herschel looked up and down the road. "All right. Don't do anything crazy now. This here's my livelihood."

"Promise," Jay said. He eased out of the lot toward Nutley. The road was a wide ribbon of asphalt with aged and empty factories on one side and the concrete wall of Route 21 on the other. He eyed the speedometer and kept it to the limit. His old street was the next left over the border. He could cruise past the old house, maybe park outside a while. Grab a pear off the tree.

"You're doing okay," Herschel said. "Ha. It's the other people on the road you gotta worry about, sometimes it feels like they're all out to kill you."

"I'm used to that," Jay said.

A police siren blipped from behind. A gray cruiser filled the rearview, hidden flashers flickering blue in the grille.

"You gotta be kidding me," Herschel said. "Should've known not to drive into Nutley. Pull over."

The ice cube stuck in Jay's throat told him to do otherwise.

"Stop the vehicle," the cop barked over the loudspeaker, and blipped the siren a second time.

Jay white-knuckled the wheel, his work boot hovering between the brake and the gas.

"What're you doing?" Herschel said.

Okie woke in Jay's head. *If you ain't carrying contraband or got a serious warrant, running is a dumb play. You can't outrun a radio. My last stand, I had a machine gun in my lap and a trunk full of cash. Had no choice. But there's shit-for-brains in here serving time for running when they had nothing to run for.*

Jay braked to a stop.

"About time," Herschel snapped, and killed the ignition. "Keep your hands on the wheel. Let me do the talking."

The ice cube sank to Jay's gut and bloomed into a nest of cold snakes. The officer appeared in the driver's side mirror. Suit and tie, tall and lean. Close-cropped brown hair.

Jay unsnapped his seat belt and popped the door locks. Pressed his shoulder to the door. A different voice than Okie's told him to hip-slam the cop with the door and bounce his head off the sill. Snap his neck, take his piece and be gone.

The same voice that told him Joey had needed killing.

"License, insurance, registration," the cop said. Flashed a Newark PD badge.

Jay choked back the snakes in his throat. "Ain't got none, officer."

Herschel leaned over. "I was giving him driving lessons, sir."

"I wasn't talking to you," the cop said. "And I have a feeling Black & White Taxi isn't a licensed driving instructor. Out of the vehicle, peckerwood."

Jay glared at the cop. He stepped out with his hands up.

Gray around the temples. Hairline receding like surf at low tide. A smirk slashed across his sharp face. He pushed Jay's shoulder toward the hood. "Assume the position, jerkoff."

The same old big mouth. He had beefed out into a hockey goon with a regulation cop haircut.

Herschel leaned over. "Officer, I have registration and insurance."

The cop slammed the door in Herschel's face. "Stay in the vehicle."

Jay kept his shoulders loose. "You gonna arrest me, you dumb Polack?"

The smirk faded, and the officer's hand drifted toward his shoulder rig. "What did you say, asshole?"

"Aw shit," Herschel said, and raised his hands.

The blinking red eye of the Avionics Tower glared from the beacon of ribbed gray steel as they rattled into town in a truck carrying everything they owned. Andre drove with slow precision, mindful of the limit. Mama Angeline kept her arms folded most of the way, tight-lipped over the sale of her Renegade. Jay sat between them, craning out the windows, chasing rock 'n roll on the radio dial on the two-day drive from St. Martin Parish.

"They got swamps here too," Andre had said, as they circled the football stadium. "And no gators to bite you. I bet they got crawfish and sac-au-lait just like home."

They moved into a cookie-cutter Cape Cod, one of three crammed on a lot neighbored by a truck repair shop and a lumber yard. Across the street was a white-sided A-frame inhabited by a squat old Italian woman who peered through her blinds like a mother warthog deciding whether to remain hidden or flay the intruders with her tusks.

They unpacked late into the night, then drove until they found a place called Rutt's Hut that was open late. They took home a tray of hot dogs and ate them on the back porch with cups of Coke and watched the last innings of a local baseball league play out as the sun sank low.

"This ain't a po'boy," Mama said. "But it's pretty damn good."

The next day Mama Angeline rang their neighbor's doorbell with a plate of fried chicken and potato salad, and the aged woman's wrinkles creased into a smile. Andre liked the Italians, you knew where you stood with them. If they didn't care for you, they made a face like they'd stepped in dog mess. But if you got along they stuffed you full of good food and wine, put an arm around your shoulder, and told you they knew a guy who could hook you up with whatever you needed.

Andre got a job with Mr. Strick, a sandy-haired construction foreman who drove a silver Porsche with pop-up headlights. He bought dilapidated old homes on big lots and split them into smaller properties. Mama Angeline took a cafeteria position at the International Avionics company clubhouse. It was kitchen work, but it came with invitations to the summer picnic and full roam of the campus, which included an Olympic pool, a nine-hole golf course, and a duck pond beneath the communications tower which doubled as an ice rink in the winter.

Jay was urged to be friends with the Strick boy. Matthew Junior read adult books and wore khakis and short-sleeve collared shirts like his father. Matt was at home in the sickly green light of his IBM XT personal computer while Jay preferred to explore the creeks that wandered the town like veins on the back of an old man's hand. He caught a big brown crawfish and brought it home for Mama to cook, but it tasted like mud, and they spat it out. Jay was fixing to pack a bindle and camp in the woods that summer when the company pool opened and everything changed.

The rippling pool was caged in sixteen-foot green chain-link to keep teenagers out at night. Executive cabanas sat under the trees, and the rest of the folks arrived early to stake out spots the shade.

Angeline strutted in wearing a yellow bikini and bug-eye sunglasses. She ignored the stares and hopped on a chaise lounge among the executive wives. Jay scratched the melted-wax scars on his back as the boys in the water sized him up. Angeline prodded him with her big toe. "Jump in. You can leave your shirt on."

Jay cannonballed at the six-foot line and splashed into icy silence.

The chlorine tingled his nose and eyes. He'd only swum in swallow fishing holes off Bayou Teche, never in water so clear and cool and empty of life. The waves above flickered crystal, and the water's embrace muted the buzzing in his head, leaving him to marvel at this newfound quiet at the bottom, all alone with his heartbeat.

The lifeguard grabbed him by the wrist and pulled him to the surface. "If you can't swim, you gotta stay in the kiddie end."

"My boy can swim just fine," Angeline called from behind a folded paperback. "Jay, quit fooling around. Show him you can swim."

Jay dived under and swam from the wall of the kiddie side all the way to the diving boards, waving as he tread water.

The lifeguard gave a nod and returned to his wooden aerie.

Jay climbed out by the diving boards. His eyes fell on a cheeky girl in a blue bathing suit in the line for the twenty-footer. Long black hair, cobalt eyes, a defiant pout to her lip.

"Take a picture, it'll last longer," she said.

"Hi. I'm Jay."

"So what?" She rolled her eyes and climbed the ladder. "Creep."

Her dive was the most graceful thing Jay had ever seen. He waited for her to climb out and dive again, but she free-styled to the far side. Didn't even look over her shoulder at him as she got out and dried off in the shade.

Jay swam to the shallow end, where a trio of boys his age huddled to squint and scan.

A chubby black-haired boy who wore a white tee to hide his fat, and a pair of dusty-haired twins, tall and lean. One quiet, the other brash, holding court with a permanent sneer.

"See, Tony?" The soft-eyed twin said, nudging the chubby kid, nodding toward Jay. "He wears a shirt, too."

"Whatcha all looking at?" Jay asked.

"The boobs on that blonde," Tony said.

The boys basked in the magnificence of a full pair of breasts barely constrained by a bikini top. They were the broad palette for a spray of freckles, which the trio seemed to be counting. The woman they belonged to shook her bleached Fawcett locks and rolled onto her stomach, to their groans of dismay.

The tall twin clucked his tongue. "Those aren't boobs, Tony. They're tits. Big, beautiful tits."

"She sure is one hot canary," Tony said.

"Canary?" Jay asked. "You calling her a bird?"

"Yellow bikini means canary, *dupek*," the bigmouth twin said. "The stuck-up girl by the diving boards, with the Phoebe Cates titties? She's a bluebird. Get it?"

"I reckon," Jay said.

"You reckon? I got an e-rection for that canary," Bigmouth said, nudging his twin brother, who did not take part in the ogling.

"She's a real peach, ain't she?" Jay said.

"Those are a lot bigger than peaches."

"I'd suck on those for a week," Chubby said.

"Well, she's my mama," Jay said. "Why don't y'all go for a swim and stop making her feel uncomfortable?"

Chubby froze.

Bigmouth slapped the water and splashed Jay in the face. "It's a free country, redneck. I'm gonna stare at her big boobs all day."

Jay leapt on him and pounded his ribs. The kid tried to knee his nuts, so Jay bit his shoulder and left a ring of marks. His twin brother tried to pull them apart and got an elbow in the chin as they thrashed against the wall.

"Boys! Settle down." Mama Angeline held them both by the ears. "Thank you, Jay, but I can fight my own battles. What are your names, boys?"

The chubby kid was Tony. The bigmouth twin's name was Billy, and his well-mannered brother was Brendan.

"And where's your mother?"

"My mother dropped us off," Tony stammered. "She had to go to Bradlee's. But she works here, I swear."

"Why don't you boys make better sport," Angeline said. "I bet Jay here can make it to the deep end and back before any of you can. You beat him, without cheating?" She leaned over with her arms folded and whispered, "You can rub tanning oil on my shoulders."

Tony's eyes bulged.

"Well? Go!"

The boys attacked the water. Jay kicked their asses.

Billy held a grudge for a little while, but the three became fast friends. Sharking the pool, fishing sunnies out of the Mud

Hole and carp out of the grimy Passaic. They climbed the rusted dinosaur skeletons of railroad trestles and roved on their Huffy bikes like kings, exploring their twelfth summer's universe of boundless possibility before anyone told them their place.

"You heard me, Billy boy."

"Detective William Zelazko to you, peckerwood," Billy said.

"I heard you were a prick cop like your old man," Jay said. "The horse apple don't fall far from the tree."

"Get in the cruiser."

Jay narrowed his eyes. "I maxed out, if you recall. No parole, no probation. Full citizen."

"In the front," Billy said. "To talk. This ain't a roust. Think I'd come alone, with your jacket?"

Jay ducked by the taxi's window. "Sorry, Hersch. Gotta do what the lawman says. I'll find my way home."

Herschel exhaled slow and scooted to the driver's seat. "You're something else, you know that?"

Billy waited in the cruiser with the air blowing max. After Jay sat shotgun, Billy stared at Herschel until he pulled away.

"Newark ain't candy-ass Nutley," Billy said, "and I'm not my father. I'm here as a friend."

Jay stared at the street corner, where condos had replaced the old electroplating factory they had explored as children. Inside, information was currency. He'd learned not to give it freely. He wanted to know who sent the goons after him on freedom day, but if Billy wasn't aware of them, there was no need to clue a cop in that he'd assaulted two men. "How'd you even know I was out?"

"You know this town," Billy said. "Bello used the news of your upcoming release all over the last election. Not that anyone ran against him, except that crazy guy with all the Roman statues in his yard. But he thinks aliens built the Coliseum."

"I could move back," Jay said. "Nothing stopping me."

"Oh yes there is," Billy laughed. "Remember, I'm the nice one. The official welcoming committee won't be so friendly."

"You're a regular bucket of sunshine," Jay said. "I can't even go see my old house?"

"I'll drive you up there, you want." He held up a finger. "One time. I'm here doing you a favor. You never were good at knowing when the world handed you a favor, but you're gonna learn today. Nutley is off limits."

"I'm a citizen with a job. You can't even bust me for vagrancy. And this ain't Newark."

Billy grinned. "I figured you'd hit up Tony first."

"He promised me work, and I took him up on it."

Billy huffed through his nose. "You think he wants you there? Quit fooling yourself. Here's a reality check, you're nothing but a bad memory. No one wants you here. Not even your friends. They want me to kick your *dupa* out of town, so don't be a complete asshole about this. This was negotiated."

He slapped Jay in the chest with a fat envelope, and let it drop into his lap.

Jay frowned at the blank manila paper.

"Open it."

"What's that?"

"That there is your walking papers," Billy said. "A ticket to New Orleans and twenty-five grand. Enough to start over."

Jay held the envelope out. "That's mighty white of you, but unlike your shitbird old man, I'm not for sale."

Billy flared his nostrils. He took a slow breath. "You're already bought, asshole. You think your early release was mercy from the state?"

So that's where the two months came from.

"Matty and my father, playing games. They didn't want Bello to have to deal with you. But they're fuckin' stupid. Bought you a plane ticket, first. And I told 'em, you been a jailbird since you were fifteen. You don't got a driver's license, no picture ID. How

37

you gonna get on a plane? So it's the grey dog, but it beats walking."

"Well fuck y'all very much." Jay flipped the envelope into Billy's lap. "I made more working in the damn wood shop." He'd spent most of it in the commissary, but that was true.

"Don't think you got privileges because we pissed in the same pool. I'm using the velvet glove right now," Billy said, and raised an uncallused hand. "You want the fist, you'll get the fist. Think anyone cares what happens to a shittums like you?"

Jay stared down the hood.

"So open your ears. Take the money," Billy said, jabbing Jay's stomach with the envelope. "Hop the next bus to N'awlins. Last time we checked, your folks were in some shit-swamp called Hopedale. Go have a teary-eyed reunion and disappear, for the good of everybody."

Jay took a deep breath and tugged the envelope from Billy's hands. He stared at it a long time. Squeezed the cash like fruit for ripeness. Felt its weight. The promise of seeing his folks swelled in his chest. He killed the feeling before it reached his face.

"Listen, bro," Billy said. "It might not look like it, but I think what happened was pretty fucked up. But what you gonna do? It's the way of the goddamned world."

"That why you're a cop?" Jay said, tapping his knee with the envelope. "To make sure it stays that way?"

Billy raised a palm and put on his television face. "I assure you, without me involved, this transaction would be a lot less diplomatic. Matty's got his own security, real operators. I believe you met? They wanted to black bag you and throw you in a private jet."

So the prison chauffeurs were from Matty. "Let 'em try."

"I told them I'd take care of it," Billy said, eyes drifting toward Jay's old street. "Because you stood up for Brendan."

"How is he?"

"Good," Billy said. "Real good." A tic played at the corner of his mouth. He gave the steering wheel a quick kneading.

Neither Brendan nor Billy had testified at his trial, but Jay hadn't expected their father to permit it. His temples burned as he saw little Matthew Strick in the witness chair, lying through perfect teeth. The feeling in his belly turned sour.

"If you're Matty's messenger boy," Jay said. "Pass this on to the little shit." He dropped the envelope on the floorboard. Jay unzipped his jeans and reached into his boxers.

"The fuck are you doing?"

"Y'all gonna piss on me," Jay said, "Then I piss on you."

The hot splatter hit the envelope like a wet raspberry.

Billy reached cross-draw for his sidearm and Jay pounced. He shoved Billy's elbow and pinned him to the door, then gripped his wrist and pulled Billy's arm around his own neck. One of his cellmates had fought MMA. They'd traded some moves.

Billy swore while Jay snaked his other arm against Billy's throat and eased into a blood choke. Jay pressed in, nose to nose. Smelled the stale cigarettes and old coffee on Billy's breath as he struggled in vain.

His eyes rolled back, and he sagged against Jay's side.

Jay wriggled his arm free and extracted an ugly Glock from Billy's shoulder holster. Held it in his lap while he shook off his pecker and tucked it away. He fumbled with the pistol until he popped the magazine, racked the slide and ejected the round from the chamber. Cars weren't the only mechanics he'd learned, and Okie had been a strayed Marine who learned to kill in Korea.

Jay squeezed the Glock's barrel inside Billy's belt until the muzzle hit crotch, then slapped him hard across the face.

Billy mumbled and fluttered his eyes open.

Jay jabbed his groin with the Glock. "If I remember correctly, you got a pretty small pecker. But I doubt I'll miss at this range."

"Easy," Billy said. He wrinkled his nose. "Aw, you pissed all over."

"Now you listen, my so-called friend. You tell Matty that money ain't gonna fix this. I paid twenty-five years in blood for what your fathers did to me."

Billy sneered. "You think I'm gonna let you go after my father? He's an asshole, but he's my asshole."

"Well, your asshole's gonna get a big surprise."

Billy gritted his teeth.

Jay smiled. "I scare them, don't I? Good. Let them be scared for a change. Fear's good for you. It shows you who you are. Some of us could never protect our brothers, so we gotta play hero, try to make it up to ourselves. Isn't that right, Billy boy? You wanna play hero today?"

Billy narrowed his eyes. "Don't burn your bridges."

"Hell, I'll burn 'em at both ends. I know how to swim."

"You killed him, Jay. Not us. And we paid for it, too."

"Not hardly enough," Jay said. "You think I was playing with my pecker while I did my time? I learned some law. About a little thing called conspiracy to obstruct justice. Not to mention conspiracy to commit murder. There's no statute of limitation on either of those, and y'all are in up to your necks."

"No one'll believe you," Billy said. "You know what you're up against?"

Jay ground the gun into Billy's crotch until he winced. "All that means is you got plenty to lose. And I got nothing. You took it all."

"We didn't—"

"My family!" Jay said. "Ramona, too. I did what none of you had the heart to do. Your fathers let that sumbitch beat and rape and torture you every day! He got what was coming, but instead of the truth, your old man chose his job. Strick and his father chose money. No way he'd get all those houses built without Bello greasing the wheels. And seeing me reminds y'all of what they done. Well take a good look."

Billy gritted his teeth and said nothing.

"Now I'm gonna walk away and you're gonna turn tail. And if you or anybody else pushes me around they're gonna get pushed back so hard their head's gonna pop out their ass." Jay reached back and pulled door handle. He stepped out and left the Glock in Billy's pants.

Billy drew the pistol and sighted on Jay's chest. He tilted the weapon and saw the empty magazine well. Checked the chamber and sneered.

Jay grinned. "Next time you come for me, you better bring more gun."

Billy drew a spare mag from his right armpit, slapped it home and racked the slide. He sighted on Jay's face. "You come after my family, you're gone."

Jay breathed slow, stared through Billy's angry rictus. "I died ten thousand times in there. Your old man's gonna get what's coming to him. Matty's is too." He tossed the other magazine onto the seat, kicked the door shut and headed for the street.

Billy lowered the pistol and holstered it. "Stay away from my brother, stay out of Nutley, and stay out of my fucking face!" He gunned the pedal and peppered Jay with gravel as his cruiser roared away.

Jay pointed his boots back toward the repair shop.

He had never known trouble until he met Tony, Matthew, and the twins. No bully came for him more than once. Mama Angeline taught him to throw hard and early, and Papa Andre taught him to stand up for those who couldn't.

Principles that built not only strong bonds of friendship, but also of enmity.

CHAPTER 6

Even at a dead stop the Hammerhead felt like freedom. More so than his first day walking. Tony had painted over the shark's cracked purple and rusted chrome with black so flat it absorbed light. It slipped through traffic like a revenant shadow, its driver a ghost from the past pale as a fish's belly from his years inside.

Driving felt like navigating the prison yard. Pedestrians dared you to hit them, crossing slow. Fancy sedans cut you off like it was their birthright, trucks bullied around the weak, and everyone avoided the banged-up beaters whose drivers were far beyond caring. Commuters fought over the tiniest patch of space and risked collision to deny anyone else a chance to get ahead.

Welcome to Nutley, the green sign said. But not to him.

The Hammerhead's big block champed at the bit. Jay goosed the pedal, all his teenage prison dreams alive. The beast spoke to him, humming through his fingers on the steering wheel.

You and me, we're gonna start some shit.

The streets were torn up with construction. Andre used to joke that New Jersey only had two seasons: winter and road work. Nutley's main drag was sliced stem to stern in the heart of town as utility trucks performed surgery on the main intersection.

Memories teased the back of Jay's mind as he cruised through town. The street where Matt got his dreaded nickname. The junk lot where Joey Bello's picador games of torment began. The park where it had all ended in blood.

The death shroud lifted as he crossed the border and climbed the hills of Montclair. The dividing lines were a jigsaw, but each town had its own character. Montclair had been considered bohemian with its antique shops, punk record store, and restaurants that served more than burgers, Chinese, or pizza. The quirky edges had been polished off and the gentrifying denizens eyed his loud ride with curious disdain.

Ramona's address brought him to a Tudor mansion on a ridge overlooking Manhattan. It looked half as big as Rahway prison and nearly as imposing. Behind it sat a six-door garage of newer vintage and a stable at the end of the driveway. A horse paddock stretched from the carriage house to the edge of the property, and a young girl in English riding gear trotted a roan pony along the fence posts.

Jay parked beneath a weeping willow and followed the steps, slabs of Liscannor slate, to the entrance. A gate of wrought iron ivy barred the thick oak door. He knuckled the doorbell. It tolled deep within.

He breathed his four fours and brushed stray crumbs from his jeans.

"May I ask who's calling?" A woman's thick Irish brogue issued from nowhere.

Jay looked for a camera and found none. "A friend of Ms. Crane's."

"Your name please."

"Tell her it's Jay. I came to pay my respects and nothing more."

Jay gave her two minutes and counted off the seconds. At a hundred and eight the lock thunked and the door eased open.

A slender woman with an auburn ponytail and a brick of a chin held the door and glared at him through the wrought iron bars. Not Ramona.

"Sir, you'll have to leave." The voice from the intercom.

"She won't tell me herself?"

"I'm sorry."

"Not as sorry as I am," Jay said. "What's your name? I'm Jay."

"Erin," she said.

"Erin. Would you tell Ramona something for me, please? Tell her I was a sorry son of a bitch for what I did to her, and I'm even sorrier now, for coming here and disturbing her."

Her eyes flicked to her left, behind the door. "I will."

"Thank you," Jay said. He held a bouquet of purple hyacinths and gold daffodils. The florist had said they were for asking for forgiveness. "Reckon she don't want these, then. I'll just leave them here. Maybe the horse can eat them. Wouldn't want to walk downwind if it did. Probably give him gas something fierce."

Erin bit her lip. "I'll relay your message, sir. Please go."

"All right. I don't want to cause you any trouble. I'm going now," Jay said. "Tell Ms. Crane I'm sorry I shooed my blackbird away. I was a damn fool."

He turned to walk toward the car, just like he'd turned his back on her in prison so he could serve his time alone. Each time she had left the visitor's room it felt like reliving his first night behind bars. He couldn't take it and he couldn't tell her.

"Jay."

Ramona's voice rang through him. Jay turned and studied the slate flagstones. They were patterned with rivulets, fossilized worm tracks from eons ago.

"Do you want to talk or not?"

He walked back slow, studied her like an apparition. She stood pressed to the gate, pinned him with her cracked cobalt stare. The breeze rippled her blue sundress and the bars framed her raven bob-cut. The years had smoothed her like a river stone, brought out flecks and patterns of detail. He had expected surprise, but she'd known he was out and steeled herself for this moment. It showed in the tendons of her throat, the set of her jaw.

"I'm glad you're free," Ramona said. "But there's nothing for you here."

"I didn't come looking for anything," Jay said. "I was raised

44

to apologize when I've done someone wrong."

"You're forgiven," she said. "No penance required."

"Thank you, Blackbird. It'll ease my guilt, but not my regrets."

"Don't call me that." She wrinkled her perk of a nose. "We're not kids anymore."

"I'm sorry, Ramona."

"I'm sorry, too. I'd say we could be friends, but I'd be lying. We have nothing to talk about."

"I heard you became a lawyer," Jay said. "I'd like to discuss a certain case."

She stretched her lips in a thin grimace. "I no longer practice criminal law."

"How about civil, then?" Jay said, and held the bars, leaning close. "Conspiracy to obstruct justice. Willful withholding of evidence. Violation of civil rights."

"I specialize in business and environmental law. Who would you be suing?"

"That friend of ours who took the witness stand to drive in the nails. Perjury. There's no statute of limitations on that if I recall."

"I'd have to recuse myself from your case I'm afraid."

"Because of our prior history?"

"No, Jay. This is ridiculous." She sighed and shook her head. "Am I your first stop on the tour? I'm married, you know. Nobody told you."

"Tony told me," Jay said. "I can come back when your husband's home, if you'll be more comfortable."

She twirled her hair around a finger and chewed on it. "Anthony always was a fucking coward."

"Tony tried," Jay said. "He didn't have the heart for it."

"And he still holds a torch," she said. "He threw away a fortune in a fit of childish pique. Out of jealousy. Did he tell you that part? I guess not. Now he plays with cars like a little boy. So, have you seen Matthew yet?"

45

Jay narrowed his eyes. "That backstabbing piece of shit better run if he sees me first."

"He's the one you blame for all your troubles?"

"I did what I did," Jay said. "Never denied it. But when it came time to tell why I done it, everyone clammed up. Y'all left me flat, and that stung. But only Matty turned on me."

"Try to see it from his side. It would have destroyed his father."

"Maybe his old man deserved it," Jay said. "Tricking me into a confession with a load of bullshit about a high-priced lawyer."

"Do you love your parents?"

"You know damn well I do," Jay said, and gripped the bars.

"You have no idea who they are. Ask them why you they brought you here. Why they abandoned you and everything they owned during your trial."

"Leo Zee threatened them," Jay said. "I went along to save them."

"Maybe you should have saved yourself," Ramona said. "I tried, and look what you did to me."

Jay rolled his eyes skyward. A gray cloud shaped like a fist punched out the afternoon sun. "You want to know why I stopped coming on visiting day?"

"Not really, no. For you, I switched to law, and interned in the public defender's office. We might've cut your sentence. But you threw me away."

"I was protecting you."

"I can take care of myself, Jay. Take a look around. You never thought you deserved to be with me," she said, twisting a knot of her hair. "And you found a way to convince yourself."

"That's not it at all," Jay said. But she was right. He'd said it enough. *You deserve better.*

She bit the twirl of hair she'd twisted around her knuckle, shook her head in a rueful grin. "Then what was it? You know, I don't care. This was a lifetime ago, it was a road not taken. And there's no way to take it now. I'm sorry Tony didn't tell you.

You love your parents? Well, Matthew loved his too, and you tore his family apart. You want to know what they really are, you can ask him when he comes home."

Jay white-knuckled the bars as a cold shot of vodka hit his belly.

"But I'd prefer you leave before he gets here," she said.

Jay looked at her bare feet, nails painted blue. "Are you happy?"

"Don't insult me."

Erin returned and tapped Ramona on the hand. She whispered, "Saoirse's done with her riding lesson," and hurried away.

"It may not look like it, but I'm working today," Ramona said, smoothing her dress. "And I'm happily married. I would've fought for you, and waited. I was young and stupid then."

Jay swallowed and stared at the worm tracks fossilized in the slate at his feet. "Matty offered me twenty-five grand to walk away. Now I know why."

Ramona clenched her teeth, then shook it off. "That asshole."

"That's what he is. He used me, Ramona. People aren't real to him, they're like little players in the game he's always playing."

Ramona smirked. "You haven't figured out why you're free, have you?"

The corners of Jay's eyes wrinkled.

Ramona broke a half smile, shook her head. "You think Martins & Shaw did all that work *pro bono*? You're not innocent. No DNA exoneration, no death penalty to appeal. You're an anniversary present."

Jay squinted his eyes, a confused child.

"I knew Martins from my public defender days. But he's not cheap. When my funds ran low, I had no choice. I went to Matthew. And he let me have you."

Jay ground his molars like two icebergs calving.

"Not that I want you," she said. "But I wanted you free, once the Miller decision made it possible. I've lost cases, but yours I never got to try. Martins is good, but I did a lot of the work for him."

"I didn't let you try because you wanted me to rat on my own parents. What did you expect?"

"For you to trust me. Like I said, Jay. I knew I could win your case, and I did. That's all. The condition was, you go to Louisiana. Now I can't tell you where to go. But I'm sure you've figured out that you're about as welcome as a cock in a convent back in Nutley."

Jay huffed through his nostrils. Couldn't help it. She was a different woman now, but was still the girl he'd once trusted with everything he hid from the world.

"You'll be fine," she said. "You've got half your life ahead of you. It took too long for me to learn it, but you taught me an important lesson. If I listened to mother and had forgotten you, I'd have gone to Cornell and stayed with architecture. I'd be designing cities instead of convincing dead-broke towns to give us tax credits for another ugly office park that'll we'll raze in ten years. It's like you're fresh out of high school. Don't waste it, Jay. Run while you can."

She pushed the oak slab closed on silent hinges and fluttered her fingers through the shrinking gap. "Fly away, little blue jay."

The bolt snapped home, loud as the gates slamming shut on the prison tier.

Jay left the flowers at the oak door. In the car, he kneaded the wheel like a leather-wrapped throat.

In the rearview, the young girl dismounted her pony onto a set of wooden steps, and jumped into Ramona's arms. Jay rested his forehead on the wheel, ran Okie's words through his head.

"There's plenty things worse than killing somebody," Okie said over a cigarette, his smile gone devil. "Find what they love and take it away. They'll wish you killed 'em, every night of their sorry-ass life."

CHAPTER 7

Summers at the pool drowned out the chaos of his past. Cruising through the cool clear water, young Jay lost himself in the spider webs prismed on the bottom by the sun. The diving girl in the blue swimsuit captivated him in a queasy-belly way he didn't understand. She sprung off the six-footer and breaststroked to the end, as if performing for hidden Olympic judges. Tony and the twins didn't know her name, only that she was the daughter of a big boss at International Avionics.

"She's got grade-A tits," Billy said. "Gonna miss 'em tomorrow, when our dad gets his medal. He blew that carjacker *away*." He made finger pistols and two-gunned an imaginary target.

"You told us five times already," Jay said.

"Squeeze her boobs, I dare you." Billy lunged at Jay and attempted a double purple-nurple. The two of them tussled and splashed until Jay wrenched Billy's tit and he cried mercy.

"Why don't you go ask what her name is?" Brendan said.

"I will," Jay said.

Tony said, "You're gonna get our moms fired."

"Just call her bluebird," Billy laughed.

She reminded Jay more of a red-winged blackbird, the way her white shoulders reddened in the sun. He hurried to meet her as she climbed out of the water.

"I know, your name's Jay." She smirked and cut away. He filed in behind her. She was taller than him and the boys and bore her awkward frame with pride. He followed her to the twenty-foot board.

She turned at the ladder and looked him up and down, from

his flint-chip eyes to the road map of veins on his muscled little arms. "I changed my mind," she said with a wry grin. "Your turn, creep."

Jay looked up at the diving platform. It looked as high as the Avionics tower. He gripped the ladder and planted his foot on the second rung.

"If you fall wrong, you'll break your neck," she sang.

"When the ambulance comes? Tell me your name before they take me away."

She rolled her dark blue eyes. It drove the weakness from Jay's legs as he pumped all the way to the top.

The wind tickled between his legs as he teetered on the end of the board. Down below, Mama Angeline stood and took off her shades. Brendan pointed, Tony gaped. The twin towers of the World Trade Center gleamed in the distance. Behind him, the lone Avionics tower winked red. The lifeguard hollered that he was too short and should come down. Jay held his nose and walked the plank.

The water hit him like an open hand.

He'd learned to swim in the bayou. Dark water. Sunken roots snagging his feet, and who knows what else down there, slippery and sharp. He'd learned to hold his breath, to calm down and hold his bubbles in.

The sting all over his body cooled in the water as he sank to the bottom, hoarding his air in the ear-popping silence. Blackbird cut through the diamond-speckled waves, cheeks puffed, blue eyes wide.

The concern on her face drove the pins and needles away. Jay pushed off the bottom to show her he was all right. He reached for her hand.

The big tanned lifeguard snagged him and heaved him out like a catfish. Then he banned Jay to the kiddie pool for a week.

"Girls don't like show-offs, Jay," Mama said at the dinner table. "Well, that's not true. I reckon maybe we do, but show-offs wind up wrapping their car around a telephone pole. And the quiet fella who takes wood shop gets the girl."

Papa Andre chuckled and ruffled Jay's hair.

Saturdays, Mama Angeline and her work friends—Tony's mother, their supervisor Big Teresa, and her husband Harold—brought casseroles of jambalaya, sausage and peppers, and slow-cooked ribs and ate them in the shade by the company pool.

A gray horseshoe of hair was all Harold had left on his head, and a pink starfield of razor nicks marked his puffy brown neck. Jay liked Harold because his fingernails looked like the backs of shiny almond beetles and he often talked of his time in the war.

Teresa enveloped Jay in her pillow-soft arm. "That girl you never stop looking at is Mister Crane's daughter," she said. "Name's Ramona Beth. Go on over and bring her a Coke."

Angeline said, "Son, you better cool off with a swim first."

The women snickered, and Jay's ears burned. He jumped in the pool for a few laps. He didn't want the diving girl to call him a creep. Mama Angeline had told off many a man who'd whistled at her on the street, or roared alongside and honked as they rode in the Jeep. Jay remembered one who'd blocked them in at the grocery store, and sat on the hood of his Malibu with a curled-lip smile. "Lemme buy your boy a comic book, and take you for a ride."

Mama smiled and aimed the Colt Diamondback she kept under the seat. They left the man gaping, a stain spreading from the bulge in his leisure slacks. "Man who can't control himself's not much of a man," she'd said.

When the women wandered into the clubhouse, Harold waved Jay over. "Go get us a couple Cokes." Jay got them from the cooler.

"You like that girl, don't you?"

"I guess so," Jay said. "I want to talk to her, but she's always mad at me."

Harold cracked open the Coke bottles on the side of the table, took a slug and smacked his lips.

"That's a woman's way," Harold said. "Girl like that you better get early, 'cause soon there'll be a line. When I was younger, I was a ladies' man. Started in the army."

Harold smiled at the sun through the trees. "Them French gals were something. After we got done liberating them, we had a time. This one gal, a little thing, thin and delicate like china. She was always peeking at me from upstairs in the madam's house, but she wouldn't take my money. You know why?"

Jay shook his head.

"A white soldier wanted her all to himself. He told her us black men had tails."

Jay screwed his eyebrows. He'd seen black children swim naked back home, and they didn't have tails.

"Yep, like a monkey. Now where would I hide a tail? My back pocket? I was young and headstrong. So I let her think what she wanted, and stopped calling on her. But before we shipped home, I went back for one last taste of hay for the donkey, and you know what? She asked for *me*. She had to see for herself."

"Was she sorry you didn't have a tail?"

Harold broke into a deep laugh. "Yes she was, at least at first." He took a long draw from his Coke. "Don't chase your blue-eyed girl around so much, is what I'm trying to say. Women got a bit of cat in them, they get curious."

"Mama Angeline says men got some dog in them."

"Can't say she's wrong there. I'm a good dog, now that I found my Teresa."

Jay swam his laps while Ramona strutted to the diving board. It hurt his neck not to turn and look at her. He played with the boys, and didn't use the diving boards. He held his breath for time at the five-foot mark and watched aquamarines roll on the surface.

White arms cut the water past him. Jay lost his count as she kicked by in a royal blue one-piece. She doubled back, braided hair following her like a water moccasin.

Jay fought the fire in his lungs until he was near choking before he kicked to the surface.

"What were you doing down there, creep?" Her forehead was lined with thought. "Watching girls like a pervert?"

"I can hold my breath for two minutes," Jay gasped, holding the pool edge.

"You weren't down there that long."

"I counted a hundred twenty, that's two minutes."

"You must count fast," she said, legs kicking as she treaded water.

"You can time me."

"That's dumb," she said, pointing her nose at the boards. "You wanna race? Let's go."

She ducked under and zipped off like a seal. Jay splashed behind her, but never caught up. They met at the ledge in the deep end, and she kicked off the wall for the return lap. She kept her head down and breathed from the side, bobbing like a sea serpent. Jay swam his heart out, but couldn't keep pace.

Ramona doubled back and met Jay in the shallow end, barely winded.

"Don't make the lifeguard come in and drag you out like a baby," she said, and shook water from her ear.

"I'm fine," Jay wheezed.

"What's your name again?"

"Jay."

"That short for anything?"

"Just Jay."

"Jay what?"

"Jay Desmarteaux. It means two hammers."

"No it doesn't. I know French. It means 'of the hammer.'"

"Close enough." Jay coughed.

She slapped him on the back. "Jay Desmarteaux, you need to take swimming lessons."

"I know how to swim."

"You're fast, but your form is lame." She climbed on the edge of the pool and sat with her legs dangling, kicking, leaning over to talk.

"I'm from Louisiana," Jay said. "We have to outswim gators and snakes."

"There's no snakes in a pool, dummy." She laughed. "You sound like that Cajun cook on public television."

"I do not."

"Say 'guarantee.'"

"Guarantee," Jay said.

"I thought you all said *gah-rawntee*."

"Papa Andre does sometimes," Jay said. "You gonna tell me your name?"

"You didn't need an ambulance," she said. "So I don't have to tell you."

"That's not nice. That could've been my dying wish. Mrs. Teresa told me anyway. Your name's Ramona Beth Crane."

"Ugh, don't call me Beth. What's your middle name?"

"Ain't got one."

"Don't say 'ain't.' It's not a real word. Why don't you have a middle name?"

"Couldn't afford one."

She wrinkled her brow for a moment, then smirked and flicked water at him with her toes. "My dad says your mother livened up the cafeteria," Ramona said, wringing out her braid. "He took home some of her gumbo. It was so good."

"You hungry? Mama brought fried chicken," Jay said. "I always have a drumstick and a breast, you can have my drumstick if you want. I'd rather have the breast." His ears turned red when he heard the words come out of his mouth.

Ramona laughed and splashed him. He splashed her back,

and she launched in and dunked him. She was soft but strong. They tussled underwater, laughing and tickling and pinching until her foot jabbed his crotch. They swam away, embarrassed and exhilarated.

Ramona climbed out and slapped the water. "You'd better come out of the water. There's snakes," she snickered.

After Jay swam it off, he found Ramona wrapped in Mama Angeline's beach towel, nibbling chicken and laughing with the older women. Harold snored in a lounge chair.

Jay pulled two of Teresa's ribs from the rack, and licked the sauce off his fingers.

"Thought you wanted chicken?" Ramona snorted and poked him.

Ramona came to the pool when she didn't have riding lessons, or the dreaded piano lessons with her Irish great uncle. She taught Jay a proper dive and how to swim freestyle. She spoke stilted French and Jay answered in Cajun patois. When they went to the kitchen for Cokes she held his hand.

The leaves had gone gold at the tips, the breeze edged with cold. Ramona said that on Labor Day, the maintenance men would haul out the pool cover. They swam all day, racing and playing games until their friends went home. Then she dragged him to the clubhouse to get sodas.

Her lips had gone blue. She pushed him against the chipped white siding of the clubhouse and pressed her lips to his. Closed her eyes and gripped his wrists. When her eyes popped open, Jay stared into the cracked blue. She kissed him again, heart rabbit-quick in the swell of her chest, and Jay decided this was where he belonged.

She broke the kiss with a smack. "Don't tell a soul or I'll cut your little bird off."

Jay nodded, wide-eyed.

"School starts next week," she said. "Maybe we'll have the same homeroom."

"I hope so, Blackbird."

"You're supposed to kiss me back, you know."

Her lips were cold and he warmed them.

CHAPTER 8

The sun shot blades of light through the big oaks that ringed the bowl of the athletic fields behind Jay's old home. He sat atop the concrete steps, eating a pair of Rutt's Hut rippers and sipping coffee, working up the strength to walk the cracked sidewalks and knock on the door and beg for some memento of his past before leaving this cursed place forever.

The house looked the same. The garages had been torn down, Andre's workshop erased. The little workbench Andre had built for him to hammer out his rage had likely been broken apart for scrap.

Jay stared down the steps to the baseball diamond and soccer fields where they'd played as children, swinging stripped tree branch swords and dirt clod grenades. The pear tree they once climbed for the tough, tart treats remained, the scent of fallen fruit thick in the air.

Honey bees half-circled him, caught in the whirlpool of his bay rum aftershave on their drunken search for rotten pears. After the Berlin Wall fell, International Avionics sold its campus. He'd driven through the maze of crushed little townhouses that replaced it. The clubhouse was now the Umbria Americana Pavilion, a private dining club and recreational facility. The pool remained, but indoors. Ringed with chaise lounges, filled with tanned mothers, splashing children, and sagging middle-aged men. He watched through the glass until a squat woman stepped out and asked for his membership card.

Jay asked how much it was to join. She told him they weren't taking applications.

The town hadn't wanted him when he was a kid and it didn't

want him now. The Challenger had a full tank. He would drive south, find his folks.

Do his best to live well.

He bit through the frankfurter's crispy fried skin. Mama Angeline called this place the armpit of the nation, but acknowledged that rude as New Jersey was, the people knew how to eat. He would miss the hot dogs and the pizza, the diners and their Bible-thick smorgasbord menus. And Tony, who had told Mama Angeline that if Jersey was the armpit, then Louisiana was the crotch.

A horn barked from behind. A large black truck butted the Challenger's rear bumper.

Jay finished his hot dog slowly, interrupted by frequent jabs of the horn. He took his time, then sauntered to the black GMC Denali, coffee in hand.

The tinted window descended to reveal faded gray wisps feathered back over a glaring skull. Leo Zelazko had become a distilled version of his younger self, the inefficient layers sloughed away. A pepper gray goatee covered his chisel point chin. Lean to the bone, his lips a perfect line. None of the softness of his son.

Jay squinted a smile. "You dinged my bumper. Hope you got insurance."

Leo blinked gold-eagle eyes. "I see you take after your so-called parents, Joshua. Squeezing this hot-rod out of Anthony Giambotta. If you think you deserve something for what you endured, you should have taken your vindictive friend's offer."

"My name's Jay, you emaciated prick."

"Let's see your driver's license," Leo said. "And prove it. Oh, you don't have one? I know. You need a birth certificate to get one nowadays, thanks to the ragheads who blew up the Towers." He nodded to the empty space in the sky where the World Trade Center had been. "And if you had your birth certificate, you'd know that that's not what it says. A man should know his name, his calling."

"Leo suits you fine," Jay said. "You being a big pussy and all."

Leo spoke in measured tones. "I would consider it a challenge to pit myself against a man twenty years my junior, who's had nothing better to do but pound weights and defend his asshole in the prison yard, but it won't be with swamp trash like you. Because you're going to get in the car you extorted out of your fat guinea friend and drive it out of town."

"I'm a free man, unlike some." Jay sipped his coffee. "Big Man Bello's still got you by the short and curlies, I reckon. Must hurt something bad, being his whipped dog all this time."

"No worse a sting than that of the fatherless whelp, Jesse. No, that's not your name, either."

"My name's Jay, shitbird."

"Want to see your birth certificate?" He popped the glove box and ruffled papers.

Jay stood on tiptoe to peer within.

Leo produced a well-worn service revolver and aimed it at Jay's chest. Braced over his crisp uniform sleeve, the dark eyes of hollow points stared from the cylinders.

"You remember this," Leo said. The Smith & Wesson Model 36 he'd used to dispatch the carjacker when he became the town hero. Grown men would ask to touch the checkered wood grips as it rode in his holster. "It's what put down the last animal stupid enough to threaten the sanctity of this town."

The shooting had entered suburban legend. A stolen Mustang packed with joyriders from Newark totaled out on the border. The driver ran and evaded police in the tight-packed Nutley side streets until he found a young woman returning from the late shift at the Avionics factory and carjacked her at gunpoint.

She intentionally crashed her vehicle at the Kingsland park bridge where police converged, and her captor fled into the park. Officers Zelazko and Carnahan gave chase through the chestnut trees that gave the town its name, and emptied their service revolvers after cornering the gunman by the waterfall. The story made the state paper on the year Jay arrived, and again when the carjacking victim married her savior, Officer Stanley Carnahan.

"You should've filed the sights off before you stuck that in my face. It'll hurt less when I shove it up your ass." Jay broadened his smile, raised his coffee. The old man was smart. The hammer was down, but Jay had nowhere to go. If he tossed the coffee at Leo's eyes and ran, he'd have a clean shot at his back. Dive under the truck, he'd get flattened when Leo reversed.

"Enough of your jailhouse bravado. Mayor Bello is unaware of your early release. I had to call in a lot of favors for that to happen. You will be out of the state before he and his wife are the wiser. Consider the weeks shaved off your sentence my gift of pity. You don't even know what dog fucked your bitch whore of a mother."

Jay thumbed the lid off his coffee.

Leo cocked the hammer with the sound of cracking teeth. "It ruins a boy, to be raised without a father. Leaves him unanchored in the storm of adolescence. The prisons are full of fatherless wreckage like you, washing up on our shores. The hospital records said you had chlamydia and a prolapsed rectum. That must have hurt as almost much as your real father tossing you aside before birth."

"My father is Andre Desmarteaux," Jay said. "You ruined his name, 'cause you were too greedy or chickenshit to put Joey Bello in a cage."

"I know you want to kill me, Jason." He smiled. "Jacob. Furious with the rage of the fatherless. You should focus that anger on the people who dragged you here. You never belonged here. We'd like to go back to living like you never existed. You're a stain we scrubbed out of the mattress."

Leo levered the shifter into gear and reversed, keeping the

sights trained on him. The truck lurched forward, and knocked Jay aside.

"I ain't going anywhere, you son of a bitch!" He hurled his coffee cup as the truck roared away. He stalked back to the Challenger and wiped the coffee from his hands.

CHAPTER 9

The driveway of his old house was empty. Jay rang the doorbell with his knuckle.

No one answered.

He pulled on a hairnet and a pair of blue nitrile gloves from the drugstore around the block. Okie had been obsessed with forensics. "You can't get away with shit nowadays," he'd said. "They find one red cock hair and you're done. Might as well climb into a big Ramses condom and cut eyeholes before a job."

Jay hopped the fence and walked to the cellar door, ducking by the hedge. He taped over the casement window. Looked around and cracked it with his fist, then peeled the glass back before shimmying inside.

The dank unfinished cellar contained a shop sink and storage boxes stacked on cinder blocks. The cellar's familiarity washed over him like a drug. Phantom scents wafted from what had once been Mama Angeline's kitchen upstairs. He crept up the steps and eased the knob open.

Walking through his old house now inhabited by strangers felt like the impossible reality of a dream. The carpets replaced with polished hardwood, paneling torn out for bright pastel paint. Here and there the house he knew shined through. A gouge he had left in the molding, playing with a screwdriver. A built-in bookshelf he'd built with Andre on a breezy autumn day.

Jay's bedroom was now an office, cluttered with paper and a stocky beige computer tower. He padded upstairs to the master bedroom. Andre had built a platform bed with a sunburst maple headboard, and the new owners either appreciated its massive beauty, or couldn't be bothered dismantling it. Jay knelt to stroke the grain, and it felt like shaking his father's hand. The wood glowed a soft ruby beneath the rich brown.

Two steps up to a sunk-in mattress, now spread with a stranger's sheets. Jay pressed the panel by the headboard. The wood eased in, then popped open to reveal a hideaway.

Jay blinked at what lay inside the cubby.

Two of the few things Jay had been forbidden to touch. The tomahawk Andre had taken home from Vietnam, and the combat knife with the finger grooves cut in the handle, so sharp that Andre's arm hairs used to pop off before its edge. Jay hefted the Lagana war hatchet's worn hickory handle with reverence, his reflection warped in the hand-hammered blade, the edge scratched from field sharpening.

A worm turned in his stomach, as if he could smell his parents' fear. They had left everything.

In the matching nook on Angeline's side he found two rolls of cash wrapped in desiccated rubber bands, a tiny zip bag of ancient weed, and a yellowed envelope.

The envelope was not sealed. Jay peered inside. It held several Louisiana driver's licenses, with names like Evangeline Anne Calvin. Andrew and Antoinette Demonde. Birth certificates to match.

No birth certificate for little Jay, but there was a faded check made out to Joyce Anne Calvin from Kuhn Law Partners, for five thousand dollars.

Jay tilted his head and studied the documents and puzzled through their meaning. A door creaked downstairs and clicked shut.

Jay tucked the cash and papers into his pockets, stuffed the knife in his boot, and eased the nooks closed. He froze by the door and heard a woman lumber into the kitchen cursing to herself, slamming cabinets as she put away groceries.

He could run straight out the front door but Leo Zee would find out he'd been here when she called the cops. And what if he left a cock hair someplace?

The bedroom window offered a sheer drop. The master bath opened to the back porch roof, but the window was a mere sliver, no way he'd squeeze through.

He eased down the carpeted steps one by one. The woman in the kitchen was putting away canned goods and having a lively argument with an absent male who apparently did nothing but scratch his balls and fart up the couch. Jay timed the squeaky third step with one of her cabinet slams, and padded past the kitchen to the downstairs bathroom. He hid behind the shower curtain while she swore up a storm.

The fella wasn't there to defend himself, but he *had* left the toilet seat up.

Jay gripped the hatchet and waited for the woman to plop her ass on the farted-up couch.

The bathroom door hit the wall.

"Useless lazy *bastard!*" The toilet lid slammed, then squeaked as she sat on it.

Prison had robbed Jay of all expectation of privacy. The first time he'd used a private toilet again outside he had lingered and wished for a newspaper. Now he sank with dismay as he heard the woman ruffle pages.

Jay covered his mouth as she did her noisy business.

He hoped it wasn't so bad she needed a shower. From the sounds she was making, he considered it a distinct possibility.

Jay relaxed once she washed her hands. Then she announced, "No, I'm putting the lid up! *You* can put the damn thing down."

She stomped to the other side of the house. Jay crept out carefully, peering out the door. The head of the tomahawk hooked the toilet lid, and it slammed with a hollow thunk.

"Dammit!" She doubled back.

Jay padded into the kitchen and cellar steps, pulling the door shut. She slammed the lid up again and headed back to the parlor. Jay took a deep breath and leaned against the damp concrete wall.

He used an upended bucket as a stool to squeeze out the cellar window. The casement fell in with a crash as he scrabbled out onto the grass.

"Hello?" echoed from the cellar.

Jay ran rabbit over the fence without looking back.

He left the tomahawk on the passenger seat as the Hammerhead choogled back to Tony's. He gripped its smooth wooden handle like he was squeezing Papa Andre's hand.

He would find them. But he wanted answers first.

Tony had fired him like a hate-seeking missile. Jay homed in on the big man's office and mechanics skipped out of his way. Tony slouched over his desk staring at an invitation card with a chocolate frosted donut stuck in his mouth.

Jay slammed the door behind him. Yellow invoices twirled off the desktop.

Tony coughed out the donut, choked, and reached for his coffee. "Don't you fucking knock?"

Jay gripped a handful of Tony's work shirt and sat on the edge of the desk. Tony wheezed donut crumbs and squirmed in his chair. His donut hit the floor and rolled behind a filing cabinet.

"Saw Ramona," Jay said. "Imagine my surprise, she's married to someone we know. You didn't think to tell me?"

"I'm sorry," Tony coughed. Jay leaned in as he tried to muscle out of his grip. "Gimme some coffee. Please."

Jay pushed the chair away and plucked a chocolate frosted from the box of Entenmann's donuts. It was ice cold.

Tony coughed into his sleeve and gulped the coffee, winced at the burn, and coughed some more.

Jay bit through the donut's chocolate shell. "That was a real jag-off move."

"I said I'm sorry," Tony said, wiping his mouth on his sleeve. "You want coffee? No, you don't like my coffee."

"Talk, Tony." Jay crunched his donut. "Talk real good."

"I wanted you to punch Matt's face in," Tony said. "Like he deserves." He grinned and reached for another donut.

Jay slapped his hand. "Thought you were on a diet."

Tony glared.

"You trying to get me back in prison for assault?"

"Ramona won't let him press charges on you. I want him to get what's his, like you said."

"I don't like being used. Next time clue me in."

Tony sighed and sank into his chair. "I'm taking a damn donut." He took one from the box and bit a quarter off in one bite, before it could be snatched away. "They're so good straight from the fridge," he said, chewing beneath Jay withering glare. "When you were gone, Ramona was all upset. I wanted to help. You know, to like watch over her for you."

"Right."

"But she was too good for us. Then in college, I blew up like a whale," Tony said, and took another bite. "The dorms were stocked with Doritos and Mountain Dew. We stayed up all night coding and playing Quake. When Uncle Sal died, rest his soul, Ma had a fit at his funeral. Said I was gonna break her heart and die before she did. She stopped cooking for me. You believe that? An Italian mother, not feeding her only son." He threw his hands up, and sent crumbs flying.

"So I lost the weight. No pasta, no bread. It was murder," Tony said. "I hit Gold's gym, beefed up, and now I'm looking good. The skanks who never had time for me start smiling at me. I'm thinking, if I ever had a shot, it'll be now. So I ask around. Then I hear Ramona's with the guy who squeezed me out right before he made millions."

"And helped put your buddy in jail."

"Yeah, that too." Tony sipped his coffee, wrinkled his nose, and tossed the half-empty cup into the trash. "It hurt, you know?"

Jay rubbed chocolate off his fingers. "My heart bleeds.

Ramona described things differently. Said you left Matt's firm in a huff, when she starting seeing him."

"Yeah, well maybe. Why should he get her? He already has everything." Tony held a stack of invoices for Challenger parts. "You like pulling the blood brother act when it suits you. I think you can spare a little sympathy."

"Another old friend of mine said, 'sympathy's in the dictionary between shit and syphilis.' Don't ever set me up like that. You try and use my temper, you'll find it cuts both ways."

"Okay. Said I was sorry."

Jay took the invitation Tony had been looking at. "What's this?"

"The big reunion."

Jay read the card. A silhouette of a boy in a tux and a girl in a prom dress, with *Save the Date! 25 years, Class of '89!* in garish neon. The date to be saved was a few weeks away.

"You going?"

"Fuck no."

The reunion was at the Umbria Americana Pavilion, with an '80s motif and cover band. *Wear a swimsuit under your dress or tux! The pool is open!*

Jay tossed the card on the desk. "Leo Zee found me at my old house. He said some things I need to check out. Whatever happened to his partner?"

"Officer Stanley? He retired. Heard he got divorced. He was a crossing guard awhile, but you know." He wiggled an imaginary bottle by his lips.

"You got any spare toggle switches, and a couple hydraulic cylinders, like for a hatchback?"

"Sure," Tony said, and plucked another donut from the package. "Right next to the money tree. Take all you want."

CHAPTER 10

The Hammerhead rolled onto the grass beneath the power lines a hair above idle, the double-baffled mufflers puffing a muted bass note. Headlights out, Jay flipped the new toggle he'd installed that cut the brake lamps and interior dome light. He killed the engine and popped another switch. The rear cushions rose on silent hydraulic cylinders, revealing a hidden compartment.

Andre's tomahawk sat inside atop a duffel bag full of kit. A big screwdriver from Tony's shop, a slim jim for car doors, duct tape, WD-40, a pack of nitrile gloves and another of hairnets, a cheap pair of flip-flops.

He sat in the dark with the door open while he taped a pair of flip flops over the soles of his work boots to mask the tread, then wrapped a pair of plastic shopping bags over them and tied them around his ankles. Pulled on a hairnet, put a trucker cap over it. Slid Andre's tomahawk handle in the back of his pants.

He disappeared into the suburban jungle behind the rows of houses, following a jogging path until he came upon the backyard of retired police officer Stanley Carnahan. A daylight creep of the house had shown no sign of a dog or security system, only the faded Pontiac in the driveway and multiple entrances shielded from view. Jay slipped around front, hidden by a weary mimosa tree. A television throbbed inside, lights splashing over closed curtains.

He raised the screwdriver to pry the door open, paused, and tried the doorknob first. Okie always said never do more work than you have to.

The knob turned and the door pushed in.

Okie also said that cops had the worst security.

68

Jay eased the door open. He breathed his four fours before padding into the kitchen. The house was one of Strick's cookie cutter jobs, a mirror of Jay's own. He eased toward the doorway, pausing as the television flickered over a figure curled on the couch like a baby.

Stanley Carnahan. A beefy, red-faced Irishman, with a quick smile, good with kids. The good cop to Leo's iceman. The one who said it would all be over when Jay's younger self signed the confession, that he could go home with his folks.

Jay had never seen them again.

He slow-stepped onto the dull brown carpet and peered at the man. A spray of broken blood vessels across his face, the nose cratered from hard drinking. A sour smell caught in the back of Jay's throat. The man looked to have his thumb in his mouth.

He felt a wave of embarrassment for the man. On closer inspection, the thumb was nickel plated steel. The twin of Leo's revolver. The muzzle between his lips.

Stanley's eyes popped open. He pointed the revolver at Jay and cracked the hammer back.

Jay stood still as stone.

"Boy, did you pick the wrong house," Stanley said, licking dry lips. Squinted at Jay's hairnet. "Sit your ass in the love seat, Paco."

Jay did as he was told.

Stanley winced as he hunched on the edge of the couch. The once-handsome man had melted into a haggard golem of his former self, but the gun never wavered.

"You a junkie?" He studied Jay's silent face, and his slick lower lip quivered. "Oh, God. It's you."

Jay flexed his thighs and triceps. No way he could launch out of the mushy old cushions with any speed.

"Leo told me you were getting out," Stanley said. "Said he'd take care of it. He likes to take care of things. Not gonna put the blame on him, though. I went along, and you're right to be here. Turned you into a damn predator in there, didn't they? You came for the weakest first."

Jay slouched a notch, head lowered. A practiced motion that had inspired pity in many soft hacks and the occasional social worker. He drew his gaze back to scan the room for makeshift weapons. Spotted a half-empty bottle of Tullamore Dew standing sentry on the end table.

"You can talk, kid." Stanley winced. "Guess you're no kid anymore. Say something."

"Why," Jay said.

"Come on. You said you did it." A dry laugh. "Even if you had help. A poor kid from out of town? None of them were gonna pay when you were there to burn."

Jay chewed his lip.

"You did what we should have. Bello's kid was a damn monster, or close enough. We should have put him away. Or put him down. They gave the little bastard a memorial, did you see that? Across from the police station. Had to see that every damn day." Stanley thrust out his chin. "Leo, he liked riding high, being the town hero. And Brendan had been through plenty already. A trial...he'd been through enough."

His eyes went rheumy.

"You ever been a hero? I guess not. It feels real good." He rested his elbow on his knee, held the gun steady over the opposite wrist. "That poor dumb ghetto kid thought we were gonna arrest him. Held up his hands like it was some teevee show."

The story went that the carjacker had a gun. Kids pointed out the gouge in the chestnut tree where his shot went wild.

"Leo shot first. That's how I remember it, but your mind does that kind of thing to help you live with it. We emptied into him. We'd run a mile through the trees. Panting. Firing after that, it was like...coming."

He ran his free hand through his hair.

"Captain Rasp shows up, says 'where's the weapon.' Leo said

it must be in the water. Cap says 'keep looking,' and drove away. We kicked some leaves around, started to shit our pants. Then the captain comes back. Lo and behold, they bagged the weapon."

He picked at the revolver's hammer with his thumbnail. "He paid my wife a visit in the hospital that night, the good captain. She wasn't my wife yet. She isn't now, either." His lip curled with a twinge of pain. "Rasp made sure she was on the same page. That the boy had a gun.

"It felt good, that's the worst part. Like it was right, pulling that trigger," he said. "*How dare he come to our town.* Now anytime I feel good I see that kid's face coming apart as he slides into the water. But not his eyes. Not his eyes. They're always there."

Stanley licked his lips. "You ever see the Bello kid?"

"All the time," Jay lied. He eased his hand along the arm of the couch, toward the bottle. No, Jay didn't see Joey Bello. He saw himself. Hacking apart the monster he was terrified he might become.

"So, who had it worse. Him or you?"

Jay tilted his head.

Stanley raised the revolver a hair. "Talk."

"Reckon he did," Jay said. "I'm still kicking."

"For now," Stanley said, with a huff of abbreviated laughter. "So how bad was it? My brother's a CO in Riker's. He says they're a bunch of animals in there."

Some were, but so were some of the hacks. "You watch your step, you get along," Jay said. "Can't show weakness. But that's the same anywhere."

"You said it," Stanley said. "Look at me. Did my twenty without another promotion. All because I wouldn't kiss Mayor Bello's ass. Think that'll cover my tab with Saint Peter?"

Stanley Carnahan had signed the confession as witness, but didn't testify at Jay's trial like Leo had. Jay stretched as he breathed. Watching the black third eye of the gun barrel.

"No, didn't think you would." Stanley grimaced and leveled his aim on Jay's heart. "I should pull this trigger, shouldn't I? You're not gonna let this go. You're here to give us what we deserve."

"I came to talk," Jay said. "Your door was open."

"I saw your face," Stanley laughed. "If you wanted to talk, you should've brought a six pack. No, you had other plans."

"I'm looking for my family," Jay said. "Thought you'd know something."

Stanley grinned. "If I knew a damn thing we wouldn't be talking here. I'd have moved to Carolina, like *she* wanted." He gestured at a picture of him and a curly-haired woman on the table. "No, you didn't come to talk. You came because we let Joey use that school like his own private torture chamber. I mean, when we shot that stupid joyriding kid, Leo said that he would've killed somebody eventually. That all we did was nip the bad in the bud. But that's not for us to do." Stanley jabbed with the revolver. "That's for God to do. Right?"

"My mama said everyone should get what they got coming to them in this world," Jay said. "Just in case they're good at lawyering come judgment day."

"Trust me, we get what we have coming. A lot of cops eat their guns." Stanley licked at his teeth, looking at the photo of him and his former wife. "Playing God leaves a bad taste in your mouth." He turned to Jay, his face gone blank. A killing face.

"Before you do whatever you have to do," Jay said, "Tell me what happened to my folks."

"They weren't your folks," Stanley laughed, flicked his eyes down. "They were using you—"

Jay leaped with a roar and the couch rocked with the impact. Stanley shuddered beneath the assault. They traded grunts and screams as Jay wrenched the revolver inch by inch until he jammed the barrel into Stanley's right eye socket.

A groan bubbled past Stanley's lips as Jay curled his thumb

over his trigger finger. Jay stared with two nailhead eyes.

"You go to hell," Jay said.

The report slapped him in both ears. Hot splatter blew back his hair. Stanley's body clenched and his head bobbed like a baby's, thick red pabulum pulsing out the mouth. His skull out of shape like a hardboiled egg that had rolled off the countertop.

Jay exhaled slow. Wiped his face on his sleeve, and washed away the tang of blood and gunsmoke with a slug of whiskey. His ears rang like the hearing tests they used to give at school. He wiped off the bottle on his shirt and left Carnahan twitching as the room filled with the earthy stink of his bowels letting go.

PART TWO

PROBLEM CHILD

CHAPTER 11

After the pool closed, Jay and Tony would fish for bullhead catfish in the creeks or play Atari with the twins, killing pixelated purple spiders until their mothers shooed them outside to ride their bikes. They met at the Lyndhurst bridge to watch Latino men fish for eels and carp in the brown slick of the Passaic. No one caught anything, so they rode through the jungle of the Avionics grounds until they came to the gates of the town dump.

Humps of mulched leaves rolled from one end of the fenced lot to the other. They rode through the maze, jumping their bikes over the hillocks. Battered old appliances stood in a row, stripped of parts. At the labyrinth's end was a sheltered spot overlooking the treetops of a valley below. A small campground littered with teenage artifacts. Crunched beer cans, condom wrappers, cigarette butts, and empty packs of e-z widers.

Tony and Billy toed at the detritus with a sort of reverence. Brendan wrinkled his nose. Jay was about to ask if they wanted to ride to the arcade when they heard voices from around the next curve.

"I bet some girl's getting nailed," Billy whispered. Tony nodded, and they rolled their bikes forward. Jay and Brendan followed.

A large woman's bra, yellowed with sweat, had been strung in the limbs of a sumac tree like a double-barreled slingshot. A pack of seventh-grade boys stood around the tree, passing around a pair of frilled women's panties.

A freckle-faced boy with broad shoulders shuffled from foot to foot, holding the pink triangle of fabric to the sun, stretching the elastic. Peering through the stain which blossomed across its crotch. After a moment's study he pressed the garment over his nose and mouth and breathed in deep as if chloroforming himself.

Their bikes skidded to a stop, sneakers dragging in the dirt. "That's Joey Bello," Brendan whispered, hunching behind his brother. Jay had seem him in school, ice blue eyes with flat black river stones for pupils, knobby little fingers with nails chewed short, always wrapped with Band-Aids from where he'd had his warts frozen off.

"That's good pussy," Joey Bello said with a knowing nod. He held out the panties to skinny Greg Kuhn, who wore his baseball cap pulled down low.

"Whatchu looking at, faggots," Bobby Algieri said. Sluggo crew cut, cheeks pocked with early acne. "Sixth graders. Think you're big shit. When middle school starts, you ain't nothing." The boys huddled and grinned, a mass of sneers beefed up by an extra year of growth.

"You little virgins ever smell pussy?" Bello held out the panties. "Buck for a sniff."

"You're sniffing on dirty drawers?" Jay said, and wrinkled his nose.

"Fat boy's digging in his pockets," Bello laughed.

"I was scratching!" Tony said.

"Jerking off," Bello said. "You were jerking off!" His voice rose in pitch to a cackle. He plodded closer, waving the panties. "C'mon, fifty cents. I know you wanna smell it. What about you, *Brenda*?"

"Shut up," Brendan said.

"You wanna smell 'em? Or are they yours?"

"Shut up, Joey," Billy said. "I'll get my dad."

"You'll get your *dad*," Joey sang. "Fag. I bet the redneck wants some." He sneered, jabbing the drawers at Jay's face.

Jay snaked sideways and dropped his bike. "Get them dirty bloomers away from me, you sick bastard."

"They're your mom's, you hillbilly faggot."

"Don't you talk about my mama!" Jay thrust his face forward with his nostrils flared.

"What are you gonna do about it, mama's boy? Your mom's so poor she showed me her titties for a dollar." Bello looked back to his crew huddled behind him. "Anyone got a dollar?"

"Shut your mouth, you panty-sniffing freak!" Jay launched at Bello and swung wide. The bigger boy ducked back and laughed. Nicky Paladino, tall and lean, grabbed Jay from behind and heaved him up. Jay lashed out with kicks, his face red.

"I'm gonna get my dad," Billy snapped, and rode away. Tony's eyes darted between the six older boys and the gate.

"Hold him," Bello said. "Gonna stuff it down your throat. Maybe some pussy will knock the fag outta you."

Bobby Algieri and his brothers grabbed for Jay's limbs while Joey Bello aimed the wad of stained fabric at Jay's seething mouth.

Nick screamed and held his arm. "He bit me!"

"Only girls bite," Bello laughed. "See? He's a faggot."

Nicky wrinkled his nose at the choppy crescent of tooth-marks. "Gonna beat you for that."

Brendan dropped his bike, eyebrows knitted in righteous anger. He shoved Joey into the leaves. "Stop it, Joey," he said. "Or I'll tell."

Jay squirmed and kicked his way out, and turned on them with balled fists. The Algieri brothers blocked the exit while Joey climbed out of the leaves.

"Or you'll tell *what*, faggot? That we caught you staring at our meat while we took a piss in the park?"

"You were—"

"He wanted us to ram it up his rear," Bello said. He and Nicky flanked their prey. "You still want it, don't you faggot?"

Brendan's eyes darted for an exit.

"You're not going anywhere, *Brenda*."

Tony kneaded the handles of his Huffy. "J-Joey, I think you got shit stain on your lip."

"The fuck you say, fat boy?"

"Those panties got skidmarks. You got shit on your uh, mouth. I th-think you all do," Tony said.

Bello glared at the panties in his hand and made a face. Greg Kuhn squirmed like a slice of bacon on a hot skillet and rubbed his mouth on his sleeve.

"Let's book!" Tony said. The three of them biked for the tight curve between two leaf mountains and bowled the Algieri brothers out of the way. Nicky jammed his stick into Brendan's spokes.

Brendan yelped as his bike somersaulted into a leaf pile. Joey Bello laughed and pushed Brendan's face in the leaves.

Jay skidded to a stop and ran back.

Bobby Algieri wiped his mouth on his palm, smelled it for signs of shit. "He's lying."

Bello and Nicky dragged Brendan over the mulch pile by his kicking feet, laughing as the leaves went under his shirt. The Algieri brothers pinballed Jay between them, shoving him back and forth while Greg Kuhn laughed.

Tony knocked the cap from Greg's head and ran off with the beanie underneath.

"Hey!"

Tony ran to the rock-strewn edge. "I'll throw it!"

"If you drop that you're so dead, Tony!"

"Let us go!"

"I don't care what you do to his Jew hat," Bobby Algieri said. His brothers pushed Jay into the leaves and Bobby, the oldest and biggest, sat on his back. "You bite, we'll stuff turds in your mouth."

Greg clenched his fists at Tony. "Give me my *kippah*!"

"Take it, Greg. Why are you being such a jerk?" Tony set the beanie on a discarded washing machine. "You were so cool in computer class."

"Shut up," Greg said, and snatched back his *kippah*.

Joey Bello and Nicky walked from behind a leaf pile,

laughing and slapping. Nicky dragged Brendan's jeans through the dirt. Joey held out a pair of white BVDs.

"You better wear those panties, Brenda," Joey howled. "Or you're walking home naked, queer bait. You'll get reamed by every fag for miles."

Nicky snorted and watched the path with a twitchy little grin. He had plain handsome features, but his expression made his face seem waxy and flat as a mannequin's.

"Come on out," Joey said. "We ain't leaving until we see you."

"Go to hell!" Brendan yelled from cover, his voice shaking.

Bello wadded Brendan's briefs and threw them over the ledge. "Whoo! There go your underwear, fag! Better dance for us, or your jeans go next."

"What the hell's wrong with you?" Jay said.

Bello bent and flicked Jay's nose. "You like that Crane cunt, don't you? Greg, tell the redneck how you kissed that slut."

Greg squirmed his lip. "That was fourth grade," he said. "Spin the bottle."

"I bet you could feel those big tits up any time you wanted."

Tony's face went red, and he charged Bello with a roar.

"Whoa, mad elephant," Bello laughed, skipping back. "You're too slow, you fat piece of shit. You like that cocktease?"

"Fuck you, Joey!"

"Tony Baloney!" Bello said. "You'd crush her."

"You're fat, too!"

"Not as fat as you, you fat fuck."

"Fatty fatty two by four," Algieri chimed in.

"Four by eight," Joey said.

"Hormona," Greg said. "That's what the other girls call the stuck-up bitch."

Bello laughed. "Hormona. I bet she'd moan with Tony's fat ass bouncing on her." He jabbed Tony's stomach with his finger. "She'd love your fat cock."

Jay struggled, and Bobby ground his face into the leaves. Jay snarled and spat.

Tony swung wild and missed.

Bello cracked him across the mouth. "Don't ever try to hit me, fat boy."

Tony touched his nose and stared at the blood in his hand, jaw quivering. Bello rammed both palms against Tony's chest and knocked him to the dirt.

"Get him, Greg. Hold him, Nicky. Sit on his back, stupid."

Bello crouched by Tony's face. "It was a compliment when I said you fucked that slut. No girl will ever love a fat tub of shit like you."

Tony trembled. "Fuck you, Joey. We're gonna tell everybody you sniff filthy underwear."

"Oh yeah?" Bello smiled. He unzipped his pants took out his penis. He took a cowboy stance in front of Tony's face. "Hey, *Brenda*. Come get a free show."

Greg squinted and laughed nervously.

Bello grinned. "You faggots aren't gonna say shit."

Tony wrenched his face away as the hot stream hit. He buried his face in the dirt and howled.

"You sick son of a bitch!" Jay hollered.

"Gah, you're spraying me!" Greg scrambled away. "I'm going home."

Nicky shook with silent laughter and held out Brendan's jeans for Joey to piss on.

Red police lights flared off the leaves. A siren blipped.

"Come on out and wear your jeans now," Bello laughed, in that forced high pitch. He threw the jeans toward Brendan's hiding spot, and slowly zipped his pants.

The Algieri boys leapt off Jay. Nick Paladino stood, unable to conceal his grin.

"Brendan!" Officer Leo Zelazko marched around a leaf pile, his sharp jaw set. Billy jogged behind. "Brendan, where are you?"

"I'm not coming out until everyone's gone," Brendan called.

Tony sobbed, wiping his face on his sleeve. Jay spat leaves and picked up a branch like a club.

"Desmarteaux!" Officer Leo snapped. "Put that down."

"But they—"

"Now! Or I'll drag your mother out of work to come get you."

Jay threw the stick into a leaf pile.

"The rest of you, scoot. I catch you trespassing again, I'll make your parents come get you at the station."

"Sure thing, Officer Zee," Bello snorted, and walked past him. Nicky followed.

Billy gaped as his father ignored their tormentors like ghosts. "Dad!"

"Go on, get out of here." Officer Leo waved each boy away with a hand, as if smacking them upside the head. He turned to Jay and Tony. "That means you boys, too."

Tony and Jay collected their bikes, leaving Billy to stare at his father.

Jay looked back and saw Brendan creep out, hands cupped over his crotch as he shuffled to his piss-soaked jeans.

Jay and Tony rode to the water fountain by the park's baseball diamond, where Tony washed off as best he could. The ride home was empty of Tony's usual spur of the moment questions and exclamations. He kept quiet until they passed through the abandoned electroplating plant at the bottom of Jay's street, the air tickling their nose with chemicals.

"You swear not to tell?"

Jay stopped his bike in the metal-stained dirt. He fished his bone-handled Case knife from his pocket, that Papa Andre had given him. He unfolded the blade with his thumbnail.

Tony circled around him. "Wanna play mumblety-peg? Sorry about your toe last time."

"Shut up a minute."

For once, Tony did.

Jay slicked the blade's silvery hand-honed edge along his palm.

"Jesus, what you do that for?"

Jay beckoned with the knife point. Tony edged closer, staring at the red welling in Jay's life line.

"My folks saved me once," Jay said. "From someone a lot worse than Bello. So he did what he did. And when we're older and stronger, we'll make him pay. I promise you that."

Tony nodded.

Jay passed him the knife handle first.

A trash barge on the Passaic sounded its horn as it approached the bridge. Its lowing echoed through their chests as they ground their palms together and bit back winces.

CHAPTER 12

As the harsh July sun cut through the trees, Jay stared at the memorial. A simple plaque on a stone inhabiting a triangle between city hall and the police station, it portrayed a smiling young man swinging a baseball bat, the all-American boy.

Joseph Bello, Junior 1971-1986
Only the Good Die Young

Jay's breakfast turned to acid. He scored the metal with Andre's blade, and walked around the corner to the car.

RAPIST.

Jay lost himself in the work. There was plenty of it. As the sun crept toward noon, he adjusted the idle on a Camaro while Tony argued with a customer, circling a silver BMW.

"Knew I should've gone to the dealer." The owner knuckled the groomed scruff that covered his weak chin.

"You brought your own parts," Tony said. "And it took three hours longer than what I charged. Far as I'm concerned I already gave you a discount."

"You know Beemerfest is next week, at the Hermitage," Beemer Guy said, and tilted his head. "I know people."

"I'm sure they know you, too." Tony chewed his lip and tugged the invoice from the man's hand. "Make it two hundred even."

While Tony reprinted the invoice, a Nutley police cruiser parked in front, blocking half the driveway. A cold fist twisted Jay's insides. *Cops can smell outlaw,* Okie said. *Just like we can smell law.* A man with a shaved head and a Roman nose stepped out of the cruiser in full uniform.

Jay didn't recognize him. The anger on Tony's face melted into despair.

"Tony Baloney," the policeman said.

Tony ran the customer's credit card, and avoided the policeman's eyes. "What can I do for you, Officer Algieri?"

"Oh, just a friendly visit. I thought your customers ought to know that you employ a convicted felon."

"What?" Beemer Guy looked around him, as if masked thugs were about to spring out and grab his wallet.

Algieri pointed to where Jay worked on the Supra. "That scumbag. He killed a kid."

"What the hell?"

Jay wiped his hands on a rag and walked over slow. "That was a long time ago. I did my time."

"Did you work on my car?"

"No," Tony said. "I did. But he's certified."

"Certifiable," Algieri snickered. "He could be copying your house keys, you wouldn't even know."

"I wouldn't let you wash my car, much less work on it," the Beemer Guy said, and peeled out of the lot.

Algieri gave a gargoyle smile. "I got nothing to do but sit here all day." He walked back to the cruiser and sat inside.

Back in the office, Tony tore the wrapper off a protein bar and gnawed off a chunk. "Believe that shit?" he said through a mouthful of chocolate tar. "Why you think I left Nutley? Fuckin' Bobby Algieri kept pulling me over. 'Just a roadside check, Tony Baloney.'"

While Bello cut with cruel words, Bobby Algieri hung back with a sneer, audience to the humiliation.

Tony picked up a hand gripper with a spring thick enough for a bear trap. With a snarl, he clamped it closed, held it there. Veins on his arm bulged. "I could crush his head, but he's a cop."

Jay pushed the door shut. "He only watched. Nicky Paladino was the one who got away."

Tony huffed and switched hands with the gripper. "He still works at the ShopRite." He crumbled the wrapper and spiked it into the trashcan. "Can't even shop there. Ma does it for me. Think I want the cunts who laughed at me in high school ringing me up at the register?" The vein in his forehead pulsed. "Bobby fucking Algieri. When he pulled me over, I wanted to back over him and drag him for blocks."

"Easy, Tone. You're fixing to turn green and smash stuff."

Tony laughed, let out a long breath. "It was what, almost thirty years ago, but I feel it every time I drive through town. Cross the bridge, where they threw Brendan's hat in the creek. Or pass Church Hill, or even the high school. I can see Bello staring from the steps. I still hear his voice in my head, sometimes. I use it when I work out, you know? To get that last rep."

Jay opened his mouth and Tony held up a hand.

"Why didn't I stand up for myself? It's like I deserve it, for not having the balls to hit Bello in his fucking ugly face."

Tony made a fist and stared at it, like he might take a swing at himself.

"We were only kids, Tone."

"Yeah, what the hell did we know?" Tony kneaded his temples. "What could we do, the Safety Dance?"

Jay shifted to his other foot. "I'm gonna finish up under the hood. You gonna be all right?"

"I'm fine," Tony said. "Sometimes I wish I was more like you." He tore open another protein bar, peanut butter this time.

"No you don't," Jay said.

Outside, he ignored Algieri's attempts at cold glares. He'd been a coward, a hanger-on, an observer. Jay knew the type. Fall guys, too shit-scared to rat. Safe in a crew, as long as they stayed useful.

A green Cherokee Sport pulled in the lot with the windows open, Pearl Jam loud on the stereo. Billy Zelazko stepped out of it, in running clothes. Officer Algieri frowned at him.

"This isn't your jurisdiction," Billy said. "Why don't you go home."

"It ain't yours, either."

"My father know you're here?"

Algieri grinned. "Who you think sent me?"

"Still a Giants fan, Bobby?"

"Course."

"Box tickets, preseason. Go home."

"But the chief—"

"You did what Pop wanted. I'll talk to him."

"It ain't right, him being here," Algieri said. "We were just boys being boys. But he's psycho."

"Go home, Bobby. Check your mailbox."

Algieri gave Jay his cop glare again. "I know you don't got a license. I see you in town, that's a four-hundred-dollar ticket, and I'm calling a wrecker. Every single time." He drove out, flipped on the emergency lights at the intersection, and roared back toward Nutley.

Tony walked out of the shop, taking wary steps. "Thanks, Billy."

Billy sighed. "Thought this was done. And this is my last favor. You know this scumbag pissed in my car?"

"I'm right here," Jay said. "Ain't going nowhere."

"Jay," Tony said. "I dunno, maybe you should. You know, lay low a while."

"Thought this was low," Jay said. "I'm trying to make a living here."

"Yeah, well so am I." Tony looked at the ground.

"I'll be in Saturday, Tony. For the brake job." Billy said, and climbed into his Cherokee. "Hopedale, Jay. Take the ticket. This is only gonna get worse."

He watched Billy drive away, and Tony drag his feet back to

the office. Worse was where he'd been most of his life. If they wanted to kill him, they should try kindness.

Jay held the pay-as-you-go flip phone open with the post office number punched in, but did not stab send. He'd seen cellular phones in prison, but never used one. Couldn't get over putting his ear next to something that had been wrapped in a condom and hidden inside somebody's ass.

Mama Angeline's last letter had come five years ago. He thought of what to say. Hey, this forty-year-old con wants to drop in at your next crawfish boil and crash on the couch.

The memories of his folks were a faded Polaroid deteriorating in the attic of his mind, chewed by the rats of doubt fed by Ramona's harsh words. He'd been closer to Ramona than any human being, even Mama Angeline.

Questions clawed at the back of his brain. The answers gnawed at his stomach. If his folks were dead, or his memory had faded in the light of another child's smile, he wasn't sure he wanted to know.

He hit send.

The phone thought a moment before it rang. He stared at the blank ceiling, the tone rattling in his head. On the seventh ring, a woman's voice answered.

"Post office, may I help you?"

"Ma'am? I hope you can. I'm trying to find my people. They lived down there before the storm."

"Well, that's no trouble dawlin', ya not the first been looking." Her voice was scratchy with nicotine, and had that New Orleans "Yat" accent which resembled the Bronx more than a Southern lilt. It brought a smile to Jay's face. "What's ya name, now?"

"My name's Jay, ma'am. I'm looking for Angie Desmarteaux. She'd be about—"

"Hold on, I got someone at the counter."

Her phone touched wood. Jay closed his eyes, listened to the muffled sounds on the other end. Felt the summer heat radiate through the receiver, smelled the thick air. It turned to ice as he saw tombstones bearing Angeline and Andre's names in his mind. Bodies in floodwater, bellies bloated and white.

"Who were ya looking for now?"

"The Desmarteauxs, ma'am. Angeline and Andre. They'd be about sixty. Andre's a woodworker, makes real fine furniture and the like. Angeline, she's got blonde hair..." Jay spun his wheels, and realized he didn't know what his Mama would do for work. She could cook, but most women in bayou country could. She could shoot the face off a playing card at twenty feet, and sometimes she bought and sold jewelry. Folks were always coming by for her opinion on this ring or that necklace, but she didn't wear any herself, not until they moved north. Then she and Andre each wore a thin gold band. "She might be working at a jewelry store. Got a good eye for stones."

"Hmm, don't know dem," she said. A fingernail tapped the handset. "I can ax at church. Lemme get an inkpen. Gimme a number to reach y'at."

"I'd be real grateful, ma'am."

He gave her his number. She told him her name was Cindy, and said he should call back next week. "We having a *cochon du lait*. Don't ya worry now. I'll find someone who knows."

He thanked her and closed the phone.

He called Martins' office next. A young woman answered and told him Martins was with a client. "Tell him it's Desmarteaux."

"Oh, wow. He's been having us call all over the place looking for you."

"Well you win the prize."

He waited.

"Like crazy," Martins said. "That's how you've got us here. Where the hell are you?"

Jay liked Martins. He had a full beard and a bald patch on top, like someone had used his head for a pencil eraser. A good sense of humor and a jaw like a pit bull.

"I'm working at an auto shop in Belleville," Jay said. "All good here."

"You know what I mean. You weren't supposed to cycle out until August."

Jay told him what Billy had said about Leo Zelazko and Matty Strick gaming him out to avoid confrontation with the Bello family.

"Well, I don't usually file complaints for my clients getting early release. Looks like we're all done."

"They're threatening my boss," Jay said. "Trying to get me fired. I want to file harassment charges."

"And you're in the right. They shouldn't be doing that. A lawyer can take care of it, but it won't be me."

"Come on now, you got the big win of getting me free. Now you gonna let me swing? I know Ramona was paying for it."

"Uh—"

"She told me," Jay said. "No bad blood. You ain't the first one who ever lied to me."

"Jay, it's not like that. Your case was important. We'll be using it to help a lot of men like you, who did things as kids, and got put away for life."

Wasn't the first time he'd been used, either.

"Martins," Jay said. "You won the war, but they're gonna kill me here in the peace. A man's got to work. Now, I ain't got her money, but I can pay something."

"No offense, Jay. Our hourly rate? Unless you're fixing Ferraris…"

So that's how it was. Jay thanked him and let him get back to work.

CHAPTER 13

Jay had met Cheetah on his first day in juvenile prison at Annandale farms. A little smart-assed four-eyes named Alfonse, who had earned his name for how fast he'd hotwired the cars his crew took for joyrides. The guards paid back his smart mouth by sticking him with a strapping, cold-eyed cellmate named Feature. Jay had the cell next door.

He hadn't anticipated sleeping his first night through, but the nightmare music of Cheetah failing to fight off his cellmate's advances made sure of it. Jay shouted for the guards until he was hoarse.

The next morning, Jay picked a fight with Feature on the basketball courts. Feature was a head taller and had an easy twenty pounds on him. The boys crowded around to watch the new kid get pounded and to shield the fight from the bored guards.

Jay couldn't box yet, but he knew how to fight mean.

Feature had speed and reach, used both with cruel precision. Snapping quick knuckles to the ribs, the point of the nose.

He popped Jay's head back. Jay let the tears run free. Lighter fuel to the flames smoldering in his opponent's eyes.

Feature flashed a smile and threw hard. Jay lunged to take the punch on his hairline, like Papa Andre had taught him.

The crowd winced at the crack. Feature yelped and clutched his busted knuckles.

Jay leapt on him like a wolverine with a cattle prod up its ass. By the time the guards pulled him off, Feature had one eye puffed shut and a chunk bitten out of his chin.

Jay bared a bloody smile as the hacks dragged him away.

No one bothered him or Cheetah after that.

After they graduated to Rahway prison, they kept their friendship on the down-low. No one crossed the color line in the open. They communicated through a sister named Rene, little brother to one Verdad Hernandez—corona of the Latin Kings— who ruled from his roost in the SHU, the Secure Housing Unit. Jay fell in with an old outlaw named Okie Kincaid, and Cheetah found Mack, a Brick City construction foreman and sometimes fight promoter who ran the yard's boxing ring, where Jay and Cheetah could talk freely as they sparred.

Jay knew Cheetah ran strip clubs for the Italians, and that meant selling women and drugs. He wanted to break clean, but the citizens didn't want him. He needed papers to operate in their world, and Cheetah could get them. Maybe he knew a mechanic shop that would overlook Jay's record.

And maybe he'd gotten over their last bout.

Cheetahs dangled like a lure between Newark's train station and the Prudential Center, where the Devils hit the ice. The building was painted flat black with a stripe of purple neon ringed around the top like a hat band. A garish painting of a curvy woman in a leopard-spotted bikini leered from the wall.

Jay touched the brass door handle where the paint had been worn off. One summer day as kids, he and Tony rode their bikes to a go-go bar called The Red Shingle, a brick dump with windows painted over black. They scraped the paint with a penny and peered in at men slouched over beers while a skinny woman in a bikini danced a bored little jig, until a sallow bartender with crusty elbows came out whipping a dishrag. They ran, and Tony flipped the finger. The bartender gave chase.

Tony yelped when the bartender caught him and wrenched a handful of chub. Jay doubled back to find the man tripped to his knees and hawking up a lung cookie. "Little fuckers," he panted, and wiped a brown rope of slime from his yellowed mustache. "Like them titties, don't you?"

They mounted their bikes. The bartender slumped against the brick wall and lit a smoke. "Hey, fat boy." He gestured with his cigarette. "Go into that drugstore. Five bucks, they'll sell you an electric pussy. That's the only trim you'll ever get."

They left the man laughing and wheezing.

"Think they really sell one?" Tony asked on the ride home.

"Don't reckon I want to find out."

Jay felt the same worm twist in his gut that he'd felt that day. The only time he thought of sex without it turning sour was with Ramona.

He pulled the door handle.

It opened on a dark atrium, where a bald tree trunk in a sleeveless black shirt leaned on a metal stool, thumbs dancing on the screen of his phone. There was a sea urchin of black hair living on his chin, and his meaty forearms were graffitied with expensive Japanese ink. He looked at Jay like he was a freshly deposited turd.

"I'm here to see Cheetah," Jay said.

"Come back later," the bouncer said, and went back to his phone.

"I called," Jay said. "He'll want to see me." He peered around the man's juiced physique. An empty bar beckoned through an open curtain.

"Whoa, is there a fuckin' problem?" The bouncer planted a palm on Jay's chest.

It was no problem to snap the man's thumb and knee him in the balls. Kick one of his skinny legs out from under him. Crash his head into the stool, bounce it off the floor a few times. Okie talked a lot about delayed gratification, Headshrinker Shit, he called it. How you had to picture the reward, to ease the waiting. He told some story about marshmallows. You could get one marshmallow now, but if you waited, you could get two marshmallows later.

"No problem," Jay said, and cracked a smile. A man's eyes felt kind of like marshmallows before they popped under your thumbnails.

The bouncer pushed him back a step. "Then come back later."

"Tell Cheetah I'm waiting," Jay said, on his way out.

"I'm not that moolie's secretary," the bouncer said, and went back to his phone.

Back outside, Jay rounded the corner to the parking lot. A silver Mercedes G55 and a coffee-colored Coupe DeVille land yacht hugged the wall. There was a newer model Cadillac sedan, the one with the monster V8, and that big SUV they made. Jay had only seen those in magazines. He ran a hand along the polished paint. The building was unpainted brick in the rear with a blackened exhaust fan and a Dumpster flanking an open kitchen door.

In the kitchen, a short Latino in a dingy apron unloaded a green rack of glasses from the dishwasher. He looked up as Jay approached.

"*Donde esta* Cheetah?" Jay said.

The man pointed through the kitchen.

"*Gracias*," Jay said, and dodged men in aprons on his way into the club proper. Dim blue light from above froze the room with a dreamlike gloaming. Black walls and blue velvet curtains, with matching low-back chairs ringing stages skewered with chrome poles. The air vibrated with a dull bass thump from hidden speakers. A tickle caught in the back of Jay's throat, the chemical buzz of air freshener and old perfume over spilled booze and human funk.

Curtains covered three doorways. The fourth was lit with restroom signs. In one corner of the ceiling, one-way glass allowed a view from above. The boss's office. Where Cheetah ought to be.

Jay stepped through the curtains nearest to it and bumped face-first into a topless mahogany statue.

"Oh shit!" The dancer skipped back and folded her arms over her breasts. She was as tall as Jay in her stocking feet, with a glow to her rich brown skin.

"Sorry, ma'am," Jay said, and tore his gaze away. Heat flushed his ears, and his boxers went snug.

"Ma'am? I look old or something?" she laughed. "You're red as a beet."

"Been away awhile," Jay said, admiring her white thigh-high stockings and pale blue boy-shorts. "I'm looking for Cheetah's office. My name's Jay." He'd seen her breasts. Only polite that he introduce himself.

"I'm Leticia," She pointed over his shoulder. "The office stairs are on the other side."

A thin Asian girl in a Betty Page wig appeared at Leticia's shoulder. "Hey. Get the fuck out!"

Jay stepped back with a quick bow. "I was just on my way."

A flare in Leticia's eyes made Jay snap around.

The bouncer charged across the room like a tattooed bull. "You motherfucker!"

Jay juked left, skipped into boxing footwork. The bouncer kicked a chair into his legs and looped an overhand right to Jay's ear that jumbled his vision.

The pain lit up Jay's eyes, swept aside the down-low tingle from his first glimpse of real-live bare breasts in a quarter century, stoked a fire of indignation in his gut. His hands launched into a flurry of muscle memory. Two jabs to the bouncer's throat and neck, a left hook to the ribs, and a chain of body blows as the big man covered up.

The bouncer roared and crushed Jay into a bear hug, plowing through the curtains. The dancers screamed as the men hit the floor, tangled like lovers in the sheets. Painted toenails scampered and pink heels kicked at their faces.

Jay pounded the bouncer's nose back with his palm and kicked his way out from underneath him.

The Asian dancer clocked Jay across the head with her shoe. "Get him, Randal!"

Jay clinched, and Randal the bouncer heaved him onto the make-up counter. Lipsticks and bottles tinked on the floor as he pinned Jay to the mirror and threw wild hooks.

Jay gripped Randal's bullet head and dug both thumbs into the folds of his eyes, knuckle deep. Two marshmallows about to pop.

Randal screamed and clutched his face.

The ragged shriek of the women halted Jay from scooping out a tablespoon of brains. Okie's calming voice broke through the haze of fury. *Face ain't worth dying for. Or doing a stretch.* A celly named Leif Dunham had fought MMA, before he'd cracked a skull in a street fight. They'd cross-trained. He scoured his memory for one of the moves, and scrambled around Randal's shoulders and snaked a forearm under his chin.

The bouncer stumbled through the curtains with Jay on his back and tried to scrape him off on the door jamb. The Asian dancer followed, swinging her stiletto heel as they swayed across the main floor.

Two men exited the stairs, one thick, one thin. Cheetah, a lean chestnut middleweight in a summer suit. Mack ballooning a turquoise tracksuit with a matching golf cap. Cheetah tilted his head, regarding the tussle with cool eyes.

Jay sank the choke deep and smiled over Randal's shoulder. He clamped down until the bouncer crumpled to his knees. Randal slumped with a gurgle.

Cheetah swept a hand over his shaved-smooth head. Sharp eyes took in a scene that should not be, and quickly made sense of it. "Welcome home, brother."

Jay extracted his arm and took Cheetah's hand, pulling him in for three hard slaps on the back.

The dancers piled through the curtains and stared at Randal's wheezing bulk. "What the fuck," the Asian dancer said.

"It's all over, ladies," Mack said, around a dead cigar.

Jay brushed his rumpled shirt. It had split between the shoulders.

"You all right?" Cheetah said.

"A few love taps," Jay said, and nudged Randal with his shoe. "Who's the jag-off?"

"He comes with the club," Cheetah said.

Randal coughed and groaned. He put a hand to the ground.

"Hear that, big fella? The boss knows me." Jay rubbed the back of his head. His palm came away red. He wiped it on his torn shirt.

"He ain't the boss." An old hawk-nosed bruiser with gray wings in his slicked-back hair held open the curtains for a hulking silhouette behind him.

Dante Mastino had hound-dog eyes, a forehead that recalled Easter Island moai, and hands fit for scooping gravel pits. His hand-tailored suit hung off him like cave bear pelts. He surveyed the wreckage.

"So you're out," Dante said. "The one-man walking shit-storm."

Jay had met Dante when he did five for perjury. Did the man a favor that could never be repaid. One Dante had never expected to with Jay being a lifer. Gears turned behind Dante's eyes.

"Your boy swung first," Jay said. "He had it coming."

Dante prodded Randal with a loafer. "This fuckin' jooch. Get him up, Vito."

The old hawk helped Randal to his knees.

"You interrupted a meeting. Cheetah and I," Dante said, "we're discussing the future. I'm guessing you didn't stop by for a drink and some tits."

"Could use help with some paperwork," Jay said. "I'll pay the same as anybody else."

"Later," Dante said, furrowing his brow. "We can take care of anything. You being out, this changes things. We could use someone like you right now."

Jay knew what Dante wanted. With the life sentence, Jay had

put his fists out for hire until Okie knocked sense into him.

Cheetah said, "Give him a second to breathe. How long you been out?"

Jay weighed his response to avoid offense. "Few days. Had to take care of citizen shit. I'm here to see old friends, maybe do a little business. Things ain't like they were before. If they were, I wouldn't be out. And I aim to keep them that way."

"What, you don't want to work for me?" Dante said. "You always thought you were too good for us."

"I never said that," Jay said. "But I don't work for no whoremasters."

"Whoa," Cheetah said. "Cool down, everybody. We should celebrate. Come on, to the bar."

Randal shook his head clear and blinked the wooziness out of his eyes. "Motherfucker."

"Get him some water," Dante said to Vito. "We'll be at the bar."

"How you doing, sweet cheeks?" Jay said to Randal. "You gotta learn not to mistake patience for weakness. An old friend of mine taught me that. Now I taught you. It's a good lesson. Don't take it the wrong way."

Cheetah laughed and led Jay toward the bar. "No more of that. That boy is Frank Dellamorte's nephew. That's why we keep him on, even though he's an asshole."

Jay held a bar napkin to the spot where the dancer's heel had gouged his scalp, to staunch the drip. "So, you miss me?"

CHAPTER 14

Jay was bussed to Rahway a year before Cheetah, and entered the chilly cruciform edifice without a friend in sight. A concrete bunker with four wings, where the inmates walked free on three open tiers. Jay had bulked up some, but not enough. He'd heard tales that kiddie-rapers got a broom handle shoved up their ass until it came out their mouth. That was the first prison myth he saw shattered. If the short-eyes were tough enough, no one did a damn thing about them.

For example, Feature held court in the mess hall with a big crew, when by all rights he should've been piked at the gates as warning to all his predatory kind. He wasted no time. Dumped Jay's tray on day one, and said if he went down easy, all was forgiven.

Jay's answer was to break the handle of a plastic spork off in Feature's cheek.

Within a week Feature and his crew cornered him in the shower. Jay took three of them with him to the infirmary, but not before they took what they wanted.

An orderly with a Norse rune tattoo whispered in Jay's ear while he sank below the hospital bed in a morphine haze. *White men need to stick together in here. We can protect you, bro. Birds of a feather flock together. They'll be running trains on your ass like Grand Central.*

Jay's jaw was swollen shut. He closed his eyes in answer.

He woke to a black trusty sweeping the floor, knocking the broom against his bedside. *Soon as you can walk, we're coming for seconds.*

Jay plugged his ears while the trusty told him everything Feature had planned.

In the morning, old bikers with grizzled beards huddled around his bed reciting hate-filled bullshit. Called themselves the Heimdall Brotherhood after the whitest god of the Vikings. Jay nodded his bandaged head in agreement. *Survival*, he told himself. Like he'd pretended to love The Witch. *A tattoo is a scar by choice, and scars are armor. Enough scars and the witches and monsters can never touch the real you inside.*

The tattoo gun was made from a smuggled electric toothbrush. Their Norse arrow emblem speared on his right deltoid. *This is Tyr, the warrior god*, a Viking lord said, and slapped the fully decorated Thor's hammer on his meat slab arm. *Kill one of the mud people, you'll get your hammer. Start with Feature. We'll get you the shank. Then you're protected.*

When Jay hobbled back to his cell, a hack told him to report to the library. Italians played chess in one corner with pieces made of toilet paper mâché. A few cons pored through outdated law books.

A rawboned old coot ran the place. He wore his white-streaked hair back in a ponytail, his face scruffed with a red pepper beard that barely hid a star-shaped scar in his right cheek.

He sneered at the tattoo on Jay's arm, which still wept blood. "You fell for their play," the old man said. "You dumb shit. You're gonna need to be a whole lot smarter to last in here. This here's the best job in the joint. How you think you landed in shit this sweet?"

Jay gripped the shank in his pocket. "I'll die before I pay for anything that way, geezer."

The old devil smiled and rolled his sleeve. The faded tattoo of a viper's head stared from the back of his left hand, its fat copperhead coils looping around the forearm. "A rattlesnake's only got one play," he said. "The bite'll kill you dead, but you can corner one in an open field. Because it's too damn stupid to back down."

He flexed and the viper's tail flicked, death without warning. "Name's Okie Kincaid," he said. "I got wind of how you tore through Feature's boys. I can make a good boxer out of you."

"And what if I don't want to?" Jay made a point in his pocket with the shank.

Okie laughed. "Don't make me shove that down your throat." He skipped back into a boxer's stance, nimble as a mountain goat.

"You ain't touching me and walking away," Jay said. He held the blade low.

"You think that's a gift? The Hitler Bitches got wind of a cell search coming," Okie said. "Then it's on your jacket, not theirs. You shank Feature, it costs them nothing. It gets you a death on your jacket."

"I'm in for life anyway," Jay said. "Got nothing to lose."

"You got plenty," Okie said. "A man's nothing but what he *does*. You wanna be the sucker who does other people's shit work, you go ahead. Feature's crew runs hooch, the HB boys must want to take over."

Fear and confusion jerked Jay like a puppet. He lunged with the blade.

Okie juked left and hit Jay in the liver. The shank clattered to the floor. He scooped it up and hid it away. When Jay caught his breath, Okie pointed to a wall of stacked boxes filled with mildewing books. "Unbox those, fiction on the left table, non-fiction on the right."

Jay limped to his task.

After he stacked the books, Okie told him how the white power gangs eyed the new fish for good muscle, and paid gangbanger wolves to put the scare into them. "You ain't the first, and won't be the last."

"I can't let this go."

"The hacks will be watching you," Okie said. "And no one

thinks you're a punk. Not after the damage you did. You made four on one look like even odds, and you can't even fight. Not yet."

Okie hid the shank in the library, and sure enough, a cell-to-cell search went down that week. The night after, Wing Four woke to howls and gurgling screams. In the morning, Feature and two of his crew died in the infirmary puking their guts. Rumor from the orderlies was that someone dumped a bottle of Drano in their last batch of toilet-tank hooch. The mix stunk so bad they couldn't smell the poison before their throats had liquefied.

Okie winked at Jay across the mess hall, and sipped from an invisible flask.

Jay followed him to the yard's boxing ring to train.

Footwork came natural. He'd danced the Cajun two-step with Mama Angeline from a tender age. Hardest part of sparring was holding back when his opponent wanted to take his head off. Learning patience and timing. His cheekbones thickened over time. His knuckles grew prominent, his body lean. He saw the rhythm in every movement.

Okie learned to box in the Marines, where he'd also learned to steal. When they fled Korea, he kept right on stealing weapons and morphine from military depots to arm and fund bank robberies across the Midwest. He worshiped the Depression-era outlaws, and while free, he'd made a pilgrimage each year to the desolate highway in Bienville Parish where Bonnie Parker and Clyde Barrow were gunned down, to piss on the marker dedicated to the lawmen who'd done it.

"When I was a boy, they paraded their corpses through town. Laid 'em on a slab in the drug store. I snuck in and put my finger in a bullet hole in Bonnie's leg." Okie smiled. "She was a beauty, but both of 'em were dumb sumbitches. No one should ever know an outlaw's name. Copperhead's deadly 'cause he gives no warning. Strikes, then fades into the leaves and disappears." Okie flexed the tattoo on his arm.

He wasn't the best boxer himself, nor the best corner man, and his third-strike life stretch for armed robbery proved him a terrible thief. But as the adage goes, he was a great teacher. And Jay soon followed his every word.

"Don't watch the eyes," Okie coached. "They lie. Watch the heart, the plane of the chest. Keep your head down. Sink at the knees! Like your balls are a pair of watermelons."

CHAPTER 15

They drank and talked old times at the bar, but Dante's eyes were somewhere else. Worried, and not hiding it well. "I got a meeting with the Fox. You throw the Cajun a nice party tonight. Maybe he'll remember who his friends are." Jay shook his hand before he left. Dante showed the wounds plain in his eyes.

"You hungry?" Cheetah said.

"I'm always hungry."

They got in Cheetah's Benz G55, a silver Jeep for rich folks.

"Told you Dante took care of us," Cheetah said. "Rene, too. It's Raina, now."

"No shit?" Jay said. "How's he look?"

"She," Cheetah said. "And call her Raina, all right? Don't make a big deal about it."

"Sounds like you're riding a gravy train with biscuit wheels."

"Sure wish it was." Cheetah let out a long sigh, and his slim fingers worked the teak steering wheel. "The club's a washing machine for Frankie Dellamorte's money, but we still need bodies through the door. Newark's changing. Dante sees things my way. Lose the girls, expand the kitchen. Make it a sports bar during the week, and a dance club on the weekends. Run book if you got to. How's that sound to you?"

"Real smart," Jay said, leaning back in the seat.

"Well, Frankie doesn't see it that way. He's been running things at the port from his castle in Livingston so long, he can't see that a strip joint won't have much of a future, least not there by the Rock. Not when the Hustler Club's looking at putting one of their steakhouses in the hotel around the corner."

Jay half-listened, people-watching through the window tint.

"We'll throw a little party at the club tonight," Cheetah said.

"Let's get you out of prison clothes. My gift to you, to make up for not being there to get you myself."

Cheetah's haberdasher had a corner shop in Silver Lake. He fitted Jay in fine Italian wool that camouflaged the bulge of prison muscle. He needed an hour to hem the pants and take the waist in on the jacket, so they grabbed dinner at the Priory, a brownstone that had once been a church but now served soul food that nourished both the body as well as the spirit. A woman sang jazz in the back, framed by a stained glass window.

Jay worshiped over a plate of fried catfish with red beans and rice. He chewed slow, with his eyes closed. All he could do not to cry. The tang and spice brought back images of Mama Angeline and Papa Andre working through a mess of crawfish boiled crimson, potatoes, and corn cobs piled on newsprint spread over their kitchen table.

"We're in something good here. You should be part of it."

"The life's not for me, brother," Jay said, and flaked off a piece of catfish with his fork. He told him about his folks up and disappearing, and Cheetah looked at the sunset blazing the stained glass. All Cheetah had had was his grandmama, and Jay had been there when Cheetah learned of her passing.

"Seems I was better off with no one to lose." Cheetah frowned. "You're gonna need work to keep the cops off you."

Jay savored a bite. "Got work. What I do need is papers. Stuff that'll pass more than a glance. The cops are already so far up my ass I'm tasting badge polish."

Cheetah laughed. "You went right back to where you killed that boy. All I did was jack cars, but I haven't been back to Baxter Terrace, not even to look. If I see one of the bangers who used to push me around, I might throw all this away, to put him in the ground."

"I'm just looking for my folks. Not trying to rub it anyone's face."

"You find anything?"

"They're back in Louisiana, best I can see. Storm hit them."

Cheetah nodded. There was nothing to say.

"Where you working?"

"I told you about Tony. The mechanic?"

"You're gonna be a grease monkey?"

"Papa worked with his hands." Jay steered back toward business. "I don't have my birth certificate or my social. So I need a driver's license, insurance, the works."

"I'll get Mack to hook you up, but that won't be cheap. Not even with friend prices."

"I'm good for it. Hell, what I did for Dante, he ought to pay."

"He always pays what he owes, but he sees it as a down payment on the next favor."

"Then he can keep it." Jay laughed, and chased the last bit of rice and beans around his plate. "Save a man's ass, and he acts like I'm trying out for the position of number one punk."

Back at the club, Leticia swung flagpole on the second stage for a crew of drunk suits while Beyoncé thumped from the speakers. The blue lamps highlighted her muscled legs, stiff as wrought iron. The men flicked crumpled bills and snickered to each other. The crowd had an edge to it. Men hyped on vicarious adrenaline, eager to make women perform for their benefit. Mack leaned back to the bar, his cigar bobbing as he watched the patrons. Cheetah patted Jay on the shoulder and beelined for the office. "Have a drink, in your new suit. I got a few calls to make, then we'll celebrate."

Jay had to admit, the suit felt good. He'd never seen Andre in one, had only worn one himself in court, but those had been cheap, scratchy things. *A man in a suit can get away with anything*, Okie had said.

Jay eyed the jeweled rows of glass bottles behind the bar and settled on Wild Turkey. His Papa's drink. He lifted the glass, clinked with Mack, and tasted the whiskey's smooth fire. It warmed his face and brought him back to his last drink with Ramona, and her anger and her tears on the night he walked the tracks to meet her a final time. Waited below her window while she dressed and slipped out the back porch with a blanket and a bottle of Jameson's. They walked hand in hand to their secret spot in the park beneath the railroad trestle, where they'd met nearly every night each summer. Away from the frowns of their parents and the knowing glances of their friends. A little further each night. Careful and tentative, as if disarming nuclear weapons.

Jay slammed the whiskey back. It bloomed in his belly and out through the skin and sent memories fleeing. Cheetah walked to the bar with a slender Latina on his arm, a tall angular beauty sheathed in black. She regarded Jay coolly and offered her hand.

"Raina. You look sweeter than a Ruston peach," Jay said, and bowed to kiss her broad knuckles.

"Thought you said you'd die of heartbreak when I left you," Raina said.

"Hope kept me alive."

Raina laughed, and Jay saw his old friend's face break the surface. She pulled Jay in tight. "You had your chance, *papi*," she said, rocking him side to side, pressing her cheek into the corner of his neck.

Cheetah called to the bartender, who left a bottle of Johnny Walker Blue and four glasses. Cheetah poured, and raised his glass. "To my brother Jay, free after twenty-five years."

They drank, and Cheetah quickly refilled their glasses.

"*Mi familia's* back together," Raina said, and patted the corners of her eyes.

"Almost," Jay said. The liquor ate away at his joints and softened the edges of his vision, turning the night into an old home movie on Super 8. "To Okie Kincaid," Jay hoisted his glass. "May the crazy old son of a bitch be neck-deep in pussy and corn liquor, wherever he may be."

Mack chuckled and Raina slapped Jay's shoulder, and they all drank.

Okie wouldn't have liked the party. He was all business, a pure outlaw. He counseled Jay to drink in moderation, and bed only strange women he never planned on seeing again. His meticulous lessons bordered on paranoia. *An outlaw's like a coyote. Everyone wants him dead. In our case, being paranoid's just seeing the true natural order.*

The DJ segued into "I Touch Myself" by the DiVinyls and announced the new girl as Stacey. She wore fire orange curls and a sleek emerald teddy. Sharp nose and strong thighs, with a foxy grin that said yes, but not with you. She leapt on the pole like she owned it, and danced for herself. Patted the hands that tucked bills in her garter like dogs on the head.

Jay stared as the dancer worked her set. Felt as giddy as a boy, riding his bike down a monster hill with no brakes. Raina smiled and slinked away toward the dressing room.

Cheetah palmed Jay a bankroll. "Walking money."

Jay pocketed it without counting. "Thanks, brother."

"Me and Raina," Cheetah said. "Got a house in Forest Hill. Big yard. We want to adopt. Now that's tough with my record, but we had hers expunged."

"You'll make great parents," Jay said. "Reckon I ain't much use as a character reference."

"Things take time," Cheetah said. "Time and money. Another reason the girls have to go. They don't give too many kids to folks who run titty bars."

The DJ announced the next performer as Mariko. The dancer who'd clocked Jay with her shoe strutted out in a schoolgirl uniform and huge eyeglasses that made her look like a cartoon goldfish. She twirled her plaid skirt and flashed red satin beneath, eliciting hoots from the crowd.

A woman nudged behind him, soft breasts pillowed against Jay's shoulder blades. She smoothed his suit over his shoulders, squeezed his arms. Stacey, the redhead. With Raina beside her.

"Still got your nose open for your big-tit bitch," Raina husked in his ear. "Stacey's gonna take you to the VIP room. Make you forget all about her."

Jay didn't want it like this, but there were gifts one couldn't say no to.

Stacey flashed him a grin and took him by the hand, bouncing ahead barefoot. Jay floated after her on a cloud of whiskey through the curtains into a private corner of the VIP room, where she pushed him into a low-slung leather chair.

"You've been away a long time," she said in a clipped Slavic accent, and placed his hands on her breasts. Jay groaned at the soft flesh, his head lolling forward. "I'll make you feel like a free man." Her broad hips parted his knees as she pressed in close, unbuttoned his shirt and ran her nails over his chest.

Jay leaned back, let her soft skin and musk perfume distract him from her bored eyes.

"So strong," she said, and ducked to rub her lips over his nipple.

Jay shivered and kneaded the back of her thighs, cupped her behind. "Might go back to prison, if you were waiting when I got out. Where you from, Stace? Guessing it ain't Long Island."

"Ukraine," she said, and tweaked both his nipples.

Jay winced and hunched over. She pressed a finger to his lips, stepped back to let her teddy pool at her feet. She reached behind herself and unsnapped her satin brassiere.

Jay studied how her perked white breasts held their shape once released. "Sweet mercy."

Stacey smiled and the light caught the sun spots and crinkles a moment before they vanished behind her show-face. She climbed into his lap and rubbed her breasts against his cheeks. He closed his eyes to relive his last night of freedom with Ramona, her strong swimmer's legs pinning him to the ground. He breathed slow, to keep his control.

Stacey gripped him through his pants with one hand and unbuckled his belt with the other. She slinked to her knees and thumbed the head of his erection through his boxers, ran her silk curls down his chest and taut belly.

Jay dug his fingertips into the chair's leather arms. The wood creaked beneath his grip. She opened the window of his boxers and hot breath seared his penis. Hot sulfur filled the air, and his hands clawed into fists.

"What is wrong?"

"Just dance," Jay said. Teeth chattering.

"It's paid for."

"Sit in my lap," Jay said. He forced a sly grin.

She shrugged, and straddled him in the chair. Grinding while Jay gripped her behind and buried his face between her breasts. The skin so soft he might disappear into it. He screwed his eyes shut against the rage inside, images flashing across his eyelids. Brushing the locks from Ramona's face, leaving her beneath the trestle sleeping. Walking home in the morning chill to the police cars waiting.

Jay kneaded Stacey's hams and shuddered. Clutched her close and muffled his cries in her chest. He drove against her satin-sheathed crease until he collapsed dead.

She pushed his face from her cleavage. "Like a little boy."

Jay gave a flushed grin and caught his breath. Watched as she bent over to reholster her girls in her brassiere, and wiggle into the teddy.

"My name's Jay, Stace. What's yours? For real, I mean."

She smirked.

"I won't follow you around. Just want to know."

She mussed his hair. "Oksana."

Jay took her hand. "Thank you, Oksana." He left two of Cheetah's hundreds in her palm. "You tell 'em I gave you a wild ride." He watched her leave, and breathed his four fours until he knew it wouldn't do any good.

He staggered past a bouncer who said, "Zip your fly, bro," into the blue lights and thumping music, floating like a ghost over battlefield slaughter as he slow-walked to the bar where Cheetah squeezed his shoulder and said words he didn't hear.

Randal exited the men's room with Mariko, rubbing his nose while she wiped her lips. He shot Jay a look. Jay ignored him. *Play the game,* Okie said. *Hell, act afraid a little. Like you're squeezing in a turd. Some dogs gotta bark, and that's the only way to shut 'em up.*

Cheetah and Raina came back downstairs, smelling of sex and weed.

"You look green," Cheetah said. "You O.D. on pussy?"

Raina rolled her eyes. "*Pobrecita.* He's not used to living."

"I need some air," Jay said. "I'm gonna bunk early. Some of us got to work in the morning." They smiled and embraced. Jay felt no fear from them, like he had from Tony, Billy, and Ramona. He thought about it as he walked to the Challenger. How he'd fought in two different wars, with different friends. One crew had made it home, while the other was still shell-shocked. He fished for his keys, wondering which battlefield had been worse. Rahway had been hell, but a predictable hell of violence.

Joey Bello had wounded all his childhood friends in unique ways. Jay had thought on it endlessly in his cell. Why had Matty turned on him after Jay had set him free. It made no sense, but people rarely did. Matthew's secret smile from the witness stand burned into Jay's eyes like the rictus of a mad creature about to feast on his insides. And yet Ramona loved him. Jay's teeth clenched at the thought.

A door slammed shut. Jay stopped and scanned, back in coyote mode.

Three shadows emerged from the black Cadillac truck and crossed the parking lot, cutting off the street exit. Even with drink-dulled senses, Jay recognized Randal's silhouette. Two gym rats flanked him. Top heavy with skinny legs.

One flipped a billy club length of heavy gauge electric cable. Another slapped his palm with a miniature baseball bat. Randal sneered and swung his arms, stretching. Gave Jay that you-ain't-shit look Bello had been so fond of using.

Okie's counsel echoed in Jay's ears, but he ignored it. Instead, he shucked his suit jacket and sank at the knees, hands held in guard. "Know what they call that shit on your face, Randy boy? Prison pussy."

Randal charged bare-fisted and Jay leapt to meet him. Traded a knee to Randal's gut for a beefy shoulder to his own. The gym rats closed in. The cable thumped Jay's ribs and the ragged end tore shirt and skin.

Randal slammed him into the bricks and Jay sucked wind. He covered up and fists pounded the meat of his forearms. His head bounced off the wall and the pain went far away like distant artillery. Randal plowed an uppercut through Jay's guard, and blood splashed bright salt in the back of his throat.

The air turned sulfurous and the night misted red.

Jay launched a head butt to the chin that staggered Randal back. He pounced with a wild snarl, the gym rats' clubs beating a wild rhythm across his back. He sank his teeth into the side of Randal's head like a piece of overripe fruit.

Randal shrieked melody while Jay bit down and tore.

"Get him off me!"

Jay pushed himself away and grinned bloody around the mouthful of Randal's severed left ear. He panted, his breaths flicking the hanging lobe.

The gym rats stared fish-mouthed while Randal chased his own tail, blood pattering to the pavement, his ragged scream punctuated with sharp yelps each time he reached for a chunk of his face that was no longer there.

Jay reared back and spat. The ear rolled past its owner and Randal ran after it.

A gym rat raised the length of cable and stepped forward, tentative. The end of his weapon gleamed ragged copper.

"Fuck with me again and I'm taking eyes," Jay hollered, and ripped off his shredded shirt. Blood poured from his nose and ran over his scar-puckered chest. "You ain't nothing but meat on my table!"

They piled into Randal's Escalade and lurched out of the lot, jumping the curb.

Jay reared back and his howl echoed off the bricks.

CHAPTER 16

Jay woke in bed with his face to the wall, his heart thundering. He was too amped to sleep. He threw his legs over the side of the bed. The alarm clock read 1:47 a.m.

Cheetah had been pissed about the fight. Like he was supposed to take two beatings in one day from that jag-off. Raina refereed, pushing them apart like always.

Jay stood, stretched, and fell to the floor into a push-up and banged out fifty. Then five singles for each arm. Getting his blood up drove the ache from his ribs. He took a hot shower and finished it ice cold, more a distraction from the pain than anything else. Patted his face dry and looked in the paint-flecked mirror. His cheekbones had some puff to them, rouged with abrasions. His knuckles wept a little blood. He covered the cuts with exes of tape.

When he woke nights as a boy, he'd sneak out for a walk and do some thinking. Inside, there were nights he never thought he'd walk free again. This night was as good as any other.

Outside the apartment, he plucked a hair from his head and licked his fingertip. He stretched the hair across the space between the door and the jamb and swiped his wet finger across it, gluing it with spit. If anyone opened the door, he'd know.

Jay kept his foot light on the pedal and rolled the Hammer-head through Branch Brook Park. The cherry blossoms had gone with spring, and left the branches grasping like twisted hands from the earth. The road crossed the stream below, and he cruised to a stop. Killed the engine and walked along a crooked path along the water.

He soaked in the night's emptiness. Crickets and leaves ruffling in the summer breeze. The quiet of the small hours had always brought him peace. The magic hour, Mama Angeline called it. She'd sat on the bayou smoking weed in the moonlight, serenaded by spring peepers and bull gators. Jay would join her, or sneak past and walk the roads, quiet like an animal on its nightly rounds while man slept.

He followed the creek's trickle. One boot before the other. If Mama Angeline was alive, maybe she was a grandma now. Maybe she cut her hair short like older women seemed to do. He thought of how her letters had hurt, with their poetic ambiguity. Disguising herself as if hunted. Knowing the letters would be read before they got to him.

Voices through the trees cut short his reverie. Midway between street lamps, the ruby glow of tail lights made brief twin embers through the trees. Human shapes in the quarter moonlight. Footfalls in the leaf litter. He pulled back the hood to give his eyes free rein.

A fit man in jogging shorts beckoned with a wave from between trees. Sharp nose, carved legs.

Jay loosened his shoulders and kept walking.

The man loped closer, half a smile on his face. "New here?"

"Out for a walk," Jay said.

"Sure." The man smirked.

Jay strode past him and followed the worn asphalt trail as it dipped and doubled back under the bridge. Lamps set in the concrete painted the walls in shadow. Jay stopped as he saw figures in the tunnel.

A kneeling silhouette pantomimed an urgent act of supplication.

Jay's fists clenched and the air turned to ice in his lungs.

"Fuck off," the standing man said.

Jay stalked back toward the car. He snorted out the night's sudden sulfur stink, even though he knew it originated in his mind.

The jogger he'd met earlier loitered outside the streetlamp's yellow light. Jay flashed him a prison yard glare and passed him in a headlong gait, smoldering.

The jogger spat in the leaves. "Fucking pig," he said, and ran into the trees. Several cars came to life, lights flashing amber as they pulled away.

Jay found the Challenger where he left it. He reached for the door handle and pulled his hand away as if stung. A used condom drooped over the door handle, dripping. Jay wiped his hand on the back of his jeans.

In the morning, Jay asked a girl at the drug store for some touch-up paint he could use on his face. She had some fun dolling him up. Mack had said to see his woman Yvette at the DMV in an hour.

When Jay made his way to the end of the line, she had all the cheer of a prison matron who'd learned her dog died. She took Jay's photo and his envelope of cash, and two hours later he had a license, insurance card, registration, a handicap sign for the rearview mirror, and a printout of the home addresses he'd asked for. Jay dropped the handicap sign in the trash and stood outside peering at his license photo. Looked like a mug shot.

The phone buzzed in his pocket. Unknown number. He flipped it open and listened.

"Hey, Creep."

Ramona's voice tickled in his chest.

"I talked to Matthew about the bribe," she said. "That was pretty shitty."

Jay said nothing.

"If you want to grab some disco fries, I'll tell you what I know about your parents. I don't know what it will help," she said. "But I think you should know. And that's all I can offer."

She said to meet him in a train station lot. Jay drove there and waited, listening to an AC/DC mix tape Tony had left in the

Challenger until a blue Aston Martin DB9 pulled nose to nose with him.

Ramona grinned above the wheel from behind black shades.

On the highway, she winced at the red marks on his nose and cheek. "If I wanted to help you, I should've gone to med school." She weaved through traffic and drafted behind a box truck, the spy-car's nose to the bumper.

"Way you drive, it's good you're a lawyer," Jay said. "Maybe you can teach me sometime."

Ramona wore navy slacks and lipstick that gave her the prim air of a strict schoolteacher. "I trained on the Nürburgring," she said. "Driving here's easy. Just expect everyone to behave like a complete jerk or a total idiot."

The Tick Tock Diner gleamed in the fading sun, a castle of red and chrome on a rise of highway crushed with strip malls. Her favorite after-school haunt, sitting around a plate of fries with milkshakes. She downshifted and swerved into the parking lot.

They sat across from each other in a red leather booth. Waitresses cruised the aisles as Dion belted out an appreciation of the roving life. Jay flipped through the tableside jukebox's offerings. Wandering had begun to sound like a good life choice. Ramona ordered cheese and gravy fries, and Jay a vanilla malt with a cheeseburger and onion rings.

"This place never changes. That's the one thing you miss when you travel," she said. "A good diner where you can get waffles, cannoli cake, or a plate of disco fries twenty-four-seven."

Diners had always seemed like a dream to Jay, with their menus thick as a phone book. Like a deal with the devil, offering anything you could possibly want. Okie always said if he'd busted out, they could shoot him dead soon as he got two things: a face full of a big bouncy woman, and a truck-stop meat 'n three in his belly.

Jay raised his water glass in a silent toast.

"What's that about?" Ramona said. She tapped her phone and tucked it away.

"Thinking on what you said, about starting over."

"Never saw you as a mechanic," Ramona said. "Thought you wanted to build houses."

"I already knew carpentry," Jay said. "So I learned everything they taught in there, and plenty they didn't."

Ramona smirked. "Well, I suppose it's good you kept busy. Mother always said you didn't use your full potential."

"She said a lot of things," Jay said. He pumped a few quarters in the juke. "Thought you never paid her any mind."

"She wasn't as dumb as I thought."

The waitress brought his milkshake. Jay jabbed his straw into the shake and took a hard draw, until his head flooded with malt and vanilla. "Oh, that's good." He spun the cup so the straw faced her.

She inspected the thick contents, white flecked with tiny specks of vanilla bean, before she ducked and took a sip. "I'll tell you what I know."

His eyes flicked to her cleavage and he hauled them back up. "I'll take what I can get. I just want to find my folks, but now I'm curious why everyone wants me gone so bad. Feel like I'm the only one who doesn't know the punch line."

"Well after what you did, you can't expect a homecoming parade."

"All I regret's going to jail for it."

Ramona looked into his eyes. "Don't say he 'needed killing.' From his parents' perspective, so do you."

Jay took another draw at his shake, licked his lips and smiled. "Maybe so, but it don't mean I'll let 'em put me down."

She looked away.

"So, you had something to tell me?"

"Matthew's parents split during your trial," she said. "He won't talk about it. Rumor was, Mr. Strick gave his wife herpes. Remember Donna DeVane? She told me she used to blow my classy father-in-law in his Porsche when she was a sophomore."

"He's a real charmer. What's this got to do with me?"

"The night your parents left town, your mother went to Matt's house. She told his mom something that made her go after his dad with a lead crystal ashtray."

Jay looked into his shake. Mama Angeline caused a minor scandal when she arrived in town with her Fawcett cut and tied-off shirts and cut-off jeans. Strick couldn't keep his eyes off her, but few men could. "You saying they…"

"All I know is Matt hates her, and he testified against you because of it." Ramona swirled the ice cubes in her water glass. "You know how he idolized his father. They didn't get much in the divorce. His father's lawyers were too good for that, and Matthew's been paying him back for it ever since. It's what drives him, and I keep him sane. I'm not asking you to forgive him, just understand him a little. He's as angry about that mean little town as you are."

"Still can't imagine you and him. He must've changed a whole lot."

"He grew up," Ramona said. "He's got the same fire in the belly you always had. But he uses it differently."

Jay sipped his shake. Watched the endless stream of traffic go by until the waitress brought their meals on white platters.

"Can I get a Coke?"

"Make that two," Ramona said.

Jay put an onion ring on his cheeseburger and took a large bite.

She twirled a gravy-soaked steak fry in strings of melted cheese and bit the end off. "Damn," she said. "This isn't El Bulli, but I do like my gravy fries."

"Trade you a ring for couple."

"Knock yourself out, there's no way I can finish this."

The waitress brought their Cokes. Ramona sipped hers. "Beloved strange chemicals."

"You always said the town dumped Valium in the drinking water."

"If they didn't, they should have. That place was uptight," she gave a husky laugh. "You know that Nutley was once considered boho? My art teacher, Miss Foote? She said the houses by the Mud Hole used to be an art colony, started by...what was his name. He painted portraits of Harlem, in the 1850s. Now they'd burn his house down."

"They'd at least talk and give him dirty looks." Jay traded her an onion ring for a scoop of molten cheese atop a crisp French fry.

The jukebox kicked into an '80s tune by the Cure. Ramona frowned at the speaker and kicked Jay under the table. "Did you play this?"

"I kinda feel in between days myself." Jay grinned and tucked into his burger. They ate in silence while the juke spun through the music of their youth.

"I'm sorry I pushed you away," Jay said while she sucked the cold dregs of his milkshake. "Friend of mine's woman got stomped real bad in the prison parking lot. Like, wish she was dead bad. I didn't want anything like that happening to you."

"No use crying over it now," Ramona said, tilting the cup to get the last sips.

"Thanks for this," Jay said. "You're the first one's been honest with me."

They walked to the car, the highway twinkling with electric stars. It brought him back to their nights sprawled in the grass holding hands. Thumb circling her palm until she'd pounce, tickle and kiss. Lips hot against the pulse in her neck.

She blipped the Aston Martin unlocked.

"Tried to swim in the old pool," Jay said, "But it's private now."

"We have a pool in the yard. I bet you still can't swim." She leaned against the driver's side.

Jay took her hand, and she let him. He pressed his lips to her knuckles.

"We could've raised some hell, Blackbird."

Ramona smiled with sad eyes. "You and me against the world." She stroked his cheek, fingertips over the abrasions. Arms around his neck as she rested her head on his chest. He slinked his arms around her waist and held her close, her soft curves molding to his muscle. Nuzzled in her hair, his head flooded with violets. He kissed her scalp, felt fire bloom inside.

She pushed him away, slow but firm. "No, Bluejay."

Jay sat silent in the passenger's side as she shifted through the gears. She dropped him by his car and pulled away fast.

CHAPTER 17

Jay memorized the addresses Yvette had given him and burned the papers with a Zippo. Strick's house sat on a parcel of farmland fronted by identical barn-shaped mansions built close together along the county road. The wrought iron gate read Strick Farms, tall and spiked. The view from the street revealed little except a manor shrouded by red maples.

The satellite view of the property from Tony's computer had shown a dirt road leading to a barn at the rear of the property and squares of tilled fields. He nosed the Challenger up the dirt ruts and K-turned to point downhill.

He killed the engine, depressed the brake pedal, and reached under the dash to pop the hidden switch. He took what he needed from the small duffel inside and eased the seat down until it clicked. He slipped on his creeping gear and jogged behind the barn.

Perfect rows of pine trees stretched off to the forest. Babies at one end, bushy saplings at the other. Jay followed a trail behind the house and spied the open double garage. A mineral gray roadster and a chromed-up motorcycle sat inside. According to the DMV records, Strick owned the Harley, and the bank owned the Porsche.

Strick's words echoed from the chasm in Jay's stomach. The lies and empty promises.

The front door clicked shut and sandals crushed the grass. Jay cut back to the garage in time to hear the Porsche roadster snarl to life and spin in reverse with a sandy-haired man behind the wheel. The driver buzzed toward the gate, his nub of a ponytail bobbing to the stereo.

Jay ran for the car.

The Hammerhead bogged down the dirt road, the road race springs too low for the ruts. The Porsche blew past him on the road, framed by a break in the trees. Jay jerked the pistol shifter and gave chase, but Strick was already gone.

Jay gave it pedal and the big engine ate up road. Took air on a crest and came on the Porsche tailgating a minivan. He downshifted and let the engine clear its throat, leaning on the brake as the Porsche's rear bumper approached fast. Nosed to a stop with a car length to spare.

The Porsche took the Hammerhead's roar as challenge and revved in neutral to answer.

At the first opening in the oncoming traffic, Strick veered into the opposite lane and barked through the gears. Jay followed with a squealing plume of smoke.

He fought to keep the nose straight until the Hammerhead chirped into third. The Porsche rabbited through the curves ahead, and Jay scraped roadside brush and worked both pedals to keep the Challenger's ass from sliding out from under him. Nearly lost a mirror to an oncoming truck, and the little gray two-seater disappeared around the bend.

Breaking out of the curve into a long uphill straightaway, the Porsche waited a quarter-mile ahead at a stoplight. Jay buried the nose in the pavement with both feet on the brake, skidding alongside in the shoulder.

Strick the Elder twisted his sandpaper complexion into a familiar sneer. Thinning hair pulled back, belly gone to seed. A burnt-out star twinkling his damnedest to defy the impending dark.

"You didn't think we were racing, did you?" Strick said, and broke into a smug grin.

Jay winked through cheap shades. "Got you beat in a straight line. But that's not good enough, dealing with a crooked piece of shit like you."

The turkey tracks around Strick's eyes deepened and his gray-toothed smile melted away.

"Next time, we race for pinks, old man." Jay peeled through the red light and hit the onramp, leaving two black scars across the asphalt.

Jay white-knuckled the wheel, heading to Tony's shop. Fire burning in his gut. *Leave everyone else out of it,* Strick had said. *And we'll take care of you.*

They'd been caretakers, all right. The graveyard kind.

At a stop light, Jay frowned at the buzz in his pocket. He dug out the phone and thumbed open its silver clamshell. "Hello."

"Gonna need you to work the club today," Cheetah said, hurried. "We're short a bouncer because of you."

"I'm kind of tied up." Tony had said he could work nights, after hours, when no customers might see the pariah.

"I don't care if you're half-dick deep in angel pussy, get your ass in here."

Muted horns filled Cheetah's office with yearning and pain. Jay found him sitting on the couch, kneading his temples with delicate fingertips, listening to Marvin Gaye sing his heart out.

"The way you do *my* life, makes me wanna do a lot more than holler," Cheetah said. He folded his hands, rested his chin on them. "You couldn't just bust Randal's ribs? Had to go all Tyson, bite his damn ear off?"

"They had clubs." Jay untucked his shirt, showed black leopard spots haloed in mustard yellow. "Anyway, Holyfield was head-butting."

"Evander did no such thing, but even if he did, who got the shitty end of the stick? The big bad-ass who poured gas on the fire. Except Holyfield's corner couldn't shoot Iron Mike in the head and cremate him. Randal's can. And will."

"They want a war over this shitbird, they'll get one."

"No they won't, because you're gonna apologize," Cheetah

said. "Frankie Dell wants a sit-down. Frankie fucking Dell. I ran his club eight years, I've never met the man. And I don't want to."

"He wants to talk, we'll talk. This is on me, brother."

"Everything's easy with you. You have no idea what we could be walking into."

Jay grinned. "I'll burn that bridge when I get to it."

Cheetah navigated the clogged backstreets constricted by a gooseneck of the Passaic which gave the Down Neck neighborhood its name. "If we walk out of here, you gotta chauffeur Leticia in that redneck ride of yours."

"No problem."

"Dante's got his nose open for her," Cheetah said. "But keep that on the DL."

Jay had met Dante at the chess games Okie held in the library. Another Italian, Big Kenny, made a crack when Dante lost his white queen.

"If she'd been black, you'd of protected her," Kenny laughed, and Dante's hound dog eyes went wolf dark. "What? So you like the eggplant. Who doesn't like eggplant? I bet Cajun Jay likes eggplant. You coon asses are half moolie, right?"

Jay flattened Kenny with a hook to the jaw. Okie swore at him for bruising his hand, but Dante repaid the favor by handling the betting on Jay's fights. They got flush with cash and contraband, and Jay used his share to work in the auto shop and get his certifications.

"Dante is married to Frankie Dell's goddaughter," Cheetah said, turning the wheel. "But he always keeps a tall sister on the side. When Frankie got word about his last piece of strange, he put Dante in charge of the recycling center at the port. Where they shred plastic, aluminum cans, like that.

"Do-nothing job, but you gotta show. He takes Dante to dinner to congratulate him, then they drive out there. Where they got his girl tied up, all beat to shit. Brutalized," Cheetah said. "Got her feet-first in the mouth of this big machine that grinds tree stumps into fertilizer. And Frankie asks him, do you want to spend the rest of your life with this woman, or my goddaughter?"

Cheetah pulled into the parking lot of a Portuguese steakhouse with a terra cotta roof. The scent of charred flesh thick in the air. "Made Dante pull the switch himself, is what I heard." He turned to Jay. "Think on that before you go making any smart talk in here."

The restaurant boiled with loud men and the clatter of silverware. A gorilla with a flat top led them beyond the louvered doors of a private dining room done in dark red and faded gold.

Two men sat in bespoke chalk-striped suits, alone at a table for twelve. Dante sulked. Beside him sat a mottled stone bullfrog sporting a coiffed silver pompadour. Paper-skinned hands folded on the white tablecloth with nails like glass claws. Sharp eyes above a thick-lipped frown as he picked over one platter splayed with tentacles of fried calamari and another of eggplant rollatini.

Flat Top gave them both a cursory frisk and removed the batteries from their cell phones.

"Sit," Frank said, popping a ring of calamari into his mouth.

Cheetah sat. Jay remained standing.

Beads of sweat pearled on Cheetah's neck. Frank chewed loudly, and Dante smoldered.

Jay stepped forward and offered Frank his hand. "Mister Dellamorte, sir, my name's Jay Desmarteaux."

Flinches all around. Flat Top's meaty hand eased under the flap of his jacket. Dante and Cheetah stared, lips parted.

It took five heartbeats before Frank curled his fat lips into a tombstone smile, hauling the trawler net of his sagging neck. He pondered Jay's palm a moment before he held out his own liver-spotted hand, a signet ring gleaming from a finger.

Jay squeezed his hand lightly, then sat.

"Jay. Is that short for Jason?"

"Just Jay. Sir."

"Pleased to meet you, Jay," Frank said, watching the imprints of Jay's fingers disappear from his flesh. "Dante tells me you come from New Orleans."

"Around there."

"I've never been there," Frank said. "The humidity is no good for me. I prefer Napoli. The Mediterranean climate is perfect."

"A friend of mine's mother used to tell us to go to Napoli, when she got mad. Never got around to it."

Frank shuddered with a silent laugh, and then sipped his wine. "Ah, she must be Calabrese. *Va fa' Napoli*. Well, you should go to Napoli, some day. The people there are direct. You know where you stand with them."

"Sir, that's something I appreciate," Jay said. "That and good eggplant." He forked a piece onto his plate, cut it in half and took a bite. "And this here is real good, Mr. Dellamorte."

"The boys call me Frankie Dell. Or the Silver Fox, behind my back. Call me Frank."

"Thank you, Frank."

Frank tapped his empty glass with his ring. "Dante."

Dante snapped his fingers at Flat Top. A waiter rushed in to pour ice water and wine.

Frank looked to the server. "Four steaks on the stone. And another bottle of Amarone." When the waiter left, he turned to Jay.

"I am told that you and my nephew are in dispute," Frank said, lifting a glass of arterial red. "Normally we would not speak over this. It would simply be handled. But Dante says you were helpful during his time away, and deserve a chance to redeem yourself. Convince me."

"Randal and I had us a little tiff. I put it aside, but he wouldn't let it go. He and a couple friends set on me with lead pipes. No disrespect, but you come swinging like that, you're gonna get hit back."

Frank stared into his eyes. "My nephew is prone to such things, but he is still my nephew. My blood. Do you understand?"

"No disrespect, but if he was anyone but your nephew? He'd be bobbing in the Passaic about now."

Frankie remained stone still.

Jay caught Cheetah's side-eye.

"I didn't go snapping their necks as they ran," Jay said. "I didn't chase them down, and I didn't creep in their bedroom windows and gut 'em like fish, which is what your garden variety shitbirds would've got. Now I apologize for hurting your nephew. But I've been watching my back for a week, wondering if that boy's gonna take a shot at me, or if my car's gonna explode. You can ask Dante. In situations like that, I was taught to take what a good friend of mine called 'pre-emptive revenge.' Meaning, if a sumbitch has it out for me, it's safer for me if he wakes up dead. But I let your nephew slide. Out of respect."

"You had a problem with him, you should've come to me," Dante said. "It never should've gotten this far."

"Excuse me, Dante," Cheetah interrupted, "I planned on telling you at the next pickup, but Randal's been dealing again, and brought in some of the Russian's girls. With the Rock around the corner, that brings a lot of heat."

"We pay you to deal with heat, Alfonse," Dante said. "Talk to our lieutenant."

A knock at the door. Flat Top looked to Frank, who held up a finger.

"You will treat my nephew as if he is my own flesh," Frank said, leveling the finger at Jay. He nodded to Flat Top, and the waiters brought platters trailing the bite of charred meat. Each man received a square of butcher block topped with a thick stone tile glowing dull red, crowned with a chunk of sizzling ruby prime. The servers knifed each cut into four slabs and capped them with garlic butter.

A glare from Dante sent the servers back to the kitchen.

Frank breathed in the crematory fumes and struggled out of his chair. "It is what it is. I'm going to use the *baccausa*," he said. "When I return, I'd like two things. My steak medium rare, and for you and Dante to come to an agreement. Take care of the low-hanging fruit, gentlemen."

He turned to Dante. "Medium rare. Not medium." Frank lumbered toward the doors, and Flat Top opened them for him.

Dante flipped his own steak, barely seared. He snapped a finger at the guard. "Outside."

Flat Top closed the doors behind him.

Dante carved the butter-soft meat, dark juices spilling over his plate. "It is what it is. You like that shit? Don't even know what it fuckin' means. He spews shit like that all day long, like the Dalai Parmigiana." He hawked a stringy oyster of spit onto Frank's steak.

"Low-hanging fruit. He can suck my low-hanging fruit." Dante popped a chunk of his own Pittsburgh blue filet into his mouth and chewed while the other steaks sizzled away.

Jay shook his head and flipped his own.

"We got a few minutes. The Fat Fuck Fox pisses sitting down," Dante said. "Trickles like a leaky faucet. Got a prostate the size of a grapefruit."

"Don't wanna ask how you know that," Jay said.

"Because I got my head stuck up his ass." Dante sneered. "You ain't changed one bit. Balls like fuckin' steel. Frankie likes that shit. That's how I got the job slicing his steak." He flipped the slabs on Frank's plate, mopping the dregs of spittle. "Don't think it buys you jack shit."

Jay popped a flower of fried squid legs into his mouth.

"Dante, you know how Randal is," Cheetah said, and pressed on his steak to force the blood out.

"You could tear both of that mamaluke's ears off and fry 'em on that fuckin' stone for all I care." Dante plated Frank's steak and cut it into little cubes. "Believe this shit? At least I don't gotta wipe his ass."

"Not yet." Jay chewed a piece. "How 'bout you remember the riot, and we call this even. I'll be out of your hair and Randal can go play King Shit."

Dante glowered. "Because I already doled out your chips for that."

"How you figure?"

"Your buddy back in Nutley, the mayor." Dante smiled. "He got talking with a knockaround guy who said he could call a hit on you in Rahway. Guess who the mook came asking to? Let's say he fell down some stairs after a poker game, and you had nothing to worry about."

"Funny how that works. I'm owed a debt, now I'm the one in hock."

"It is what it is." Dante snickered. "So we're even." He turned back to his steak. "Next order of business. You like working with your hands, don't you? So you work off your debt down the docks, where Randal is too good to dirty his mitts."

"What kind of debt we talking about?"

Dante shrugged. "That's up to the Fox, but the pay's pretty good there. You'll be out from under this nut in no time."

Flat Top opened the doors and Frank waddled to his seat, tucked a napkin over his silk double Windsor, and dug in to his little cubes of steak. "Perfect, Dante." He chewed, dabbed his lips with a napkin. "So are we past this unfortunate impasse? I do not want my wife getting another call from her sister."

"Yes, Frank," Dante said. "We can put Jay down by the port."

"Good," Frank said, mopping a chunk of steak in the juices on his plate. "In the union, they pay a man for loss of limb or

131

ability. Dante, find out what we pay for an ear. That's what he pays my nephew."

Dante nodded.

"Alfonse," Frank said. "We need more cars in the parking lot. Get your people to park there. Give out free cognac, if you must. As long as the lot looks close to full, if someone were to photograph it."

"I'll take care of it, Mr. D."

"Now, Jay." Frankie looked up. "I'm told my golfing partner is an acquaintance of yours."

Jay tilted his head. "And who might that be?"

"A young man named Matthew Strick."

Jay set his fork down. "We're acquainted."

"And you harbor him a grudge."

"You could say that," Jay said, a quiver in his upper lip.

"He asked me to speak with you," Frank said, jabbing little pieces of meat onto his fork. "As a favor, for a business partner. He's doing wonderful things for the union pension fund. Thus, you will consider him, and his family, as you would my nephew. Are we understood?"

Jay smiled, knotting his fists under the table. "Oh, we are."

"You will work off your debt and leave for New Orleans. My friend Sally Jiggs runs things down there. He'll have work for you."

Jay bobbed his chin with a nod. "You tell Matty hello for me."

Frank smiled back. "I will, on the golf course. He'll be pleased." He reached across the table and smacked Jay's arm. "Dante, put Jay in a truck at Ironbound Carting. He has that prison physique, like a fighting dog. Standing around watching whores is no good for him." He broke out the tombstone smile. "A little manual labor will cool that temper of yours."

* * *

Dante grinned at Jay while he stuffed Frank in the back of his angry-looking black Cadillac. He mock-kicked the old man in and shut the door. The Cadillac rumbled away with a throaty chuckle.

Jay rode back in silence.

"Have fun playing garbage man," Cheetah said, loosening his tie. He turned the air conditioning to max. "Least he didn't invite you over for a barbecue."

CHAPTER 18

Jay brought Taylor Ham sandwiches to the garage next morning, but Tony waved him off, sucking down one of his shakes. Before business rolled in, Jay installed baffles in the Challenger's mufflers to quiet the beast's roar.

His phone went off as he tightened the clamps.

Louisiana number.

Jay nearly dropped the phone answering.

"Hell-hello?"

"Jay dawlin'? It's Miss Cindy. Where y'at?"

"Doing just fine, good to hear your voice, ma'am. Good morning."

"Wish it was better, baby. I axed around for your Angeline and Andre, came up dry."

"Well, thank you for looking."

She cut him off before he went further. "I put a bug in everybody's ear at the *cochon du lait*, we'll see what shakes out. Even told my hairdresser, One-Eyed Evie. She knows everybody."

"I'd be worried she'd cut my ear off," Jay said.

"Yeah, you right. But she ain't nicked me yet. Makes a good gumbo, too."

Jay could smell the heady scent of a roux. The scars on his back tingled. "You're killing me, Miss Cindy. Could you air mail me a bowl?"

She laughed. "Ya need to come on down where you belong," she said. "I got to open the post office now, but I'll ring you soon as I hear a peep, all right?"

"Thank you, Miss Cindy."

Jay snapped the phone shut, and went to see if Tony's mood had improved.

* * *

"How's Ramona doing," Tony said, moping over his black coffee.

"Just fine." Jay poured himself a cup, took a sip, and winced. "What do you put in here? Cockroach turds?"

"Go to Dunkin Donuts, you don't like it."

"Maybe I will. You want me to get you some Raid?"

Tony sighed. "For the roaches in the coffee?"

"No, for the bug up your ass."

Tony rolled his eyes. "You come and go as you please, you run up a big bill. And now you're gonna be gone for two weeks. You want me to dance the tarantella?"

Jay dumped sugar and creamer into his cup until he could choke the coffee down, and sat on the edge of the desk. "Seems like something else is bothering you."

"You a psychic, now?" Tony swiveled his chair away.

"Tone…"

"Did she ask about me?"

"She asked how you were, and I said you were good."

"How's she look."

"Damn fine," Jay laughed. "I'm not gonna lie."

Tony looked into his cup.

"She told me about my folks some, that's all. She's a lawyer, now. Environmental law. Makes me want to take a shit on an endangered species, so she can defend me in court."

Tony sniggered. "You asshole."

After Tony left for Sunday supper at his mother's, Jay installed a panhard bar beneath the Challenger and a strut brace on top to tighten the turns. Gave it a test drive and yanked the wheel on a curve. The rear gripped better and the nose went where he pointed it.

Jay found a deli across the river and had the gray-haired

woman behind the slicer make him a Yankee approximation of a roast beef po'boy. He ate it in a park on the Passaic where the trees upriver masked the Jersey sprawl of little houses and old industry, and for a brief moment you could believe you were in a wild place.

His phone buzzed. Maybe Miss Cindy wanted to chat.

"You want me to show you how to handle that old clunker of yours?" Ramona said.

"We can't all have James Bond cars," Jay said. "But I'll take a lesson if you're offering."

He met her at the Upper Montclair train station. Across the lot, the elite huddled at cafe tables to brunch and complain. Ramona leaned on her Aston Martin, sipping a barista's large iced concoction. She wore a liquid blue skirt and sleeveless top, aviator shades, and wedge sandals. Her legs flexed definition beneath the plush as she strutted to where Jay waited in jeans and a white athletic undershirt.

"Put a shirt on. You look like an extra from *Grease*."

"Got no air conditioning," Jay said.

"Scooch over. I need to get a feel for this thing."

Jay obliged.

The vinyl seat squeaked beneath her behind, and she smirked at the safety harness. She lifted the center strap between her knees. "Doesn't this crush your nuts?" She left the strap hanging over the seat, like a dog's tongue.

"They're doing just fine, since you asked."

"Well, hang onto them."

She broke the tires loose. Brunching heads snapped up and glared as they squealed away with a burbling growl.

She took the rolling hills of the interstate that cut through the Watchung mountains. "You accelerate into a turn, but don't let the rear end get away from you," she shouted over the wind, her bangs whipped back. "You feel it low in the seat when you take a turn too hard. Drive with your butt."

She downshifted, feeling out the gears and shift points. Tony had built the car for drag racing, and the suspension kit Jay added could only tame it so much. They took a rise and passed a cluster of traffic hogging the left lane. Ramona smashed the horn with her palm. "Bear right, fuckers!"

She took the exit to Newark, into Branch Brook Park. The Hammerhead disappeared into the canopy of old oaks and twisted cherry trees, the intestinal curves of roads looping around the lake.

"This heap's pretty tight," Ramona said, and pulled over. "Drives like Dad's old GNX." Her father had caused a minor scandal by parking a gloss black Buick Grand National among the Audis and Volvos of Alexander Avenue.

"Switch," she said, unbuckling the lap belt and squeezing over his lap.

Jay stirred deep down as her soft body brushed past his. He buckled in and left the center strap hanging. He doubted he could buckle it tight at the moment.

"Take it slow," Ramona said. "Feel it out."

Jay took off easy and built speed. The park bustled by the water, but the woods remained empty. He let himself become attuned to the feedback through the seat. She corrected his hands on the wheel, pressing close. He doubled, tripled back through the park, slaloming through the double-S curve at growing speed.

"I think you're ready to hit the highway," she said, and squeezed his hand around the pistol shifter. "Still can't believe you drive a car with an idiot stick."

Jay grinned and gave the Hammerhead more pedal around the lake. As they came over a rise, a little maroon sedan drifted into their lane.

Ramona yelled and Jay swerved around with a squeal of

rubber. Behind them, the other car hit the water.

Jay pinned the brakes. Ramona braced her palms on the dash.

"Go," she said. "I'll call nine-one-one."

Out the back window, the maroon sedan bobbed ass-up in the lake like an old turtle seeking deeper water.

"Get moving," she said, thumbing her phone.

Jay knuckled the wheel and watched the car spin lazily in an undercurrent. He could hear Okie telling him to stay cool and roll on out of the park, but wilted under Papa Andre's disappointed gaze.

"Jay, I can't be involved in this—"

He thunked the shifter into reverse and smoked the tires back the way they came.

Two teen boys had dropped their fishing poles and pointed at the fraught young face pressed to the rear passenger window.

"Mister, we can't swim."

Jay kicked off his work boots and trotted toward the water.

"Jay!" Ramona called.

He didn't answer. He snagged a shore stone and hit the water running. Weeds caught at his arms as he stroked, and something thick slithered past him as he gripped the door handle. He slapped the window.

"Open the door!"

The woman inside answered with shouts of hoarse panic. The water lapped over the front windows. Jay tried to clamber on the trunk and slipped. He raised the rock and punched through the driver's window.

Water rushed in and he followed it. The woman kicked away from the water, eyes white with terror. A second after Jay saw the child seat in the back, the green water swallowed them and the baby whole.

The woman kicked at his face as he tugged her out by the feet, wrapped an arm around her hips and pushed her to the surface. She gripped his neck for dear life. He took a gulp of air and shoved her away thrashing, and dived through the weeds back to the car.

The sun gave the water a dull jade haze. Strips of water grass gripped his throat as he went in the open window. He made out black shapes in the murk and groped his way into the back. Felt something squirmy soft and tugged it. The baby was strapped in.

He reached for his boot, and knew Andre's combat knife lay useless on the Hammerhead's floorboard.

Jay wriggled his fingers beneath the straps and braced, pulling hard, lungs beginning to burn. His heart throbbed, a cruel fist crushing the back of his throat demanding air. He could endure this for minutes. The baby could not.

The car seat strap popped and his head hit the roof, bubbles bursting from his lips. He clenched his chin to his chest to keep from breathing, clutched the child, and kicked his way out blind. Shoulders got caught on the window frame. His drowning body jerked of its own accord. The sun was a dim green spot in a black jade murk.

He burst to the surface with both hands thrust high, wheezing a breath and thrashing toward shore. Ramona hooked an arm under Jay's shoulders and kicked back in a lifeguard stroke.

"Take the baby," Jay gasped. "I'm good, I'm good."

Ramona swam with the baby held high.

Jay sucked air, struggled to shore. "We got her, we got her."

The mother sat spitting water and clutched for her squalling child. The little fists shivered as the boy gurgled water. The woman squeezed her baby tight, moaning relief, before she knocked Jay back in a crushing embrace. The baby's cry was a triumphant wail.

Jay patted the woman on the back, his face lit with camera-flashes as he stumbled sopping from the scene, teens following him with their phones. Ramona smoothed her dress and wrung out her hair on the way to the car.

Jay kicked out of his jeans and collapsed in the passenger seat.

"We should get moving, Blackbird."

Ramona peeled away as emergency sirens echoed through the trees. She looped to an empty field and slid the car onto the grass. They stared at each other across the seat, breathless.

The water pearled her chest with a mild sheen. She gripped Jay through his boxers and kneaded him, leaping into a kiss. He clutched her with a groan and peeled her shirt over her head.

She yanked his boxers, and his erection bobbed free. "This is still mine," she snarled, ducked to wet him. Jay gripped her nape and kissed her hard. Tugged off her panties and pulled her atop him. She winced deep as they joined.

He buried his face in her breasts as she pinned him with short, fierce jabs until he roared with half a lifetime of pent energy. Clutched her against him, eyes screwed tight.

"That's my Bluejay," she panted.

Jay carried her to the back seat without a pause. She reached to brush the hair from his eyes as he slid under her skirt a second time, her smile feral.

CHAPTER 19

In middle school, the boys and girls shuffled into pecking orders they didn't understand. Jay's denim jacket got looks from Ramona's preppy friends and her designer clothes got sneers from his. They held hands in the hall and kissed in secret.

Her parents thought boys were a distraction and held the threat of Catholic prep school over her head. In study hall, she palmed Jay a hand-drawn map directing him through the park, from his backyard to her bedroom window.

After dark they met on her porch and walked the tracks of the Erie line, where moonlight bathed a hideaway nestled in the trees. She glossed his lips with strawberry kisses while their sneakers dangled off the railroad trestle, legs tingling from the height. Jay kneaded her shoulders, thumbs circling. She moaned into the kiss, pressing her chest to his. Her warmth seeped into to him and Jay felt safe in the world. He weaseled his thumbs under her bra straps, soothing the red-lined skin. He rubbed his lips over her throat, her pulse hot.

He closed his eyes, feeling real for once. Not the demon boy who still woke some nights screaming. Mama Angeline would stroke his hair and smoke a cigarette, swirling orange squiggles in the dark with its ember. After the Witch, she'd had to chase him down some nights, crush him to her chest until he stopped thrashing.

Ramona pushed him from her breasts.

"Sorry," he said, his mind fuzzy.

"You want to see them?" She adjusted her straps. Eyes sharp.

"No," Jay lied.

"I know you do. I felt it in your jeans."

His face flushed red.

She pulled her shirt over her head. Brassiere glowing in the starlight.

Baby fat softened her grown-woman curves. Her grin twisted wry, the left side screwed into her cheek. She sank to hands and knees and prowled closer, eyes bright.

Jay swallowed as gravity wrestled with her brassiere.

She knelt beside him, her breasts level with his trembling face. She ran her hands through his locks and thrust out her chest.

Jay shivered as he saw himself throwing her belly-down on the dirt, taking her like he'd watched the Witch be taken. Gator claws tickled his neck, and sulfur tinged the air.

He scooted back wide-eyed.

A tremor played across her face. She hugged her knees and rocked behind them. "I'm a freak, aren't I?"

"I'm the freak," Jay said. He crawled to her side. "You deserve better than me. I'm broken."

"I'm the one who's broken," she said through the shield of her knees. "Mother wants me to cut them off. A birthday present, she says. Fix my nose, and make these pert." She weighed her breasts in her hands.

They were nearly as large as Mama Angeline's, and garnered the same hungry stares from men and envious sneers from other women.

"There's nothing wrong with you, Blackbird."

"You'll say anything," Ramona said, letting them drop. "They make you do it. Maybe Mother's right."

Jay furrowed his brow at the prospect of the proud diver beauty wanting to cut herself. Other girls in school had acne, gangly limbs, breasts out of place with their chicken legs. Ramona reminded him of the paintings in art class that made other boys snicker.

"Lisa had it done," she said. Her older sister Lisa went to

college in New York. "With her shirt off, she looks like a burn victim."

Jay looked away. His scars flushed hot.

"I'm sorry," Ramona said, her brow perked with tender regard. Stroked his puckered back under his shirt.

"It's all right." He could barely feel her touch beneath the thickened skin.

The two of them looked over the trestle-edge at the empty road below.

"You knew me before I got these," she said, looping an arm around his neck. "You liked me, right?"

"You know I did."

"Well? Is Mother right? Was I prettier before they ballooned?"

"I like 'em just fine," Jay said. She locked eyes until he shrugged. "They're part of you."

Her mouth became a thin line. "Take your shirt off."

He obeyed, shielding the pink-edged flames scarred across his back. A shotgun spread of cigarette burns glinted on his chest and belly. He told the other kids they were chicken pockmarks. Behind the pool clubhouse, Ramona had showed him the scar she got on her thigh from falling off a horse, and he showed her his. And they had kissed each scar.

"Hands behind your back."

Jay sat on his palms.

Ramona stood and twirled, glowing in the starlight, shoulder blades speckled with beauty marks. Her smooth skin rose in goosebumps beneath the breeze's tickle.

She straddled his lap and kissed him, eyes open and locked on his own. Pushed him onto his back with her breasts. In her games he wasn't allowed to budge, and that suited him fine. Behind the poolhouse they studied each other through barter, but only she was allowed to touch. She would guide his hands.

She slid out of her garment and spilled warm over his chest and face, enveloping him.

Jay imagined swimming with her in an endless pool of blue. They could breathe it, and knew each other's thoughts. The water was cold but they were warm. She touched him and it never hurt. The familiar swelling betrayed his excitement but his lips never wandered from her heart.

She tugged his hands free and put them to good use.

CHAPTER 20

Ramona's scent lingered in the Challenger as Jay wended the maze of streets at the port. They had unleashed the desperate ferocity their younger selves had discovered, and it still radiated from deep inside him. Leaving her a second time was not in the cards.

Staying meant giving Frankie Dell satisfaction.

Weaving among trucks while jets roared overhead, he passed a snowy mountain of rock salt and the Seaman's Church before he found Ironbound Carting on a concrete spit that jutted into Newark bay. The office trailer floated in a mire of asphalt amidst a Lego skyline of shipping containers. He parked next to a black Benz.

The truck depot stank of rot, and a low buzz of chemicals stuck in his throat. Jay practiced drawing Andre's combat knife from his boot, reverse grip like a shank. He tucked it under the hem of his jeans and headed to the trailer.

Men in dirty jumpsuits lined outside the trailer's single window. Rickety steel steps led to a beat-up aluminum door on the other. The door was unlocked.

Inside, a haggard man with red eyes and a yellowed white mustache sat at a steel desk by the window, sliding the wheels of his office chair back and forth on cracked linoleum tiles. He stabbed at a smoke-stained keyboard while peering at a smudged computer monitor. A steel box next to it whirred and spat a ticket, which he tore off and handed to a driver out the window.

Across from him, two men sat on an ass-worn leather couch in front of a flat screen television. One was a dirty blond stork, the other puffy and red-faced, receding hair swept back in a fuzz, as if he'd braved a sandstorm to reach this oasis.

"Whoa," Red said.

Stork pointed to the window. "Get your jobs out there, pal."

"Dante says you boys got a job for me," Jay said. "Didn't say nothing about waiting in line."

The two men exchanged glances before they introduced themselves. The stork's name was Oscar, and the red-faced man was Paul.

"Have a seat, buddy," Paul said. "We got satellite teevee."

"There's beer in the icebox."

"Dante said I'd be working a truck."

"He sends a lot of people here, none of them work a truck," Oscar said. "You gotta have a Waterfront Card to work a truck."

The television showed two jag-offs dragging a body around a beach house. The trailer smelled of old smoke and men in close confinement. He'd rather put in a day's work than smell these guys' farts.

"This came from Frankie Dell," Jay said. "He says I'm supposed to haul trash."

Oscar called to the man working the window. "Mustache, we got a short crew? Find a truck for this hard-ass. See how long he lasts."

Mustache hammered at the grungy keyboard. "What's his Waterfront number?"

"Just find a three-man truck and put him on it. *Weekend at Bernie's* ain't good enough for him."

Mustache tip-tapped and the printer spat a ticket. "Chris got an empty seat."

Oscar called the truck on the radio.

"You'll work a half shift," Paul said. "Come back after lunch. We fish for striper."

"Can't eat it, cause of the dioxin," Oscar said. "You see these guys with coolers full. Try and tell 'em it's loaded with Agent Orange, but they don't speak no English."

"Ain't gone fishing in a dog's age," Jay said. "A whole pack of dogs."

"You can use his gear," Paul said. "He never catches shit anyway."

"He scares 'em away with his damn aftershave." Oscar turned to watch the television screen, rolling a bottle between his hands.

A truck horn blared.

"That's your ride, garbage man."

The rear loader was once white but now caked with soot. A sunburned bald driver in front and two beefy workers in do-rags hanging on the back. Jay climbed in the passenger's side.

The driver's name was Chris. His head was shaped like a pink bean, and his lips never seemed to fully close. "Hope you got gloves. Your hands are gonna get destroyed."

"I'll manage," Jay said.

"When there's junk outside the can, you go toss it in."

"Okay then."

They switchbacked the streets along the piers, seeking out Dumpsters overflowing with trash. Jay hopped out to help toss in a stack of busted pallets and old computer monitors, then watched the truck crush it with its massive claw.

An older man with a ready smile worked the crusher. His partner was a silent hulk, wide as a door frame, who flung pallets like playing cards.

"Everybody likes to see stuff get chomped," the old one said, and offered Jay a stained glove. "I'm Abdullah."

"Jay," he said. "*As-Salamu Alaykum.*"

"*Wa-Alaikum Salaam,*" Abdullah said, laughing in surprise. He gave Jay a spare set of gloves and helped him get on the riding deck. "Hang on real tight."

"Who's the big fella?"

"Don't mind Denny," Abdullah said. "He don't talk much."

Abdullah showed Jay how to hitch a Dumpster and dump it. Let him chomp a rusted steel desk into twisted sculpture. They dumped the load on a barge pier, and Chris said it was break time.

"I could go for a cheeseburger," Jay said. "How 'bout y'all? On me."

"You sure about that?" Chris said. "Denny can eat the whole cow."

"Don't gotta pay for me," Denny mumbled.

"If you're buying, we're going to Krug's." Chris drove them to Ferry Street and parked the truck on the sidewalk of a back street.

Krug's Tavern was an old brick house with a neon shamrock outside and a long mahogany bar infused with the scent of seared beef within. A poster of Jake LaMotta, the Raging Bull, graced the wall above the grill. The cook served thick slabs of cheeseburger on Kaiser rolls, and the four men ate them on a picnic table out back, grease running down their arms.

Jay tilted his head with a nod. "This here's a damn good burger."

Denny got three. They looked like White Castle sliders in his hands.

Chris got a radio call and finished his meal in the truck.

"What you doing hauling trash anyway?" Abdullah asked between bites.

"I plan on making a big mess," Jay said, "Reckon I better know how to clean it up."

Abdullah held the burger in front of his mouth. "You watch out for those boys in the trailer," he said. "Seen them take wrenches to a driver for the dock boss. Never saw that boy again."

They lumbered back to the truck with heavy bellies.

"Thanks," Denny whispered.

Chris dropped the men off at the union office. Denny waved to Jay as the truck moved on, and Abdullah looked away. Chris turned the radio up and beelined across the asphalt.

"My car's over by the trailer," Jay said.

"Paulie said to drop you on the pier," Chris said, eyes flicking away. "He, uh, said the stripers are running."

Ahead, the concrete horizon broke to the water's gray chop. The Benz was parked by a row of moorings. Paul sat on one of the iron toadstools, smoking a cigar and holding a brown paper lunch bag. Oscar the Stork leaned on the hood of the car, surf rod in hand.

Sweat gleamed on Chris's upper lip.

"They fixin' to kill me, Chrissie?"

The tremble in his eyes said enough. Jay threw his body into a liver punch, followed it with two more. Chris dry-heaved, face bent to the steering wheel. Jay stomped the accelerator and jerked the wheel toward the Benz.

Oscar and Paul snapped their heads up as the truck veered their way. Paul waddled like Costello, holding the lunch bag. The paper burst and the windshield starred twice before he disappeared beneath the truck's nose with thump and a scream.

Oscar did a funny little dance, stuck in place until the truck crumpled the Benz like tinfoil and punched it and him into the waves.

The air brakes hissed and the truck slammed into a mooring with a shudder.

Jay hit the dash with his shoulder and his right arm went numb. He clawed for the knife in his boot, but his fingers didn't work. He needn't have worried. The truck's rear wheels had flattened Paul's middle. Blood pooled on the concrete as his life twitched out through his limbs. Jay found the pistol not too far away.

He poked the muzzle into the truck's cab, where Chris wiped vomit from his chin with a wad of fast-food napkins.

"Don't go anywhere now," Jay said, and stepped to the edge of the pier. The Benz slowly bobbed into the gray-wash of the bay. Oscar tread water and clutched the bumper for purchase.

"Are they biting?" Jay called.

Oscar swore over the slap of the waves. Seagulls cried and circled overhead.

Jay aimed and blew out the passenger window. The pistol packed more wallop than Mama's old Colt. The kick drove the pins and needles from his hand.

Oscar fish-mouthed and dived under. Jay fired until the window shattered and the bay sucked the car in. When Oscar didn't surface, he winged the pistol into the chop.

Jay dragged Chris out of the truck by his collar. Slapped him around until he helped him heave Paul into the crusher. Jay pulled the lever and the body disappeared into the truck's maw.

Chris wobbled and gripped the side of the truck.

"Cheer up." Jay patted Chris on the cheek. "Teach me to drive this thing, and you won't have to crawl in after him."

Across the channel, cranes lifted their booms like giant steel fingers clawing from the sea.

Dante's Cadillac sat parked by a trailer tucked in his own private corner of the container yard.

One foot on the brake and one on the gas, Jay butted the hauler's bashed nose against the trailer until Dante burst out of the door raging, his belt and fly undone, hands upturned into claws. "Guess which asshole will never drive a truck on the east coast again!"

Jay drowned out his words with the air horn, then yanked the dump lever. The rear of the hauler rose and disgorged Paulie's wrecked body onto the hood of the Cadillac and buried both in a waterfall of crushed refuse.

Dante dropped his jaw and stumbled back.

Jay hopped out of the truck. "Your boys missed, Hound Dog." He raised a wrecking bar over his head.

Dante ran back into the trailer. Jay splintered the door jamb with two thrusts and chased him through the tumbled furniture.

Dante collided with a bottom-heavy truck bunny gathering her clothes, glossy braids flailing.

Dante fell to his ass and kicked with his loafers, bare skin squeaking across the tiles.

Jay straddled him, iron bar across his throat. Stared glassy-eyed while the Hound Dog's face ballooned purple. A lock of hair fell in his eyes, and Jay blinked it away. Dante bucked and gurgled.

"Frankie's next," Jay said. "Then that dumb shit Randal, for starting it all." Jay put his weight on the bar.

"Hey, mister," came a woman's voice from behind.

"Just walk away, honey."

"He ain't paid me."

Jay ripped Dante's wallet from his pants, scooped the cash, and held it over his shoulder. "Take it all. He won't be needing it."

She snatched the bills and ducked out the door.

Dante wheezed and held out a finger.

Jay let up a notch. "Better make it good."

"Not me," Dante gasped. "Frankie."

"He didn't give you the job?" Jay prodded the crowbar point against Dante's throat. "Guess you only cut his steak."

Dante coughed. "If I wanted you dead, asshole, you'd be landfill."

Jay dug the point under his Adam's apple. "Take care now."

"Easy, you crazy fuck."

"You're the negotiator," Jay said. "Let's see you lawyer your way out of this one."

"I know better than to threaten you, you psychotic prick." Dante licked his lips. "Why you think I palled up with you inside? You're an animal. A hate machine. Killing's all you're good at. Aim you at something and you tear it apart, don't find nothing but shreds in your teeth. We'll go back and forth until there's nothing left."

"Reckon so." The corner of Jay's mouth curled. "Get to the chorus, Hound Dog."

"You got a thick skull. I won't kill you 'cause I can use you."

Jay dragged the crowbar point to Dante's eye. "Tell me again who's killing who."

Dante grimaced and screwed his eye shut. "Ice Frankie, and all is forgiven."

"So you're gonna let this slide? Don't sound like you." Jay wiped his forehead. "I know how you goombahs like it. I do your shit work, then you whack me to settle the books." He raised the bar with both hands.

"Whoa, think a minute," Dante said, showing his palms. "You took a gigantic shit around here, you gotta split town anyway. I'd pay an out-of-towner ten gees. If that's not enough for you, take the drop money from the club. Then disappear, because we will come looking."

Jay crinkled his eyes. "Keep your money. Hand the club over to Cheetah."

"You crazy? That property alone's worth four mil, easy."

Jay wagged the crowbar. "And your life ain't?"

"*Cazzone!* It's not my decision to make. I'll see what I can do, that's the best I can give you."

"You just figured out what your life's worth." Jay dropped the crowbar to the floor.

"Mind getting off my chest? If I wanted a peckerwood sitting on my face, I'd work the trucks like that twat you gave my wallet."

Jay stood. "Your Italian hot dog's showing."

Dante smirked and clambered to his feet. "Tomorrow night, we'll work out the details. Or as Frankie would say, *we'll take care of the low-hanging fruit.*"

"Where can I find the foxy sumbitch?"

"Frankie? He's beached like a whale by his pool." Dante belted his slacks. "What, you're going now?"

"Call and tell him you punched my ticket." Jay slipped the

combat knife from his boot. Dante had hound dog eyes, but a wolf soul you didn't turn your back on. "You and Cheetah better work things out," Jay said, wagging the blade. "Or I'll take care of *your* low-hanging fruit."

Frankie Dell's castle lay nestled in the hilly woods of Livingston at the end of a one lane road. Jay pulled Chris's trucker cap low as he approached the gates. Dante had yammered out the code for the keypad, warned him about the security cameras. The pack of black Neapolitan mastiffs, the incinerator in the woods.

The sprawling white villa peeked through the trees at the end of a meandering drive, protected by barred gates. Jay shifted the garbage truck into low gear and roared ahead. The truck's battered grill plowed on through and twisted the iron bars to sculpture.

Statues of the Dellamorte family lined the path in white marble. A cherubic grandmother with a double chin. An equestrian of young Frankie looking dour and Napoleonic. Jay turned the truck around and knocked the horse off its pedestal. The legs shattered and the beast rolled into the grass over its rider.

Jay reversed up the drive, gears whining.

Flat Top opened the front door to investigate the truck's loud beeping. Jay grinned from the driver's seat and gave a little wave. Flat Top ducked inside and slammed the door.

The truck jounced over the steps and crashed through the columns and the broad door. The rear demolished a wide staircase and the entire front of the house shuddered as the truck rocked to a stop. The front end stuck out through the splintered doorway. Terra cotta tiles rained from the roof and clattered off the hood like dinner plates.

Jay kicked the truck door open. The floor creaked and the truck jolted as the joists gave. He jumped out and ran around the side of the house as the truck boomed through to the wine cellar with a crash and plume of dust.

A tiled pool gleamed aquamarine, surrounded by palms and cabanas. Frankie sprawled in a chaise lounge, flabby crepe paper arms hanging off the sides, silver mane shining over the top. A young blonde girl sat in his lap wearing a satin red bikini top and nothing else. They both stared back at the house.

Jay ran for them with the tomahawk held low. The girl shrieked and ran bare-assed across the patio.

Frankie gawped and flopped like a mottled albino walrus. Jay's reflection loomed in the silver fox's tortoiseshell shades.

"*Va fa Napoli*," Jay said, and slammed his elbow under Frankie's nose. The chair snapped flat under the weight. Frankie moaned through a jumbled mouthful of shards.

Jay dragged him by the pompadour to the pool's edge.

Frankie spat chunks of shattered bridgework. Jay held him under and clusters of denture sank to the bottom flashing pink and white. He yanked him by the hair and chopped Andre's hatchet into the back of his neck. The steel crunched through bone and the Mediterranean blue water flushed crimson.

PART THREE

LIVE WIRE

CHAPTER 21

Jay met Rene his first year in Rahway. The queen was a fine observer for Okie's plays, her doe-eyed flutter perfect for cozying up to the hacks. A skill she required to keep the steady flow of what Okie called her "titty medicine."

"I got you moved to a new cell," Okie said. "You're bunking with a sister named Rene."

No big loss. Jay's celly's snore resembled a top fuel dragster, and his feet smelled like Frito's corn chips.

"He needs protection. I want you to pretend this queen's your punk, to keep the jockers off her. You do that, the Kings will lean on the Hitler Bitches, take the heat off you for a while."

Jay scratched at his Tyr rune tattoo. "How much I gotta pretend?"

"You don't gotta suck dick," Okie said. "Just let it be known he's your property. His brother's Verdad Hernandez. Latin King royalty, but he's stuck in the SHU for good."

Verdad was a three-foot-wide slab of flat-eyed meanness, who earned his name when a crew threatened to knock Rene's teeth out and make her their suck-dog. He told them, "You look at my brother again, I'll feed you each other's balls. And that is *verdad*."

They hadn't taken him as a man of his word.

Verdad's word was bond, and he earned a triple life sentence to prove it.

A wiry little Latino awaited Jay in his new cell with full lips and soft skin. Sprawled in the orange plastic chair, chatting about Madonna with another queen two cells down. Wore a red bandanna and lipstick, a tied-off shirt, and jeans cut so short the white pockets showed. When Jay stepped in, Rene winked and pointed her perkies his way.

Jay set his box of things on the table and eyed the top bunk, where a Snickers bar sat on the pillow.

"This yours?"

"Welcome home, *papi*."

"Thanks. Name's Jay."

"Rene."

Jay reached to shake. Rene offered a hand knuckles up. Jay obliged with a gentle squeeze. "I hear you need a friend."

"I need a *papi*, that's what I need." Rene licked her lips, showing small, chipped teeth.

Jay took a sheaf of magazine pages from his box, and held out one of a model who reminded him of Ramona. "You got nice ones, buddy. But I like hers better."

Rene peeked at the picture and sat cross-legged in the orange chair. "Those titties look like fake plastic fruit," he said. "Besides, she's paper and my fresh peaches are right here." Folded her arms together, making a snug little cleavage. "Tell me you don't wanna stick it between these peaches."

Jay gave an appreciative nod. "You make a strong argument." He stacked his paperbacks on the desk.

"You the kind who's gotta take it, aren't you."

Jay grabbed Rene by the shirt. "I ain't gonna be your *papi*, but we're gonna act like it," he whispered. "Gift from your brother."

Rene's eyes went wet. "*Mi hermano.*"

"You want your candy bar?"

They split it.

"Shit, why didn't you tell me sooner," Rene said, and sank back into the chair with a heavy sigh. "Been giving you my best bottom game."

"It was fun watching you work, Peaches."

After lights out, Jay gripped himself and thought of Ramona while Rene gave an Oscar-worthy performance in the bunk below. The line of jocks gunning for Rene's peaches evaporated when word went round that the sister had hooked up with the crazy Cajun who'd put Feature and his entire crew in the dirt.

When the Brotherhood stomped Verdad's woman in the parking lot, Jay held Rene while she cried. The hacks said they should've backed the ambulance over her, put the woman out of her misery. Verdad let it be known he wanted the kind of revenge that only a riot could bring. Jay traced his warrior-rune tattoo, and told Okie he had an idea how to start one.

CHAPTER 22

Jay got to the garage before sunrise. The door was locked, and Tony nowhere to be found. He took Andre's tomahawk out to the back and practiced throwing it at a stump. Steel rang as he found the ancient muscle memory, the weight in the shoulder, the snap of the wrist.

The Hulk Truck rumbled to the lot. Jay waited for Tony to mosey through his opening-up routine before joining him, leaning on the corner of the desk, and sipping his lunch-truck coffee.

"What's on your mind, Tee?"

"Nothing," Tony said. "Just the life of a businessman."

"You can keep my pay. Put it toward what I owe."

"You don't owe me anything," Tony said. "Thought we went over that. I owed you, now we're even. So don't insult me."

"Okay then."

Tony jabbed at the keyboard. A familiar beat came out of the tinny speakers. An old INXS song that had remained Tony's mantra: "Don't Change."

"Nothing else bothering you?"

Tony blinked and pursed his lips, getting words ready to spit.

"Me and Ramona, ain't it?"

Tony sighed, as if Jay let the air out of his tires. "It's good having you back, pallie. Really it is, but this old shit, I thought I was done with it, you know? Now we got the reunion, and I wanted to go and show everybody I'm not Tony Baloney anymore, but now I'm thinking it's not the best idea. Bobby Algieri'll be there, shooting off his mouth. Nicky Paladino, too."

"I'll make sure Nicky stays home. He ain't no cop."

"Then it'll be somebody else. It wasn't only Bello and his

160

crew, you know. The whole school went along. We were Tony Baloney, Hormona, and the Redneck Runt."

"I forgot about that one."

"Yeah, well good for you. Not all of us can. What did Joey call Billy?"

"I don't recall."

"Think he just called him Brenda, like his brother. Then said 'Oops, wrong faggot.'"

"Sounds about right." Jay took a bite of his buttered roll. "You want to grab that pizza tonight?"

"Nah, you know what, I'm busy," Tony said. His chair hit the shelf as he stood. "Maybe I should've gone to prison, so I'd be over this shit."

Jay chewed his lip to keep from speaking his mind. He'd seen big fellas like Tony do their time. Most begged for protective custody.

"And you can take the day off," Tony said. "Not that you're here half the time anyway. I need some time alone."

"Tone," Jay said.

Tony stopped by the door. "You fucking her?"

Jay narrowed his eyes and sipped his coffee. "You can be a gentleman or we can talk outside."

"Yeah, thought so." Tony stomped into the service bays. A tool clattered to the floor, and a mechanic swore in Spanish.

Nicky Paladino stood by the tall front windows of the ShopRite, flashing his gap-toothed smile as he handed an old lady rolls of quarters, then returned to staring at the pert little ass of the girl working lane five.

Jay watched through a pair of cheap sunglasses from the lot across the street, between bites of a ripe peach. Pimply teenagers wrangled the carts as the supermarket closed. Jay gnawed around the peach pit and spat it out of the car, then carried his shopping bag across the street.

The store employees parked on a roof lot atop the building. Nicky's black Corvette straddled two spaces. Late '90s model, but waxed pristine. Jay ice picked a front tire with Andre's knife. The car settled off-kilter with a long hiss. He hit the other three corners, sheathed the knife, and waited behind a delivery van.

Nicky had been a stockboy in high school. Jay remembered helping Mama Angeline get groceries for a cookout, and Nicky grinning at the two watermelons in their cart. With Jay in earshot, he offered to help her carry her melons to the car. Angeline said he didn't look strong enough, and grabbed Jay's belt when he went after him. Said he wasn't worth the trouble.

Jay slipped a twenty from her purse and bought two rolls of quarters. When Nicky followed them into the parking lot with two snickering cart boys, Jay punched him in the balls and whaled on him until the coins rained a jackpot.

Mama Angeline wasn't pleased. "I can handle myself, son," she said in the Jeep.

"I didn't want you getting in trouble for using your Colt," Jay said.

She chuckled. "That piss-ant ain't worth a nickel's worth of lead, much less the change you dropped."

Nicky strutted toward his Corvette. He'd lost an inch of hairline but kept the same sneer on his face, like he had seen photos of you on the toilet, or had heard something involving your sister and a zoo animal.

The expression melted into an open-mouthed glower as he noticed his tires.

"When I find the dickless little shit who did this, he's fired," Nicky announced to the lot and dug out his phone.

Jay came around the van and sapped him in the kidney with a bag full of Campbell's soup cans.

Nicky yelped and fell to hands and knees, phone skittering

across the asphalt. Jay swung overhead, cans clanking as they hit doughy flesh. Nicky curled and whimpered.

Jay crushed the phone with three stomps of his work boot. "Face to the dirt, you piece of shit."

"Take my wallet, take it, take it."

"I'm not here for your money, Nicky."

Jay put a knee to the small of Nicky's back and drew the hatchet from his belt. Yanked Nicky's belt and sliced through his navy chinos, baring dingy briefs.

Nicky jerked and yelped as the spike pricked flesh. "Oh fuck!"

Jay ground his face into the ground with a knee. The soup cans rolled in circles around them.

Nicky blinked as a pine cone bounced off the pavement past his face. Then a second, and a third. "Fuck, oh fuck." The fear left his face and his lip twitched like a cat scenting prey.

"Awful jagged, ain't they? Except your ass is so wide I could kick one of those cans of Chickarina up there. You wanna play kick the can?"

Nicky gritted his teeth. "Do what you're gonna do, fuck-face."

"Careful what you ask for, Nicky." Jay gripped him by the hair and put the blade to his soft neck. "I'm here to talk about your rapist buddy from high school."

"You killed him," Nicky groaned. "What do you want from me?"

The blade rang as Jay scraped it over Nicky's stubble. "Some might say I left the job half done. But your sorry-ass life ain't worth a murder beef." He let Nicky's chin drop to the asphalt.

Nicky grunted. "You don't scare me."

"You don't know me anymore. I ain't the boy who left town. Now, what made Joey so scary, shitbird?"

"His father."

"Scary enough you felt safe playing your sick games with the town hero's son."

"Mr. Bello has something on everybody," Nicky said. "Joey said his father had his hand up Leo Zelazko's ass like a Muppet."

Jay peeked up like a gopher, saw no one, and crushed down again. "He's still pulling Leo's strings. Why?"

Nicky laughed. "Find out where Zee goes after work every day."

"This ain't no joke, freak. Unless you wanna walk home leaving a trail of shit and blood, talk."

"Jesus," Nicky said. "What you gonna take? Matty Strick took it all. I had a fucking business. I'm forty years old and I work with pimple-faced little shits who talk behind my back. If you're gonna do it, get it over with, 'cause I'm fucked already."

Jay read the psycho vibe coming off Nicky. In prison, the sickest had no fear. Pain was something that happened to other people. The strong inflicted it upon the weak, and threats rolled off them like piss on porcelain. Jay switched gears, spoke their language. "I don't wanna kill you, Nicky. I like watching you suffer. When we were kids, you were on top. Now it's my turn. Like you two did Brendan." He jabbed the axe point between Nicky's ass cheeks. "He brought it on himself. I turned out a lot of bitches like him in prison. You would've done real well in there."

Nicky looked beneath the cars for approaching feet. Rested his cheek to the pavement when he saw none. Predatory daydreams swirled in his eyes. "Joey made it so easy. We got away with anything back then."

Jay recalled Joey Bello's all-knowing smile beneath the blue-ringed bulls-eyes of his fathomless stare.

"We did whatever he wanted, and people let us. It was better than sex," Nicky said. "Like getting a blow job, *all the time*. The best kind, when they don't wanna give it, but they know they have to, and they start to get into it, about halfway through—"

Jay bounced Nicky's face off the asphalt. "I can't believe you're walking, and I went to jail."

"You hacked my friend to pieces," Nicky choked.

"So why should I follow Leo Zee. What am I gonna find?"

Nicky chuckled. "Know why I'm still alive? Because I know to keep my mouth shut. Joey never learned that, he liked to throw things in people's faces. It's better when they only think you know. You get to watch it fuck them all up inside."

Hate rose in Jay like a fever. It would be easy to bleed Nicky out on the pavement. Or at least reacquaint him with those pine cones. But he had a feeling both of them might enjoy it. Jay wiped the blade on Nicky's briefs, and tucked the hatchet away. "I want you to do something for me, shitbird."

"Whatever you say," Nicky said. "Just leave me the fuck alone."

"You're gonna tell the mayor that the one who really took the axe to his boy? He never served a day. I was paid to do his time for him."

Nicky looked over his shoulder, trying to read his eyes. Jay had learned to lie from the best.

"You rat on me, I'll toss your head into the Mud Hole with the snapping turtles," Jay said. He punched Nicky in the kidney, and when his mouth gaped open he jammed a pine cone past his big white teeth.

He left Nicky gagging and spitting.

CHAPTER 23

Jay pushed off the wall of Ramona's pool and swam to the shallow end without breaking for air. The water was heated, the pool bottom textured to mimic Caribbean sand. Perched on a ridge of the Watchung mountain chain, they overlooked a carpet-roll of forested hills terminating at the jagged teeth of the Manhattan skyline.

Ramona walked onto the sprawling patio holding two glasses. She sat at the pool's edge, slow-kicking the water in a blue Jantzen swimsuit.

Jay surfaced between her knees.

"I hope Pappy Van Winkle is to your taste," she said, handing him the glass. "We're fresh out of Wild Turkey."

Jay savored its slow fire. "It'll do."

Ramona sipped her negroni. "This won't last," she said. "You know that."

"I'll take what I can get."

They drank and counted birds crossing the patch of blue sky. "Did you hear about Stanley Carnahan?"

"I read in the paper that he took the lead pill."

"That's one way to put it." She stared at him through her sunglasses.

"If he checked out from the guilt, he dug his own grave far as I'm concerned."

"He's still a person, Jay."

"Ain't we all?"

"Jesus. How bad was it in there?"

"Wasn't no picnic," Jay said. "You don't know what you got until it's gone, and they take everything. There's not much you're allowed to do, but there's ways you work around it."

"Kind of like us," she said.

"Wasn't the same."

"You remember Mother. She wanted to control everything about me. It sure felt like prison. Maybe that's why our trysts were so sweet. Forbidden fruit."

"Well, our courtship wasn't exactly encouraged, but I never got the 'stay the hell away from my daughter' speech. Your father liked me well enough." Mr. Crane had invited Andre over for a beer. Said his own father had been a bricklayer, and he'd "carried the hod" for him summers as a teen. Had Andre build them a china brake, which he used as a liquor cabinet.

"What did you see in me? I was such a snotty little brat."

"Attitude," Jay said. "You flipped the whole world the finger."

"I remind you of your mother," she said, and drained her drink.

"And why'd you smile on a poor boy like me?"

"You were a little gentleman," Ramona said, setting down her glass. "And you're cute." She marched to the diving board with that same defiant step and executed a perfect jack knife.

Jay swam to meet her halfway, and she surfaced in his arms. He held her as she kneaded his muscles, cataloging his new body. Water dripped down the scarred marble of his skin. The old constellation of burns, cut with ragged lightning bolts left from scratches and shanks and tussles. She traced them with short painted nails.

He flexed his arm around her waist, bringing her close. Put his lips to her widow's peak, and she pulled him down for a long kiss that muffled their quiet shudders.

"Damn you, Jay," she muttered, biting his ear, his neck. "Why."

Deep down he knew that it never would have lasted, that he could never give her what she'd been born to. That no matter whether she cared or not, it would dig at him, the way people's eyes would pinch when seeing them together, as they measured what she must have thrown away for him.

But if she wanted to pretend awhile, so would he.

She pushed away and untied her top, and swam away with thin smile. He followed, and she swerved to brush and tease, shimmying out of her bikini bottom. Jay shucked his trunks and gave chase. The water muted colors like an old photograph, lensing them to their younger selves. She cut away and he followed, trailing behind. His power no match for her speed and grace.

She doubled back and he caught her in the shallow end, sliding against her sleek skin. She snapped her thighs around his erection and kissed him, fierce.

He carried her to a chaise lounge. The years had speckled her chest with freckles, tiger-striped her hips with stretch marks. He kissed each new landmark, and all the familiar ones, breathing her in while she gripped his hair and shuddered.

She tugged him up, and rolled to her elbows and knees.

A twinge, down deep. "I want to see you," Jay panted, and nudged her hip.

She rolled to her back and crossed her ankles around his behind, heels pulling him in deep. He stared in her eyes, like the first time she'd kissed him and all the times after, where he was safe, rocking and matching her motions until he was lost, rippling, seizing, collapsing, burying his face in her neck.

She curled her lips back and freed a languid sigh.

His hands made lazy sweeps over her curves as the clouds scrolled by. When they first met, they spoke in dares and challenges. A tennis match of misunderstandings and appeasements. Now their language had become muscle memory, in the absence of anything to say. He traced the fine scar lines beneath her breasts.

"I had the reduction," she said. "Tired of the judging. They're the first thing anyone sees, and then they think they know all about you."

"People always gonna judge you on something."

"Imagine if you had to walk around with your cock length tattooed on your forehead."

"Then everyone would call me 8-Ball."

"You wish," Ramona said. Gave him a measure, a squeeze. "Did you...have sex in there?"

"No," Jay said. "Unless Howard Jones concerts count."

Ramona laughed. "I haven't thought about that in ages. Howard Jones and Billy Joel."

"What is love anyway," she sang, and watched herself work. Jay lay back and relaxed to her quickening touch.

Ramona would spread a blanket in the grass behind their garage shed, bring a bottle of Jameson from the liquor cabinet Andre had built for her father, and an armful of pillows from the guest room. Some nights they talked while he rubbed her shoulders, others she lay waiting to pounce him, her hand plunging into his jeans for a possessive squeeze.

The first time she took him to a Howard Jones concert, Jay froze like a deer in the headlights. His head was under her shirt, hands kneading her behind. She asked if he liked that, took his silence for the affirmative, working faster until he hunched against her, shuddering. She walked him through how to return the favor.

They phased between mad-rabbit marathons and long spells of making out and talking under the stars. That night she huddled in her denim jacket despite the heat. Jay plucked a firefly's glowing ember from the grass. Crawled onto the blanket, and kissed her hand.

He stuck the firefly's jewel to her ring finger. "Wanted to get you a diamond," he said, resting his head in her lap. "But they didn't have one big enough."

"You're so corny," she sighed.

That day at school her kisses had been needful, but tonight she didn't pounce. He kneaded her shoulders the way she liked, got no response. Some nights she wanted to control his every move, other times she expected him to take the lead.

"What's wrong, Blackbird?"

"Nothing," she said. "I'm cold."

"I'll warm you up," he said, and cupped her breasts through her shirt.

She flinched and pushed his hands away.

He waited for the flint to go out of her eyes, then sat close, not touching. "What's wrong."

She stared into the woods a long time. After a time, she stood.

"This what you want?" She pulled off her shirt and reached behind to unsnap. She spilled out, revealing pinch marks fading to yellow bruises in the cream of her skin.

Jay blinked.

She pulled her shirt on and stomped toward the house.

He caught her wrist. "Who," he snarled.

Her face broke into a silent rictus.

Jay spied the old man in a worn tweed suit on Ramona's porch, rocking his chair with a Waterford glass of whisky. He had a thick cobblestone jaw, and saliva sparkled in the corners of his mouth. His snores rumbled out horse nostrils like the rattle of cicadas.

Ramona's great-uncle Seamus visited a different relative each year, cycling through a large Irish family that had scattered after the Great Famine. She liked his stories of Ireland, and how his slender pianist fingers could effortlessly coax jaunty traditional ballads from her mother's Chickering upright. She begged for lessons as soon as she could talk, learning from his lap, skipping to the liquor cabinet to refresh his glass.

When she was too old for his lap, he sat beside her, and he corrected her with a pinch to the behind. For a while she thought it was cute, that maybe that was how they behaved in what her father reverently called "the old country." This year's visit, Uncle Seamus had waited for her mother to head out, before he pinched a bit more, as if measuring a fattened calf, and Ramona slapped his hand.

Uncle Seamus slapped her back, and good. Gripped her by the wrist while he pinched her hard in tender spots, telling her how a temptress like herself should be washing laundry with the Magdalene nuns. Whiskey breath misted her ear. He said no one would believe her. That he'd tell her mother he saw her whoring around with that American boy unless she took off her shirt for him.

Jay waited for her mother's Volvo wagon to back out of the drive. Ramona said she'd tell her mother she needed a new bra fitting, and that they would argue again about the reduction before eventually leaving for the mall.

When they did, Jay crept over the porch railing and shoved the old bastard's rocking chair down the front steps.

Seamus hit the paving stones face first, the chair clattering. His trembling hands pawed at the lawn, moans muffled by the grass. Jay put his knee on Seamus's shoulder, gripped his wrinkled right thumb, and bent it back until it cracked. Then the other one, like pulling a drumstick off a chicken.

"You won't be pinching no more, you cruel old bastard."

Seamus groaned, beige vomit oozing from his lips.

Jay righted the chair and walked back to his bike. He pedaled home fast. Mama was making a shrimp boil.

A week later, they clutched one other on a blanket beneath the summer stars. Ramona wore nothing but Jay's denim jacket and her knee-high striped socks, lolling sated in his arms. Her scent lingered on his lips and he breathed it in like a drug.

Ramona relished in telling him how they had found Uncle Seamus face down in a pool of his own sick. Mother called an ambulance, and made her visit him in detox at Mountainside hospital. He had the shakes bad, and for his own health, the family decided his visit would be cut short this year.

She gave a sly grin and worked her hand inside Jay's pants.

Jay sprawled on his back, a marionette with the strings cut. He couldn't touch himself this way without seeing the Witch and the Gator man slavering from behind his eyes, but Ramona could. She drove away his old dreams, festering with sulfur and oil and Vaseline, and replaced them with visions of her swimming naked in a blue bayou circled with water lilies.

She dragged her nipples down his belly, her breasts pillowing his erection in warmth.

Their eyes locked.

"Tonight I'm taking you to a Billy Joel concert," she said, and ducked.

Electric heat bolted down his spine.

Fingers with broken nails brushed back his bangs. Revealed the Witch's rotten smile. Just a kiss, just a kiss. The boy grabbed the doorknob and the Witch yanked him by the ankles. Dragged him along the moldy carpet toward a pair of oil-stained work boots.

The Gator man.

Jay woke to Ramona choking his name. Found himself gripping her hair with one hand, the other knotted into a fist. Her irises flicked side to side, seeking escape.

Jay let go. Scanned her face. He had not struck her. "I'm sorry," he gasped.

She watched shivering as Jay collected his clothes and walked naked into the woods toward the railroad tracks.

"Jay?" A hoarse cry.

"I'm broken," he said. "You deserve better."

He pulled his clothes on as he walked home. The Witch had stolen this from him, and nothing he could do would get it back. Jay wished the Erie freight train ran tonight. He'd lay his head down on the cold tracks as it thundered by to smear him from the earth.

CHAPTER 24

Leo Zelazko lived a life of rigid structure. Jay watched the police lot with binoculars from across the par, as Leo pulled his GMC Denali out of the Nutley PD lot at six p.m. each day in civilian clothes and took the main drag toward Route 3. Jay drove to Leo's house and scoped the driveway from the right-of-way beneath the power lines. Leo arrived home about two hours later, entered the side door without disarming an alarm, and took his unfixed Doberman for a jog.

On the third day of watching, Jay approached Leo's door five minutes into his dog walk.

A lockpick gun provided by Mack popped the rear door in fifteen seconds. The house had changed little since Jay visited as a teen. It smelled of dog now, but the kitchen was eat-off-the-floor clean. The living room a museum to late '70s wood and brass, the den a revered warrior's retreat.

Up the hardwood steps, the twins' room had been converted to an office decorated with Brendan's track trophies and photos of Billy graduating from police academy. The master bedroom was still as a tomb. Another of Andre's handmade platform beds, with sheets folded military tight. Jay knelt by the side with an indentation in the pillow and pressed the hidden release. The cubby opened, revealing a tactical flashlight and two speed loaders of .38 hollow points, but no pistol.

He closed the cubby and eyed the beige monolith of the gun safe.

Billy had liked to brag about his father's gun collection. Jay had been raised around guns, so didn't much care. He ran a blue glove over the safe and tested the door.

Locked.

Leo was not as careless as his partner. His secrets had already been leveraged against him.

For many years Jay had fantasized about killing Leo each night. Bare handed, with his carpenter's axe, Mama's Colt, kitchen knives. As he aged, he preferred to imagine his tormenttors in their own prison cells, weeping. Sinking into hollow, bird-chested travesties of their former selves, and finally swinging from a knotted sheet, jerking and choking as they splattered the floor with their own piss and shit.

Now he saw how to realize his fantasy.

Take one of Leo's guns and kill Bello with it.

The Denali was locked in the garage. Leo might leave the revolver in the glovebox. Jay searched for a spare set of keys in kitchen drawers and jacket pockets, but found none. He locked up and left the way he came.

Tony had a lockout kit.

Jay waited in a parking lot along Leo's evening route. The kit from Tony's shop sat in the compartment under the rear seats. Jimmies and door wedges, everything one might need to gain entry to a locked vehicle. When the Denali roared by in the left lane, Jay gunned it onto the pockmarked shoulder. He dodged a fallen muffler and passed cars in the right lane, then fell behind a cluster of traffic where he could follow his prey.

They crossed the Passaic, passed the Meadowlands arena, and took the Turnpike south. Jay weaved between trucks as the Denali became a dot far ahead in the Gordian knot of concrete twists by the airport.

When the Turnpike split, he followed Leo into the truck lanes.

The Denali raced ahead in the left lane, hugging the guard rail. Jay flattened the pedal and cut into the shoulder, kicking up busted glass and trash. A tractor trailer's horn lowed as he blasted past it on the rumble strips. Jay eased back in front of a tanker in time to see the Denali slam on the brakes in the left shoulder, then lurch through a break in the guardrail back onto the cars-only side of the highway.

He'd been seen.

Horns wailed as Leo bulled his way into the car lanes.

Jay swore as the Denali vanished into the heat mirages far up the highway.

He didn't feel like hearing Tony mope about Ramona, or want to think about his best friend had mooned over his girl the years he was away. He took a shift bouncing at Cheetah's, eager to deal out a beating.

The clientele behaved themselves, to his chagrin.

As the club closed, Jay left by the front doors and scanned the streets. His hackles tingled. He let his eyes adjust and made out a man in black against the wall of the alley, watching the club's rear door.

Jay soft-stepped in the shadows, then jumped and looped his arm around the man's throat. Hooked a half-dozen kidney punches, then pulled the man down into the choke.

Jay knelt to search the man's wallet. A second later his eyes exploded white. Jay flopped next to the unconscious man like a fish. Felt someone zip tie his wrists and bag his head, give him another jolt, and toss him hogtied into the back of a truck. They yanked the barbs of the Taser out his back and rumbled away.

Jay recovered his breath and tested his bonds. His hands went numb as he felt for a door handle.

If they'd wanted him dead, he'd be dead.

Unless they wanted him dead slow, for an audience.

A short time later the truck stopped. The lift gate opened and an octopus of limbs pinned him. Snips popped his ankle bonds. He moved to kick and they jammed his ankles to his ass.

"We're going for a short walk and then your hood will be removed," a deep, authoritative voice said. "You will be released unharmed if you cooperate. If you don't, we'll use the Taser or compliance holds, neither of which will be pleasant."

"Okay then," Jay said through the hood.

They steadied him on his feet and walked him into a rattling elevator that smelled of concrete dust. The doors opened and they led him into a cool room. Pressed his chest to a wall and pulled off the hood.

Jay blinked at the dim light. Inhaled the familiar sweetness of coolant and the scent of fresh oil. The faded tang of exhaust hung in the air. They spun him around.

Three beefy men in black turtlenecks and work pants. Two he recognized from the black truck on freedom day. The new guy rubbed his neck.

Beyond them, rows of vehicles parked beneath concrete supports. A Matchbox display of classics and rarities. Jay recognized a red Mercedes 420SL convertible, an Alfa Romeo Spyder Veloce, a bathtub Porsche. A Corvette ZR-1, a vintage Countach with the wing, a classic Jag XKE ragtop in British racing green. A rich gentleman's collection of dust-binned toys.

A thin man in a gray suit walked from behind the three soldiers. Sharp cheekbones and a knob of a chin, skin smooth as a baby's ass, hair in glossy short curls.

"You can remove the bonds," the suit said. He turned to Jay. "He's taking a call. Then he'll meet with you."

A guard reached behind Jay with a multitool. Brush Cut held the Taser at low ready.

"Who's he?" Jay said.

"You'll see," the suit said.

Jay rubbed his freed wrists and said to the grunt, "Sorry about the ribs. Didn't have a knife."

The man ignored him and stood relaxed by his compatriots. All three springy on their feet, ready to go. The driver Jay had made puke held a collapsible baton.

"I wish you were armed," the suit said. "Then you'd be off to jail and out of my hands."

Jay heard a muffled argument and scanned the room slow. Squinted as he recognized the robin's egg blue Triumph TR6 that Ramona's across-the-street neighbor had been restoring. Beside it, a 1984 Porsche 928S in *Risky Business* silver, coated in layers of dust.

Matty's father had owned one exactly like it.

A tall man sat in it, gesticulating as he argued into his phone. Matthew Strick. Jay took a deep breath.

"Who are you, Matty's court jester?"

"You don't recognize me?" He removed a Nat Sherman cigarette from a platinum case, and lit it without offering. "Greg Kuhn."

Jay tilted his head and smirked. "Thought that brown nose looked familiar. You got it up a new ass."

Greg arched his eyebrows, then straightened them with a roll of his eyes. "You haven't changed much. Matthew and I started working together in college."

"Tony said you squeezed him out."

"He didn't have the spine for it."

"Didn't recognize you without your Yankees cap," Jay said. "What do you hide the beanie under these days?"

Greg laughed and patted his head. "We're not the same people we were in middle school. Well, maybe you are."

Let them think that.

"I should thank you for what you did," Greg said, puffing. "I tried to, but you refused my gift. Rude. Why would you do that?"

"Because this ain't about money."

"Oh, it's always about money," Greg said. "Money is the great measurable. Worth nothing on its own. Just paper with a high linen content, some special ink. Its true purpose is to quantify the ineffable. Everything has its price."

"Every thing maybe," Jay said. "But not every one."

"Such principles," Greg said. "Matthew thinks people should get what they deserve, and he's already decided you deserve nothing. No matter, I'm prepared to quadruple my original offer, if you'll say your goodbyes and close this unfortunate chapter of our childhood."

"How much is that again?"

"A hundred thousand."

"Boy, a hundred gees." Jay cracked a smile. "What's that look like?"

Greg held out his right hand as if gripping an overstuffed sandwich.

"Looks like it would just about fit."

"Where?"

"Right up your ass, which is where you can stick it."

Greg smirked, shook his head. "Don't hold out for more. More than that, and it costs less to deal with you differently."

Jay looked at the guards. "He's skimping on your life insurance."

"Nothing so crass. You're employed by a known criminal. The county sheriff would be happy to shut down your pal's strip club and jail you all for human trafficking. We made a generous contribution to his reelection campaign."

"See," Jay said, "the more you want me gone, the curiouser I get. What's a little old boy like me doing to bother a couple of rich jag-offs like you?"

The charged conversation inside the 928 rose to a crescendo before coming to an abrupt end.

Greg rolled his eyes. "That, right there."

Matthew Strick sprang out of his father's old Porsche. He stopped, took a breath, and tucked his phone away.

He had put on height since school. Six-foot-two of slender gym physique with bespoke gray herringbone painted on his rangy limbs. Sandy blond hair brushed straight back. Lines at the corners of eyes and mouth, stress cracks from practiced glares of contempt. Soft gray eyes behind slim gunmetal frames.

Jay leveled a glare that Matthew returned with equal intensity.

"You keep eye-fucking me rich boy," Jay said, "and we'll see if your rentboys can drop me before I bite your throat out."

"Charming as always," Matt said. "You should've taken Greg's offer."

Greg moved to speak.

"It's all right, Greg. I'm accustomed to your attempts at behind-the-scenes manipulation. You think you're a *consigliere*, it's cute."

"Matthew, it was my money—"

"Your money?" Matt laughed. "That's hilarious. You've been riding my coattails since college."

Greg tightened his jaw. "And you've been stubborn just as long," he said. "Pay him, get rid of him. He's affecting your judgment. And that affects your money *and* mine."

"How about a cool million, Matty boy?" Jay said.

"You're not getting a dime," Matt said. "Greg credits you with freeing him from that piece of human excrement, but I see it differently. You stabbed my father in the back after he dragged your white trash family from the swamp to civilization. We took you in, gave you work. And when it came time to pay the piper, you showed no loyalty."

"Maybe your definition of disloyalty is different than mine," Jay said. "I told your old man I'd keep my mouth shut in return for a lawyer. I held up my end."

"What did you expect, my father to throw me to the wolves? Besides, your bitch mother soured that deal."

"I ain't no rat, but you're abusing the privilege. There's no statute of limitations on this shit."

"Go ahead, Jay. I triple fucking dog dare you," Matthew said. "It won't change a thing, and what hurts me, hurts Ramona. You know, *my wife*." He bared perfect white teeth. "I know she still pines for her little damaged piece of white trash."

Jay cracked his knuckles. His hands curled to fists. Red tickled the corners of his eyes.

"Is this necessary?" Greg said.

"Y'all bring me here to piss me off, show me how much power you got? Got your lawyer threatening to lock me up again. If I go inside again, there'll be a damn good reason. And don't think your muscle can stop me before I get it done."

Two guards moved to flank him.

"What, like Frank Dellamorte?" Matt said. "That was more than I expected from you and your little piss-ant street thugs. But it was a good move, a good move, Jay. I was wrong to have Frank pressure you."

Jay betrayed nothing.

Matt waved his hand. "No, I should've gone straight to targeting the few things you care about. Tony doesn't have much, but he did well with the scraps we left him. He'll be pushing grocery carts like Nicky Paladino, if you're not careful. Bobby Algieri thought joining the Nutley cops would protect him, but he hasn't had a single promotion. He's almost got his twenty years in, the poor bastard."

Matthew smiled. "Mouth-Breathing Bobby doesn't know what's about to hit him come retirement. He's made a lot of enemies, and when they testify to what he's been up to, the town will be clamoring to nullify that pension of his."

"Couldn't happen to a nicer guy, could it?" Jay said. "I'd admire you, if I didn't know what a backstabbing piece of shit you are."

"It's all about perspective. You know the story about the frog and the scorpion? The frog—"

"The frog had it coming," Jay said. "And so do you and your old man."

"Your cunt of a mother already did enough damage."

Two guards each gripped Jay by a shoulder in anticipation.

"I'm fine," Jay said through gritted teeth. "Nothing this shit-bird says is gonna get to me."

Matt smiled. "You haven't changed. I remember how you'd froth at the mouth, like a rabid animal."

"Are we done?" Jay said. "You can go back to sticking it to

your old man, and acting like you hit a triple when you were born on third base."

Matt smiled. "If I was born on third, I've hit a few grand slams since then. I ought to thank you, though. When your redneck mother tore my family apart, my father tried to buy back my love. Contingent on getting my degree, of course. And I cinched *summa cum laude*. But the school instituted one higher honor, *egregia cum laude*."

"We called it egregious come louder," Greg said.

"And all my father could say was 'wouldn't it have been great if you'd been the first to get that honor?' Belittling prick," Matt spat. "Now he's a sharecropper. He pays some Piney to grow Christmas trees on the back forty and drives a white-trash Harley. A pathetic old fuck trying to live like *Easy Rider*."

"You sure showed him," Jay said. "We done with your therapy session?"

"One question," Matthew said. "Will you accept Greg's little offer?"

"Nope."

Greg sighed.

"Good," Matt said. "I'm not done with you yet."

"And I ain't even started on you," Jay said.

Matthew laughed. "You're gonna have to do better than boning my wife."

The guards leaned hard on Jay's shoulders.

"She told me all about it," Matt smiled. "And afterward, we fucked like rabbits." He thumbed at his phone, and held it so Jay could see. The video was from a high angle, but excellent quality. Ramona sprawled on the chaise lounge gripping fistfuls of Jay's hair.

Jay felt the ground waver like when he'd stepped onto the twenty-foot diving board at the pool.

"You've done wonders for our marriage," Matt said, leaning closer. "I want to thank you for never letting her suck your cock. She makes up for it every chance she gets. I've had the best the world has to offer, but your Blackbird is a *savant*."

Jay furrowed his brow. The guards gripped his biceps.

"Know who taught her?" Matthew said, "My father."

He laughed with a broad smile. "Introduced her to his architects, then taught her the art of the blow job in this baby"—Matt patted the hood of the Porsche—"on the rides home. Hope you enjoyed our sloppy seconds."

Jay felt his nostrils flare with quick breaths. "What the hell is wrong with y'all?"

The world moved slow, as if Jay were underwater, only hearing his own heart. They led him to the truck, and dumped him in the strip club parking lot. He lay there among the dried-out rubbers and broken glass, rubbing his wrists and staring at the dead night sky.

CHAPTER 25

Matthew Strick had skipped two grades, making him both the smartest and the smallest boy in Nutley Middle School. The bell rang and students filed in. Behind Jay, Matthew and Tony talked computers, arguing over Apples and Ataris and Commodores.

"Hey, runt," Joey Bello said. He hawked a gob of spit on the back of Matt's head. "That's for ruining the curve." The rest of his crew laughed.

Matt flinched and scowled. He pulled a handkerchief from the pocket of his corduroys and wiped his hair.

"Sniff any dirty drawers lately, shitbird?" Jay said.

"Piss-Face gave me his mother's," Bello said.

Tony flushed red.

"Yours next, Strick," Bello said, and flicked Matt's ear. "Bring them tomorrow. Fresh from the hamper."

"You're revolting, Joseph."

"And you're a little queer," Joey said. "Ask Tony what happens if you don't bring 'em." He shoved Matthew and strutted away.

That night in the workshop, Jay eyed the tools on his side of the pegboard. Andre had given him his own set of chisels, rasps, and planes as he taught him woodwork. Even a carpenter's hatchet, which resembled the Vietnam tomahawk. It wasn't well-balanced for throwing, but would stick if you lobbed it right. Behind the garage, Jay and his father would take turns throwing their axes at a stump.

Jay hefted it, thought of what it could do to Joey Bello. The wide blade, heavy hammer head, and claw on top for removing nails made it resemble a strange medieval weapon.

After Angeline and Andre saved him, the Witch's squirming white eye sockets had filled Jay's retinas with every blink. Sunday morning when the church bells rang, Mama Angeline found him bawling.

"Why you crying, son?"

"Am I gonna go to Hell?"

"You already been there, honey. And we got you out."

"I mean when I die."

Mama Angeline laughed, kissed his forehead. "You think Hansel and Gretel went to Hell? No, they got a hero's welcome. Got a cloud all their own." She crushed him to the plush of her chest. "What you did wasn't no sin."

Jay wasn't sure if he cared anymore, but he knew he was supposed to. While the Witch slept, he had prayed for help every day, but none came. He slipped the hatchet into his book bag. If God was there, he wasn't answering. He helped those who helped themselves.

In study hall, Bello flicked Matthew's ear, leaving a red welt. "Pay up, Strick."

Matt ignored him.

"Tony Baloney, tell the runt what happened at the dump."

Jay felt the red mist coming on. He gripped the hatchet's leather-wrapped handle.

"Tell him, or I will." He flicked Tony's ear next.

"Ow! Asswipe."

"Now I'm telling, you fat piece of shit."

Jay eased the axe handle out of his bag. Bello's hand rested on the back of the chair. Jay thought of smashing those warty fingers flat.

The talk cut to whispers as Jay kneaded the leather-stacked

handle. He felt the world draw in, like it had the morning he'd done the Witch.

Assistant Principal Chapman strode down the aisle, the fluorescent lights gleaming off his pate. "Joseph Bello. Come with me."

Joey gave an indignant sneer. "What did I do?"

"You know what you did." Chapman's thick mustache squirmed in disgust. "Your father's waiting in my office."

Joey Bello hunched as if struck, kneaded his wart-scarred hands. Everyone turned to stare. Joey puffed up for his perp walk. The sneer returned to his bright, freckled face as Mr. Chapman led him away.

Matt smiled. "I told Principal Chapman about Joey's sick little collection. The moron keeps them in his locker."

When Joey Bello got a three-day suspension, Jay returned his hatchet to the peg. Matt invited Jay, Tony, and the twins to his clubhouse that weekend. It was built as a miniature of their own oversized home, with power, a ladder to a sleepover loft, and steel shelves for Matt's books and hand-painted miniatures. His mother brought a tray of snacks on crackers, a pitcher of homemade lemonade.

The boys sat in folding chairs around a power line spool, papers in front of them covered in chicken scratch. Matt wanted to teach them to play Dungeons & Dragons. Tony flipped through the manuals while Brendan pored over the bookshelves.

Jay daydreamed through Matt's lecture on the rules. On a nice day, he'd rather be fishing or exploring an old factory. Tires hit the gravel drive hard and an engine whirred to a stop. They all looked up from the game.

A car door slammed. Boots on gravel. The double doors shuddered open, revealing Mr. Strick in khakis, rolled-up sleeves and work boots. Rimless glasses perched on his thin nose. Tight smile biting back words. "Hello, boys. Having a good time?"

"Yes, sir," Matt said, shrinking into his chair.

"Matthew," Mr. Strick said, and beckoned with a manicured finger. Matt stiffened and walked outside. His father put his hand on his nape, and walked him around back.

The twins looked at each other. Tony snatched a handful of snack crackers and chowed nervously. Jay padded to the wall, and heard voices held low in anger.

"The son of the goddamn building inspector."

"It's not fair!"

"Yeah, well life's a bitch. Give him your damn lunch money, or whatever he wants. Take money from the jar."

"He doesn't want—"

"Matthew," Strick gave a weary chuckle, "you're supposed to be smart, so start acting like it. If his father gets called to the school again, you can kiss this little clubhouse goodbye. I'll use it for storage. Am I understood?"

"Yes, sir."

"Now go play, while Daddy works."

Jay slinked back to his chair.

"What did they say," Brendan whispered.

Father and son returned, faces red. Tony stuffed another cracker into his mouth and crunched loudly. Matt slumped into his chair.

"Have a great time, boys," Mr. Strick said, sweeping back his thinning hair. His Porsche kicked gravel against the doors as he roared out the driveway.

Matt pruned his face like a baby about to bawl. He stabbed a pencil into the tabletop until it splintered to pieces.

They walked convoluted paths to avoid Bello's haunts, and Matt and Tony brought notes from home that allowed them to use the computer lab instead of gym. The twins had hockey practice, so Tony, Jay, and Matt cut through the greens of the First Presbyterian church to hide their lessened numbers.

Church Hill was the school's unofficial fighting grounds, where rivals were called out to put up or shut up. Passing through it risked bumping into Guido toughs gathered to watch a grudge match, but it was the quickest way to bypass the Krauszer's convenience store where Joey bought cigarettes.

There was no fight that day. Jay had thought about calling Joey out. He knew some dirty tricks. He could let Joey bust those warty knuckles on his skull, then poke him in the eye and knee his nuts. But Andre told him that he had to stay out of trouble and that this wasn't his fight.

A familiar laugh came from over the rise.

Bello and crew perched like jackals on the brownstone steps to the church's little cemetery, passing a filtered cigarette around like a joint. The smoke and a link of fresh dog shit in the grass gave the air the scent of a freshly trampled battlefield.

Matt thrust his chest forward in a defiant march, his mouth a stiff line. Jay loosened up, rolled his shoulders, and wished he hadn't left the hatchet on the pegboard. Tony planted his feet. "Well if it ain't the faggots who got me in trouble," Bello said. He blew a plume of smoke. His flat blue eyes stared through them.

They walked past, showing no fear. Holding onto the thin rope of belief that they had fought back, and now it was over. Let the insults roll off, like they had been told by the adults.

Matt took a deep breath halfway up the block. Tony grinned.

Jay heard the slap of sneakers on pavement too late. Tony hit the grass with a whump.

Bobby Algieri scooped Jay under the armpits and swung him to the ground. Dogpiled him to the church lawn, put a knee between his shoulder blades.

Matt bolted. His short legs didn't take him far. Nicky and Joey dragged him back, whimpering.

"Nobody likes a snitch, runt," Joey said, puffing his smoke to a bright cherry. He held the ember to Matt's ear.

Matt squirmed away. "Scar me and my Dad'll sue!"

Joey stomped Matt in the gut. While he groaned, Joey flicked his butt into the grass, and ground it out under his shoe. He limped back with a little smile, keeping one sole off the grass.

Joey lifted one knee to show Matt the treads of his sneaker stuccoed with dog shit. He lowered it toward Matt's face.

Matt shrunk into himself and wrenched his face away. "N-no!"

"My father says rats eat shit," Joey said.

Matthew wretched and coughed as Joey ground the shit-smeared toe of his shoe against his mouth. Nicky laughed in high-pitched little whoops as Joey wiped his sneaker clean on Matt's powder blue shirt.

Matt dry heaved and wailed. Greg Kuhn looked away, his face wrenched.

Tony gagged in sympathy. Jay seethed and clawed at the grass.

"Runty Matt Strick," Bello said. "Now you're my fuckin' doormat." He chuckled and kicked Matt hard in the balls.

Matt rolled to his side and vomited on the church lawn.

"This is what happens if you snitch on me," Joey said. "Tell *all* your faggot friends." He walked away with Nicky rubbing the back of his neck like a prize fighter.

The Algieri brothers shoved Tony into the grass and jogged after their leader.

Greg Kuhn blinked at Matt's curled form. "I'm sorry," he said, and ran the other direction, back toward school.

"Catch up, Jew-bagel," Bello hollered. "Where you going?"

Tony looked away while Matt cried and smeared his face clean with his handkerchief. Jay offered his undershirt, but Matt ignored him and stared at Bello and crew, slapping hands and laughing.

CHAPTER 26

Jay stood in a corner of the club, reading the swarm of bodies like he was still in the prison yard. Fear in their body language, the macho posturing of men drunk on overpriced liquor and the power of a handful of dollars. The trapped eyes of dancers working the hustle.

A black girl with a racetrack's worth of curves had stage two, working a handful of businessmen. Oksana/Stacey had a single customer, a short man with big arms and thinning hair atop an angular head. Nursing a Bud, giving her a hyena stare at the watering hole. He tucked a bill into her garter and pinched her behind. Jay slow-walked over. The man wore carpenter's jeans and smelled like he came straight from work. Something about his face made Jay's teeth grind.

Dante and Vito entered with two young soldiers in sport coats and skinny jeans. The kids eyeballed the room, on tiptoe like a pair of meerkats.

Dante cupped Jay's face like a puppy's. "This fuckin' guy."

Jay pushed him away slow.

"Give us a private room with Leticia," Vito told Raina.

The soldiers stood guard while Jay and Cheetah joined Dante and Vito in the private dance room. Leticia climbed onto the tiny stage in a green sari and bikini bottom with matching spike heels.

"Close the curtains," Dante said, and smiled at Leticia. "Now you can show everything."

Leticia parted her lips barely, blushed and smiled. But not in the eyes.

Dante peeled ten hundreds from his wallet and tossed them on the stage. Leticia bent and worked the stereo.

189

"Drink," Dante said, and hoisted his glass of Jack.

They drank. A bouncy song came through the speakers, and Leticia wrapped herself around the pole, leaning back so her hair brushed Dante's lap.

"Now what we talked about, there's a hitch or two."

Jay made to speak and Vito raised a finger. His jacket bulged under the shoulder.

Jay wished for Andre's knife, but Cheetah made him leave it in the car. Said he caused enough trouble unarmed.

"Relax," Dante said. "The bosses are all fucked up over Frankie. We can't change nothing until the shit settles, that's all."

"Okay then."

"Now speaking of Frankie, may his shit-stained soul rest in peace, that crazy move with the garbage truck offended a lot of people. Made the news. The top tier don't like that."

"Top tier, huh?" Jay smirked. "You gonna talk dangly fruit and shit?"

"Honey, turn the music up a bit," Vito said.

Leticia leaned out from the pole and raised the volume, then untwirled out of her sari.

"*Minga*," Dante said. "Look at this beauty. Dancing here when she ought to be in magazines."

"Buy a magazine, we'll put her on the cover," Cheetah said, sipped his scotch. "We'll call it Ebony and Italy."

"She's gonna be hostess once we switch this place around," Dante said.

Cheetah kept his poker face as Dante snatched Raina's dream away.

"But first we have to deal with Jay's mess," Dante said, as Leticia splayed her long legs over his shoulders. He slipped off her heels, set them on the stage. "Those garbage trucks cost a shit-ton, and it kinda ate up the money we talked about. In fact, you're about eighty gees in the red."

Cheetah sucked teeth.

"Funny how it works with you fellas," Jay said. "I get you promoted, and suddenly I got a mortgage."

"You didn't say you were gonna total a garbage truck," Dante said. "Those things cost a quarter mil. You're getting friend prices."

"I got a little issue with your math," Jay said. "Say we call it even."

"It's out of my hands," Dante said. "I'm second banana with the union. The truck was family property, Jay. I play games with union money right now, it'll look bad." He looked at Leticia, bent backward from the pole in a slow spin, her breasts swelling out of her top. "You're pretty hot, babe. Why don't you cool off a bit." He plucked at the center of her top.

She reached behind herself and untied the bow.

Dante licked his fingertip and put a sparkle to both her nipples. "Like blackberries on *tartufo*," he said, tracing over her heart. "You really are gorgeous." He ran his finger over the blood orange wedge of her pursed lower lip.

Jay cleared his throat. Let his eyes go out of focus.

"If you split town, you leave Cheetah with the bill," Dante said. He patted Leticia on the behind, and she hugged the pole, rubbing herself against it, eyes closed tight.

Cheetah smirked. "Still selling cars to the Russian? Jay's good with cars."

"I'm gonna need soldiers," Dante said. "I could use an animal like you."

"That's not what I had in mind," Jay said.

"Yeah," Cheetah said. "He's a mechanic, if you haven't heard."

"Then hit 'em with a monkey wrench," Vito said, ending on a snicker.

"You jack a truck, it better not be at the port." Dante stood and ran a finger along the back of Leticia's thigh. "You fellas can go. Send in a bottle for the lady."

Vito opened the curtains and waved them out. Before the

fabric closed, Jay caught Leticia shimmying out of her bikini bottom, and Dante bending inspect her like a prize mare.

Jay chewed ice cubes, the liquor gone sour in his mouth. Oksana lap-danced her customer in his chair, and his callused hands left red prints on her thighs. She called him Eddie, and fake-smiled as she pushed his hands away, but never gave the bouncers a signal. Eddie disturbed Jay on a cellular level.

The way Joey Bello had.

The other bouncer was a big footballer, kept eyeing the game on the bar television. Jay told him he was heading to the bathroom. Inside, Jay splashed his face with cold water, to quench the fire in his temples. His scabs had healed, leaving new pink skin. He pressed a sheaf of paper towels to his face.

He was no Eddie.

But how far had he been from Joey Bello?

Jay saved his torment for the strong who abused the weak. Okie winked from the mirror. *And therein lies all the difference.*

On the floor, Oksana was gone. So was her customer. Jay veered from the VIP Room, where she was surely giving Eddie everything Jay had denied himself when she'd offered it to him. The Witch had ruined that for him. His hands knotted into fists as he passed the dressing room.

"Eddie, you can't be here."

The whine of a spoiled child. "You said you liked me best."

"Later, I'll dance for you, special."

Jay pushed through the curtains. Eddie had Oksana by the wrist. She winced, and fire bloomed behind Jay's eyes.

Jay twisted Eddie's arm back and ground his elbow into the pressure point at the bottom of his triceps. Eddie's face wrenched like a child baffled by its first acquaintance with pain. Jay muscled him out the rear door, using his face as a ram.

Kicked him in the ass and sent him sprawling on the asphalt.

Eddie tensed without a sound. Jay felt a tingle down his

spine telling him to run, thinking he'd cracked the man's skull. Then Eddie rolled over with a choked scream, and reached for his gravel-studded forehead with a trembling hand.

"No touching the girls," Jay said, and slammed the door.

Oksana waited in the hallway. Angry, but wary. Familiar with violent men. "You did not have to do that."

"Yeah, I did." Jay looked away, and walked past her. "Shouldn't have, but I did." He punched the bricks, the pain that shot through his arm his first act of contrition.

CHAPTER 27

With the windows down, the summer scent of fresh-cut grass and wild onions smelled like forest nymph perfume. Jay coasted the Hammerhead into the parking lot of Wise Owl Academy. The institutional brick gave him a chill.

The one-story school was set in a suburban neighborhood of post-war Cape Cods on snug lots. Jay parked between a Honda and a Volkswagen, nose to the chain-link fence. Beyond it kids played tag and others sat in the speckled shade of mimosa trees listening to the cicada racket.

A large boy with a childish face loped to the fence and hit it with both hands. He gawped at the Challenger. "That's a nice car," the boy said.

"That she is." Jay smiled.

The boy had an ursine build and freckles with a look of permanent awe. Jay remembered playing with the Down's syndrome kids in grammar school and wondering where they disappeared to in later grades. Schools like this one.

"Can I sit in your car?"

A fit man in a polo and khakis approached, patting one of the students on the shoulder. The spectacled mirror of sandy-haired Billy Zelazko, with the swagger traded for tenderness.

"That's up to your teacher," Jay said.

"Mindy," Brendan called. "They need you to play the game."

"Hi, Mister Zee," Mindy said, and pointed. "That's a really nice car."

Jay leaned against the fender. "Hello, Brendan."

"Oh shit," Brendan said. His strong jaw quivered.

"That's a bad word," Mindy said.

"You're right Mindy," Brendan said. "I shouldn't have said it."

The two men nodded at each other through the fence.

"Mister Zee, can I sit in that car?"

"We don't get in cars with strangers."

"But he's your friend."

"Just because someone knows your name doesn't make you friends."

"When's lunch, Mister Zee?" Jay asked. "I'd like you to educate me. In history."

Brendan tapped out a rhythm on his thighs. "C'mon, Mindy. Recess is over soon."

Another boy with a peach fuzz mustache ran over. He pointed his finger like a gun and blew a loud raspberry at Mindy.

"Robbie! Say it, don't spray it!"

Robbie laughed and ran with Mindy chasing after him.

Brendan took a measured breath. "Jay, that's part of my life I don't talk about anymore."

Jay narrowed his eyes. "I didn't talk for twenty-five years. All I want for that's a few answers, and they're in short supply. Your brother's being a real prick."

"That's Billy being Billy." Brendan squinted through his glasses at the green roll of hills in the distance. "Thirty minutes," he said, and walked away.

Jay followed Brendan's Subaru to the shaded gravel parking lot of a hiking trailhead, not far from the school.

"Get out, we'll go for a walk," Brendan said. "Otherwise someone'll think this is a pickle park."

Brendan led him along a well-worn path to a split boulder that rose from the grass like a plated turtle's back. The forest was old pine plantation left to grow wild. Trees in neat rows.

"What's a pickle park?"

Brendan sat on the rock. "A place where gay men hook up in unfriendly areas. If they're in the closet." He held out his left hand, flashed a thin gold band. "Which I'm not."

Jay found a misplaced birch scarred with teenagers' initials and leaned on it. "Think I ran into one on a walk the other night. Gave me quite the surprise."

"I sympathize with what you must've gone through," Brendan said, removing his glasses to wipe them on the hem of his shirt. "But I hope you didn't come here thinking I owe you something."

"Why does everyone think this is about money? My father worked with his hands, but it's not like I came from hunger."

"Then what do you want? We did what we could, Jay. We were kids."

"How about the same loyalty I gave you? Maybe I wasn't born here, but I jumped in to fight for you. Because y'all were my friends."

Brendan sighed. "Leo placed me under psychiatric care, after…you know. Even if I testified, it wouldn't have mattered. Do I think your sentence was fair? No. But they had to do something."

"You of all people," Jay said. "I thought you'd be on my side."

"Jay," Brendan said. "What you did was wrong."

"We did," Jay said. "Maybe not you, but it wasn't just me. And we did the world a favor."

"It was *not your place*," Brendan said, raising his voice. "If the right belonged to anyone, it was mine. And you took it from me, along with any chance of moving past this shit. You want me to fawn over you?" Brendan huffed. "For what? Giving me nightmares about a kid who's dead *because of me*. Thanks for that."

Jay hit the tree with a quick jab cross, and his knuckles flecked red. "You weren't as forgiving back then."

"I called Billy before we came out here. So calm down."

Jay snorted, rubbed his knuckles. "Figures."

"Nothing we said would have changed anything. They didn't believe us then, and they won't believe us now."

"You ever wonder why?"

Brendan rolled his eyes. "Because he was the son of a big shot. You know the type. 'I know a guy.' Bello was that guy. Still is, probably."

"And that made the town hero cop's kid fair game?"

Brendan sighed. "Do you remember my father? He broke bricks with his bare hands. For *fun*. I told him we were outnumbered. Know what he said? 'Bring a baseball bat.' He didn't get it."

The only time Joey Bello had ever looked scared was when his father got called to the school. Even when they'd pounded his face in, he had mocked them. He'd dealt with something much worse.

"He said it would toughen me up," Brendan said. "Leo knew I was gay before I did. He didn't say 'gay,' of course. He said I was 'different,' and that meant I'd have to be stronger."

"Matty had to eat shit 'cause his father needed Mr. Bello," Jay said. "He was in charge of zoning and building and whatnot, but you got worse. A lot worse. No one else dared to fool with you boys but Joey Bello. You don't think Joey's father had something on your old man?"

Brendan folded his arms. "No one ever got close to him. I tried to run with him one morning, below the power lines. He took it as a challenge. I nearly caught him, but he disappeared. He can push himself harder than anyone I know."

If anyone could have caught him, it was Brendan. He set the freshman record for the 880-yard run, and the trophy sat in the school case until it was vandalized. Joey Bello scratched out the second *n* and changed the name to 'Brenda.'

"I left him to his own misery," Brendan said.

"Pardon me if I'm not as forgiving."

"I don't forgive him," Brendan said. "I pity him. Revenge is part self-loathing, you know. Blaming yourself for allowing yourself to be hurt, and taking it out on the transgressor. You have to grow past it. You think the Bellos are satisfied? They wanted you executed."

Jay smiled. "They tried. And I don't mean legally. They hired some goombah to hit me in there."

Brendan frowned and looked at the dirt. He found an old pine cone, pondered it, and tossed it into the dry brambles. "Do you blame them?"

"Them I don't care about. The rest of the town thinks I went plumb crazy. They need to know what Joey was."

"Is that why you're here? My partner and I want a family. It's difficult enough without our names in the papers. Billy won't like it," Brendan said, turning stony. "You dragging me through this again."

"Your brother don't like me as it is," Jay said. "And he's gonna like me a lot less. Kinda funny, him being a homicide detective. He's got what you call hands-on experience."

"He doesn't deserve that."

"We all got our hands dirty. We did what we were best at."

"Billy told me. Not that I wanted to know." Brendan sighed, removed his glasses, and kneaded the bridge of his nose.

"Bren," a voice called from behind them on the trail. Billy.

"I have to get going, Jay." Brendan headed back. "Maybe you paid more than you should, but don't play innocent. If you didn't bring that hatchet, Joey would still be alive."

"And he'd leave how many more like you, huh? Ever think about that?" Jay followed him back to the lot. Billy stood waiting with one hand beneath his blazer. Next to his twin, his eyes looked all the more hollow.

"Thanks, bro," Brendan said in passing, and patted him on the shoulder.

"We're having dinner at Ma's Sunday," Billy called. "Bring Kevin."

"We have plans," Brendan said, climbed into his car, and pulled away.

A second officer, a muscular black man swelling the sleeves of his blue uniform, sat on the trunk of the Challenger. They had it blocked in with an unmarked squad car.

Jay tilted his head. "Did I break some bullshit law, Officer?"

Billy drew his service pistol. "I told you to stay away from my family."

The hood of the Challenger burned Jay's cheek as Billy's partner zip-tied his wrists, the plastic rasping like a viper's hiss.

"They find bodies out here in trash bags all the time," the officer said. Wisps of tattoo ink peeked from his snug shirt sleeves like serpent tongues. "You run with Cheetah Plunkett, right? Maybe we'll do you here, and drop a throwdown in his club. Take care of two shittums in one day."

Jay grabbed for his nuts behind his back, and the cop bounced his face off the sheet metal.

"Easy, Drake," Billy said.

"What's this 'shittums' you're calling me?"

"A shittums is what y'all are," Officer Drake said, and gave Jay a rough frisk. "We lock 'em up, and the lawyers keep shitting 'em out."

He tossed Jay's car keys on the hood. Threw his money clip in the dirt. "He's clean," he said, then looped his arms through Jay's and lifted him up, keeping clear when Jay snapped his head back. "But he is one sneaky motherfucker."

Billy stuffed a haymaker in Jay's belly. After a thought, he sank two more.

"Still swing like you're scared," Jay heaved.

Drake gripped the cuff chain and lifted Jay's arms behind his back.

Jay bent to keep his arms from breaking. Gritted his teeth and put away the pain.

"Hit him when he tries to breathe."

Billy wrenched his face and dropped punches. Jay fell to the gravel wheezing, saliva dangling from his chin. "That better, asshole?" He panted. Drake folded his arms and stood behind him.

Jay spat and missed. "You two wouldn't last five minutes as Rahway hacks. You two are real cute."

"There was a burglary at your old house," Billy said, catching his breath. "You get nostalgic?"

Jay huffed a breath. "You still stick kielbasa in your pants so you know what it feels like to have a dick?"

Billy lunged with a punch. Jay took it on the forehead. Billy growled and clutched his knuckles, stumbling away.

Jay laughed his way into a coughing jag that didn't quit until he tasted copper.

Drake cocked a fist, feinted. Threw a hook that clipped Jay's shoulder and brushed his jaw. "Boy can box," he said. "Want the Taser?"

"Not yet," Billy said. He squatted out of kicking range, looked Jay in the face. "They found Stan Carnahan with a bullet in his brain."

Jay kept his eyes dead-steel seas. A catbird broke the silence with its cry.

"Postman smelled the stink. The cat ate his lips and earlobes," Billy said. "That's loyalty for you. Looked like suicide. He was a drunk, his wife split, they wouldn't let him work as a crossing guard no more. Only a matter of time. But I got a feeling you paid him a visit."

"Must've had a guilty conscience," Jay said. "That'll get you every time. I heard he and your old man planted a throwdown on that carjacker kid. Some heroes."

"You don't know who your friends are," Billy said. "That's your problem. Carnahan was on your side, or tried to be. Nutley don't have much in the way of forensics, but I pulled some strings, got Newark to lend some. If you were there, we'll know."

Jay watched turkey vultures coast overhead through the blue.

"Boy's con-wise," Drake said. "Won't say shit. Want me to sweep the car?"

Billy nodded. "What we gonna find, Jay-Jay?"

"Your balls, maybe. Might've rolled under the seat," Jay said, and rested his head against the fender.

Drake popped the trunk, swept under the rotten liner and tossed the spare. Opened the passenger's side, dumped the papers from the glove box, searched under the seats and beneath the dash, flung out the worn floor mats. He tugged hard at the rear seat cushions.

"Nothing," Drake said. "Better if we had a dog. This old heap is solid. We taking him in?"

"Fuck 'im," Billy said. He tossed the car keys into the woods, jerked his head toward the squad car. Drake got into the cruiser and closed the door.

"What you got is the best you're gonna get," Billy said. "You got a job, a car, a roof over your head. The American Dream. Let shit go."

"Ain't gonna happen," Jay said. "Your old man shafted me, sent my folks on the run. Which might've got them killed. His partner blew his brains out. Now it's his turn."

Billy raised a fist, gritted his teeth. He fought himself still. "Next time we'll find something, you know that, right? Don't make me do this. I don't want to."

"I ain't making you do shit."

"Mayor Bello's gonna come after you, then all this shit gets dragged up again. Wake up. Matty already destroyed everyone. He's even got Bello shitting his pants." Billy laughed. "Who you think owns the street construction company that's got the whole town ripped to shit? You should partner with him, maybe he'll let you have a three-way with Big Tits."

"He send you?" Jay kicked at him.

"No, this is family business. I told rich boy he's on his own, after you pissed on my fucking floor mats."

"His rent-a-cops dragged me into a van, brought me to his toy garage. In case you want to arrest him for kidnapping."

"I told you," Billy said. "Sniffing after that high-class tail. You think you were gonna marry her, coming from some trailer park with your redneck white-trash family? You were lucky you got into her skeevy panties."

"You sound like our old friend Joey," Jay said, and flopped back against the car.

"Fuck you," Billy said. "You act like we abandoned you. Ask Tony, sometime. He biked his fat ass to the station, thinking he'd tell the truth about Joey Bello, be the big hero. He didn't know my father was the one covering it up." Billy rubbed at the torn skin on his knuckles. "They hung Tony out the window until he pissed himself. That's what you're up against."

"I don't scare that easy," Jay said.

Billy shook his head. "You wanna kill yourself, do it somewhere else." He walked to the cruiser and drove away.

Jay pushed himself to his feet. He bent over and held his numb wrists high as he could. He slammed his forearms into the back of his thighs, like he'd learned. Six tries and the zip-tie snapped. He rubbed the deep welts on his wrists as he stepped through the brush, searching for his keys.

CHAPTER 28

Jay watched the angry hornet of Matt's Lamborghini disappear up the road before he eased the Challenger in the private drive and parked by the stable. The horse was unsaddled, chasing a fat little goat around the paddock.

Erin the au pair sat on the fence smoking a cigarette. She regarded him with a smirk on her lips and narrowed eyes, a showgirl who'd caught a young boy at a peephole to her dressing room. She wore a tweed skirt and a smart blouse. Crossed her legs as he joined her on the fence.

"You missed the lord of the manor," Erin said, letting her brogue out. "He was in fine form."

"What about the lady?"

"She's inside with her daughter," she said. "I wish you'd leave them be."

"Then they should've left me to rot in there," Jay said. "I didn't ask to be her cat's paw."

Erin rolled her eyes. "Look at you, thinking you're Johnny Depp. They've been at it long before you came around, but you're certainly no help." She tapped the ash off her cigarette. "It's Saoirse I worry about."

"Smoke?"

Erin handed him her half-smoked Marlboro and lit herself another. Jay pretended to smoke it, like he used to in the yard.

"She a good mother?"

"That's not why you're sniffing around, is it?"

"Hey now. I walked away."

"But you know she'd pad after you. She told me all about your star-crossed romance," she said. "Sad, it was. But you've had your fun, the both of you."

203

"I came to say goodbye."

She perked an eyebrow. "Really now."

"An old friend once told me to never butter another man's biscuit."

"That's what makes the world spin," she said. "We all want what the other one's got."

"Can she leave?"

"Of course she can," Erin said, and clucked her tongue. "But she'd lose everything. Our lady knows the law, as you'd expect. And she'd rather not put little Sair through all that. Mr. Matthew was living in New York until you came along. Maybe once you're gone he'll move back."

"Starting to feel like a marital aid."

Erin tutted. "What did Mick Jagger say? We can't always get what we want. You got more than most do."

Jay watched the riderless horse play with its goat companion. "What do you want?"

"I've got what I want," Erin said. "But not to myself."

Jay thought on it, and looked at the ember of his smoke.

"My family, we lost everything in the famine. The Cranes took us in," Erin said. "But there's a price for everything, you know. I graduated from Trinity College, but here I am, like my ma before me, my gran before her. Squiring the Cranes. Common people like you and me, we should get our happiness where we can, and pray to God our betters don't envy us."

"I had everything I wanted for one summer, but I threw it away. Because I couldn't let something bad be."

Erin blew smoke, which hung in the dead July heat. "Was it worth it?"

"Hell no."

She gave him the same sideward look Herschel the cabbie had given him when he learned who he was. "Why, then?"

"Reckon the kind of person we hate most is the one we worry about becoming."

She tilted her head and shrugged.

Jay stubbed the cigarette out on his boot. "Tell her I came by," he said, and hopped off the fence.

Erin gave him a noncommittal nod. "Gimme your fag end." When he squinted, she added. "The butt. Can't have the goat eating them. This one don't eat cans, she eats good as the bloody queen."

Jay looked over his shoulder. "Where did you say his lordship was headed?"

Jay straightened his tie and walked the winding drive to the Balthus Field Club's ivy-strangled brownstone. A turquoise Ferrari parked at the club entrance, and a young valet sweating in a brass-buttoned jacket parked it among the neat rows. Jay spied the parking spaces. Matt's Lamborghini flickered yellow among the silver and black high-end sedans.

Inside the clubhouse, the air was ice cold and the dark wood decor signified wealth with discretion. Between two urns, a stiff young man behind a lectern with an open journal.

"And who are you visiting, sir?"

Jay didn't like his smirk or his shit-brown eyes, but smiled anyway. "I'm here to meet Mr. Strick, but I'm running late," he said, and tapped his watchless wrist. "Can you tell me what hole he's playing?"

"I'll call the caddymaster, but you won't be able to play in a suit, sir. If you are without, we rent shorts and rubber cleats in the pro shop."

"That'll be fine."

"May I tell him who's here to see him?"

"Mr. Duke."

The man picked up a white phone, pressed a button. Jay plucked a membership pamphlet from beside the guest book.

"He's on the upper course, end of the twelfth. Will you please sign the guestbook, Mr. Duke?"

Jay studied the map of the course until the valet plucked a

key from the numbered board and left to retrieve a car.

"Know what, they're almost done," Jay said. "Tell him I'll catch him next time."

The man's bullshit goodbyes slid off Jay's back as he hit the doors.

Jay plucked the three bull-emblazoned Lamborghini key fobs off the board and keyed the buttons until Matt's Gallardo Spyder flashed its tail lights. He keyed the ignition and the drop-top's engine whirred to life. The valet jogged over. Jay chirped the tires in reverse and left him skipping aside. He honked the horn and scraped through a row of pines onto the teeing ground.

Jay smiled wider than when he'd caught his first catfish. The top folded back, and he goosed the clutch and let the engine spool, a Pelé kick to the hornet's nest beneath the hood. Players in white shorts and caps stared as he roared by spraying grass. He fishtailed past a pair of greensmen who dropped their tools and gave chase. He sprayed them with divots and gunned over the hill, slaloming around the sand traps.

He pulled behind a threesome of gray-haired old men wearing huge sunglasses. "You fellas seen Mr. Strick?"

A man with a bullfrog chest and Groucho eyebrows pointed across the water hazard, where four men in a cart hugged the silver pond.

"What in hell are you doing?"

"Playing through." Jay laughed, and buzzed down the fairway.

He revved the engine as he got close. Matt gophered up and stared.

Jay cut the wheel and stomped the pedal, circling the golf cart in screaming donuts. Matt, Greg, and their two older, puzzled passengers covered their heads as the tires hosed them with clods of grass and soil. The cart wobbled to a halt near the water hazard.

Matt mouthed "Motherfucker," and calmly retrieved his phone.

Jay let off the pedal and babied the yellow demon out of the dirt ruts. He waved at Matt and let the Lamborghini roll toward the water.

Matt shoved Greg from the wheel and veered the cart to intercept his car, eyes wide.

The Lambo bumped the cart and the passengers grabbed the roof poles. The engine drowned out Matt's curses as Jay nosed the cart down the embankment into the water.

Matt and his passengers splashed out, slipping in the muck.

Jay smiled and flipped them the finger. He spun the car around to give Matt one last shower of mud, then roared back the way he came, dodging angry picadors waving seven-irons.

Sirens echoed through the trees as Jay flew out the club entrance onto the street. He straddled the county road's double yellow line, dodging traffic on both sides. He dropped the hammer on the interstate and howled out the window with the wind buffeting his face.

At the shop, Tony stood beneath a green GTO. Jay rolled into the service bay and let the Lamborghini's engine scream. Tony dropped his wrench and swore.

Jay grinned behind a pair of Matt's shades with carbon fiber frames.

Tony blinked. "The fuck did you do?"

Jay told him as they raced down the Parkway toward the airport. Tony worked the paddle shifters, laughing as Jay regaled him with the story of his *Blues Brothers*-style raid on the country club. The wind rushing past reminded Jay of how they used to coast down suicide hills on their Huffy bikes.

"Feels good to stick it to that prick," Tony shouted over the stereo. He'd brought his iPod, and put "Don't Change" on repeat. Jay pointed him toward the looming hangars of the

Newark airport cargo area. They pulled into a storage lot rowed with identical Nissans half-sheathed in white transport wrap. Empty shipping containers lined the other side, shielding them from view.

Vito stood by the open doors of a red "K" Line forty-foot-high cube box. He held out a hand, and Tony braked. Vito knelt by the front bumper with a cordless drill and whizzed off the license plate bolts.

Tony frowned at the container's cargo. A Mercedes sedan with the license plates removed.

"Time to ditch this ride," Jay said. "Unless you wanna take the slow boat to China."

Dante stepped out of his Cadillac, nodding appreciatively.

"This makes us even," Jay said.

"I'll let you know what the bosses say," Dante said. He nodded toward Tony. "Who's the jooch?"

Jay slapped Tony on the back. "This is my *cumpari*, Big Tony. Performance specialist. Y'all ought to let him tune that Caddy of yours."

Tony flicked his eyes from Jay to Dante. "That a CTS-V?"

"Does the Pope shit in the woods?" Dante popped the hood. "It's got balls, but this prick on my cul de sac's got a Benz AMG." He grinned and cocked his head toward the container. "Well he *used to*, but I'm betting he buys the same damn thing with the insurance money. When he does, I want to leave his ass in the dust."

Tony peered at the sleek beast's heart. "I've worked on 'Vettes with the same engine. The right supercharger, a new chip. Shift right, you can beat him no problem. Come by the shop sometime."

Dante waved Vito away. "You fellas go ahead." He turned back to Tony. "Get in, I want you to hear how it bogs down sometimes."

Jay hitched a ride in Vito's black '89 Roadmaster. The old bruiser had a suicide knob bolted to the wheel and drove the land yacht in slow, sweeping curves. His arms were mottled with sunspots like a caramel granite countertop.

"Relax, cheech," Vito said. "You can take your hand off the pigsticker."

Jay hadn't noticed his fingers drifting to his boot, where he'd stuck Andre's combat knife. He set his fists on his knees.

"You been out what, a month? I did a ten spot up in Ossining, back when you were a little Cajun tadpole. Takes a while to adjust, but not everyone out here's gunning to stick a spoon handle in your throat."

"Reckon Frankie's people would."

"Randal's making noise, but not getting any traction." Vito spun the wheel like an old salt. "Frankie stepped on a lot of backs to get where he was, and only paid back his own blood. Most of them are limp dicks at do-nothing jobs."

A cabbie using a phone cut them off to make a red light. Vito stomped the brake. "Your sister's ass," he yelled out the window, and shook his head. "You see that prick?"

"Driving here's been an education."

"People don't give a shit," Vito said. "That fucker dinged my Buick, I'd kick that phone down his throat. Other day, I saw some mamaluke using an electric razor on the turnpike. Broads putting on makeup, like it's the powder room. They do that shit where you come from?"

"Maybe." Jay said. "Left when I was a kid." The Witch years were a plain of broken glass in the geography of his past. He recalled toddling on a porch between his folks before the Witch stole him from their Jeep, but little else.

"You're a good kid. I was you, I'd get my ass back to the land of cotton."

CHAPTER 29

Jay was beneath a Honda changing the oil when Tony hollered that he had a phone call. He let the oil drain, wiped his hands on a shop rag, and took the call in Tony's office.

"Hello," the woman said. "We've never met, but I saw you on television the other day."

"Who is this?"

"That was heroic. It reminded me of my..." she paused as her voice caught. "My Stanley," she said. "My name is Margie Carnahan."

"I'm sorry for your loss," Jay said, flat.

"Yes, it's terrible. He was too good to be a cop," she said. "He had a lot of guilt, and I know he'd want me to do this. I have something to tell you."

She said she'd meet him at her condo and gave him the address.

Jay threw Tony a wave, and Tony swiped his hand from his chin in return, Italian sign language for see if I care.

Carnahan's funeral had been a week prior, and there'd been a big splash in the paper about the fallen hero. Retold the fairy tale of the young officer marrying the maiden he'd rescued, and mentioned his role as arresting officer in the case of the horrific axe murder that rocked the town twenty-five years before.

A sidebar rehashed Jay's trial and questioned his quiet release from prison. A blurry photo of Jay drenched at the lakeside, from the internet video. "Axe murderer dives for redemption."

He wondered what she had for him. On the day of his arrest, Jay had been carrying the jack knife Andre gave him on his tenth birthday, a Case redbone trapper. He sure did want it back.

Her condo was on River Road. He slowed as the approached the parking lot.

A black Ford pickup swerved in front of him, tail lights flaring red. Jay swore and slammed the brakes, nosedived inches from the bumper. He gripped the wheel and bit back his breaths to keep from jumping out to pound the driver's face in. He punched the horn.

The Ford's backup lamps flashed white. Jay blinked as the bumper crunched the Challenger's nose. Glass tinkled on the pavement.

Jay threw the shifter in park and stomped toward the truck.

Officer Bobby Algieri stepped out in uniform, grinning above the muzzle of his service pistol. "Put your fucking hands on the hood, asswipe."

Jay curled his lip, hands bent into claws. Blood thumped in his temples. The hatchet and knife were in the seat compartment. His hands ached for them.

A clunk from behind. Leo boxed in the Challenger with his Denali.

"Make a move," Algieri said. "I wanna shoot you so fucking bad."

Jay slapped his hands on the hood.

"We fooled you," Algieri said. "That was my wife, retard."

"Shut up, Bobby." Leo marched, his manner stiff, face taciturn. He snapped his elbow and extended a collapsible baton, and whipped it across the back of Jay's legs.

Jay cracked his chin on the fender as his legs turned to water. A wallop across the shoulders emptied his lungs. They heaved him to the pavement in front of the truck.

"You killed him," Leo said, raising the baton. "Same as if you pulled the trigger. You should've left the state. Knew he wouldn't be able to handle it."

"You're next," Jay wheezed.

Leo kicked Jay in the gut. "Stop following me, and stay out of Nutley."

Jay fell to his back, covering his face.

"Learn, Joshua," Leo said. "Learn."

"My name is Jay," Jay shouted, hunching in a protective curl.

Bobby Algieri dumped a sheaf of tickets on Jay's chest. He hawked deep and spat before leaving.

Jay crawled to the Challenger. He gripped the curls of traffic summonses and used them to wipe the slick mess from his face. He slumped in the dirt and let the tickets blow away in the afternoon breeze.

"*As-Salamu Alaykum*," Cheetah said, sporting his new kufti cap in the yard.

"Pork chops and bacon," Jay replied. The sleeve of his shirt rolled up, flashing the Tyr rune of the Heimdall Brotherhood.

"So that's how it is. All you white devils are the same."

Ears perked and the yard watched.

"Save it for the ring," Jay said. "You're all show anyways, jumping around throwing punches for points like a bitch."

Cheetah threw hard and Jay staggered. The hacks shouted warnings over the PA as they tussled in the dirt. The yard seeped closer, eager for blood, until a guard pocked the dirt with a rifle round.

Jay ran back to the Brotherhood, and Cheetah's rep rose in rank as the Grape Street Crips, Sex Money Murda, and the Disciples put their force behind him.

Dante said they should settle it in the ring. He pitched high odds for the Cheetah, whose technical game impressed the purists. They called Jay a one-trick pony, a knockout artist who wouldn't go the distance. Cheetah had a steel jaw and had never been sent wobbling to his knees, much less dazed against the ropes.

The Ragin' Cajun against the Brick City Cheetah.

It was on.

As fight day approached, the air in the yard became electric. Cells were tossed and searched. Blacks ganged whites in the yard. Whites shanked blacks in the mess hall.

Verdad put silent protection on both Jay and Cheetah. The Latin Kings stood poised to eat any territory lost in the war. When Jay asked Okie why the warden didn't call a lockdown, the old con laughed and scratched his chin. "Why you think? He's betting too. So are the hacks. They know it's gonna be one hell of a fight. Hear they're gonna videotape it." Okie flexed the arm with the copperhead tattoo, and the serpent flicked its tail. "We'll be riding high."

The morning of the fight, guards arrived at Jay's cell a half hour before the mess hall, and escorted him there alone. He ate all he wanted, splattering a plate of scrambled eggs with ketchup and hot sauce, flanked by hacks loaded for bear.

A man sat across from him. He wore a brown suit with a badge on the pocket. The top of his head was bald as an egg, with a horseshoe of dusty hair around the back. Bristle broom mustache to match. He folded his pudgy hands and sat across from Jay on the plastic orange bench.

Jay smiled at Warden Jeffers through a mouthful of eggs.

"The natives are restless about your fight this afternoon," the warden said. "You got the population all worked up over it." His voice was thick, like he had a throat full of snot. "Your associates Dante Mastino and Leroy Kincaid have something planned."

"Don't know any Leroy," Jay said.

"Your trainer."

"Leroy, huh?" Jay chuckled. "I gotta rib him about that. We call him Okie." He ate another forkful and washed it down with black coffee.

"I don't give a damn what you call him, but you're losing this fight. We haven't had a riot under my tenure, and I plan to keep it that way. I know you're playing both sides. Spoke to people at Annandale who told me you and Alfonse Plunkett were thick."

"Alfonse? I don't know no Alfonse."

Warden Jeffers narrowed his eyes. "Let me appeal to you as a white man. We're outnumbered here four to one, by people like the fellows who sodomized you. There are plenty who'll gladly take their place, and I can ensure they have every opportunity to have a go at your scarred asshole."

Jay lowered his fork.

The warden leaned closer, smiled wide. "So, give them a good show. Three or four rounds. Then eat a punch and play dead. Or they'll be running trains on your ass until they call you the Lincoln Tunnel."

Jay stared into the warden's watery brown eyes. "Y'all kiss your mother with that mouth, or just use it to lick her dirty hole?"

The guards choked Jay with their batons and held him back. The warden bruised his soft hands on Jay's hardened cheekbones and scuffed his patent leather shoes on his ribs.

Rene passed the word from cell to cell. The Ragin' Cajun would throw the fight.

The air hummed as Jay climbed into the ring. Fresh stitches made a prickly third eyebrow on his forehead. Shrewd bettors pointed, and packs of cigarettes changed hands. The towers bristled with riflemen, scopes scanning the crowd.

Cheetah jumped and raised blue gloves. Black fists pumped in response. Jay slammed his red gloves together. A weak cheer rose, swallowed by jeering. Cheetah had three inches on him and resembled the lean cat of his name. Speed which had blossomed into rapid fire bursts on the heavy bag under Mack's direction.

Okie rubbed Jay's shoulders and smiled. He loved a good scam. They had communicated through Rene, choreographed their moves through sparring partners. A violent opera rehearsed to enrage its audience.

The bell rang, Jay charged in swinging and ate several of Cheetah's stiff jabs. Cheetah racked points while Jay tagged the body hard. In the third, Jay bent Cheetah in half with a hook to the ribs, and the crowd leapt to its feet. Cheetah opened the cut over Jay's eye with a flurry of blows. Okie stuffed it with Vaseline, and ironed his face with the end-swell. In the fourth Jay took a combo that sent him to his knees, and he wobbled through half the standing eight-count before the dour, pockmarked ref waved him back in. Half the crowd chanted his name when he raised his glove. Jay couldn't make a middle finger with his hands taped, but he knew the warden would catch his meaning.

In the sixth, Jay clinched every chance he got. Bets changed hands. It was the longest fight the Ragin' Cajun had ever fought, and the Cheetah hardly looked winded. In the seventh, Jay found a second wind, chasing Cheetah with combos, but was no match for the quicker man's footwork.

Thirty seconds into the eighth, Cheetah caught Jay in a corner and teed off on his swollen face. The ref stalked over. Okie raised the bloody towel, looking as devastated as the boy about to shoot Old Yeller. The yard thundered with the stomp of a thousand brogans.

Jay clinched, ate a hook, and rebounded off the ropes. Launched an uppercut that put an inch of air between Cheetah's soles and the ring.

A collective gasp sucked the air from the prison. Jay chained cross-uppercut-hooks and drove Cheetah to the ropes on shaky knees. The ref shoved Jay away. Cheetah tumbled, glove catching on the top rope. Bettors swore and pleaded.

The guards watched through their rifle scopes.

The glove slipped. Cheetah fell face first to the ring floor.

"Bullshit!" broke the silence. "Cheatin' motherfuckers!"

The crowd rushed the ropes. Rifles cracked and tear-gas grenades popped and pinged. Okie tackled Jay into the corner as sirens wailed. The old copperhead laughed and dragged Jay through a phalanx of Latin Kings that had formed to protect them.

"You did great, kid. You should get a damn Oscar for that shit."

Jay leaned hard on Okie's shoulder. He knew he hadn't acted, and neither had Cheetah. They had both gone full bore. Driven by hidden resentments and rivalries, disputes over the final count in their long-running poker game of debts owed and never repaid, inner fires kept smoldering by the uncrossable color lines of the prison yard.

What was meant to last five rounds went eight, until Cheetah proved to himself that he could take out the friend who had once saved him. He'd long realized that Jay only had one speed, all or nothing, his strength and his weakness. In that moment, Jay mad-dogged him with a suicide punch, ensuring that Jay would never learn the downside to his strategy until the day he died.

The yard erupted into a thousand little skirmishes. Wing Four roared with anger. Toilet paper embers floated and swirled like blazing snowflakes from the top tier. Okie and Mack hurried their fighters toward the Secure Housing Unit. Hunters with scores to settle stalked the tiers. Their targets paced in anticipation, or sat empty-eyed in their cells, resigned to their fate.

CHAPTER 30

"Wouldn't be doing this, but school's starting soon, my little girl needs new clothes," Herschel said.

Jay squinted through binoculars at the endless roll of traffic from the passenger's seat of the beat-up green Crown Vic. They were parked in a hotel lot on Route 3, along Leo's afternoon route.

"Plus she wants a dog. House on the block got robbed, and she says a dog'll protect us. Wrote it up with statistics and everything, like it was homework."

"Wish I'd had a dog, I was her age," Jay said.

"Yeah, me too. If wishes were fishes, we'd all be in riches." He sipped at a Coke leftover from their Popeye's chicken haul. The scent of the carnage still lingered in the car. "Saw your ass on the news. Jumping in to save that girl."

"Thought they blurred it out." A black truck passed, and Jay checked the license plates. Not Leo.

"Real convenient," Herschel said. "Making you the hero and all. How much you pay her to drive into that lake?"

"You have a doubting nature, Hersch." Jay said. "Your mama should've named you Thomas."

"Ha, that comes with the job. You get old ladies who play senile, say they left their money on the kitchen table. They go in to get it, and lock the front door on you. It's easier to put them on the no-ride sheet than to call the cops over a fifteen-dollar fare."

"I paid in advance. That should get me some points."

"See, that's compensating," Herschel said. "Like when my daughter gets in trouble in kindergarten, she cleans her room before I get home."

Jay scanned another license plate.

"Well?"

"Well what?"

"You gonna tell me, or not?"

"Have you considered maybe that it was pure chance, me being there?"

"Ha," Herschel said. "My cousin Errol, he's a junkie. Stole his mama's television more times than I can count. How his skinny ass carries the damn thing, I don't know. What I do know is he's always got a story. Some huge guy he owed, from when he was in County? He came knocking, said he was gonna beat his ass if Errol didn't give him twenty dollars. That's why he had to pawn your shit. And you can get it back, here's the ticket. Thing about a junkie. They'll steal your stuff, then *help you look for it.*"

Jay had heard a thousand stories like that inside. Some cons just had a way with reality, making it fit their needs.

"I ain't no junkie, Hersch."

"Didn't say you were." Herschel leaned back. "No Rutt's dogs, next time. They went right through me. Had to pull into a gas station, dancing like Urkel all the way to—"

"There he is," Jay said. "Left lane. Let's go."

"I see him." Herschel pulled out of the lot, using a panel truck for cover. He merged in behind a kid in a hopped-up Civic and passed when the car slowed down. "Ha. Everyone thinks we're the police."

"Hang back," Jay said. "He's got good eyes."

"Probably heard that loud-ass hot rod of yours."

They followed the Denali toward to the Turnpike, where Leo cut to the truck lanes like before.

"Careful now. He slipped over to the car lanes on me last time."

Herschel used tractor trailers for cover. "The lanes all go to the same place," he said. "He does that, we can still follow him."

They didn't have to. Leo pulled into a service area five miles later.

Herschel hugged a truck's bumper and followed it into the lot. Leo rolled to the truck's side where rows of semis were lined up. The flat-roofed service building advertised Roy Rogers, Starbucks, and ice cream. Leo parked the Denali and walked toward the entrance.

"Find a spot where you can see the doors of the building," Jay said, and checked his duffel.

Herschel found a corner spot with a good view. "Just taking pictures, right? I don't want no trouble."

"Just taking pictures," Jay said. "Call me if he's coming."

Jay walked across the parking lot, wearing work clothes and a trucker cap. *No one sees a working man,* Okie had taught. *Get yourself a clipboard, a hardhat, you can go anywhere. Any trouble, blame the boss who sent you.*

Jay crouched between the Denali and the hedges with Tony's lockout kit. It consisted of a rubber wedge to pry the door from the frame and a long extendable hook to pull the inside handle. According to manuals, the 2012 GMC Yukon Denali had no factory alarm system, and Jay had spied no aftermarket kit. A brick through the window would be easier, but that would ruin the surprise.

He stood on the running board and stuck the wedge in, muscled the door open a half-inch. Slipped the hook in and levered it toward the lock, like those claw games at the boardwalk where you fumbled to win a toy.

Jay felt a buzz in his pocket. He let the hook fall and checked his phone.

No calls. It was a phantom vibration.

He tried again. The steel scraped the paint inside the door jamb, and the hook slapped the seat. Jay took a breath and aimed the hook toward the handle. It tickled the plastic, wavering. Got it around the handle, pulled, and it popped off.

Jay swore under his breath. Closed his eyes, breathed his four fours to steady his hands. He opened his eyes and lifted the hook.

He blinked. The red button indicated the doors were unlocked.

Police got the worst security, Okie always said. *We robbed more banks with cop shotguns we nabbed right out of cruisers than I can count.*

Jay opened the door and sat on the plush leather seat. Okie never expected Jay to use his knowledge out in the world, but taught him to kill time. He would've laughed his ass off at all the time Jay wasted without trying the door handle.

Jay popped the glove box. Found the owner's manual, nothing more. He frowned and flipped through the papers.

The phone buzzed in his pocket. No mistaking it this time. He ignored it and felt around under the driver's seat, poked his head under the dash. Tugged at all the spots he'd learned to build hideaways. Some would never open without the car running. Or you had to press buttons in sequence, have the radio on. A good builder could put one anywhere, but Jay doubted an installer whose customers were mostly drug dealers would build one for a cop.

His phone buzzed again. Jay sighed and sank back to the seat. His hand fell on the console, and something sharp bit into his latex glove.

Sitting in the cup holder was the nickel revolver, snug in a pancake holster. Jay put it in a zip bag like evidence. Looked up and saw Leo crossing the parking lot.

Jay ducked into the footwell. The phone vibrated its insistent warning. Jay gripped the pistol through the plastic and waited for the door to open. Breathed slow. Imagined himself making Leo eat the gun like his partner. It would work, but Billy would know who did it, and come gunning for blood. No, he had to stick to the plan.

He counted five and peeked. The door didn't open. He scanned the lot slow. Picked Leo up at the edge of the truck line.

Jay took a deep breath and flipped open the buzzing phone. "Well that was a thrill."

"You're crazy," Herschel said. "Called you three damn times. Let's get out of here."

"Hang tight a minute."

Jay exited the truck and low-ran toward the row of steel road dogs. The air thick with raw diesel and exhaust spice. Leo headed toward a red-nosed semi towing an Old Dominion chassis. Jay came along the side of the rig and hunkered beneath the trailer, following Leo's patent leather shoes. They paused before a pair of mustard work boots.

The air took on a new sulfur tang.

The men stepped onto the running board and disappeared inside the cab.

Jay took little steps, the thrum of the engines hypnotic. He gripped the mirror and pulled himself up. Froze as gator claws dragged along his spine.

He forced himself to peer in the driver's window.

Leo sat in the passenger's seat, legs wide. Pants at his ankles, baring ghost-white runner's thighs. A trucker-capped head bobbed rapid between them.

With one hand Leo stroked the country boy's neck. With the other hand, he slapped his own scarecrow face side to side, leaving cheeks red with welts.

The sight of his adversary bare and unarmored flooded Jay's mouth with bile. He flipped open the phone and pressed the camera button.

Leo's eyes snapped open and met Jay's through the glass.

Jay hit the pavement in a sprint.

Herschel's car wasn't there. Jay ran serpentine through the rows of cars. "Dammit, Hersch!"

Two pairs of feet slapped the pavement behind him. The trucker hollered "Thief!" and clanged a tire iron along his trailer to rouse the troops.

Jay ran for a car with an open door. He could toss the bald driver and get the hell out of there. A car mirror clipped him as he rounded the row of cars. He raised his fist to throw.

"Get the hell in!" Herschel said.

Behind them the trucker came running with the tire iron. The tail lights on the Denali lit and tires shrieked as Leo reversed.

Jay dived into the cab's musty rear seat.

The cab balked at the hard corners, wobbling on the side-walls of its tires, transmission slamming into weak downshifts as Herschel floored the pedal. They crossed over the grass and squealed out the southbound exit with the Denali charging behind them.

"Move this heap! Want me to drive?"

"I told you these old cabs don't burn rubber unless they're on fire," Herschel said. "First damn thing I said when we met."

Out the rear glass, the Denali's angry grille homed in like a missile on afterburners. Leo's piercing eyes and devil goatee loomed in the windshield. The truck nudged hard at the rear bumper. The cab spun sideways. Herschel palmed the wheel, punched the gas pedal to get them straight again.

"He's trying to spin us out," Jay said.

"No shit!"

Jay clambered into the front seat. Leo rode the shoulder for the next pass. Herschel squeezed between a slow minivan and a sedan, the drivers honking bloody murder.

"Slam the brakes when he gets close," Jay said. The truck filled the passenger's side mirror. It lurched toward their rear bumper. "Now!"

Herschel stood on the brakes.

Body panels thunked and squealed like nails on chalkboard. The truck shot forward and took their passenger's side mirror with it.

Herschel gunned the gas again. "Damn, he's crazy."

The truck's brake lights seared red, the rear bumper rocketing toward their windshield. Herschel yanked the wheel and passed. Jay bounced off the dash.

"Hersch, cut on through the divider," Jay said. He pointed at a tiny opening ahead. Approaching fast.

"We're doing eighty!"

Jay took the revolver from his pocket. "Then I gotta shoot him."

"What the hell? You said—"

"Yeah, and that girl in the lake? She crashed 'cause of me," Jay said. "That's why I saved her. But I ain't saving this sumbitch."

Herschel shook his head, pressed his lips tight.

"Do it!"

The Denali roared ahead, one lane over. Leo gripped the wheel, raptor eyes glaring.

Herschel swerved hard right. The Jersey barrier loomed like an approaching iceberg, and flew past. The driver's side mirror exploded. Cars leaned on their horns and swerved as the cab kicked dust and trash in the cars-only lane's shoulder.

"Try that!" Herschel said with a hoot.

Tires squealed and the Denali torqued with the turn. Leo's eyes bulged as the truck plowed into the concrete with a chest-thumping crash. The black behemoth crumpled in on itself. Air bags filled the interior like swollen marshmallows.

Herschel stared at the wreck in the rearview mirror. Jay gripped the wheel and eased them into the left lane as tires shrieked and traffic clotted in the truck lanes.

"You said no trouble," Herschel said. "I'm gonna lose my job over this." He surveyed the damage with worried eyes while Jay popped the dents out of the Crown Vic.

"I'll order mirrors from the junkyard," Jay said. "Put them

on tomorrow. It'll look fine." He tucked another of the old hundreds into Herschel's palm.

Herschel pulled away in the battered cab, shaking his head.

Jay released the hideaway compartment in the Challenger and buried the baggied revolver underneath his duffel. He opened his phone and stared at the photo he'd taken.

The town hero liked to cruise the pickle parks. Bello Senior had likely met him there, and hated that part of himself. Saw it in his son, tried to burn it out of him with the embers of cigarettes held to his warty fingers. The son learned from the father. Took out his rage on Brendan, and any other boys who stirred his loins.

Jay texted Tony the photo.

So that was what Joey Bello had been grinning about.

CHAPTER 31

Jay and the boys marked time in school while dodging their tormentors, and escaped any way they could, via the Punisher's twin .45s or umber hulks slain by the roll of twenty-sided dice with Iron Maiden wailing heavy metal myth from a boombox. Invisible forces began to draw them apart. Brendan and Billy hung out with the hockey team, Matt and Tony with the brains in the computer club.

Ramona held Jay's hand held loosely in the halls, and frowned when he talked to kids in denim and leather jackets whose fathers worked with Andre. The summer seemed to swell with importance as their fifteenth year loomed.

Saturday, Tony suggested they snag bags of broken cookies from the ladies of the Famous Amos factory like in the old days and race the wide runway of Washington Avenue on their tenspeeds. The cookies were crisp and buttery, their first taste of nostalgia made their friendship feel like one infinite summer day where they had only met in the pool that morning.

"Atari sucks," Matt said. "This Christmas, I'm getting an IBM XT." He rode a new Schwinn, a girl's model so his legs could reach.

"How can you think of Christmas already," Tony said. "I can't wait for the pool to open. Then it's prime titty time."

"Standard mountain time," Matt said.

"I hope Ramona comes back this year," Billy said. "Can't wait to see those."

Jay veered his bike over and smacked Billy in the head.

"Watch it, asshole."

"Then watch your mouth."

"Billy's jealous," Brendan said. "If he were a gentleman like you, he'd have a girlfriend too."

Jay had never thought on it much, but he guessed she was his girlfriend.

They cruised through the park and cut into the grass to dodge the joggers. Kingsland Park was split up the middle by the Third River. Ducks went bottoms-up to nibble weeds, and fat carp drifted below. Upstream it widened enough to fit a small island, connected on both sides by picket fence bridges. The isle hosted a gazebo shaded by decorated trees, and the path was usually empty enough that they could put on some speed.

The twins shot ahead, long limbed and swift. Matt and Tony lazed behind, talking computer games. Jay pumped the pedals to catch them. The twins stopped after the bridge, squinting into a copse of dogwood trees.

Billy waved for them to hurry, eyebrows high with drama.

Jay coasted to a stop beside them. Brendan stared into the trees. Billy put a finger to his lips and pointed.

Boys kneeled in the bushes.

"Don't reckon I want to see this," Jay whispered. He turned away, and Brendan tugged his handlebars.

"Listen."

"Say it!"

Joey Bello.

A young boy kicked at the grass with his sneakers. A larger boy on his chest.

"Say it, you little faggot," Joey said. "Say it and we'll let you go."

A slap, then Nicky's trademark giggle.

"Say you want to suck it," Joey said. "You fuckin' little queer."

Jay ditched his bike and hit the bushes running.

Bello kneeled atop a young Vietnamese boy who lived on Jay's street, who everyone called Jon. Nicky Paladino stood grinning, hand kneading the crotch of his sweatpants. Bello had his fly undone, a wad of white briefs jutting out.

Jay's eyes misted over red. He hit Nicky with a tackle. He tasted salt and iron and his fists bounced off Nicky's ribs. He heard yelps, felt sneaker points bounce off his back.

Jay reached behind and him grabbed his assailant's nuts. A loud groan and the kicks went away. One of the twins hit Bello hard. A rope of snot boloed into the grass as a fist hit Joey's round face. The enraged attacker fell on him. Joey panted and squealed, covering his face.

"Just leave me alone!" Brendan said, throwing his fists. "Leave me alone!"

Nicky clawed at Jay's eyes. Jay chomped his chin and slammed a knee into his crotch until Nicky crawled away dragging his face in the dirt.

Tony and Matt watched, hands frozen to their handlebars.

Joey Bello curled in a ball, crying through his bloodied nose. Brendan stood over him, staring at his torn knuckles. Little Jon swore, punctuating each word with a kick to Joey's back.

Jay gripped Joey by the shirt and shook him. "The hell's wrong with y'all? Tell me!"

"Fuck you," Bello cried.

Billy led his brother to their bikes. "We better go."

Jon made fists and roared at the sky, and gave his rescuers a nod in thanks before he ran home.

They rode home through the parks, quiet for a time. Billy hooted and slapped Brendan's shoulders.

"We showed them," Billy said. "We finally fucking showed them."

Brendan stared ahead a long time, and curled his lips into a tight smile.

Jay worked the morning at Tony's. He let two of Ramona's calls go to voicemail, before he turned off his phone. The thought of her and Matt laughing at him twisted his gut.

Jay lost himself in working on a late model GTO, a honey of a sleeper. He drove to the diner and bought a grilled chicken salad for Tony and a cheesesteak with fries for himself. On the way back, Billy's green Cherokee was parked in front of the shop.

Jay kept on driving. He ate his cheesesteak in the park by the river, flipping through a Parker novel at a picnic table. Okie idolized the thief, even though every single one of his heists went wrong. Something made him ignore his instincts and the job went sour, but Parker always made it out alive, usually with a cut of the take.

There endeth the lesson, as Okie would say.

Jay powered on his phone and deleted Ramona's voicemails. Tossed one of the French fries to a fat squirrel. The phone vibrated in his pocket. Incoming call. Unknown number, like all of Ramona's calls.

He held the phone to his ear. Dirty silence. Air rushing by.

"Well, say what you have to say," he said.

"Is this Jay?"

"Yeah, who the hell is this?"

"Someone who taught you better manners." Her smoker's husk had dropped an octave, but Angeline's tongue was still sharp as a new Case knife.

"Mama?"

"Well, it ain't the Queen of France," she said. "It's good to hear you, son."

"Miss Cindy found you," Jay laughed.

"That nosy old thing could find Lafitte's treasure if she put her mind to it," she said. "How you doing?"

"I'm real good," Jay said, and laughed to free the birds fluttering in his chest. "Got a job, and a car. How about you?"

"Ain't you a regular citizen? Never thought you'd walk free, son. But I'm real happy for it. Changes everything." She paused for a puff of her cigarette. "This a safe line?"

"Yeah, Mama. It's one of those pay-as-you-go phones."

"Okie taught you right. How is the old horndog?"

"Gone," Jay said, and picked at the flaking paint of the picnic table. *How'd Mama know Okie? He'd never written about him.*

"Yeah, he wouldn't have liked getting old."

Jay stared at the trees as if she were a ghost hiding in the woods, a wisp at the edge of his vision. "You knew him?"

"He didn't take you under his wing out of the goodness of his heart," she said, and broke into a coughing fit. "I was a dumb little thing in Shreveport, and he taught me the long con. He never told you?"

Jay bit his lip and hissed out the corners of his mouth. "He kept your secrets. He was good as an iron vault. That who you learned from?"

"Kinda lost track of who taught who," she said. "He did right by me. When I heard he was in Rahway, I reached out. We took care of you best we could. Now maybe you can drive on home, and take care of me for a change."

Jay swallowed dry. The more he dug, the less he wanted to know.

"Found some papers in the old house, Mama." Jay frowned out at the muddy Passaic. "Says your name's Evangeline. What they calling you these days?"

"Huh," she said. "What's it matter? You're gonna call me Mama anyways." She paused for a puff. "A lot's changed since you been away."

"Could've used more letters," Jay said. "Got real low in there."

"I know I should've wrote more, there's a lot of things happened." She sighed. Jay could smell the smoke of her Winston. "A lot of things, and a letter wasn't gonna help any."

He sensed it, like a burn mark on a photograph where Andre's face had been.

"Can I talk to Papa?"

229

"Not if you're expecting him to talk back." She hummed with the memory of distant pain. "*Defan* Andre's gone, baby."

Jay's breathing slowed to death. He didn't blink. He could see her lips pinch around the Winston's filter.

"They caught up with us, and that's how it played out. I was gonna try and call, but didn't see the good. Thought you might do something rash, get yourself killed, or worse."

Jay clutched the edge of the table. The wood creaked in his grip.

"Who," Jay said.

"You know I don't like that voice. Send that boy away now."

"Why'd we come here," Jay said, through gritted teeth.

"Why you think?" She took a long drag. "You remember. You called her the Witch. It's a long story, and I got a shift to finish."

"You owe me the truth."

"Hey. Don't you tell me what I owe. Whatever me and Andre did, we did for you," she said. "You want to know why, ask that Strick. If anyone's to blame, it's that rotten son of a bitch. He's the root of it all."

Jay took Andre's knife from his boot and ice-picked the picnic table, again and again. The fat squirrel shot up a tree. He pried out the blade out and tested the edge on his thumb. A curl of callused skin peeled away.

"Reckon I'll give him a visit," Jay said, in the voice she didn't like. "I'll be heading south when I'm done. So I better like what I hear."

She chuckled a long, smoker's laugh. "I cut hair in a salon behind Little Ray's. You come on home and we'll talk about it over a couple po'boys, but you won't like the story one bit. There's nothing about it to like."

Jay gave her silence in return.

"Love you, son. Don't forget it. We're kin, but I'd have saved you anyhow."

Jay exhaled through his nostrils.

"Be smart, now. Do what you're gonna do, but be smart about it. Then come home where you belong."

"I will."

Jay closed the phone, and slipped the knife into his boot.

CHAPTER 32

The Hammerhead cruised the dark highway at speed. The stereo thumped the opening bass notes of AC/DC's "Live Wire," as Bon Scott told the world to get the hell out of his way. Jay kneaded the tomahawk handle in one handle, the steering wheel with the other. The smooth hickory was a bony handshake, a tenuous bond to his lost father.

He hugged the hills to Strick's house and rolled up the farm road behind the rows of Christmas trees a hair above idle. Put on his kit and padded to the garage. One door was open, where the Porsche ticked as the engine cooled. The Harley sat beside it in the dark, keys in the ignition.

A little black Toyota sat parked in front of the house. Jay crept behind a hydrangea bush and peered through a corner of the window.

Two milk-white bodies glowed on the floor of the candlelit parlor. A slender woman with big dark curls spilling past her shoulders reached toward the man. Skin loose at his hip and belly, arms mottled sandstone, legs pasty and thin.

Jay swallowed and walked to the garage. They would be a while.

He pushed the Challenger in neutral to block the Porsche in.

Inside the garage, he stuck a pen light in his mouth. Set his tool box on the concrete floor by the Harley and went to work.

Andre had taught him to swing a hammer, throw a baseball, and catch a fish. Paddled him into the waters of Bayou Teche in a pirogue to fish the bottom for big cats, while Jay cast his cane pole for *sac-au-lait*. Jay's first catch was no bigger than Andre's palm, but he showed him how to remove the hook and kill it quick. They gutted it and fried the filets in Mama Angeline's cast iron skillet. Jay had eaten a lot of cooking since, but nothing in his memory ever tasted as good as that panfish did, dipped in cornmeal, sweet and crisp.

Strick's garage smelled of oil and cigarette smoke. The memories turned to ashes in Jay's mouth.

A door slammed. Jay flicked off his penlight. The woman, now clothed in a pencil skirt and a hastily buttoned blouse, walked barefoot to her car clutching a pair of heels.

Strick Senior ran naked out the door behind her.

"You want something to remember me by, try my name." She slammed the Toyota's door.

Strick mouthed silent, sad-eyed apologies through her driver-side window. The car veered out the driveway, and he chased it for a few steps, and slumped his shoulders. He ran a hand through his hair and watched the tail lamps shrink into the dark like a rocket escaping the atmosphere.

Jay padded inside and waited.

Inside, Strick poured himself a scotch from the crystal decanter, and plopped naked onto the enormous puff of chocolate leather sofa. Legs splayed, the candles lit the chicken-skin of his balls and the fine gray down of his chest. He sipped and stared out the bay window at the half moon.

Jay stepped from behind the front door and closed it with a click. "You done with your saggy-ass stargazing?"

The scotch tumbler hit the carpet and Strick froze in a half crouch. The upholstery squeaked under his skin.

"Don't get up," Jay said, and twisted Andre's tomahawk in the candlelight. The blade rippled gold. "Unless you're looking to get circumcised."

Strick cupped his hands over his genitals.

"You figure out who I am?"

Strick nodded, and melted into the cushions.

"Know why I'm here?"

"Matthew said he paid you," Strick said. "If you came looking for more, the well is dry." He waved a hand over the room. "This is all leased and mortgaged to the bone."

"I pissed on your son's money," Jay said. "And that's no figure of speech. I don't understand you folks. Money's everything to you. Maybe you roll those bills nice and tight, and fuck 'em when no one's looking."

"Can I at least put some pants on?"

"A little chilly, ain't it? No, I like you exposed and vulnerable. Like I was in the police station, when you sweet-talked me into that confession. What happened to the lawyers? You fired my father, they couldn't pay one themselves."

Strick kneaded his temples with thumb and fingertip and stared at Jay over the web of his thumb. "Bello would've destroyed me. Why do you think I moved here? The divorce tore everything apart. Your mother—"

"Careful now," Jay said, and grazed the blade over the back of Strick's neck.

"Jesus," Strick said, squirming. "I never intended to hurt anybody. I made mistakes, but I've tried to set them right!"

Jay slapped the haft of the tomahawk into his palm. "Start from the beginning. I'm tired of the bullshit."

"That one damn Louisiana job," Strick said, and ran his fingers through his thinning locks of silvered bronze. He let out a whispery sigh. "Oil men were throwing cash around like water with the embargo on. And what can I say? I love women. I thought she was on the pill, but what was I thinking, expecting accountability from a woman."

Jay tilted his head.

"Angie didn't tell you? She told everyone else." Strick threw up his hands. "Followed me here like a vengeful ghost."

"What?"

"Easy." Strick hopped to his feet. "Joshua, that's what she

called you, in her letters. Then after her sister came, she said to call you Jay."

They circled on the carpet.

"It wasn't my fault," Strick said. "I was married! Told her we'd get it taken care of, but she wouldn't listen to reason. One damn night, it's been haunting me for forty years."

Jay raised the axe, teeth gritted. "What are you telling me?"

"I did what Leo told me to do! What happened to you, Jesus, how was I supposed to know what your mother would sink to? Please, I just want to be left in peace."

Jay hunkered down, axe held loose. "You stole my damn father from me. Andre's dead now. He died with his boy in prison because of you, so start making sense."

Strick bolted for the door. Jay stuck a foot out, and he toppled to hands and knees.

Jay hooked his throat with the head of the tomahawk. "Start talking, *kemosabe*. I ain't here to count coup."

"You don't know?" Strick gagged, the shadows painting his nose into a vulture's beak. "You're, you're my son."

"Like hell I am."

"It's true, I swear," Strick said. "Why do you think I gave you a house? That crazy bitch T-boned my Challenger with their pickup truck! Why do you think I gave you the damn wreck?"

Jay blinked in the dim light, let the dust settle in his mind as the words quaked through his notion of what was what.

"So you're...my father."

"Yes! Can I get up, now?"

"Stay." Jay traced the axe along his spine. "You ran off on me once already. Reckon you'd love to hop on that hog of yours and leave this problem behind."

Strick hunched into himself.

"I know what it's like to lose a father," Jay said. "Done it twice, now. I kind of knew, deep down, I think, that I wasn't Andre's blood. They always said I favored my mama."

"She was beautiful."

"I'm guessing she still is. I just talked to her."

A confusion fell on Strick's eyes, but he said nothing.

"I don't care why you did what you did. Why you never claimed me. Knew plenty inside who never knew their old man, or wish they never had. One thing I want to ask, before I let you run rabbit." Jay said. "Ramona Crane. She would've been, what, thirteen, you started on her?"

The lines in Strick's face softened, as if cherishing an old memory. "She knew what she was doing. She was a lot older than her age."

Jay snarled and sank the tomahawk into the arm of the couch.

Strick lunged for the doorknob while Jay wrenched the axe free.

Jay swung for him and caught the door in the face. Strick ran naked for the garage, flapping down the driveway.

Jay punched the doorjamb and snarled as the jumble in his mind fell into place. Mama Angeline got the Stricks divorced. Why? She had his child.

Jay.

Joshua.

Me.

The Harley thundered in the garage. Strick wiggled the bike around the Porsche and his eyes flashed wide as Jay came running with the hatchet. He gunned the throttle and swerved onto the grass, biking bare-assed across the lawn toward the gates.

Matthew is my half-brother.

Jay fired up the Challenger and bounced down the drive, bottoming out on the pavement. The Harley's pipes rumbled ahead of him on the dark winding road. Jay squealed after him and flipped on the high beams.

Matthew Strick is my father.

The bike appeared as a red dot at the edge of his high beams.

He stomped on the pedal to close the distance.

Not my real father. Not even close.

He was a bastard son, abandoned before birth, only to be sacrificed to the law to take Matty's place in a jail cell. Twice betrayed.

They brought me here to kill the monster torturing their children. They were too weak to forsake the money-god to whom they sacrificed their firstborn sons.

Papa Andre had raised him as his own. And they had stolen him from him.

Strick looked over his shoulder.

Jay floored the pedal and nudged the hog's rear. Strick twisted the accelerator and burbled ahead.

Green eyes flickered at the side of the road. The bike's headlamp illuminated a flash of tan and white. A whitetail doe sprang across the pavement.

A shriek of rubber and the Harley somersaulted into the woods. Strick hit the pavement and rag-dolled down the pavement. Jay stomped the brakes and skidded to a halt. A red and white mess of limbs lit in his headlamps.

The adjustment Jay had made to the bike's brake piston caused the pads to seize the first time Strick hit them hard.

Jay stepped out of his blood-sire's old steed with Leo's bagged revolver in his hand.

The deer stamped its hoof at Jay's approach. When he kept coming, it snorted and kicked off into the woods.

Strick looked at him with what was left of his face. Wobbled his shattered head, reached with the gnarled red rose of a hand.

Jay bent to speak into his one remaining eye.

"You are not my father," he said, and fired.

Officer Carnahan and Detective Zelazko crowded Jay into the interrogation room and kept him awake late into the night.

"I heard what you went through, back when you were a little

kid," Carnahan said. "Of course you're angry. I'd want to kill somebody too."

"Your parents did a bad thing," Leo said. "Not as bad as what you did—and we know it was you who did it—but it's enough to put them in prison for a long time."

"But you're still a kid. They treat adults differently."

"They let kids get away with murder," Leo said. "What'd that carjacker kid get?"

"Seven years."

"That sounds like a long time now, but it's a blink of an eye."

The words blurred on the page as Jay tried to read them.

"Someone's here to talk to you. He wants to help you. I want to help you," Carnahan said. "So listen to us."

"I don't," Leo said. "I want to put you away where you belong. You *and* your grifter parents. But I'll take what I can get. So listen to what Mr. Strick has to say. When we get back, I want an answer."

They left, and Mr. Strick entered the room. Corners of his mouth twitching in nervous smiles. He sat and folded his hands. A lock of dusty brown hair fell across his dull gray eyes. He avoided Jay's face and scanned the graffitied table and scratched hardwood floor as if he'd lost something.

"Matthew was there, too. It was all his idea."

"I know, Jay. But if one of you took it all, the rest would be all right. You understand?"

"Why me?"

"I'm going to tell you something important," Strick said, and removed his thin gold frames, rubbed the lenses with a handkerchief. "About how the world works. There are people who get in trouble, and people who don't. Joey is…was…one of the people who don't. The twins are, too. Matthew. But Anthony, and your…family, you don't have that advantage."

Jay wrinkled his brow.

"Your parents wronged me, and I forgave them. Leo,

though. He's the law. And the law isn't as forgiving."

"What did they do?" Hot tears slicked Jay's cheekbones.

"That doesn't matter," Strick said. "What matters is they, and your friend Anthony, they're the kind of people who don't get away with things. Not unless you sign what Leo wants you to sign."

"But that's lying. They were there!"

"He says, with your age...you'd be out in seven years. You'll have to get a GED, but when you get out, I can help you with college. Ramona's a rich girl, Jay. A beautiful young woman. She'll want to live the way she's accustomed to, and the son of a carpenter can't give that to her. But a college boy...he could. This might be good for you. And it's the best deal you're gonna get. Because if you don't sign, they'll destroy you."

Jay wiped his nose on his knuckle.

"Didn't they give you any water?" Strick croaked. He replaced his glasses and looked around the room. "I know you've been through a lot. Matthew is weak. You, you're made of tougher stuff." He squeezed Jay's shoulder. "I had plans for you."

Jay frowned in confusion. "What?"

"Forget it for now." Strick's eyes crinkled and he squeezed the bridge of his nose. "Only you can stop them, Jay. I've got money, but Leo and Bello have power. I used to think they were the same thing, but they're not. Not always. If you don't do this, they'll destroy us all. Your parents go to jail. Your friends, their lives will be ruined. Tony, his mother. Matthew and me. The twins."

"Someone had to stop him," Jay said. The corners of his eyes turned fuzzy.

"And you did. You did! You were the only one with the guts. And you can be strong again, and save everyone." Strick's words ran out in a desperate choppy rhythm. "You're tough. Jesus, what you went through. I can't even think about it, I get sick. But it made you into a survivor. You've endured so much." His lips paled as he pressed them together tight.

"If you can take just a little bit more, all this goes away. And in a few short years, I promise I'll make it all right."

Leo shouldered in the door. "Hear that, Jay? Your friends need you. Your family. What's it going to be?"

"I want to go home to my folks," Jay said.

Leo slapped the pen on the table.

The dark of the interstate was a trench on the seafloor lit only by the fluorescent eyes of the Hammerhead. Windows sealed against the thousand atmospheres of pressure. Music throbbed against Jay's temples, his hands squeaked against the steering wheel.

Don't you say anything, Mama had said, too late.

And tonight she had loosed Jay like a blood dog at her ancient enemy. So he could learn things she should have told him herself.

Jay wondered if she knew he'd kill Strick. If after the Witch, he'd had any choice at all.

His throat cried for the burn of bourbon. His fists for the pain of a ten-round slugfest. He felt faceless and unanchored and severed from the past, a runaway spirit on the run from the underworld, fearing that dawn would shatter him into a thousand motes of shadow.

PART FOUR

TNT

CHAPTER 33

The Witch who stole the boy away from Mama Angeline and Papa Andre was a gray-faced bag of skin and bone with a jack o'lantern smile who made him call her "Mama" and fed him mayonnaise sandwiches when she wasn't snoring in front of the little television, hand dangling a burnt spoon.

The boy would sneak out to ask neighbors for food and get shooed away. Steal tomatoes from their gardens and eat them like apples whether they were ripe or green. Walk barefoot down the road in his Fruit-of-the-Looms to the roadhouse full of men who sat slugging shots and cans of beer and stank of sweat, onions, and crude.

One of them let the boy sip beer from his lap while his dirty fingernails tapped out a rhythm on his scabbed knee. Jukebox playing a song about *choogling*. The boy asked what choogling was, and the man gave him a wide gator smile.

A big Cajun lifted the boy away and carried him back to the Witch. She thanked the big man and said no, no, he didn't have to call no law. She tied the boy's ankle to the chair leg and took the man in her room. The boy watched television until the man left. The Witch slapped him good and yelled *don't you never scare me like that again.*

The Witch was often gone all night. The boy ate peanut butter from the jar with a spoon when there was peanut butter, and mustard or Miracle Whip when there wasn't. His stomach hurt so bad he'd pray for her to come back and cook him some eggs, either snotty with runny whites or burnt crisp-edged with bits of shell.

One morning the Witch came back with shopping bags.

"I'm hungry...Mama."

"I was making groceries," she said. "Gonna cook some gumbo. Memaw says you like gumbo."

The boy liked making gumbo with Mama Angeline. Papa Andre would steam crabs and pop their shells like the caps off a bottle of Coke, sweeping out hunks of meat and orange clumps of roe.

The Witch dumped flour and oil in the pot, cursing to herself as she dusted the floor white. Turned the heat on high and stirred like mad to make the roux.

"Where's the Hershey bar?" When Mama Angeline made roux she gave the boy a Hershey bar. It was his job to tell her when the roux browned to match the chocolate color. He got to nibble while she stirred.

"You don't put candy in gumbo, silly."

"I'm hungry now, Mama."

"Go find something in the fridge, I gotta keep stirring."

He tugged the silver handle of the refrigerator door and found slim pickings. Uncapped the milk jug and gave a sniff. Sour. He put it back and closed the door. He'd learned not to pour it down the drain.

The boy sat on the matted shag rug in front of the television while the Witch stirred, muttering to herself, rough gray elbows working like knitting needles. He watched cartoons, wishing Elmer Fudd would just plumb shoot that smart-aleck Yankee rabbit, like Mama Angeline said he should.

Someone rapped hard on the door.

"You gonna make yourself useful and answer the door?"

Fear gripped him by the ankles. The men who knocked talked real loud. Yelled at him sometimes. One hit the Witch and made her cry. But the quiet ones were worse.

"Get the damn door!"

The boy's bladder felt full all of a sudden. Like if he moved, it would let go. And Witch-mama would belt him again. *For your own good.*

She stomped barefoot to the door and unlocked it. "Come

on in. Sit on the couch, I'm cooking." She stomped back to the roux and went at it double time.

It was the man from the bar with the long yellow fingernails. He held a sack from McDonald's. He sat on the couch and ate the French fries one by one. The boy smelled his onion stink over the sulfur of the thick factory town air.

"Hello, boy." He held out a French fry.

The boy stared at a television commercial.

"I know you want one," the man said. "Better feed this boy, he'll disappear if he turns sideways. All your money go in your arm?"

"I'm cooking right now, ain't I?"

He put his hand on the boy's knee. The cracked calluses felt like the scales on the gator heads nailed to the walls in the fishing camps.

The room began to twist. The boy would be watching from inside the television soon. Claws traced over his pale skin. Warmth ran down the boy's leg.

"Christ," the man snapped. "Boy's done pissed himself."

"What?" She ran from the kitchen, shaking a spoon coated with roux.

The boy pulled into himself as the heat spread on the couch. Stinging him where he was still sore.

"One thing I won't abide is filth," the gator man croaked. His heavy boots headed out the door.

"Wait, we'll wash him! We'll give him a bath!" She ran barefoot onto the gravel. Shouts desperate with need.

As her feet slapped the trailer steps, the boy felt the bad coming. Fear prickled his skin.

"The hell's wrong with you?" She yanked him off the sofa and blotted the soaked cushions with a T-shirt from the floor.

A burning smell filled the room. The Witch ran into the kitchen. "Ruined," she howled. "You made me ruin it." She held the pot, the brown roux speckled black with burnt flour. "I try to cook you dinner but all you do is hate on me!"

The dank carpet swallowed his feet and held him fast.

"You wouldn't eat it if I made it anyway," she screamed. "My damn sister spoiled you! Whenever I cook, it looks like you're eating dirty fingernails!"

His eyes went watery. "I'm sorry."

"You're sorry, *what?*"

Something rumbled inside him. It boiled out before he could stop it.

"You're not my mama!"

She hurled the pot at the wall past his head with a howl, roux splashing the walls and everywhere.

A scream blew through the boy like a train whistle. His back exploded with soda pop sizzle, bubbles rippling through the skin. She dragged him to the mildewed glass shower box. "Oh no, oh no, oh no," she moaned, holding the boy screaming beneath the faucet's lukewarm trickle.

Little Jay watched from safe inside the television set as skin sloughed off the boy's back in white hot sheets of pain.

"Don't worry, baby," she said. "we'll put some butter on it."

CHAPTER 34

Jay drowned his pancakes in syrup at the Bendix diner, an old-style railroad car squeezed onto a triangle in the middle of Route 17. Flipped open the newspaper, studied the article buried in the back.

"Unidentified Man Dies in Motorcycle Crash."

Police had found alcohol and marijuana in Strick's system, but were befuddled by his lack of clothing and identification, and the scarcity of whole fingerprints due to the road rash. He was so torn up they hadn't found the bullet hole.

Jay sipped his coffee.

Strick had abandoned his boy without a name. It would be fitting if he were buried in an unmarked grave. Mama Angeline's kind of justice.

His phone rattled across the countertop. Ramona's number. He'd want to say goodbye, for good. Might as well get it over with. He answered. "You couldn't tell me?"

"Tell you what?" Ramona said. "How could I tell you anything anyway, you never answer your phone."

"Maybe there's nothing to say."

"What's that supposed to mean? Stop acting like a child. I have the house to myself, I thought you might like a swim."

"So you can make movies for Matt to jerk off to? I'm not some chew toy for you two to fight over."

The waitress cleared her throat as she made a pass with the coffee pot.

"What are you talking about? If this is messing with your head, come over and we'll talk about it. If you have better things to do, I'll swim laps by myself."

He drew in a breath to respond, but she had cut the line.

* * *

Jay lay in bed at the dead old man's apartment, reading. The yellowed white walls might've been Rahway, for all the difference. He wondered how much gas money he'd need to get to Louisiana. He could find a job in a service shop there. Or go door to door, taking jobs that shade tree mechanics couldn't handle.

His phone hummed again and he raised to throw it across the room.

Louisiana number.

He flipped it open and let Mama Angeline listen to him huff angry breaths.

"So, did you like what he had to say?" Hairdryers whined in the background among laughter and bustle.

"No," Jay said.

"Didn't think you would," she said, and puffed her smoke. "But the truth's what you wanted. Usually it hurts."

"It's true?"

"You know who your real father was," she said. "All that other one did was dip his wick. That ain't fathering."

"So how'd you meet him?"

"You'll have to ask *him* if you want to talk ancient history," she said, and paused for a puff. "Or have you had enough truth for a while?"

"He can't answer."

"That's my boy," Angeline said, hacked a laugh. "Had a feeling he'd get what's coming."

Jay kneaded his temples. "Did he really kill Andre?"

"Well he as good as did, putting us on the run like that." she said. "Just about did in the both of us."

"Aw, Mama."

Her voice took on grit. "Don't you pity him none. And why don't you go see that hard-ass cop next?" She laughed until it turned into a wet cough. "Strick went to Leo when we showed up with you. He thought up a solution, like a regular King Solomon."

"Don't care about that," Jay said. "Wish I could've seen Andre again. Talked to him."

"Okie told us what a fine young man you turned out to be," she said. "Made your Papa real proud. You know what I think about wishing, son."

She'd always said, *wish in one hand, shit in the other. See which hand gets full first.*

"How'd he...how'd he go?"

"We left Louisiana for a lot of reasons," she said. "We should've stayed gone, but that's where Andre's people are. Mine, I wouldn't piss on 'em if they were on fire, not unless I was pissing gasoline. Anyways, a job went sour. That's all there is to say, at least over the phone."

"And you," Jay said. "Butter wouldn't melt in your mouth, would it?"

"All I did was save a little boy," she said. "And I've paid for it ever since. You remember. You didn't remember much, but you remember the Witch."

"I was what, five?"

"Does it matter? We raised you right, took care of you. When no one else would. Ever hear 'how sharper than a serpent's tooth, to have a thankless child?' Well that tooth's cutting right now."

"Strick said you shook him down."

"I'd call it child support," she said.

"But...but you're my mama. Aren't you?"

"How dare you? Listen, son. You want to judge me, do it to my face. I'll be waiting."

The phone hit the receiver like a slammed door.

Jay ran his thumb over the buttons, thought about what she said.

But before he left, more men needed killing.

* * *

The sally port protecting the SHU was abandoned, the gates locked. Jay and Cheetah slumped against the cold green walls, exhausted from the fight. Okie put his fingers in his mouth and whistled through the bars.

"I got lucky," Jay said.

"No you didn't," Cheetah said. "I got smart."

Mack shifted from foot to foot, cracking his knuckles.

A heavily tattooed barrel-gut buffalo lumbered to the locked gates. Four muscled Latinos backed him up. Verdad kept his receding hair tied back in a thin ponytail. He gave them a death stare. "Where's my sister?"

"Ran off with Dante to Ad Seg," Okie said. "We did our part."

"Not all of it," Verdad said, and turned his broad back on them.

Okie, Mack, and Cheetah traded glances.

"I'll get her," Jay said, stretching his taped knuckles. "Let them in."

Verdad narrowed his eyes to octopus slits. "Don't come back alone."

Jay put a taped fist through the bars. "He's my sister too."

Verdad punched Jay's knuckles with his brown tattooed meathook. He opened the gates, and Jay turned down the corridor. Mack slipped him a shank.

"Kid," Okie called. "Be careful."

"Save it," Jay said, and jogged wearily toward Wing Four.

Jay tested the shank on the crumbling plaster. Slim spring steel wrapped with duct tape. Solid. The roar of the riot echoed through the walls like a savage ghost. The gates to Ad Seg lay open, the guardroom rifled. Two big-armed Italians sat inside, wincing between gulps of hooch.

"Welcome to the jungle," one sang, and laughed. "Had to beat the mool, didn't you?"

"Seen Dante?"

The men traded glances. "He's on a date. Best leave it alone."

Jay raised his fists, shank held out like an ice pick. "Where?" They told him.

Three cells down Jay found Rene curled on the floor, cupping her face. He knelt and cradled her to his chest. "You're okay, sister. Come with me."

Rene trembled. "Hope they didn't make me as ugly as you."

Jay helped him to his feet. "Hell, you're making my pecker hard as this shank here. Dante do this?"

"Kenny and some friends of his," Rene said. "Took him that way."

Jay passed her the shank and they stalked down the hall. As they passed the familiar solitary cells, ice crystals formed in Jay's belly. Four white walls that became movie screens for his nightmares. A choked off keening echoed from the only open door.

Dante's fish-belly white legs kicked at the floor and a rivulet of blood trickled toward the center drain. Two cons sat on his arms while Kenny, the big-nosed bastard Jay had clocked out, ground a bloody nightstick deep between his cheeks.

Rene fell on Kenny with the shank, arm pistoning like the needle of a sewing machine. Jay knocked the other two sprawling with a jab and a cross. Only one got back up. His boxing-taped hands were hard as brass knuckles. He mashed their faces to shreds.

Dante howled and the nightstick clattered to the floor. He held it by the unbloodied end, and hollered for them to stop.

Jay pulled Rene off Kenny's whimpering, perforated bulk.

Dante pointed the bloodied nightstick toward the door. "Go."

Jay and Rene leaned on each other, and they staggered onto the tier.

Dante stepped gingerly toward Kenny, his legs striped with blood. The nightstick cracked flesh and bone, echoing the hallways as they made their way back to their brothers.

CHAPTER 35

The Bello house was a Queen Anne nestled in a woodsy cul-de-sac called The Enclosure, the site of a former artists' colony from which Nutley took its name. It abutted a mucky swell of the Third River that everyone called the Mud Hole. Jay crossed the railroad trestle into the park beneath a fingernail clipping of moon, carrying the baggied revolver in one pocket and the lock-pick gun in the other.

A steady hot summer rain hushed his footsteps and pattered off his hoodie as he crept along the old pines lining the far side of the pond. He spied the single lit window in the house's turret. No silhouette broke the yellow square after five minutes of watching. Jay approached the picket fence.

The Bellos had no other children. Jay recalled Mrs. Bello at the trial. A large woman with dark curls spilling over her slumped shoulders. A drained sadness in her eyes, her lower lip twitching as the prosecutor shared every gruesome detail.

Her dead hazel eyes haunted Jay's long nights in his cell at juvenile. If he saw them again tonight, he would have to close them forever. Something twinged in his gut at the thought.

To clear his mind, he thought of her husband's little smile as he pinched Joey's bandaged fingers when he took Joey home from school. The same smile Joey Junior would use when he had his prey nailed down in torment.

Jay hopped the fence. A chill in twitched his shoulders as he neared the house, as if Andre's ghost hand reached to stay him. The rear door had an awning over it, and he crouched beneath it on the wooden steps. The revolver dug into his crotch. He fed the pick gun into the lock and slow-cycled it over the pins.

Mrs. Bello's dead stare bored through him. Like he had cut

out her heart and replaced it with a nest littered with the tiny skeletons of orphaned birds. Jay rested his forehead on the doorknob.

Joey had needed killing. So had Frankie Dell, and his mother was probably a Catholic saint wielding a sauce-stained wooden spoon.

All their victims' mothers cried, too.

Okie's voice told him to shoot, not think. Two in each face. Drop the gun, and watch Leo's world fall apart from a bayou honkytonk over a mess of mudbugs and a schooner of beer.

Jay crushed his eyes shut and let the rain beat his brain in. He'd come without a plan. He squeezed the knurled grips of Leo's revolver through the zip bag, thought on Brendan's words.

Was Joseph Bello Senior his to kill?

He'd tried to whack him in prison. He might try again.

The more he thought on it the more he knew the man needed killing.

Hot breath misted his neck. A growl filled his ear.

Jay launched off the stoop and snapped the wooden railing with his shoulder. A thick Rottweiler bulled him over and clamped its jaws around a chunk of his thigh. Jay groaned and popped a quick hook to the dog's ear. It bowled over and shook its head, then snarled and charged.

Jay bolted for the fence and felt teeth graze his ass. His hand was numb. It was like punching a brick wall. The dog ripped his jeans to the knee and he tumbled over the fence and skidded down the pine-needled embankment. His boots splashed in the muck.

The dog planted paws on the fence and howled in triumph. Jay quick-limped toward the car. Mr. Bello's voice carried across the water. "Caesar, get the hell back here."

Lights flicked on through the pines. Warm blood slicked the back of his thigh. He probed the punctures with his blue-gloved fingers and plugged the biggest with a fingertip. He spread a trash bag on the seat and staunched the bleeding with a handful of Popeye's napkins from the glovebox. He loped back to his den to lick his wounds.

Jay limped to his apartment. In the third floor hallway, music thumped from one door and indignant shouts came from another. He rested his head on his door jamb and sighed. His leg had stopped bleeding, but throbbed like the dog still had a grip on him.

Okie would have had a field day. *Cons get caught for being stupid, kid. Not for breaking the law. People break the law every day, and make good livings doing it. You get too greedy for cash, gash, or payback, and that's when you go down,* Okie would have said, and fingered the star-shaped bullet scar beneath his copper-white beard.

The dog's bite felt like poison. A childhood flash lit Jay's brain, pre-Witch. Andre had a blue leopard Catahoula named Bebe. Little Jay played in the grass with her, when a fat black moccasin lunged from its stump-roots hideaway.

Bebe thrashed the snake to death, and dragged Jay back to the house by his shirt.

Angeline cradled Little Jay and swore through tears. Andre tried to siphon out the poison, but Bebe snapped at him and dragged herself under the porch. He crawled after her with a bowl of water.

Hours later, Papa Andre came out with his face red and puffy and walked alone toward the canebrake. He stomped the snake's writhing coils until there was nothing left but a mess of blood.

Andre buried Bebe, and clutched Little Jay so tight that he could barely breathe.

Jay keyed the deadbolt, turned the knob. The clack of metal on metal. He paused and stared at the spot on the white paint of the door jamb where he had slicked a hair each time he left.

The hair's absence punched him between the eyes.

Jay leapt for the stairwell.

A head-sized hole shredded the door. Splinters raked his side. He bounced the fire door open and stumbled into the corner at the top of the stairs. A masked figure exited his apartment and swept the hallway with a short-barreled shotgun. The fire door swung closed as the gunman racked the pump.

Jay's ears rang from the shotgun's report. He slid on his ass down the first flight of stairs and screamed as the wound tore open. He jumped the rest, pain jolting up his thigh. Above, the fire door hit the wall. Shouts echoed down the stairwell.

Jay burst out the exit to parking lot. A black Lexus flicked its high beams and launched forward, clipping him with the mirror. Jay spun against the bricks and ran for the Challenger, one leg dragging. Pulled Leo's gun from his pocket and forced his finger through the guard.

The Lexus reversed, spitting asphalt.

Jay fired through the baggie and the revolver bucked in his hand. The Lexus swerved and Jay staggered between parked cars.

The Hammerhead started on the first try. Jay ducked low and backed into the nose of the Lexus, bullying the sedan into a row of cars. A shout then a blast, and the rear glass shattered and pellets tore the seat cushions. He ripped the bumper off the car next to his and hit the empty street.

The blacked-out Hammerhead flew onto Franklin Avenue on autopilot. The instinct to go to ground brought him to the familiarity of his hometown. Jay flicked the switches to kill the brake lights. Behind him, a one-eyed pursuer ran the red light he'd just blown. Adrenaline flushed through his insides and worked his limbs for him.

The trestle. The tracks. Ramona.

Where he'd felt safe, once.

He stomped the brake and side-skidded past a turn on the damp macadam. Engines and squealing rubber woke the sleepy 'burb. He spun the wheel and doubled back, roaring toward his pursuer head-on. The Lexus buried its nose in the pavement. Jay toed the brake and cut the wheel like Ramona showed him, rocketed down a side street. The railroad trestle towered above.

The Lexus roared past a police cruiser, jumped the curb and cut over a corner of grass, jerked left and clipped the Hammerhead's rear corner. Jay held the pedal a second too long. The nose veered right and the fat tires gripped, shooting the Hammerhead through the hedges into the park.

Branches slapped and clattered against the paint. The car exploded out the other side and took air over the creek's brownstone banks.

Jay felt the car loft, and for a split second he thought the Hammerhead could fly like the General Lee on *The Dukes of Hazzard* and make the other side.

The car jolted with the crash and the steering wheel crunched his ribs, his forehead shattered the windshield.

Jay tumbled out the open door into the brook's dirty babble, unsure of how much time he'd lost after he knocked his head. His hands slipped on algae-slicked stones and he choked on a mouthful of the Passaic's finest. The Challenger's rear bumper was suspended on the opposite bank, its nose buried in the water.

Jay watched the stream bank, waiting for a shotgun to blank out his misery. A roil of clouds flashed gray and a thundercrack shook his spine. The sky opened up and pelted his face with hard droplets. He crawled beneath the spinning rear tire and watched the driveshaft spin out its last.

Blue police lights flickered like silent lightning, sparkling atop the water and illuminating the railroad trestle. Jay unbagged the revolver and tossed it downstream. He crawled the other way until the creek wall was short enough to climb.

Flashlights cut the rain sheets and lit on Jay's swollen face.

He held up his hands, let them drop. He felt like a filthy rag wrung dry of turpentine.

"You can *walk* on that water," one of the policemen said. "He goes in your cruiser, not mine."

Jay crawled toward the embankment. His arms felt like petrified wood. A cop with tattooed arms and bulging sleeves hefted him out of the water with a steel grip.

"EMTs, we got injuries," the officer called. He peered at Jay's eyes with his tactical flashlight, raindrops bouncing off his poncho. "You drive like that, you oughta wear your seat belt. You got a concussion for sure."

Jay cracked a smile. He flopped onto his back and curled like Bebe in the cool dark beneath the porch slats, let the rain hammer his eyelids closed.

CHAPTER 36

Seagulls circled overhead and pierced the calming shush of the surf with their cries. A gray day down the shore. A gull dropped a shell from above and it cracked on the jetty beside the boy's head, splashed his cheek with hot brine.

Little Jay studied the palm-sized clam. Pale yellow meat squirmed beneath the shattered shell. The seabird landed on a nearby rock and squalled discontent. Jay threw the clam past the bird and a trio of sharp beaks tore the flesh apart.

Andre called from the far end of the jetty, waving for help with the crab traps. Mama Angeline lay tanning on a towel, naked and asleep, her arm across her face. Jay felt his eyes drawn to the darkness between her legs. He covered his eyes as he stepped over.

Andre worked in silence. Jay pulled a clothesline rope and slowly drew a cage from the water to see what they caught. Once, a savage green eel writhed in coils until it fought its way out. The cage broke the surface, revealing a slab of blue crab attacking the bait with its claws.

The bait was a pair of human thumbs, tied to the trap with baling wire.

Andre shook the cage and dumped the crab in one of two buckets brimming with clacking claws. He thrust the bucket handles into Jay's hands and marched along the rocks toward the sand.

The weight tore at Jay's palms and shoulders as he chased Andre down the endless jetty. He hurried as his father shrank into the distance. He tripped over a gaunt, pale leg and the buckets tumbled onto the slabs of basalt, their bounty scurrying every which way.

Andre turned to glare disappointment.

Cold fingers clamped around Jay's ankle. The Witch smiled with jack o'lantern teeth.

Thumbless hands with dirty fingernails boiled from the cracks in the rocks, crab-walking over Jay's thighs, tickling up his ribs and belly to his throat.

Jay woke with a gasp, clutching his own neck with both hands. Wind whipped the rain against the bricks of the four-bunk jail cell. It smelled of sour vomit, sweaty feet, and cleaning fluid. Jay spat on the floor to get the taste of river water out of his mouth. It was the same Nutley jail cell he'd been locked in as a teen, modernized with a lidless steel toilet.

Jay sat and took inventory of himself. Prickly stitches formed a centipede across his forehead. The punctures in his leg had been cleaned and bandaged. His lower lip was puffed and swollen, and his ribs ached.

Beyond the gray bars, cops traded snaps of bravado, talking over a television show with a laugh track. Jay sat and stretched. His shoulders crunched like Bugs Bunny chomping a carrot.

"Can I get some water?"

He fell into a push-up position. Before he could snap out number one, the pain hunched him like a kicked dog and he fell to the floor clutching his side.

The rib was worse than he thought. He caught his breath and eased into position, performed three slow push-ups before he collapsed on the concrete, the impact knocking the wind from him.

Bobby Algieri's shaved head peered through the bars. He looked like a fresh-scrubbed newborn stuffed in a blue uniform. Over his shoulder, Nicky Paladino bared a wrinkle-nosed grin that made Jay wonder if he'd been watching through the one-way mirror while Jay was strip-searched.

"You want water?" Nicky unzipped his pants, stretched his wrinkled sausage taut.

The hard patter hit the concrete. Jay rolled aside and hot spray misted his shoulders.

"You get thirsty, lick that up." Algieri snickered. Nicky tucked himself away.

"Move," a voice growled, and a barrel-chested man pushed through. Mayor Bello wore a gray tracksuit and unevenly worn loafers that exaggerated his bowlegged gait. His eyelids drooped red, face turned granite with stubble.

"You killed my son," he said.

"He needed killing."

Bello flared his nostrils with two deep breaths. "Let me have him," he told Officer Algieri, without turning.

Algieri held a plastic pistol with a fat barrel. Jay clenched his eyes and curled into a ball while they hosed him with pepper spray. Fire ants rampaged over his eyelids, lips, and nostrils. Jay held his breath as long as he could, then gagged and spat as his nose flooded with mucus.

The cell door clanged open and Jay swung blindly. "I put that shit on my eggs in the morning!" he shouted, and ate a kick to the ribs. Slippery gloved hands gripped his wrists and cuffed them together. His eyes swelled shut, and all he could see was the red flare of the ceiling light.

Jay dry-heaved and a boot crushed him into the floor. He heard the crackle of a stun baton.

Bello traced the copper tines along Jay's scalp to his hackles. "You took what was mine," he said between panting breaths.

"Your boy—"

Jay writhed to the electric sizzle coursing through his spine. He had fought through a Taser once when the hacks came to drag him to solitary. He'd been in fighting shape. Now he flopped in the piss-puddle like a fish that had run out of fight.

"Mayor," Algieri said, over Nicky's muffled giggles. "You gotta go easy. Like, five seconds max."

"Give that back to me, Bobby. You let him murder your best friend. *My son.* You pussy little faggot."

"You're wasting juice," Algieri said. "I'll do it."

"Lemme do it," Nicky said.

"Your Joey," Jay groaned. "What did you do to him? How'd you teach him rape?"

"You shut your mouth!"

The shock seared behind Jay's eyes as the electrodes burned two pinholes between his shoulder blades. Jay watched himself writhe from inside a television screen tuned to static.

"He learn that sick shit," Jay panted, "from you?"

"Shock him again, Bobby."

"Sir, he can't take much more."

"An eye for an eye, Bobby. If you're too much of a woman to do it, I will. Walk out of here. No court is gonna convict me."

Bello prodded Jay's lips with the end of the stun gun. "Open your mouth, or I'll shock you in the eyes."

"Stick it up your ass," Jay wheezed. "Like you did to Joey."

The baton clubbed Jay's temple and he lost time.

When Jay stirred, he saw only yellow slices through swollen lids. Felt rubber gloved hands dabbing at him with cool cloth. Leo argued with Bello in a hushed voice.

"You should let me handle this, Joseph."

"Look at yourself, Leo. You can't handle anything. You let him kill my boy and get away with it."

"The law is the law. I've done more than I should already."

"You'll do what needs to be done," Bello said. "Get him out of my sight. *Forever.* Or you know what happens. Everything you have you owe to me. Don't forget it."

Footsteps echoed from the hall.

"Does he need a hospital?" Leo asked.

"No concussion. He needs a week of bed rest," a soft voice said. "I'll give him a sedative and antibiotics."

Jay felt a prick in his arm and sank through the jail bunk into a cool watery grave.

* * *

When they came for him, he was staring out the window of his cell at the banged-up shell of the Hammerhead sitting in the impound lot. He rolled off the bunk and landed on his feet. Three officers, none he recognized. They were wary but professsional.

Jay held out his hands for the cuffs. The floors were newly polished old wood, the molding thick and shiny. They walked him to a small room at the end of the hall, sat him in a plastic chair and locked his cuffs to a ring on the table. The door slammed behind them.

The room table had a fresh coat of paint, but the same close smell he remembered from his last interrogation. A blank sheet of glass filled one wall. Jay waved to it, and waited in the dull silence until the door opened.

Leo Zelazko favored his left leg, moving stiffly to hide the pain. His uniform shirt crisp, pants creased. He wore a foam neck brace like a foreskin around his collar. The hollows beneath his eyes were shaded gray, the point of his nose rashed from the air bags.

He slapped his steel revolver on the metal tabletop. Pits of rust freckled the barrel and the cutouts in the cylinder.

"That was a good move," Leo said. "Better than I expected from you."

"Played a lot of chess inside."

"I bet you feel at home with your king in jeopardy," Leo said. "Because this game you're playing, it's slow-motion suicide. You've forced my hand. I have retrieved my property, but if you want to walk out of here, I need something else."

Jay smirked. "A blow job?"

"Let's not dance around it, Joshua. We searched your phone. It's clean, but I subpoenaed Tony Giambotta's phone records. He received a photo message that day." Leo reached back and rapped on the door. "Send him in."

263

The door cracked open. Officer Algieri guided Tony through the door. Tony hunched beneath the guiding hand on his shoulder, eyes darting.

"Sit, Anthony," Leo said. He turned and looked at Officer Algieri until he left and closed the door silently behind him.

Tony sat and folded his hands on the desk. His work shirt was dark at the armpits.

"Your phone's with our forensics geek," Leo said. "But why don't you tell me what you did with the photo Jay sent you."

Tony blinked at his folded hands.

Leo sighed and took the revolver. Flipped open the cylinder to six empty chambers.

"I don't know what you're talking about, Officer Zee."

"Don't tell him shit," Jay said. "You ain't under arrest. He's trying to scare you into giving him something."

"This isn't questioning, per se." Leo took a .38 wadcutter from his belt and inserted it into the chamber.

"I don't have it, Mister Zee. You gotta believe me." Tony fluttered his eyelids.

"Anthony, you never could lie." Leo turned the cylinder so the loaded chamber was one turn counterclockwise from the hammer, and snapped it shut.

"Quit jerking that gun off," Jay said. "You ain't shooting nobody."

Leo cocked the hammer and trained the barrel on Jay's chest. The thin line of his mouth curled at the corners.

"Tell him," Tony said. "Tell him, pallie." He wiped the sheen of sweat from his forehead back into his hair.

A fist knocked on the door. Leo held the revolver under the table. "Yes?"

Officer Algieri opened the door, shuffling from foot to foot like a kid who had to pee.

"Well? Out with it."

"The phone's clean, sir. Chen says there's no outgoing messages, and the card's wiped."

Leo stared until the door snapped closed.

"What did you do, Anthony?" Leo rested the revolver on the table. "I commend you on your discipline, turning all that lard to muscle. But you're not too big to hang out the window."

Tony looked away, his face flushing red.

"Leo," Jay said. "You ought to wear that neck pillow all the time, so folks know what kind of dickhead they're dealing with."

Tony blinked at him.

"Relax, Tone. Leo's a smart man. He's gonna let you go, and release me on my own recognizance." Jay leaned across the table and folded his hands. "How long you been holding me? See, I don't understand this computer shit, but Tony does. And if I don't go to the internet every couple days? That photo of you and the trucker goes all over the place."

Leo furrowed his eyebrows, and studied Tony.

Tony wobbled his chin in quick little nods.

"It goes to some folks you know," Jay said, "and some you don't. Local teevee stations, newspaper men. The Essex County Sheriff. The national police chiefs' association. Tony may be a scaredy-cat, but he's also one shrewd son of a bitch."

Leo stared into Jay's eyes. "I've broken him before."

"That's the best part," Jay said. He smiled, licked a newly chipped tooth. "Tony can't stop it. Only I can. Think you can break me?"

Leo ran his thumb over the checkered steel of the gun's hammer.

Jay met Leo's stare with dead eyes. "Tell me I'm lying."

Leo flared his nostrils with each breath. Tony squeezed his hands together as if arm-wrestling himself.

A snap like tiny animal bones broke the silence. Leo squeezed the trigger and eased the hammer down. He reached back and slapped the door three times.

Algieri appeared.

Leo gestured to Tony with the revolver. "Get this sweaty pig out of my sight."

Tony gulped air and rushed toward the door.

"You did good, pallie," Jay called. The door slammed behind him.

"You're not threatening me with anything I haven't faced off before," Leo said. "Joseph said his dog chased someone off his property last night. Then we find you with a chunk missing. It doesn't take a genius to figure it out. If you're set on killing him, none of your threats will force my hand."

"You trying to cut a deal? Because we ain't gonna be allies, not even for a minute."

"What does it take to get rid of you?"

"Tell the truth about Joey," Jay said.

"Never going to happen. Not while I'm alive, or Mayor Bello is."

"That there's the other thing that'll send me on my way," Jay said. "You two in your graves. Remember, you got until five p.m. to spring me or the photos fly."

"I can't let you walk," Leo said, tapping the desk with the butt of the revolver. "There are appearances to be maintained."

"Give me my phone call," Jay said. "I may be 'swamp trash,' but I do have a lawyer."

Leo drew in his cheeks as he thought on it. "Children have no idea what their parents do for them," he said. "What we go through."

"You hate what you are so much, you wouldn't stand up to the man whose kid tortured your son."

"Brendan was weak," Leo said. "A beating now and then, that's something you have to take if you're going to walk this world and call yourself a man. If my boy had the strength to keep his nature secret, today Joey Bello would be a fat turd working for the water department, like the useless son of any other politician."

"If you'd stood up for your boy—"

"Little Joey was a saint compared to his old man," Leo said. "You were supposed to stick a number two pencil in Joey's eye, but you got distracted by finger-banging that high-breasted Crane slut behind the pool clubhouse."

Jay ran the cuff chain through the eyehook on the desk.

"Yes, I knew about that. Not much happens in this town I don't." Leo said. "Pussy makes you weak."

"That why you prefer random trucker dick?"

"I'm no faggot," Leo laughed. "Didn't you read any history in prison? Spartan warriors only took wives to make children. They were iron men, who worshipped manhood. Their women had to dress and cut their hair like men to get their dicks hard. The bitches slept on the floor with the dogs."

Jay arched an eyebrow. "So you're a warrior, not some punk who can't admit he loves the brown-eye? I got a sister with ten times the heart as you. Did her time pre-op. She told me all about self-hating guys like you."

"I doubt that," Leo said.

"First you go for suck jobs," Jay said. "Then you pitch. Maybe give 'em a reach-around, and say it's the heat of the moment. But soon you want a little taste, to see what it's like."

Leo blinked slowly.

"She said those guys sucked her cock better than anyone," Jay said. "Their eyes rolled back while they choked on the damn thing. Called it 'stick pussy.' She had to be real careful not to call 'em gay though, or they'd beat her worse than any fag-bashing son of a bitch ever did. So tell me, Leo. That why you got a mouth like a chicken's ass? From sucking stick pussy?"

"Oh, Joshua," Leo said. "That is your birth name, by the way. Do you know the irony in hearing that come from you?"

"My folks called me Jay. That's good enough for me."

Leo laughed. "Those people aren't your real parents."

"They are to me."

"You nicely evaded the question, but that's fine for now. I'm tired of toying with you, and with your real father dead, his secrets are fair game. It took them a while to ID the body. What was left of it, anyway. They're keeping Mr. Strick on ice until they notify Matthew. His other son." Leo raised the gun. "You should've shot him with this, but I imagine you were saving it for Bello."

"That's a good story, from the man with the real reason to kill them."

"It would have been a good play, if you'd managed to pull it off. But answer me, because I want to know. How does it feel to kill your own father?"

Jay's eyes floated left. He dragged them back to center.

"So you knew," Leo said. "It makes sense, knowing your history. You know your past, but you're afraid to believe it. I could see the ache in your eyes ever since you were a boy. The things inflicted on you, no child should endure."

"Like Brendan?"

"Brendan had it easy," Leo snapped. "It's not like his own father threatened to hang him with his belt. Or cut off his balls and toss them in the furnace."

"That's—"

"You want to know where you came from? Shut up and listen," Leo said. "I've been holding this for thirty years, and I'm only telling it once."

Jay clenched his teeth and released a long sigh. He leaned back as far as the chain would allow.

"Your father was a charming prick, at least women seemed to think so. Strick the prick." He smiled. "But he was weak. A gash hound. Your mother was a typist at an oil company. Seventeen, a real beauty. Not the bottle blonde bitch you call mother, her little sister."

Jay frowned.

"Her name was Joyce Anne Calvin. Religious girl. Strick said the first time he put moves on her, she said she was saving herself for marriage. He took it as a challenge. And sure enough, once he stuck it in, that's all she wanted. He sneak-fucked her every time he could, and eventually knocked her up. That was her lie to herself, that if he married her, it would wash her sins away. It's all in her letters. He tried to buy her off, but her parents weren't poor white trash like you. They expected him to do the right thing.

"Now, the right thing would've been to have it taken care of, but she was in love. Thought he'd change his mind once he saw his beautiful baby boy. When she found out he was already married, she went off the deep end. Ran away from home, got strung out on heroin by some animal. Her parents put her in rehab and got her older sister out of jail to raise you. The one you call Mother."

Jay furrowed his brow in thought.

"She and her common-law husband Andre were small-time grifters, the black sheep of the family. They raised you until you were five years old, when your mother supposedly found Jesus again and got clean. But your aunt and uncle, they didn't want to give you back. So your grandparents had them locked up, and handed you back to your mother. You remember any of this?"

Jay licked his dry lips. The memory of the Witch stealing him from Mama's Jeep faded into storybook colors.

"She didn't stay clean for long. Threatened to come knocking on Strick's door, so he had his lawyer cut her a check. When the money ran out, she started selling her pussy. And when no one wanted to fuck a used-up junkie whore, she started selling you."

Leo bored his golden eyes into Jay's. "We both know what happened next. You killed her, like you killed your father."

Jay swallowed dry.

"The report says she fell asleep smoking and burned in her trailer. But I spoke to the coroner," Leo said. "She suffered over a hundred stab wounds, all in the face. Her eyes were gouged out. Not that she didn't deserve it."

269

Jay studied the scar lines across his knuckles.

"Your aunt and uncle, the people you call your parents, they found you. And they smelled money. They came here to put the squeeze on Strick, and he asked me for help. So I put out feelers, greased a few wheels, and figured out your story."

Jay parted his lips, and Leo cut him off.

"I hoped you'd beat Joey so badly he'd never bother my son again, but the demented little shit knew better than to hurt you."

The struggle to comprehend his past played across Jay's face. Pinballs with human faces careened off each other inside his head.

"It's a pity you and Matthew hate each other. If you worked together, you could have driven us all to suicide long ago. Like poor Stanley." Leo crinkled his eyes at the edges. "What bullshit. My guess is, you stuck the gun in his eye. You have a thing for eyes. Because they see what you did as a little boy, as your mother's whore."

Jay rested his eyes on the revolver. Willed it to go off and blast his brains out.

"Tell me, Joshua. When you're done with us, will you hunt down all the creatures who fucked you? I hope you will," Leo said, and holstered the weapon. "I have leads. They're a quarter century old, but they may help."

The scratches in the scarred tabletop swirled beneath Jay's eyes.

Leo stood and smoothed his slacks. "I'll trade them, and your birth certificate, on your word that the photo is destroyed. And if you break your word, Tony will pay for it. Forever."

The door slammed and Jay's head hit the table like a sixteen-pound sledge.

CHAPTER 37

After the riot cooled out, the prison stayed on lockdown for months.

Verdad took over the prison hooch operation and paid back the Heimdall Brotherhood for what they'd done to his woman. Okie's crew would be well rewarded for their part in firing the riot to cover it all. Jay would get protection against the Brotherhood, and Cheetah got access to a Latin King lawyer who could get his sentence cut. Mack's wife was given a job at the Wayne DMV. And once lockdown was over, Okie had been promised a visit from a busty female in a private cell. The guards who'd won big on the fixed fight would take care of it.

"All us outlaws are titty babies, missing our mama's milk. Just wanna feel a pair of warm titties again," Okie said, one cell over. "That or some of them meat pies they make in Louisiana. Could go for a whole sack of those."

Jay concurred. As a kid, they knew a gal from Natchitoches who made those crunchy pockets of delight by the batch. "You like tits so much, how come I'm celling with Peaches instead of you?"

"Aw hell, kid," Okie laughed. "The only time that one don't talk is when she's got a ramrod in her mouth, and mine's dead as Dillinger."

"I'm right here," Rene said, filing her nails with auto shop sandpaper. "*Viejo chingón.*"

"I can't figure you out, Oke." Jay laughed. "You teach me to be careful, and you raise nine kinds of hell every chance you get."

"I'm an enigma wrapped in a riddle, a regular Natchitoches meat pie of mystery," Okie said. "Don't worry about what goes

271

on in my head, the shrinks been trying to figure me out since before you were born."

They slapped hands through the bars and dreamed of their spoils like kings on Shit Mountain.

In the middle of the night, the hacks came in full riot gear. They charged Okie's cell with batons and pepper spray. Jay swore through the bars as they dragged Okie away. They came back and gave Jay the same.

The hacks dragged him past the infirmary by ankle chains and threw him on the slick green tiles of the morgue. Two stainless steel tables stood bolted to the floor, a drain on the floor between them. Cheetah sat cuffed to a table leg, hunched and shivering. The hacks locked Jay's ankle chain to the other table.

Cheetah's face glowed with sweat. Eyes red from the pepper spray. Cheeks swollen from blows. "We go down fighting," he whispered. The hardness settled behind his eyes.

Jay pushed his fear down deep, to stoke the hate-fires.

The doors slammed open and the hacks tossed Okie to the floor like a blood-streaked scarecrow. He pushed himself up with smashed fingers. Groaned through a bloody mouthful of jagged teeth. Eyes swollen to slits, cheeks ragged, showing bone.

Jay howled and leaped for him. The chain jerked him back like a dog on a short lead.

The four hacks parted to let Warden Jeffers through, red-faced to the top of his bald spot. Sweat dripped from his mustache, and blood from the knuckle dusters on his hands.

Okie rolled to his knees and held out his busted fists in defiance.

The crack of metal on Okie's cheekbone hit Jay like a bullwhip. The warden beat Okie's face until he splayed on the floor, the stomped toes of his bare feet twitching with every wallop.

"This is what happens," the Warden wheezed, spat. "This is

what happens, when you get one of my men hurt. You tell every piece of shit, they shank a guard, we'll arrest their women in the parking lot, throw her in holding with a fucking nigger rapist with AIDS. You hear me?"

Okie pushed himself to one knee with one wobbly arm. An eye lolled out on his torn cheek, his face a ruined mass of tongue, teeth and bone. Hot tears burned Jay's cheeks. The shackles cut into his ankles as he crawled toward his mentor, palms squeaking against the tiles.

Okie dragged himself toward the warden on his elbows, pulling his dead legs behind. He lifted one middle finger, shaking with the effort. Gurgled two unmistakable syllables.

The clubs rained down. A big hack fell on him with two-handed swings, mashing him into the tiles. Breath fogged their riot masks before they quit.

The last Jay saw of his prison-father was the smear of blood on the tiles as they hauled the mess of Leroy "Okie" Kincaid's body to the meat locker. He spent five years in solitary until warden Jeffers retired. Cheetah's lawyer cycled him out as promised, and Rene soon after. Verdad sneaked him books to keep him sane. Jay still wondered if they had worked or not.

Weariness dragged down Martins' thick jaw. The sickly light gave his skin green patina, like a bronze statue of an Israeli general. "Thought you said you planned on living well."

"What, this ain't farting through silk?"

Martins told him he'd been charged with property damage and reckless driving, but would be released on his own recognizance.

"Don't know when I can pay you," Jay said. "But I will."

"It's been taken care of."

"By?"

"You know." He raised his eyebrows conspiratorially.

"Give her my thanks."

* * *

The Challenger glared at him from the impound lot with busted headlights. The front fenders were bent into a sneer. A giant snowflake where Jay's head hit the windshield. River stink wafted from the front tires, and an earthy rankness rode the breeze beneath it.

He opened the door and found a fresh link of human turd on the seat.

Bobby Algieri grinned from across the lot.

Jay limped to the trunk. The lock had been drilled out, his toolbox rifled. He found a scrap of plastic trash bag and picked the mess off the seat.

He turned the key and the engine kicked to life. The fan clattered against the housing. He killed it, tried to yank the hood open, but it wouldn't budge. He called Tony's shop for a tow, called Herschel for a ride. The call to Hersch went to voice mail. He was about to start walking when the Blue Aston Martin rolled to the gates. Ramona at the wheel, her blouse cut low. Jay heard Algieri gasp from across the impound lot.

"Matt would like his Gallardo back," Ramona sad. "I wish you'd come to me before embarking on your vendetta."

"I want my father back," Jay said. "That's not happening either." He told her about Matt's videos, and what he'd said about her using him.

"That slimy shit. I'll turn the security system off when I get home," she said, and swerved down a mountain road. "You need a hot shower, real bad."

"I got nowhere to sleep, I could use a bed is all."

"Matt's been staying in our apartment in the city," she said. "And if he's spying on me again, he can stay there awhile."

"Is he worth it?"

Ramona sighed. "What do you think, your magic cock's

going to make me divorce my husband? I love him, Jay."

Jay flinched and stared into the trees flying by the window.

She eased to a stop at the entrance to their private drive. "Look at me, Bluejay."

Jay locked eyes with her.

"I loved you, too." Her eyes were hidden behind her shades. "I still do, but...not that way. We had our time, and it's not going to happen. Not like we wanted."

"That bird's flown, huh?"

"Shut up a minute," she said, and rested her head on the steering wheel. "Don't act like you conquered me. That makes it a pity fuck. Do you think I'd do that to you?"

"No."

"We have something. There's a bond there, one there aren't words for. Sometimes it feels like love, but that's not what it is. It's not love, and if you try to make it into something it's not, it'll be over."

He rested his swollen cheekbone against her shoulder.

She washed him with care in the master bathroom, a mausoleum of black marble veined with white and roiling with steam. He rose despite the aches in every joint and bone. She pressed her rump into his lap and he soaped her from thighs to breasts, weighing them in his hands, thumbing the broad pink circles to a deep red.

She shivered and craned her neck to bite his ear as his head lolled on her shoulder. The slick heat of her sex and the warmth of her silken skin felt plastic and distant, like someone else's dream. She drummed his lap with urgent bounces until he hunched in reflexive release.

She toweled him dry and led him to a guest room where another of Andre's dark hardwood beds was stowed, ornate with hand-tooled detail. Everyone had his father's work except him.

Jay collapsed into the sheets. She cradled his head to her chest, but sleep had already taken him.

A chill wind cut over the trestle and pimpled Ramona's perfect skin with gooseflesh. Jay knelt in mute supplication, breathing her scent in deep. It fuzzed through his brain like a drug. She gripped his hair, guiding him until she threw her head back, her mouth a silent rictus of pleasure.

Jay stared with empty eyes.

Ramona knelt and plunged her hand into his jeans. "This is mine."

A silent nod as she clutched him to her chest, working until he shuddered and buried his face between her breasts. The darkness and warmth smothered the insane crash of the world, her heartbeat the pounding surf of the primordial womb, and he fell asleep.

A muted thrum rocked the boy awake to the stink of sulfur.

Watch me, the Witch rasped. *It's just like a kiss.*

A big hand with grease embedded in the knuckles gripped the Witch by the hair, pushing her face against the boy.

A jolt down the boy's spine. His gumbo scars flared red.

Mmm. Don't it feel good? Now you try.

The boy ran for the door, but they dragged him back. Three cigarette burns later, he did what they taught him to do.

Jay woke with a roar and strained at the silk ties knotting his wrists and ankles to the bedposts of the guest room. The scars burned like fresh embers on his belly.

"It's all right Bluejay, it's all right," Ramona cooed, and took him back in her mouth.

The bed beams creaked with his struggles. "Don't," he groaned.

"I need this," she said, cooling his flesh with an exhale. "And so do you. Let me do this for you. The woman who hurt you is gone. Look in my eyes. Look, Bluejay. There's power in this." Her nails raked his chest, cobalt blues boring through his storm-steel eyes as she took what she wanted.

"Please," he said, through gritted teeth. "Stop."

She paused. "Most men enjoy this because they think *they're* in the position of power, but they're not. Let go, Bluejay. Give me control. I'll drive her away forever. She can't hurt you anymore."

The bonds swelled Jay's fists purple, as her soothing murmurs reverberated through his flesh. Her pursed lips cracked and her face drew thin, needle marks pocked their way down her pale arms, and her eyes burst forth with writhing maggots.

Jay bowed his spine and bunched every muscle. The left bedpost bent with a crack.

Ramona rose with a gasp. "I'm trying to help you!"

The post splintered at the base. The boy swung it like a cudgel.

Ramona yelped and kicked herself off the bed.

"She was my mother!" Jay clawed at the striped silk tie knotted around his other wrist. He roared and clubbed the second bedpost until it snapped. "I stabbed her face into chop-meat."

Ramona grabbed a robe and ran for the door as he pounded the bed to flinders.

"Now you know," Jay shouted. "That what you wanted?"

He gathered his filthy clothes and stalked naked down the hallway.

Erin cut him off at the kitchen, waving the tip of a Damascus chef knife. "You get on, now."

"What I should've done in the first place," Jay said, and pulled his shirt over his head as he walked. He turned at the door. "This place is an asylum."

"She thought she could heal you. I tried to warn her," Erin said, with a jab of the knife. "She wanted closure."

Jay slammed the door and gave it to her.

CHAPTER 38

Tony had been angry but seemed satisfied when Jay said how Ramona left him feeling like a gutted fish. "Told you she was fucked up," the big man said, and went back to banging on the Challenger.

Jay sipped Tony's shitty coffee from a Styrofoam cup and flipped through the day's newspaper.

Governor offends teachers with remark. Congress deadlocked over spending. Nude motorcyclist identified as former real estate magnate.

He read that one. Police hadn't ruled out foul play, but the odd circumstances of Strick's death were attributed to his blood alcohol level and his crumbled business empire. His family could not be reached for comment.

Either the cops missed the bullet or were keeping it to themselves.

Jay thought on what Matt had said about his father—their father—and thirteen-year-old Ramona. No wonder Matt hated Jay and his father in his bones.

There'd been times Jay had prayed for a brother. Unanswered whispers in the dark, to a deaf-and-blind Lord who'd abandoned him to the Witch and all her minions. He'd had one, all this time. One who'd preferred to let him rot in prison than admit they shared blood. Who had lied under oath to put him there.

Was there a plan to kill Joey Bello?

No, sir. Jay said "that boy needs killing." He said it all the time. We stopped taking him seriously. My father said that's just how those people talk.

Jay called him a liar and the bailiffs dragged him out of the courtroom.

The obituary listed one viewing for Matthew Henry Strick, Sr. Jay tore it out of the paper and tucked it into his pocket. The hole it made revealed another headline.

Newark Cabbie Robbed and Murdered.

Unidentified black male, age thirty to thirty-five. Shot twice in the back of the head at close range. Found in his black and white taxi on a service road by the airport. Detective Billy Zelazko said he'd been executed with a .38 caliber weapon loaded with hollow points.

Jay thumbed at his phone. Herschel's number rang and rang. He was about to click off when a voice answered, "Hello?"

"Hersch?"

A woman's voice. "Who is this?"

"Jay. I just—"

"You've got a lot of nerve, calling."

"Listen, ma'am, I'm—"

"You've hurt us enough, you crazy white motherfucker. Don't call here again."

He tried again, but it went straight to voice mail. Jay sank in the chair and contemplated the depths of Leo's self-hatred. Would he kill an innocent man to keep his secret?

If Jay had gotten Herschel killed, he thought he might hate himself as much.

At the funeral home, a line queued out the door for the fallen patriarch of the Strick family. Former business partners, home-owners. Women freckled with sunspots and lined with smoker's wrinkles. Their expressions telling whether they came to pay their respects or to confirm the man's demise.

Jay collected dirty glances as he skipped the line. He brushed past the chunky usher at the door. "I'm family."

A crowd filled the viewing room. Curt nods, eyebrows

perked in sympathy as friends caught up and smiled in the corners. The furrowed brows of those eager to curry favor with Strick the younger. The chatter faded into hushed whispers when Jay walked down the center aisle toward the stately casket.

The family sat in front on burgundy armchairs. Ramona's mother a prim and plastic statue, her dad a silver-haired smiler. Ramona on Matthew's left, his mother on his right. Their daughter, Saoirse, a deer in the headlights. The wood of the armchair creaked beneath Matthew's clenched fists.

Jay knelt before the closed oak box, his face distorted in the gleaming lacquer. He placed a hand on the cold brass furniture. Confusion twisted in his brain like a headless rattlesnake. Hate for the man who'd abandoned him, and raw sorrow for closing the door to a past he never knew existed. He folded his hands, closed his eyes, and thought of what to say to a God who had never listened to his pleas and prayers.

I live in spite of the cold son of a bitch, Okie had laughed. Jay had never given God much thought. The Witch said He was always watching, planting an image in his young brain of God as the giant atop the beanstalk, fathomless in both size and enormity, a complicit observer in the world's pain.

This old man sowed what he reaped, Jay prayed. *I know you got the same in store for me. Until that day comes, you stay out of my way and I'll stay out of yours.*

Jay held still a moment to see his words off into the void. He stood and turned to a silent room watching him like a magnificent and deadly creature that had stepped out of its cage.

Ramona held her face neutral and stroked her daughter's hand. Matthew twisted a handkerchief in his lap and bored through Jay's belly with red-shot eyes.

"I'm sorry for your loss," Jay said.

"Jay," Ramona said. "Please don't." Saoirse leaned to whisper to her, and she patted the back of her hand.

Matthew swallowed. "I thought you'd be decent enough to

leave me to my pain," he said. "You're not wanted here."

"I belong here at least half as much as you do."

"You destroyed my family," Matthew said through gritted teeth.

"Thought I *was* family."

Matthew's mother stared ice. "This isn't the time or the place to air dirty laundry."

"I ain't no pair of dirty drawers," Jay said. "You both knew, all these years. And you let me rot in there. Didn't lift a finger."

Ramona's eyes registered confusion. "What are you talking about?"

The crowd murmured and stretched to watch.

"Someone get him out of here," Matthew said, wiping his brow.

Brush Cut appeared on Jay's right and clenched his wrist in an arm lock. Jay's shoulder burned. "I'm going. Unless you want a scene, let me walk."

The guard eased his grip.

"Please," Ramona said, "Just go."

Jay bent toward Matthew. "You might want to have 'em do an autopsy. Been digging around, and I think Leo Zee might've punched his ticket."

"Please leave."

"My *real* father's been dead five years now. So forgive me if I'm not so sorry for your loss," Jay said. "*Brother.*"

Matthew tackled him around the waist with a ragged scream. They tumbled into the coffin, thunking off the wood. The room spun and Jay's stomach churned. He guarded his face as bony fists rained down.

"You're not my brother, you white trash piece of shit!"

The guards pulled Matthew toward the hall, his mother following with a prescription bottle. Jay stood and brushed himself off. Ramona clung to Saoirse. The little girl stared at the wolf who walked out of her fairy tale book.

Jay shouldered through a crowd of gasping faces blanked with fear and wrenched with disgust until he crashed through the storm door into the parking lot.

CHAPTER 39

Jay crashed on Tony's recliner, and woke to an empty house. He found a note scribbled on the pizza box saying Tony had left to open the shop. He took a long shower, hot and cold. The only towel smelled of garlic. He looked for a fresh one and found the bedroom door locked. He left wet footprints through the hallways until he found a scratchy towel in the pantry. Looked at the mess in the bathroom mirror and washed down a jumble of painkillers with an energy drink from the fridge.

Over the days, the curtain of pain slowly lifted from his world. He worked on the Challenger between jobs until it resembled a battered, beloved toy a child kept digging out of the trash can.

Tony walked over, holding a tightly wrapped sub sandwich like a policeman's baton. "Roast beef and mozz," he said. "From Cavallo's."

Jay unscrewed the dent puller from the sheet metal. "Got my hot cherry peppers?"

"Of course," Tony said. "I got a fiberglass hood we can slap on. Some fucker keyed it at the ShopRite. Nicky, I bet."

"I paid him back for you. Gave him four flat tires, and beat his ass blue."

Tony grinned and took a bite of his own sandwich.

A white van rolled onto the curb. Jay hefted the dent puller, ready to whip the screw-tip end.

A woman in a tan pantsuit stepped out of the passenger's side and walked to the back of the van.

Tony frowned while he chewed.

The woman walked backward toward them on the sidewalk, followed by a man in khakis shouldering a camera rig.

"I bet it's those 'Shame on You' people," Tony said. "That Beemer jerkoff." As the newswoman approached, Tony puffed up and folded his arms, trying to look tough. Jay thought it looked like he was squeezing out a shit.

The woman stuck the microphone in Jay's face. "This is Jay Desmarteaux, the Nutley axe murderer. It's been twenty-five years since you went Lizzie Borden on your classmate. Why did you return to the scene of the crime?"

Jay wiped his hands with a shop rag. "This is where I grew up."

"Hey, he did his time. Leave him alone."

"Are you Tony Giambotta? What possessed you to employ a violent criminal in a neighborhood full of children?"

"This is private property. You're trespassing." Tony reached for the camera lens, but the cameraman sidestepped, centering on Jay.

The newswoman circled him. "Is it true you've been frequenting a Newark strip club alleged to be owned by organized crime figures?"

Jay pointed at the cars. "I'm a mechanic. Just trying to make a living."

"Some are saying that the family of your victim has been denied justice. What do you say to that?"

"This is old news. I'll give you something fresh." He twisted the microphone out of her hand.

Jay stared into the camera's squid-like eye. "Joey Bello was a no-good rapist son of a bitch, and he needed killing."

"Cut the mike!"

"The cops and his father covered it up. You want to hear all about it, I'll be at our high school reunion this weekend."

Jay tossed the microphone and she caught it.

She mouthed *asshole* before the cameraman cut back to her. "As you can see, prison has not calmed the demeanor of the man convicted of what is perhaps New Jersey's most brutal killing in recent memory."

285

"Who's paying you, Mayor Bello or Matty Strick?" Jay said. He tucked the shop rag in his back pocket and walked back to the shop.

Later, he and Tony watched themselves on television.

"Convicted killer Jay Desmarteaux now works at a local auto repair shop, not far from where the vicious axe murder occurred. The effects of the murder still haunt the town..."

A loud beeping drowned out her words. The camera jerked to catch Tony hooking the wrecker to the news van.

"What do you think you're doing?" the newswoman screamed.

Tony hopped out of the tow truck and worked the levers to raise the bed. "You're parked on private property."

"Are you crazy?"

Tony grinned and lowered the forks under the van's chassis.

She slapped on the side of the van. "Brad, get your ass behind the wheel!"

Jay chuckled. "I swore they would've bleeped that."

The news cut back to the studio, where the perfectly coiffed anchorman nodded gravely. "A frightening scene at a local mechanic's garage." A laxative commercial came on, and Tony muted the television.

"They say there's no such thing as bad publicity," Jay said, and clinked his Rolling Rock bottle with Tony's.

Tony went to his mother's for dinner. Jay walked behind the shop with Andre's tomahawk. Rusted old wrecks lined the edge of the property, from a '56 Chrysler with a sumac tree growing through the empty engine bay, to a curvy-hipped brown Monte Carlo with the windows smashed out. Jay walked twenty paces from a thick maple stump. He took a slug from the bottle, and let fly with the axe. It sank deep into the wood. He repeated the ritual until the beer went warm.

A horn beeped out front.

The blue Aston Martin purred quietly, blocking in the Challenger. The tinted windows slipped down like pools of black oil. Ramona stared at him over the wheel.

Jay tipped back the dregs of his beer and tossed the bottle into the trash.

"Why didn't you tell me you and Matthew were half-brothers?"

"I found out a little before you did," Jay said. "Talk to hubby."

"He says it's none of my business," she sighed. "The bastard."

"That's me, technically." Jay folded his arms, muscles striped with grease like war paint.

"Will you come here? I'm sorry."

"We're all sorry," Jay said. "Poor little rich girl. Get along now. You had your fun."

"Quit being a dick," she said. "I thought it would be therapeutic. I wanted to help you."

"You can't fix me," Jay said. "Told you that."

She backed out and turned in so she faced him. "You're not any more broken than the rest of us."

"I know that now. Hell, I'm starting to feel like the most normal of the bunch. You saw what you wanted, and you took it. That's how y'all are."

She narrowed her eyes. "I said sorry. In the car, the first time, it felt like when we were kids. Like we could take on the world. Did you feel it? I wanted to give that to you."

Jay chewed his lip. "Reunion's this weekend," he said. "Go with me."

Ramona winced and shivered as if swallowing bitter brew. She pulled it into a tight grin. "Why in the world would I want to do that?"

"Closure," Jay said. "Thought you needed it."

"Some business is best left unfinished. Don't you want to hear what I came here for? It changes everything."

Jay climbed into the car.

They ate falafel and shawarma in Jersey City on a bench by the water. She wore jeans and a blue top under a short black leather jacket, some designer's take on the patched punk jackets of old.

"How does it feel to be comfortably well-off?" she said, and wiped her corner of her mouth with a wad of napkin.

"Matt's not gonna fight me over it? That doesn't sound like him."

"You're in Strick's will," she said. "It's decades old. There's nothing to contest."

"He'll find something."

"Not without my help."

They walked the piers while sailboats cut the bay in the twilight. "Is it true about you and his father?"

She clenched his hand. "You're not gonna get all weird on me, are you? That was a long time ago."

"I would've done him like I did your uncle if you'd told me."

"I know you would've," she said. "I didn't want you to."

"But you were—"

"It was a transaction," she said. "I got what I wanted, and he got what he wanted. Think of him as an ex-boyfriend who showed me the ropes."

"He wasn't no boy."

"You're talking about someone who died naked on a motorcycle," Ramona said. "He was always a boy. I know it was wrong, and I don't absolve him of responsibility. I'm just not into seeing myself as a victim."

No, she wouldn't admit that, Jay thought. No matter how true it had been.

"I'm guessing you never left him alone with your daughter."

Ramona smirked. "Of course not."

She walked ahead, turned around. "He took advantage of a precocious and overdeveloped young girl who wanted to feel like a grown-up."

"What's that feel like? Being grown up."

"I guess you don't know, do you?" She said. "I used to think I did."

"Come to the reunion with me," he said.

"Jay."

"I'm gonna tell the truth about Bello," Jay said. "Might need counsel handy."

"One thing I've learned from court," she said, "is that each person builds their own truth. From what they've heard, or seen, or believed from the beginning. Whoever controls the narrative decides what that truth is. And this one was written long ago. You won't change anything."

"They're gonna have to hear it anyway."

They held hands and watched black waves lap the spangled battleship of Manhattan.

Ramona dropped him off up the block to avoid Tony. Her engine buzzed down the highway as she rocketed away from her past.

A dim light burned in the shop, and the Hulk truck sat in the driveway. A cigarette flared by the Coke machine. Jay caught a face ghost-lit in the glow of a phone. He slipped into the shadows and padded behind the Hammerhead.

Randal's black Cadillac Tonka truck was parked around the corner.

Jay eased the Hammerhead's door open and released the compartment. Took what he needed and crept close to peek in the windows at the back of the shop.

Tony lay crucified on a work table, his face swollen and

distorted by a mouthful of dirty shop rag. Shirt torn open, chest striped with cuts. One of the skinny-leg gym rats held the Conan the Barbarian sword from Tony's office wall, and jabbed Tony in the crotch with it. Randal waved him away. He rolled the battery charger closer and clamped a jumper cable to Tony's left tit.

Gym boy tugged down Tony's sweatpants and reached in with the other clamp. Randal turned the knob of the trickle charger. Tony arched and rattled the work table with his throes.

Jay hugged the wall and followed the smell of mentholated smoke.

The stocky lookout spat on the ground and frowned at his cigarette. He blinked at the glint of moonlight off the tomahawk right before Jay cleaved his neck to the breastbone. Hot blood splashed Jay's face and the man collapsed gurgling.

Blood and breath steamed as Jay hunkered down for three more hard chops.

A squeak of brakes as a Cherokee rolled to the curb. Jay reared up with the axe.

"Freeze, asshole!" Billy cleared the distance, Glock aimed in isosceles stance.

Jay held up his hands, a slash of blood across his face. "This ain't what it looks like."

Billy drew a bead on Jay's chest. "Jesus." He wrinkled his nose and coughed into his shoulder.

"Keep it down," Jay said. "The hitters are here. They got Tony inside hooked to a car battery."

Billy pressed his face to the greasy glass, keeping the pistol on Jay. "Let me get backup." He reached for his phone and stepped away from the building.

Jay didn't wait.

The door creaked open to Tony's howls. The thick scent of oil and grease was tanged sharp with blood and piss. A blue Shelby Mustang convertible sat on the lift.

"Give him up, asshole," Randal said, and killed the juice from the battery charger.

Tony slumped to the table and gasped a "Fuck you."

Randal punched him in the nose. "You sure it's hooked to his balls?" He scratched at his stitched ear.

"You wanna check it, go ahead," gym boy said.

Randal held Tony's phone. "All you gotta do is call him."

"I'm right here, shitbirds." Jay's teeth flashed in the dark. He held the lookout's severed head by the jaw. "So's your friend."

Their jaws dropped.

Jay tossed the head underhand, landing it on the work bench. Gym boy shrieked at his dead friend's mangled face.

Jay hurled the tomahawk and charged. The blade bit into Randal's shoulder and clattered off a tool chest. Randal swore and ducked, clutching his wound. He flipped the switch and Tony bent backwards with a scream.

Gym boy pawed among the aerosol cans for a pistol.

"Drop the weapon!" Billy fired and sent an aerosol can spinning off the table.

Jay juked right and drew Andre's knife from his boot while Billy and the gym rat traded fire.

Tony bent in half, sweatpants dark with piss. Jay let Randal get away, and yanked the charger's plug out of the wall socket. Tony collapsed. "You okay, buddy?"

Randal swiped with a jack handle.

The metal caught Jay across the shoulders and sent him tumbling to his knees. Andre's knife clattered to the floor. He scrambled after it under a work table. Randal bowed the table in half with an overhead swing.

Randal flipped the table with one paw and cocked back to swat. Jay leaped to tackle and hit Randal's legs like a wall. Randal laughed and stabbed at Jay's back with sharp drops of the jack handle.

Billy ducked behind a Honda. The gym rat shattered its windows with panic fire.

Jay shouldered Randal in the groin and sent him stumbling backward beneath the Mustang on the lift. Randal cracked his head on the exhaust pipes and swung the jack handle wide. The edge of the metal tore open Jay's scalp. Blood in his eyes. Jay pressed his sleeve to it and wobbled to his knees.

Randal ducked under the Mustang and held the jack handle slugger style, smiling. "I'm gonna get made for killing you."

The hydraulic lift sank with the hiss of a dying serpent. Tony grimaced, holding the button down.

Randal swore and crouched to escape the descending Mustang. Jay gripped his ear and popped the stitches like a broken zipper. Randal screamed, jumped with the pain, and banged his skull on the car's underbody. He staggered and fell as the Mustang sank lower. The jack handle clattered to the floor.

When the gym rat locked back the slide on his pistol, Billy drilled him in the chest with a pair of double taps. The gun hit the floor and the gym rat followed.

Jay scrambled out from under the lift. Randal stared, dazed. He kicked to slide from beneath the car. Jay planted a boot on his face to halt him.

"No!" Randal screamed. "I'll pay—"

Jay stamped the words out. "Shut up and die, Randy."

Randal whimpered and tried to bench press a ton and a half of Detroit iron. Juiced muscles swelled for the challenge before his bones cracked with wet snaps. Blood strangled out his screams.

The Mustang wobbled on its springs as it came to rest.

Randal moved his mouth silently, painted black with blood.

"Aw Jesus." Billy retched into his sleeve.

Tony released the hydraulic lift button and limped toward them. One eye swollen shut, one arm flopping from the socket. His work boots scraped the floor.

Jay pressed a shop rag to the gash in his hair. "How you doing, pallie?"

THOMAS PLUCK

"What's it look like?" Tony winced at the shreds of bloody skin around his nipple, like he'd nursed a baby werewolf. "I think I got a strangulated testicle."

"Who are these guys?" Billy said, frowning at the bodies.

"Frankie Dell's boys."

Billy gave him a look. "And why do they want you dead?"

"Maybe Bello hired them. He tried before."

Tony sprayed a canister of compressed air until the can turned ice-cold, and stuck it in his pants. "Oh...that's better."

Jay dropped Andre's war tools on the table and sprayed them with carburetor cleaner.

"What are you doing?" Billy said. "This is a crime scene."

"I was never here," Jay said, and wiped off his weapons. He grasped Tony's Conan sword with a shop rag around the handle.

Tony furrowed his eyebrows. "Those fuckers chipped it." He gagged as Jay wiped the bloody neck of the severed head against the sword blade.

"Don't puke now," Jay said, and pressed the sword hilt into Tony's hands. "You're a hero."

"Aw," Billy coughed into his sleeve. "You expect me to go along with this?"

"Call your old man and see what he says," Jay said, and kicked the head toward the front door.

"I got pains shooting down my left arm." Tony winced. "Is it that arm that means a heart attack? Or the right one?"

Billy thumbed his Blackberry. "You always got an angle, and it's always bullshit. How about I call your bluff? What you gonna do then?"

"Try me, see what happens."

"I was coming to talk sense into you before Bello had you killed. Dad says he's losing it," Billy said. "No wonder, with all the shit you been up to. You went to Strick's funeral, to rub it in Matt's face? You're as fucked up as they are."

"Strick was Jay's father," Tony said. "Can we go now? It

293

feels like my left tit's trying to punch me in the face."

Billy blinked. "Strick got into your mom's bikini? Lucky son of a bitch."

"Mind your mouth," Jay said. "And no, it wasn't with Mama Angeline."

"Then how?"

"Your old man knows," Jay said. "Ask him."

The sword clattered to the floor. Tony gripped Jay's shoulder. "I uh, I don't feel so good."

Jay looped an arm under Tony's shoulders and helped him toward the door.

"Hey, you can't leave!" Billy said. "What am I gonna tell the locals?"

"Figure something out. Just remember, they call me in, your old man swings."

Billy swore and held the phone to his ear.

Tony's legs gave out, and he gripped at Jay's shirt. Jay buckled under the weight, and dragged him toward the Hulk truck.

"Put some rags on the seats," Tony said. "I shit my pants. Do tough guys do that?"

"All the time," Jay said. "I'm packing half a turd myself."

Tony squeezed his arm as he hunched over the dash. "I'm gonna die," he cried. "God's punishing me."

The truck shuddered over a pockmarked stretch of road. "No he ain't," Jay said.

"I ratted on you, pallie. They made me do it." He pressed his big forehead to Jay's shoulder. "Leo Zee said he'd kill me."

"I know, Tone." Jay took a turn hard and the truck's rear end skipped over the railroad tracks. "It's all right."

"I'm going to hell," Tony cried.

CHAPTER 40

Jay and Brendan walked home through the towering oaks of Yantacaw Park where old Italian men wearing shorts and black socks squinted down the sandy lanes of the bocce courts, jabbing fingers like stubby cigars as they argued a play. Tony and Matt had computer club, and Billy had a hockey game. Brendan scanned for groups of older boys. He'd had to quit hockey after Bello vandalized his track trophy; the opposing team started fights by calling him "Brenda," and the coach said it put Billy, their star player, in the penalty box too often.

"So, did you ask Ramona to the summer dance?"

"Reckon I will," Jay said. She had been distant. Waves instead of kisses against the lockers.

"I think Dawn's kind of hot," Brendan said. "Not Ramona hot, but you know."

Dawn was a shy, freckled girl with honey-brown curls who wore out-of-style clothes and kept her nose in a book most of the time. She didn't talk much, but she seemed nice enough.

"She's real pretty," Jay said.

"My father says girls are a distraction, that we shouldn't date until after we take our SATs," Brendan said. "I don't care. I'm on the honor roll. I'm going to ask her. You want to double date?"

"Sure."

As they topped the hill, they passed the baseball diamond and the recreation building where the coaches stored equipment. On the concrete steps, Joey Bello sat smoking, surrounded by the Algieri brothers and Nicky Paladino. Greg Kuhn had switched sides and joined the nerds of the brain trust.

Joey spread his face into a grin. "Hey, faggots."

Brendan stared straight ahead. Jay flipped them the bird.

"That's right, keep walking, faggot."

They did. Brendan shivered with rage.

"You walk like a little queer, holding your ass cheeks together. I bet your ass is so reamed you gotta squeeze all the time or the shit falls right out."

Nicky whispered something, and the Algieri brothers laughed.

"I bet you and your brother practice blowing each other," Bello called.

"Shut up, Joey," Brendan said.

"Shut up," Joey repeated, in mocking falsetto. "Shut up, Joey! Or what, faggot? Your daddy gonna shoot me?"

Brendan turned, his nostrils flaring.

"None of us are afraid of him," Joey said. He sucked his cigarette, then spat in the grass. "Big deal, he shot a moolie. My father says he taught you to be a faggot. Calls his mustache the come-catcher."

Brendan dropped his books and strained at an invisible leash.

"Ooh," Joey said. "The little faggot gonna fight? Your brother can't help you now."

Brendan sneered. "You told everybody Billy gave you the black eye, didn't you?"

"Shut up, faggot. Shut the fuck up."

"I bet you did," Brendan said with a shaky smile. "You cried like a little girl after I hit you. You're nothing without your friends."

"Shut your cocksucking mouth!" Bello flicked his cigarette and charged.

Brendan clenched his delicate fists at his sides. When Joey got in range, he threw hard. The bigger boy flattened him in the pine needles and started whaling. Jay leapt on Joey's back, but the other boys pulled him away. He clawed and thrashed and kicked until they sat on his arms.

Nicky Paladino hawked up a throat full of snot. He stood over Jay with a dull smile. "Your mom was at the ShopRite. I bagged her groceries and carried them out to the car. Then she jerked me off all over her tits." He let the loogie drop on Jay's chest like a load of semen.

Jay snarled and kicked wild. Should've kept the hatchet in his bag. Better to be thought crazy than an easy target.

"Nicky," Bello panted. "Let's give the homo a lesson."

Brendan moaned through bloody lips speckled with pine needles. Bello had him on his stomach, one arm chicken-winged. Nicky sat on his back.

Bello drew back his foot and kicked Brendan in the center of his ass. "You love it up the ass, don't you," he panted, kicking again and again. He finished with a kick in the balls.

The Algieri boys laughed.

Nicky tugged Brendan's jeans down, baring white briefs. Joey drew back and kicked Brendan in the crack until his underwear spotted red. Brendan cried into the pine beds.

"The fag's having his fuckin' period," Bello chuckled.

Nicky's eyes lit and his smile widened. Ice settled on Jay's skin. The Algieri brothers exchanged glances and stared. The youngest one said, "That's messed up."

"Shut up," Bobby said.

Nicky laughed and grabbed a pine cone. He jabbed the red spot with it. "He likes it."

Joey snatched it from his hand. "Gimme it."

Jay couldn't see. But not long after, Brendan screamed for a long time. Jay stared at the sky with his heart pounding, the clouds foaming red.

"What are you boys doing," one of the bocce players hollered, walking slow across the grass.

The Algieri boys scattered. Joey Bello gave the finger. "Fuck you, old man."

Nicky laughed, and they both walked away, slapping each other's shoulders.

Brendan pulled on his pants. Tears ran freely.

Jay ran after him. "I can get us a ride home."

Brendan pushed him away and limped toward home. "What am I gonna tell my dad?"

He spent the week home from school, recovering. Missed the track meet vs. Don Bosco, and the team got creamed in his absence.

CHAPTER 41

Jay woke with a kink in his neck, lightheaded from the ozone scent of oxygen and disinfectants. He'd slipped a nurse a hundred to stitch him and let him crash in an empty room. He floated down the hallways in the soft glow of the overhead fluorescents and the hum of distant machinery. He asked a desk nurse for Tony's situation. She told him he'd been released from surgery, but only immediate family could visit him in the ICU.

He drove to Tony's house at the creep of dawn. Looked at his makeshift bed on the couch and staggered to Tony's bedroom. The door was locked. Jay had thought nothing of it. Andre had put a lock on Jay's door after they saved him from the Witch. To make him feel safe.

He worked his way through Tony's keychain until he opened the door.

The bed was a mess, a king size with a pronounced dent in the middle. More words on the walls. Jay recognized the bad guy's blade from *Highlander*. A sack of dirty laundry to bring to his mother's.

Jay swept the sheets back, flipped the pillow. Kicked off his jeans and groaned as he hit the plush mattress. The early morning sun cut through the blinds. Nearly closed his eyes, but what he saw on the dresser popped them open.

He rolled off the bed. It was a black AR-style rifle with the stock removed and a pistol grip forearm. Beneath it were stacks of loaded magazines taped in twos for easy reloading. Pez dispensers full of deadly copper candies.

Next to it sat their yearbook, beneath a wire-stripping tool.

Stacked in an open drawer were six lengths of capped three-inch pipe with wires leading to a single switch.

Jay flipped through the pleather-bound Class of 1989. Faces were exed out in black marker, and a lengthy screed was written on the final page in neat block letters.

"Aw, Tone."

Big Mindy came running to the fence when the Hulk truck rumbled into the parking lot. The boy pumped his arm like a kid asking a big rig driver to honk the air horn. Jay obliged.

"That's a cool truck," Mindy said. "The Hulk is awesome."

"Hey, fella. Go get Mister Zee, and I'll take you for a ride."

The kid ran back toward the group.

Jay leaned against the fender and tapped an envelope in his hands. Mindy dragged Brendan back by the hand.

"You can't keep coming here," Brendan said. He wore a school hoodie and a stopwatch around his neck.

"He's gonna take me for a ride, Mister Zee."

Brendan flashed Jay a glare. "Mindy, we don't take rides from strangers."

"Aw, Mister Zee."

Jay held the envelope. "Got something for you."

Brendan crouched and looked in Mindy's eyes. "If you finish recess with no timeouts, I'll ask Miss Branigan if it's okay. But she can say no, Mindy."

"Okay!" Mindy ran off. A patch of sweat bulls-eyed the back of his shirt.

"I'd appreciate if you didn't make promises to my kids."

Jay approached the fence. "They can't have any fun?"

"They can. Unlike some of our teachers, I go out of my way to protect them. Even from well-meaning people, and themselves."

"I got something you need to see." Jay waved the envelope. "When's your lunch break?"

"I don't get one," Brendan said. "I pack a lunch, and we take turns getting fifteen minutes' peace in the faculty room."

Jay pushed the envelope through a diamond in the chain link, and leaned on the Hummer's bumper. The engine ticked as it cooled.

"What is this?" Brendan said.

"Something you need to know about your old man."

"Billy talked to me already."

"And?"

"It's all old news, Jay. It doesn't matter whether that kid was armed or not. No one's going to care. You know that town."

"Open it."

Brendan smirked, looked back at his students playing tag. He snatched the envelope and unfolded the page inside. He squinted at the pixelated photo and his shoulders pulled taut.

"Reckon Billy told you about the fender-bender your old man got himself in," Jay said. "I took that picture at a rest area out on the Turnpike a week ago. He got in a wreck trying to catch me."

Brendan lolled his head forward and stumbled a step. "I should have known," he cried, and gripped the fence. "Who's with him?"

"Some trucker."

"Well thanks for ruining my day," Brendan said. "Fuck, how did I not know?"

"He's not strong like you."

"Billy saw this?"

"Just you, for now."

Brendan knuckled the corners of his eyes. "Is this your revenge? What's the point?"

"Mr. Bello knew," Jay said. "He's had your father under this thumb the whole time. Joey knew, too. That's why things happened the way they did. That smirk he always had on his face."

Brendan straightened. "I don't even care anymore."

"It was never you your father hated," Jay said. "It was himself. I think your grandfather must've been one vicious son of a bitch."

Brendan sighed. "I teach kids here who've been through worse. And they're good inside. They don't hurt anybody. They don't make fun of the kids with Down's Syndrome. So my father doesn't get a pass, Jay. He knew right from wrong. His job was to enforce it. Don't apologize for him."

"I'm not," Jay said. "I told him about a friend of mine. Was a man, but now she's a woman. She was halfway, when we met inside. You can imagine how rough her time was. I told Leo she was a bigger man than he ever was. Because she fights like a pit bull for everyone she calls family."

Brendan raised a fist. Jay bumped it through the links.

"I'm going to the reunion," Jay said. "Gonna tell everyone what Bello did to his boy. Will you back my play?"

Brendan looked away.

"Y'all got old-time convict eyes, same as me. Like you been through a war. You've all been in your own hell since that night."

"You don't think Mr. Bello has, too?"

"We were kids, he wasn't. He knows what he did. Joey wasn't born that way." The fence links creaked inside Jay's fists. "The lie has to end."

Turkey tracks formed in the corners of Brendan's eyes. "I'll think about it," he said, and cleaned his glasses on the corner of his polo shirt.

Mindy ran over and hit the fence. "It's lunchtime, Mister Zee. Can I go for a ride now?"

"What the hell," Brendan said.

Body Shop Bloodbath, read the headline. The newspaper ran with Billy's bullshit narrative. Heroic small businessman Anthony Giambotta had been robbed and tortured by three thugs with violent criminal records seeking the combo to his safe and the keys to a custom Shelby GT500.

Jay wondered how long it would be before they made any

connection to the sword-wielding hero and the axe murder of long ago. If the truth would work its way out like a splinter, or fester beneath the skin until everyone who knew what happened was dead.

While news vans and crime scene techs swarmed the auto shop, Jay parked behind Clara Maass Hospital. Wearing his suit and carrying a clipboard, he followed a pair of pharmaceutical saleswomen and took the stairs to the open floor of the ICU. Tony lay in bed staring at a silent television. Bruises had flowered on his face and the abrasions turned to orange peel. Jay walked like he was allowed to be there, and no one questioned him.

He crouched by the bed. "How you doing, pallie?"

Tony lifted heavy-lidded eyes and said nothing.

Jay unfolded the newspaper. "You're a hero."

Tony shrugged, then winced. He reached for a plastic cup of ice water on the bedside table. Jay held it for him.

Tony stared down an empty road that wasn't there. "Lost one of my boys, too. Asked the nurse if they could give me an electrical testicle. She smiled." He hunched in a silent laugh and grimaced in pain.

"That's why God gave you two," Jay said. "Remember that? Lee Marvin, *The Big Red One?*"

"So this is what heroes feel like. Nurse said I got tons of flowers," he said. "Can't keep them in here. Ma gave them to the seniors' home. You know, the one by the school that smells like feet." He fell back, eyes half-lidded. "Who's watching the shop?"

"The cops are going over everything. I'm staying at your place." Jay leaned in close. "I found what you were working on. Took care of it, in case the police come by."

Tony fluttered his eyelids. "I'm sorry, pallie. I just…no matter what I do, I know what they all think of me. I'm the fat fuck Joey Bello pissed on." He covered his face with one big hand. "I wanted them to know how much it hurts."

Jay looked away as Tony wiped his eyes.

"You still going to the reunion?"

"Gonna raise some hell."

"You show 'em," Tony said. "Fuckin' show 'em what a piece of shit Joey was. They have to know."

"I swear," Jay said, and squeezed Tony's hand.

He stayed until Tony faded into sleep. When the nurse asked him who he was, he said he was his brother.

Jay made a final tour through town on the night of the reunion. Passed the dump where they first met Joey Bello, the font of Tony's baptism. Church Hill, the scene of Matt's dogshit blessing. The chestnut grove of Brendan's brutal rape. Last, the park where they had left Joey Bello floating downstream, his empty sockets bared to the cloudless summer sky.

If Joey's crimes had been beyond redemption, Jay's own hands were forever stained with a collage of blood. He sat in Tony's truck and studied them a good long time. The bones thickened from pounding the bodies of other men, the lace of scars draped over skin.

Okie would've said to forget the Catholic shit. *There's no penance, kid. You learn better for next time.* Mama Angeline smiled beneath big sunglasses, twirling her Colt. *You gonna let Mr. Bello walk the Earth after what he done?*

Jay decided he would not.

The idea of going to the reunion stag put a pang in his chest. He called Raina, and asked her to join him. "What you going there for? Come to the club, *mi gatito* needs you," she said. "We're short a man, but he won't ask. Don't want Dante to think he can't handle it."

"I'll come by tomorrow," Jay said. "There's something I gotta do."

"That big-tit bitch never gonna leave her mansion, *papi.* Money loves money. Forget her, my girlfriend's coming tonight.

She got an ass that'll make you forget *everything*."

"That's real tempting," Jay said. "See you tomorrow, li'l sis."

The banner outside the Umbria Americana Pavilion read *Welcome Class of '89: We Didn't Start the Fire!* The catering hall had been built around the old Avionics pool to resemble the house of a Roman patrician, columns leading to a terra cotta roof, the grounds shrouded by dimly lit gardens. Eighties synth thumped out the stucco walls. Two police stood by the front doors.

Jay walked around back where smokers had spilled into the garden. Three women chatted by a blue-lit stone fountain. He didn't recognize them, but they knew him. They turned to stare, one by one.

"Evening, ladies." Jay smiled. He flipped a quarter into the fountain before heading through the door.

The cocktail lounge was decorated in neon blues and pinks. The band at the far end played "Your Love" by The Outfield, a lonesome wail for a night of infidelity. The roof was open above the pool. The diving boards had been scrapped, the tiles replaced with marble like a Roman bath. Plastic water lilies topped with electric candles floated across the waves.

Jay ordered two whiskey on the rocks. He downed one quick and nursed the second. Old cliques huddled at tables, couples wandered the pool's edge, and singles danced by the band. His schoolmates had fleshed out into caricatures of their younger selves. Promise chipped from their faces, the youth scoured away.

Glances lingered into stares as people recognized him. He'd aged harder than they had. Pale and grinning, a gargoyle leering from the parapet of a cathedral. Jay flipped the phone in his pocket, thumbed the redial button. Mack's stubby, expert fingers had wired a burner phone to the six pipes tamped full of

Tony's homemade TNT. Jay taped the explosives beneath Randal's Escalade and filled the tank.

Jay smiled at the crowd's sneers and sipped his drink. Tonight they'd get a taste of the fear his friends had lived with every day of their lives.

Two athletic men in summer suits slipped through the crowd, trading quips and sly grins.

"Jay," Brendan called. "This is my partner, Kevin."

Kevin had broad shoulders and an outdoor tan. Sandy hair and a dimpled chin. He studied Jay with a look of reluctant resignation.

"Good to meet you," Jay said, and held out his hand.

"Wish I could say the same," Kevin said. He turned to Brendan. "I'm here because it's what you want. I'll get you a beer." He brushed past Jay toward the bar.

Jay sipped his drink. He soaked the liquor up like a cactus, welcoming its tingle. Tapped his foot to "Our Lips Are Sealed."

"They say it gets better," Brendan said, eyeing the room. "That's a load of shit. It gets bitter, if anything. You get used to it. Most people turn into bigger versions of the little assholes they were in school."

"That why you work with kids who don't really get any older?"

"Maybe," Brendan said. "They're not all angels, you know. They're still people."

Kevin returned with two bottles of Heineken. He handed one to Brendan, and held his own with frat-boy ease.

"Whoa," Brendan said.

Ramona walked alone, wearing a short dress of crushed sapphire with a black bow tied to the side. Her hair twirled to her shoulders, cobalt eyes cutting through the crowd.

"Excuse me fellas," Jay said. He left his drink on a table.

"Hey," Ramona said, wrapping her arms around him. Her lips cold and ether-slicked with vodka.

"You all right, Blackbird?"

"Just lovely," Ramona said, and took a long drink from a pint glass. She leaned against him, arm around his waist. "Relishing the opportunity to relive my misspent youth. I can't believe what they did to the pool, it looks like Caligula puked all over it."

Brendan and Kevin joined them. "Ramona, you look great."

Ramona gestured at the crowd with a sweep of her glass. "I hated these people for years. But they're just pathetic."

The partners exchanged glances. "How's Tony doing? Crazy, what happened."

"Healing," Jay said. "He got real lucky, your brother showing up like that."

As the song faded, eyes and fingers pointed from the crowd. The husky-voiced female guitarist cut from The Go-Gos to The Cure. Ramona downed her drink and tugged Jay by the wrist. "Let's give them something to talk about."

They joined the dancers in front of the band. Jay twirled her and brought her close. The couple closest to them flinched with recognition.

"Fuck off," Ramona said, and they spun away with sneers.

Her eyes sparkled beneath the strobes. The band cut into a medley, and Brendan and Kevin joined them. Then another couple, and another, until the floor was a crush of bodies. The medley ended with Billy Idol's "Rebel Yell" and the crowd pumped their fists to the chorus, jumping like the denizens of a snow globe, until Jay could almost forget why he was there with a detonator in his pocket.

When the band wound it down, Ramona led Jay off the floor and fanned herself.

"How much you tip the band to play that, peckerwood?" Billy said, and pulled Jay aside. He wore a drab cop suit. "I don't know what you've got on my father, but this ends tonight. I spent all day reciting your bullshit story."

"You should be used to lying," Jay said, and twisted his arm away.

307

A tall redheaded woman in a green dress stalked to Billy's side, her chin the beak of a predator bird.

"Kathleen," Ramona said, and leaned in for a hug. "How are the kids?"

"They're fine," Kathleen said, and sidestepped her. "How's your husband?"

"Honey," Billy said.

Ramona gave a toothy smile. "He's minding his own business. You should try it."

"Don't throw it in everyone's face and look for privacy," Kathleen said. "You have a child at home and you're out playing prom queen. I'm only here because my husband decided to bodyguard the town pariah."

Jay said, "I prefer 'outcast,' if it's all the same to you."

"Kath, you said you wanted to come," Billy said. "So be happy, already."

Kathleen looked out over the crowd. "I see some friends from the track team. That's where I'll be. Maybe I'll even be happy."

"Kath," Billy sighed. He turned back to Jay. "I should let you get killed," he said, before heading after his wife.

Kevin nudged Brendan's elbow. "I'm glad your brains aren't identical."

"Be nice," Brendan said. His eyes shot toward the door. "Oh, great."

At the entrance, Leo glared at Bobby Algieri, both in civilian dress. He pushed Bobby toward the back door with jabs of his finger, and marched their way.

"Relax," Brendan told Kevin. "I'm okay."

Leo's jacket hung loose on his shoulders, his eyes bloodshot. A transparent bandage across his nose. Kevin intercepted him.

Leo raised his hands in truce. "I want to talk to my son for a minute."

"We're done listening to you," Kevin said. "We're both tired of it."

"Brendan, please go home." Leo talked around Kevin. "That's all I ask. I promise I won't ever contact you again."

"Why would I do anything for you, after all you never did for me?"

"We can talk about that later, if you want to," Leo said. "But please. Go."

"Are we embarrassing you, Chief?" Kevin said. "We do our best to avoid you. That's not enough?"

"That's not it at all," Leo said. He shot Jay a glare of contempt. "What do you have planned, Desmarteaux? Tell them."

Jay sipped his bourbon. "Just having a good time."

Leo curled his lip. "You want to get killed, do it away from my sons."

Bobby Algieri shouldered through the crowd. Flushed with booze, with an empty drink in his hand. "Look everybody," he hollered. "It's the scumbag who killed my friend." He tossed his glass into the pool and swung at Jay.

Jay caught the haymaker on his shoulder.

"Shut up, Bobby," Leo said. He twisted Algieri's wrist into an armlock. "I'll have you on graveyard shift for the rest of your career, if you don't leave right now."

"I don't give a fuck anymore."

Leo pinched down the compliance hold.

"Ow, dammit. You're supposed to arrest scum like him, not let them shit all over your town."

A few in the crowd applauded and raised their drinks.

Billy shouldered through. "Need a hand, Dad?"

"Get this fool to the parking lot," Leo said. He turned to Kevin and Brendan. "Please go home. This will only get worse."

Billy and Leo guided Bobby Algieri out by his elbows. "Hey, that was exciting," the vocalist chirped. "The party's not over, people." The guitarist riffed into Pat Benatar's "Hit Me with Your Best Shot."

"I think we could both use another beer," Kevin said, and tugged Brendan toward the bar.

Ramona ballooned her cheeks with an exhale. "Wow. Do we have to stay here until Mr. Bello shows up?"

"They need to know," Jay said.

"Some of them do already," Ramona said. "It was an open secret. You won't change any minds. If they don't hate him already, nothing you can do will make them."

"You the only one who gets closure?"

"Don't be an ass," she said. "Ooh, I see Mrs. Molinari! Get me a fresh drink."

Jay found a short line. A spectacled man whispered behind him. "He deserved what he got." He patted Jay on the arm and walked away.

Jay thumbed the phone. Maybe Ramona was right. Nothing would change minds that were made up already. No matter how hard Tony's surprise shook them.

A familiar voice whispered in his ear. "The Stricks would like a moment alone. Will there be trouble?"

Brush Cut stood behind him.

"Don't start none, won't be none," Jay said, and scanned the room.

Matt held his chest out, but his hollow eyes told the story. He spoke and Ramona looked away, bit her lip. She voiced anger, and stared him down. Matt fell to one knee, to the pealing tones of "Sweet Child O' Mine." He held out his hand. Ramona's face broke into an embarrassed smile.

Jay had only heard the song in prison, on cheap tinny radios. When it played on some con's boombox, he would close his eyes and remember the day he and Ramona met. How his knees wobbled climbing the twenty-foot dive. The sting of the water on his skin. Ramona's eyes bright and wide as she swam for him. Her smile as the lifeguard dragged him away.

He wondered if he could have ever made her smile like that if they'd had a life together, instead of secret nights of pretending. He thought real hard, but it wouldn't take.

The dream was a lie.

Something to get him through prison. Like the Witch dreams had gotten him through the hell of knowing that his own mother had traded him for her demon needs.

Jay clenched the phone in his pocket as Ramona took Matt's hand and they skipped onto the dance floor. The hate that had kept him alive for twenty-five years gnawed at his belly, as Matt and Ramona twirled like children. His heart pounded like a fist, and his head swam with hot blood. Kevin and Brendan pushed Billy and Kathleen ahead of them into the dancing crowd.

Jay slumped alone into an empty chair. He flipped open the phone, flipped it closed.

Brush Cut said, "Don't feel bad. They're both fucking nuts."

"I'll drink to that." Jay pocketed his phone and raised his glass. The band gave it all for the song's finale, then announced a short break. Women fanned themselves and headed back to their tables. Mayor Bello walked red-faced into the room, flanked by Bobby Algieri and another officer. Leo argued with the mayor, who ignored him.

Jay took a step and Brush Cut squeezed his bad shoulder.

"It'll be better if you left with me."

The mayor jabbed a finger, and the officers marched on Jay. The crowd formed a distant circle around them. Nicky Paladino grinned from the back.

"Looks like I'm about to be escorted out." He stood and met Bello's wet shaky eyes.

"The news calls you a hero, but you can't wash your hands of my Joey's blood!"

"What about your hands, Mister Bello?" Jay slipped his hand into his pocket, flipped open the phone. "If anyone killed your boy, it was you. Joey was a no-good rapist sumbitch, and he needed killing!"

Leo raised his voice. "Get him out of here, now."

A murmur rumbled through the crowd. The officers gripped Jay by the arms and shoved him toward the door. He thumbed the send button, and shouted over the crowd.

"I got a message for all of you! You watched it happen every day. And deep down, you liked it. It was the natural order, wasn't it? The strong prey on the weak. As long as it wasn't you." Some sneered, others nodded. Some looked away.

"You let evil walk free because you felt safe, like your shit didn't stink, like you were better than everybody else. You thought once you got rid of me, it was all over. But evil never dies. It's right here. How you think Joey learned to be that way?"

"I'll kill you!" Bello struggled out of Leo's grasp.

The building shook with distant thunder. People stumbled and wine glasses crashed to the floor. A symphony of car alarms tweeted far away.

Leo grabbed Jay by the shirt. "What have you done?"

The town emergency siren wailed four bursts, alerting the fire department.

"Nothing you didn't start," Jay said. He had parked Randal's Escalade beside Joey's memorial. The pipe bombs tore it apart and left the stone a blackened faceless marker, knocked out windows in the police station and the empty high school. The fire swirled into the night sky and played off the windows.

"Now you're all in hell with me," Jay said. "Where Joey is. Where he belongs."

The crowd jammed at the doors. A woman sobbed.

Leo grabbed an officer's radio and pointed him at the door for crowd control. "Keep people inside. We don't know what's out there."

Bello lunged for Jay's throat with a roar. Leo gripped the mayor's index finger and twisted, sending him to his knees. "Officer Algieri, escort the mayor to his vehicle, he needs to call a crisis management meeting with the town council."

Bello struggled with the officer, swearing and spitting.

"Want to know who killed Joey?" Jay shouted. "You did. You made him what he was."

A gunshot boomed and the crowd rushed the doors. Billy

rushed for the shooter, and Kathleen grabbed his arm. They both fell and knocked a chair into the pool.

Bobby Algieri cupped two hands full of blood to his belly. He collapsed onto his back with confusion and tears in his eyes.

"Joseph!" Leo knelt and put pressure to his officer's wound.

"Don't move," Bello shouted. He leveled Algieri's service pistol at Jay. His pocked jowls trembled, shining with sweat. "Fucking murderers. All of you. You were all in on it, you think I'm stupid? That I didn't know?"

Billy sat on his ass, struggling with his ankle holster. Brush Cut shielded Matthew, hand lingering over his wallet pocket.

"Everybody listen," Bello hollered. "We're having a new trial. You're gonna tell everybody what really happened."

He stepped closer to Jay, but not so close that Jay could wrestle for the gun. Bello grimaced, and the gun trembled. "We couldn't even have an open coffin," he choked. "Tell the truth. Then I'm going to do what the law should have, and execute the monster who murdered my boy."

"Kill him!" someone shouted from the crowd.

"Mister Bello," Billy said. "I'll stay, but please, these people are scared. Let them go."

"Shut up! You never liked my Joey because he teased your faggot brother." Bello jerked the gun toward Brendan and Kevin, sneering. "There you are. These days men have to apologize for being men, while you degenerates flaunt yourselves in public!"

Brendan moved to stand, and Kevin held him back.

"Breathe, Bobby," Leo said. "Look at me. Mayor, this officer needs medical attention. Please."

"He let my boy die," Bello said. "Let him wait. This town ate me alive! And you brats get to inherit it. It's going to shit. All those houses your father built." He gestured at Matt with the gun. "Your father made millions, and we got the scraps."

"What about Joey," Billy said. "I thought this was about Joey."

"It was always about my boy," Bello said. "But he's dead, thanks to your friend here." He turned back toward Jay. "Tell us, you white trash piece of garbage."

Jay stepped closer until he could see the sweat glistening on Bello's trigger finger.

"You know who killed your boy," Jay said, and unbuttoned his shirt. The Witch's cigarette burns gleamed white. Bello stared. "See my scars? Just like Joey's fingers. Why don't you tell everybody how you put cigarettes out on him."

"You get warts from abusing yourself. I made him strong! You boys tattled on him like sissies, for trying to toughen you up."

"Joseph, point the gun at me," Billy said. "I couldn't take how Joey hurt my brother, like you said. Point the gun at me."

"You're a cop," Bello sneered. "You all fucking lie. Ask your father."

"Joseph," Leo said, frowning at Bobby's inert body with resignation. "Put the gun down and act like a man."

Bello lowered the pistol to aim at Leo. "What would you know about being a man, you cocksucker? You shot an unarmed kid." He turned and shouted to the room. "You hear that, everybody? The big hero gunned down that black boy in cold blood. Then he raised a little faggot who pranced around on the track team, like *that* could make the town proud. You both make me sick."

"You shut your mouth," Brendan snarled, jaw quivering. He stepped closer, in front of his father. "You want to know what Joey and Nicky used to do? They'd hold little kids down and put their cocks in their faces. Tell them to kiss it! And they did a whole lot worse to me."

Nicky Paladino gathered sideward glances from the crowd, and his grin faded.

"In your sick dreams." Bello jabbed the gun at Brendan's chest. "Why should I believe you? You're a pervert like your father."

"You know why Joey hated me?" Brendan shouted, pushing Kevin's hand off his shoulder. "Because I caught him and Nicky jerking each other off. They wanted me to join in. And when I didn't, they took it out on me every chance they got. Because they hated what they were!"

"No!" Bello snarled and drew on Brendan.

Jay sprang for it. The pistol exploded against his gut.

The room shrank like the bottom of a well. Cold, dark, full of distorted echoes. Faces flickered and gunshots slapped the air around as Billy and Leo both returned fire. Bello's shirt blossomed red and he fell. Leo stood over the body and emptied his revolver, sharp face expressionless.

Jay hit the pool like dead weight.

The water felt cool and good and the silence felt like heaven.

Black smoke rose from the hole in his belly. Jay curled around the wound. Diamonds on the water, sparkling in the sky. Breath pounded its fist at the back of his throat, a flock of blackbirds yearning to fly free. He fought to hold his breath, but air bubbles joined with the smoke.

A burst of blue hit the water. The blue-eyed girl reached for him, her dress a flower around her. The boy raised his hand and waved goodbye.

CHAPTER 42

Joey Bello plowed out the doors of Nutley High into the parking lot and headed toward Kingsland park. Tony Baloney wouldn't lie. He was a pussy. The kind of guy his father called half a fag.

The only thing worse than a fag was to be half a fag.

"The world needs cocksuckers," the elder Bello explained, puffing his cigar. "Someone's got to show the broads how to do it, cut their hair, talk to them and make them feel important. But a man's got to be a man."

Joey nodded, rubbing the dusty cauliflower of a wart on his knuckle. His father grabbed his hand. "You keep jerking off, you're gonna have warts all over. Go get some pussy. I had it by the time I was your age. Find a girl with tits on her, that means they're ready."

He puffed the ember red and brought Joey's hand close. Joey knew not to flinch.

Ever since Joey and Nicky found used rubbers along the curb behind the grammar school, they had wanted to enter that secret world. Fucking went on everywhere. All it took was a cock and a cunt.

They explored porno mags together. Smelled Nicky's sister's panties from the hamper and got dizzy from the scent. Climbed out on the roof to watch through her window as she gulped Chris Antonacci's cock. He had seen them and put on a big grin, pushed her head down.

Nicky turned white. Then started jerking off to it.

Joey joined in. The act sealed something between them.

They watched the girls' soccer team from behind the bleachers in the fields and traded hand techniques to a troop of bouncing breasts. He was letting Nicky show him a new move when Brendan Zelazko burst through the weeds on the jogging trail.

And stared a moment too long. "I won't tell," Brendan said. He sprinted away. They chased him, but he was too fast.

Joey woke in a sweat for a week, wondering what his father would do to him. It didn't matter that while Nicky jerked him off, Joey had been imagining perky little tits. His father would kill him.

Or worse.

One day at recess, Nicky was telling Algieri that if a pussy calls you a pussy, it don't mean anything, because they're a fucking pussy. And he knew what to do.

"Hey, *Brenda*," Joey cackled. "You sure had a good time watching me and Nicky take a piss. What are you, some kind of queer?" Then he charged.

Joey got hard when he beat on the little faggot. The way Brendan gasped at a punch to the ribs. How his runner's legs tensed as Joey held him down, face in the dirt. He came in his pants, grunting with every punch. That's how he knew Brendan was a faggot.

He tiptoed toward the gazebo, where Tony Baloney has told him that Brendan was giving out blowjobs. He had sweet cocksucking lips and eyelashes like a girl. It would be like a girl doing it. Practice for the real thing. It didn't make you a faggot. The one sucking the cock was the faggot.

He eyed Brendan's double-diamond calves knelt in the bushes. The familiar rush tingled down his sides.

And the axe came down.

PART FIVE

HIGHWAY TO HELL

CHAPTER 43

The boy ran through the fields with the Witch and the Gator man close on his tail. Their sulfur breath thick in the air, claws swiping at his neck. Jay leaned into his run and took flight. He circled and laughed as the monsters shrank into fierce little Atari spiders below.

He followed the Mississippi until he found Andre's fishing camp, where the scent of fish spawning rose from the bayou and the breeze whipped beards of Spanish moss in the trees.

Jay landed on the porch and Bebe the blue leopard hound tackled him into the kitchen, where Andre and Angeline laughed and pulled him in tight for a hug. His head swam with the spice of Papa's bay rum and the warm popcorn smell of Mama's hair.

Jay woke to the smell of disinfectants. He felt glued to the bed. He craned to observe his wasted body. A handcuff tugged at his right wrist and clinked against the bed rail. He was in the ICU.

A large nurse with tied-up braids brought him water. "Hello, there. How's the pain?"

A dull ache, deep inside. Fuzzy around the edges. He scratched at the patch of scars on his left shoulder, where the Heimdall Brotherhood's rune had once been. After Okie was gone, Jay confronted the Vikings in the wood shop. Put his shoulder to the sander and ground their tattoo off. He passed out and made two cons puke, but they set him free.

"Feels like someone scooped me out with a melon baller. I dunno, three?"

"Even with the Demerol, you should feel more than that." She pulled back the sheets to show him the tube drain on his right side, like a second navel. "I'll say six, so they don't cut your meds. It's harder to get it back. And I'll tell the police you're still asleep. They question you now, you'll tell them everything." She winked and hurried away.

"Thank you," Jay said, and drifted into a drugged sleep.

When he cracked his eyes again, the room was dark and quiet. The nurse had left warm broth and juice and yesterday's paper. He sipped his lukewarm meal and scanned for news of the reunion shooting, to count the living and the dead.

Jay dropped the paper in his lap.

The photo showed Cheetah's club. A massive hand had torn the roof open to reveal the scorched guts inside. A balding man with an angular face stared intensely in the sidebar.

Eddie.

The headline read Strip Club Slaughter.

Jay wiped his hands down his face.

Edwin Holtz of Belleville had shot twenty-three people, fourteen of whom died, before checking out with a self-inflicted gunshot wound.

The article said he parked a Ford F350 full of landscaping equipment in front of the club's double doors and set it ablaze. By the time the gas tank went, he had set up with a hunting rifle, pump shotgun, and three magnum revolvers in the parking lot and hunted people as they fled the flames. Bodies piled in the doorways and smoke filled the building.

Firemen arrived first. Eddie shot three of them. Police cordoned the block and traded fire from behind the ladder truck until SWAT arrived. Once the odds tilted, Eddie walked into the club and checked out with a pair of .357 Magnums jammed in his eyes.

Jay imagined Cheetah smashing out the office windows.

Lowering Raina to the roof of Mack's Cadillac and escaping into the night.

As he read the list of the dead, his hopes turned to blistered skin and bodies convulsing in clouds of smoke. Jay crumpled the newspaper to his chest, wrenched in silent misery.

He woke to a police detective clearing his throat. Balding hair trimmed close, and a flat poker face that revealed little. He asked if Jay knew anything about the Escalade that exploded in the impound lot.

"That guy who robbed Tony's shop drove a truck like that. He was mobbed up, the paper said. Don't their cars explode all the time?"

The officer stared into the grey nailheads of Jay's eyes. "You're guilty as hell," he said. "This will be a different department, now. I'd just as soon wash my hands of you."

"Your mayor tried to murder me. Why don't you question him?"

The man's lip twitched. "He's dead," he said.

"Good," Jay said. "He needed killing."

The next day they rolled his bed into a private room. Nurses checked his temperature every few hours and fed him chicken soup and ice cream. A sandy-haired doctor said he lost half his liver and fourteen inches of intestine, but if no infection took hold, he'd go home in a week or so. He told Jay he shouldn't drink alcohol or eat spicy foods for six months.

"That'll be easy, y'all don't season anything here." Jay waved his hand at the television and the curtains. "Don't know how I'm gonna pay for all this."

The doctor said it was taken care of and that he should be concerned with resting and nothing else. Tony came to visit, walking with a limp. He showed Jay the scar where they'd put in the pacemaker. "Now I got a heart like the Terminator."

"I lost some parts, myself. Chunk of liver and a foot of intestine."

Tony chuckled. "Bring it to Rutt's, have 'em stuff it and make a ripper."

"Aw, don't talk food, Tone. All I get is salty piss water." He nudged the empty broth bowl.

"I can get Ma to make some pasta *fagioli*. I'll say it's for me, so she doesn't poison you."

Jay buzzed the nurse for the urine bottle. "Police coming again," she said, after she helped him set up down there. They'd removed the catheter that morning and his pecker still burned.

Leo Zelazko walked into the room and closed the door behind him. He wore his uniform and carried a brown leather briefcase. He set the case on the table and opened the brass snaps without a word.

"Good morning to you too, shitbird."

Jay reached for the remote to call back the nurse.

Leo pressed a single finger into Jay's bandages. Sweat broke on Jay's neck as he hunched with pain. Leo tugged the remote on its cord and tucked it behind the bed's headrest.

Jay collapsed into the bed panting.

Leo held a handcuff key before his red-rimmed eyes. "Will you be a problem?"

"I'm in no shape to misbehave."

Leo unlocked the cuff and let it dangle from the bedrail.

Jay rubbed his wrist. "Thanks, been wanting a shower. I smell like baked asshole."

"Shut up." Leo took a sheaf of papers from the briefcase and dropped them on Jay's chest. "This includes a your birth certificate. Your stepmother gave it to Mrs. Strick during your trial."

Jay bent to read it. Leo adjusted the bed for him.

Certificate of Live Birth, Joshua Lee Calvin. Born July 7th 1971, to Joyce Anne Calvin and Matthew Henry Strick.

"So what?"

Leo lifted something black and heavy from the case. "This is an Ingram MAC-Ten. Still one of the best submachine guns ever made. Twelve hundred rounds a minute." He inserted a short stick magazine, tugged the charging handle to chamber a round, and set the gun on top of the briefcase.

"You gonna plant that on me or ventilate me with it?"

"I'm giving it to you. My sons survived. Brendan was grazed in the leg." Leo gestured with the machine pistol. "Otherwise I'd splatter you all over the wall. I bought it from your stepfather. It's unregistered, untraceable. Figure you can use it to complete your business with Matthew."

"That's sure tempting, but why are we buddies all of a sudden?"

Leo laughed. "Because I'm done. They found your bullet from my gun in Strick's skull, and Matthew's destroying me. The council made me resign. They blame me for the mayor's death, and they are correct. I let you torment him until I was forced to put him out of the world's collective misery."

"If you'd done it sooner, none of this would've happened."

"I'm not like you, Joshua. I'm no cold-blooded killer."

"You only shoot unarmed boys."

Leo tutted. "Carnahan's wife said he had a gun. I see one now, when I look back. Memory is a whore."

"What about Herschel?

"Who?"

"The cab driver," Jay said. "At the truck stop."

"When you caught me *in flagrante delicto?*"

Jay grinned. "That trucker was licking something, and it wasn't your damn toe."

Leo smirked.

"Herschel got shot with a thirty-eight like yours. Day after you got it back."

"I don't know what you're talking about," Leo said. He sighed and shook his head. "Your silly photo games are the least of my problems. The evidence Joseph had on the carjacker case was released upon his death. Unlike you and Tony, he wasn't bluffing."

"Damn shame."

"I'm being sued by the family. With lawyers hired by Matthew Strick. Led by the prick who got you released. The FBI wants to investigate it as a civil rights violation. Second guessing me thirty years later. Captain Rasp threw down the piece, not me. But I'm the only one left alive, so the vultures get to pick me clean for keeping my mouth shut."

"Feels bad, don't it?"

"I'm doing what you should have done. Taking my money and heading south." Leo lifted the MAC-10. "If you come looking, I'll feed you to the sharks."

"We'll see what happens when your day comes."

Leo shook with a laugh. "You never quit. That's why I'm giving you new targets. Those leads we spoke about are in the envelope. And this." He dropped a pitted jack knife on top of the papers. "It was still in evidence from when we booked you. I thought you'd like to have it."

Jay turned the Case redbone trapper over in his hand. The one he'd cut his and Tony's palms with. He tried to pry the blade open with a thumbnail, but it needed oil.

"This concludes our business." Leo set the gun in the briefcase. "I do hope you put this to good use. Matthew is one vicious little prick."

A knock on the door.

"Come in," Jay called. He turned to Leo. "I get scrambled eggs today."

Vito slipped in the door wearing a black tracksuit, holding a box of Russell Stover candies. He clicked the door shut. "Good morning, kid. A little something sweet for your recovery."

He flipped the box open, revealing a small automatic with a black tube suppressor.

Leo reached for the MAC-10 and Vito shot him in the face. The report sounded like a metal baseball bat clipping a pop fly. Leo dropped the machine pistol and fell with a choked scream.

"Sorry to do this. Boss's orders," Vito said. He racked the slide and a brass .22 rimfire shell tinked on the floor. He trained the gun on Jay and raised the volume on the television, wrapping his hand in the sleeve of his tracksuit.

Jay squirmed backward on the bed. He hurled the piss bottle and it bounced off Vito's shoulder. He reached for the phone while Vito swore.

He shot Jay through his hand. The receiver clattered to the floor.

Jay snarled and clawed for the IV pole, any weapon.

Vito racked the slide and leveled the barrel at Jay's temple. "Dante said to make it slow, but I kinda like you." The old lion curled his lip. "Even though you splashed me with warm piss."

The room thundered and the sheet hanging over the edge of the bed burst apart. Hot gases burned Jay's cheek as Vito's bullet punched through the pillow.

Vito tumbled into the wall, stitched from his left knee to right shoulder. He slid down, good leg kicking to fight his descent, slipping on the MAC-10's scattered shell casings.

Leo crawled from under the bed. The hole in his forehead pulsed a steady stream of blood. He fell to his side and shakily raised the chunky weapon.

Vito winced and bit the slide of his automatic between gray teeth in an attempt to rack the slide.

Leo aimed steady and blew Vito's head apart with a short, controlled burst.

After his ears stopped ringing, Jay heard the fire alarms. In the halls, screams and shouts. His birth certificate slipped to the floor and caught in the blood.

Leo rolled to his back. The MAC-10 thunked to the floor. "Desmarteaux," he groaned.

"Yeah," Jay pressed his hand into the pillow to stop the bleeding.

"If this leaves me a vegetable, promise you'll kill me."

"I promise, whether you're a vegetable or not."

Leo pressed a fingertip to the neat little hole in his forehead, and the blood pooled out his eye socket in thick red tears. "Like the Dutch boy at the dike."

It was an oath Jay did not have to keep. Leo bled out before the SWAT team finished clearing the hospital floor.

Jay was moved to Mountainside Hospital with a twenty-four-hour guard stationed outside his room. Leo's death ended the questioning into the shooting of the carjacker. The family's claim would be settled in probate.

A perky-nosed therapist with a long mousy ponytail had Jay make a fist. "When can I box again?"

"I wouldn't hit anybody with that hand. You'd better throw southpaw. Elbow strikes." She winked and threw a mock elbow to his temple. "Krav maga."

When she left, Jay took one of the creased paperbacks that a droopy old man carted from room to room. He was getting into one when a visitor opened the door.

Ramona entered in business attire, sharpened for court.

"Hey, Blackbird."

"Don't get up," she said, and walked over.

He stood anyway, barely wincing. "I won't be jumping in any pools for a while, but I can damn sure get out of bed."

He hugged her around the shoulders, bending to keep his stitches away. She held stiff, and patted his shoulder.

"Some guard I got. Didn't even warn me."

"He's one of ours," Ramona said. "We're also paying for your room."

"Thanks."

"Don't thank me yet," Ramona said. "I'm here purely on business."

Jay tilted his head. "That the way it is?"

"It's the way it always was. You want me, but he needs me."

"Why, so he can lie to you?"

Ramona set her jaw. "You need to see his side, Jay. He gave you three pints of blood, you know."

"I guess you can get blood from a stone."

"We saved your life. Have a little gratitude."

"Sorry," Jay said. "Guess I'm a sore loser."

She sighed. "We had something, but we were children, playing around. We remind each other of a time when we were happy. That's all."

Jay didn't know if he agreed or was simply hurt that she felt that way, but after she said it, it became the truth.

"Love is like a business," Ramona said. "It has to keep growing or it dies. Look at Matt's parents. They had something big and it fell to pieces. Because of her pride."

"I'd call it dignity."

"What do you know about dignity? You dragged us all through shit to get your revenge. If you'd taken the money, you could have made something for yourself. How many people got hurt, and how many are dead because of your fucking dignity?"

"Some things are more important than money."

She rolled her eyes. "The only people who say that don't have any."

Jay sat on the bed's edge. "Get to the point. I didn't reckon we were gonna elope, but I wasn't expecting to face you in court."

"You think this is hardball?" Ramona smirked. "This isn't even close. Regarding your claim on the Strick estate; we're prepared to make you a settlement." She handed him a manila envelope.

Inside was a sealed plastic bag holding another, stained

envelope. Jay didn't open that one. He knew what it contained, and how it would smell. "Your husband is fond of poetic gestures."

"Yes he is," Ramona said. "That's not all of it. Mr. Strick had a large acreage that he leased out, so it would be taxed as farmland. We're going to develop it as townhomes, once we wait out the county on the affordable housing mandates. If you sign a nondisclosure agreement and forgo all future claims, you'll get ten percent of our expected future profits."

"Keep it," Jay said. "I don't want it."

Her poker face might've fooled the courtroom, but Jay caught the bloom in her eyes. "I don't think you understand how much is involved."

"I said keep it," Jay said. "It'll be worth it if I never have to see either of you again."

Her face went cold. "As you wish. I'll write the contract."

Jay handed her the envelope with his birth certificate and the check Strick had written Mama Angeline. "Leo gave me these. It's all I have to prove who I am."

She flipped through the papers. "Five thousand dollars. That was a lot of money back then."

"Bad financial decisions run in the family. Tell Matty to send an errand boy, because if I see him I'm liable to take the rest of his blood in trade."

"You're so strong now," Ramona said. She clenched her fists into knots, her ears flushed. "Where was this when I needed you? We could've been together, but you chose your so-called parents over me."

"You wanted me to turn on them?"

"Matthew would have."

"I'm sure he would. You don't understand. They saved me."

"I saved you, too. Didn't I?"

Her logic was as twisted as a pit of rattlesnakes, and she had a headful of them.

Jay turned to the window and gripped the bedrail. "You're

not that girl anymore." He waved his hand. "Fly away, Blackbird."

He heard her sniff, and the angry little laugh as she bit her bottom lip. He watched a construction crew paving the road outside his window until her shoes clicked away.

CHAPTER 44

Jay changed into his jeans and work boots. It hurt to bend much but he managed. He took his soaked phone out of the bag of rice Tony gave him, and put the battery back in.

The screen was blurry, with a fat bubble of water popping from corner to corner. He arrowed down a few numbers to one he guessed was the shop and hit dial.

Someone answered in two rings.

"Ha. You're lucky I picked up, you got me in a hell of a lot of trouble last time."

"Hersch? Damn, I thought you got shot."

"Yeah, the whole family called when they heard about those cabbies. They caught the guy, too. Some meth head biker two weeks out of Rahway. I drive freelance now, for this Ryde get-up."

"You got time for a pickup at Mountainside Hospital?"

Herschel arrived in a beige Dodge minivan with a smartphone Velcro-taped to the dash. Jay had washed Matt's blood money in the sink and patted it dry with towels. It still smelled funky.

"You ever get your girl that pup?"

"Yeah," Herschel said. "Right before you got me shit-canned." He flipped the visor, showing a photo of a little girl with long braids and a serious expression hugging a bully breed puppy.

"Said I was sorry," Jay said. "When I thought you were dead, I got all tore up. Thinking of her and that dog."

"Gets his nuts cut next week," Herschel said. "Thing's a money pit."

They rolled in front of Big Tony's behind a tow truck lowering a sleek blue sports car to the curb. A man in a suit held a clipboard next to the flatbed.

"Whoa, that a Ferrari?"

"Looks like a Viper," Jay said. He dropped a sheaf of bills into Herschel's lap.

"Whoa." Herschel regarded it like a coiled snake. "You hit the lottery or something?"

"I was born rich. Don't spend it all on Puppy Chow."

"Well, uh, thanks." Herschel stuffed the cash in his pocket.

Jay slapped his hand and squeezed. "Thanks for everything, Hersch. Tell your wife I'm sorry about the hassle."

The suit approached. "Mr. Desmarteaux."

"I got business to attend to." Jay climbed out with care. Herschel waved nervously and drove away.

The suit showed Jay two copies of a five-page contract, and the scalloped blue and pink title to the Viper. "You should read this, and ideally have a lawyer present."

Jay ignored him and signed the papers.

"If that's how you want it." He punched the documents with a large round seal that perforated their signatures.

Jay took the title and the keys and looked into the Viper's interior. "That's not my real name anyhow."

"It doesn't matter," the notary said. He climbed into the passenger's side of the tow truck and it pulled onto the street.

Jay eyed the Challenger. Splotches of primer made it resemble a wild steed, a black and white American Paint.

"Holy shit," Tony moseyed over, scratching inside his shirt. "Whose car is this? That scary Dante guy?"

"Guessing from the color, it's Ramona's way of telling me to hit the road."

Tony arched his eyebrows. "Sorry, pallie. But this is a nice consolation prize." He ran a hand down the car's aggressive bulges and curves. The blue paint sizzled electric.

"How hangs the Hammerhead?"

"She's running," Tony said. "You really smashed the hell out of her. Had to put in a new radiator."

"She ready choogle on down to New Orleans?"

"If you take her easy."

Jay handed him the Viper keys and title. "Hope this'll cover my debts."

"Whoa, you sure?" Tony's eyes lit up like the day they'd met at the pool.

"You know me. I'd just wreck it." He squeezed Tony's hand. "Gonna hit the road. Find my folks. What I should've done in the first place. Stay strong, brother."

"Thanks, pallie." They hugged gingerly, two wounded beasts.

Jay eased into the Challenger and revved the engine, let the roar rumble through him. He checked the compartment. Andre's tomahawk gleamed within. There it would stay, until he could bury it in his true father's grave. He goosed the pedal and rolled onto the street.

After a few blocks Billy's gray cruiser flashed blue and red in the rearview.

Tony's mix tape snarled "Highway to Hell" on the stereo. Jay dropped the hammer and rode that highway home.

ACKNOWLEDGEMENTS

Special thanks to Josh Stallings, Neliza Drew, Holly West, Lynn Beighley, Chad Eagleton, Andrew Fader, Elizabeth Kracht and Chris Rhatigan for reading drafts of this novel. Thanks to my mother Margaret, my uncle Paul Pucci, Richard Finnegan, Peter V. Dell'Orto, Phil Dunlap, Zak Mucha, Cindy Ardoin, James Lee Burke, Adam "Pallie" Sulich and the rest of the guys down at the docks for their assistance and inspiration.

Much respect to Andrew Vachss for his life's work, and his encouragement and inspiration.

The crime fiction community is a large and friendly one. Thank you all, but special shout-outs to Allan Guthrie, Kent Gowran, Steve Weddle, Nigel Bird, Matthew Funk, Fiona "McDroll" Johnson, Sabrina Ogden, Dave White, Jen Conley, Lawrence Block, Christa Faust, Brad Parks, Hilary Davidson, Don Winslow, Eric Beetner, Bracken MacLeod, Wayne D. Dundee, Sarah Weinman, Les Edgerton, Ian Kearns, Duane Swierczynski, Todd Robinson, Glenn G. Gray, Stephen Blackmoore, Russell MacLean, Janet Reid, Scott Montgomery, Megan Abbott, and everyone else I forgot for their support.

Thomas Pluck has slung hash, worked on the docks, and even swept the Guggenheim museum—though not as part of a clever heist. He hails from Nutley, New Jersey, also home to criminal masterminds Martha Stewart and Richard Blake, but he has so far evaded capture. When not writing, he trains in Kachin Bando mixed martial arts and powerlifting. He resides in the Garden State with his sassy Louisiana wife and their two cats.

https://thomaspluck.com/

OTHER TITLES FROM DOWN AND OUT BOOKS

See www.DownAndOutBooks.com for complete list

By J.L. Abramo
Catching Water in a Net
Clutching at Straws
Counting to Infinity
Gravesend
Chasing Charlie Chan
Circling the Runway
Brooklyn Justice
Coney Island Avenue (*)

By Trey R. Barker
2,000 Miles to Open Road
Road Gig: A Novella
Exit Blood
Death is Not Forever
No Harder Prison

By Richard Barre
The Innocents
Bearing Secrets
Christmas Stories
The Ghosts of Morning
Blackheart Highway
Burning Moon
Echo Bay
Lost

By Eric Beetner (editor)
Unloaded

By Eric Beetner and
JB Kohl
Over Their Heads

By Eric Beetner and
Frank Zafiro
The Backlist
The Shortlist

By G.J. Brown
Falling

By Rob Brunet
Stinking Rich

By Angel Luis Colón
No Happy Endings

By Tom Crowley
Vipers Tail
Murder in the Slaughterhouse

By Frank De Blase
Pine Box for a Pin-Up
Busted Valentines
and Other Dark Delights
A Cougar's Kiss

By Les Edgerton
The Genuine, Imitation,
Plastic Kidnapping

By Jack Getze
Big Numbers
Big Money
Big Mojo
Big Shoes

By Richard Godwin
Wrong Crowd
Buffalo and Sour Mash
Crystal on Electric Acetate (*)

By Jeffery Hess
Beachhead

(*)—Coming Soon

OTHER TITLES FROM DOWN AND OUT BOOKS

See www.DownAndOutBooks.com for complete list

By Matt Hilton
No Going Back
Rules of Honor
The Lawless Kind
The Devil's Anvil
No Safe Place (*)

By Lawrence Kelter
and Frank Zafiro
The Last Collar (*)

By Jerry Kennealy
Screen Test
Polo's Long Shot (*)

By Dana King
Worst Enemies
Grind Joint
Resurrection Mall (*)

By Ross Klavan, Tim O'Mara
and Charles Salzberg
Triple Shot

By S.W. Lauden
Crosswise
Cross Bones (*)

By Paul D. Marks and
Andrew McAleer (editor)
Coast to Coast vol. 1
Coast to Coast vol. 2 (*)

By Bill Moody
Czechmate
The Man in Red Square
Solo Hand
The Death of a Tenor Man

The Sound of the Trumpet
Bird Lives!

By Gary Phillips
The Perpetrators
Scoundrels (Editor)
Treacherous
3 the Hard Way

By Tom Pitts
Hustle

By Robert J. Randisi
Upon My Soul
Souls of the Dead
Envy the Dead (*)

By Ryan Sayles
The Subtle Art of Brutality
Warpath

By John Shepphird
The Shill
Kill the Shill
Beware the Shill

James R. Tuck (editor)
Mama Tried vol. 1
Mama Tried vol. 2 (*)

By Lono Waiwaiole
Wiley's Lament
Wiley's Shuffle
Wiley's Refrain
Dark Paradise
Leon's Legacy (*)

(*)—Coming Soon

CPSIA information can be obtained
at www.ICGtesting.com
Printed in the USA
LVHW04s2221270818
588270LV00005B/1051/P